DEATH IN LEAMINGTON

Also by David Smith

Searching for Amber

DAVID SMITH

DEATH IN
LEAMINGTON

Cover artwork courtesy of Leesa Le May

Matador
9 Priory Business Park
Kibworth Beauchamp
Leicestershire LE8 0RX, UK
Tel: (+44) 116 279 2299
Fax: (+44) 116 279 2277
Email: books@troubador.co.uk
Web: www.troubador.co.uk/matador

ISBN 978 1784620 875 (Paperback)
978 1784620 882 (Hardback)

British Library Cataloguing in Publication Data.
A catalogue record for this book is available from the British Library.

Typeset by Troubador Publishing Ltd
Printed and bound in the UK by TJ International, Padstow, Cornwall

Matador is an imprint of Troubador Publishing Ltd

to my romantic and delicate inspiration

The Enigma I will not explain – its 'dark saying' must be left unguessed… further, through and over the whole set another and larger theme 'goes', but is not played… the chief character is never on the stage.

Edward Elgar

CONTENTS

A TENDERFOOT IN LEAMINGTON (WITH APOLOGIES TO RICHARD BAXTER TOWNSHEND)

This place from a mean, inconsiderable village, has, within the last 25 years, owing to the virtue and fame of its springs, risen into great eminence, and now justly ranks with the most elegant and celebrated watering places.

Leamington History Website, *Discover Royal Leamington Spa*

The boom years of my adopted hometown of Leamington started in 1784 with the discovery of a spring in Bath Lane (now Bath Street) on land owned by William Abbotts. He and Benjamin Satchwell decided to exploit the healing properties of the water and opened Abbotts' Original Baths. They were the driving force behind the early growth of the town.

People soon flocked to take the waters and, after a visit from the Royal Family delivered a seal of approval, the building bonanza began in earnest. In a short time speculators started to plan a new town north of the river. Although the old town continued to expand, this new town to the north quickly became the more fashionable place to live. By 1828, the population of the former hamlet of Leamington Priors had risen to over 5,000 and was still rising. In 1838, the boom town was granted the title 'Royal' by the young Queen Victoria.

Clarendon Square, where I live and where much of the action of this story takes place, is one of the town's Regency jewels. Laid out in 1832 to original plans by P. F. Robinson of Mayfair, the square consists of impressive and gleaming stucco buildings, all now listed Grade II, with oak trees planted luxuriantly in the central park. Its most famous resident, Louis-Napoléon of France, lived at No. 10 between coups and stirrings back home in Paris. Louis was eventually elected the last king of France, the last Bonaparte, but his time here was spent in seedy saloon bars, back room snooker halls and the occasional costume ball in the Assembly Rooms. It was a lucky if wasteful existence for a future *petit prince* and one that many of my contemporaries continue to attempt to emulate.

Even the most genteel of spa towns usually has a racy skeleton or two in their cupboard and by the time that Betjeman wrote his 1930s poem *Death in Leamington* the town was already past its best. When I first arrived in this town five years ago I was effectively a 'tenderfoot', though the title itself was still strange to me.

> *There was a lot of fellers as jes' hoofed it on their ten toes the whole blessed road. You can bet their feet was pretty well skinned for them by the time they got here, and naturally the other fellers who'd been before 'em and got heeled up first set themselves up for real old timers, and took the notion of calling every new arrival a tenderfoot. 'Oh, then it just becomes a newcomer pure and simple,' said I.*

Richard Baxter Townshend, *A Tenderfoot in Colorado*

But I must not get distracted. I have a tale to tell and I hope I have reassembled for you faithfully all the events of the past month or so. Well as faithfully as I can after detailed discussions with the main and many protagonists including my new friend Penny 'Dore-abella' Dore. I apologise unreservedly for the number of quotes and literary allusions, but you may know that as I am a writer, books are naturally the central actors of my life. As for the many Elgar connections, I'll leave you to solve that little enigma – certainly all the characters in this little amusement are entirely fictional, except for those that are definitely not, and they will know who they are by their inimitable peccadilloes and reveal themselves in their finite variations. You do know what I'm telling you, don't you?

R. B.

CHAPTER ONE

ALICE BANDS ALICE – (ANDANTE) 'C.A.E.'

A boat beneath a sunny sky,
Lingering onward dreamily
In an evening of July –
Children three that nestle near,
Eager eye and willing ear,
Pleased a simple tale to hear.

Lewis Carroll, *A Boat Beneath a Sunny Sky*

Royal Leamington Spa, Friday, August 30ᵗʰ, 2013

My name is Alice Roberts. I should start with the evening immediately before 'the event'. I was in the kitchen. About 7pm I remember looking up from my laptop and glancing up at the kitchen clock. It was getting late, my husband Eddie hadn't turned up for dinner and I still hadn't gone for my run. I'd been half-listening to the 6.30pm comedy slot on Radio 4 while typing my daily blog update and had not noticed how quickly the time had flown. The radio show that night was one of those slightly-too-clever satires on democracy and I remember thinking how ironically it contrasted with the news headlines that followed. They were all about the parliamentary debate on military strikes in Syria.

Already annoyed by Eddie's lateness, my blood pressure

was rising further as I listened to the politicians' sound bites and tired arguments, but I calmed down a bit when *The Archers* theme music started up. Of course, the storyline was as comfortably inane as ever: Ruth and David were saying an emotional goodbye to Pip as she left for her work placement year; David, self-important as ever, was making a big thing of packing three bags of marshmallows so that Pip could keep up the family tradition of fitting as many in her mouth as she could. Although the storyline was rubbish and I should have switched it off, I liked listening to Ruth's character, I could relate to her; strong-willed and determined, just like me. I rooted for Ruth during the 'affair' with Sam (like a good proportion of the listening nation probably) and the story of her breast cancer. She was now one of my personal heroes.

Anyway, by the end of *The Archers* I was getting slightly desperate as I stared across the red and white checked tablecloth at the pile of technical court papers that I still had to read. I remember running my fingers through my hair in frustration before closing the laptop lid.

'Where the hell is Eddie?' I muttered, but in a low voice, hoping that my seven-year-old daughter Carrie would not hear me swearing.

Our kitchen is situated at the rear of a cosy basement flat, in a row of pretty spectacular Regency townhouses in Clarendon Square, Leamington. As well as the kitchen, the three of us share a living room, two bedrooms and a restricted view onto the back garden of the main house. The flat isn't large but it is furnished comfortably, if not luxuriously and it is surprisingly light for a basement. I designed and made many of the home furnishings myself, including the dream catchers that hang from the kitchen ceiling and the cheerful starry curtains in the windows. Carrie's artwork had been spreading over the walls during the summer holiday and now decorated most of the kitchen.

I checked the level of the open bottle of Sancerre on the table; it was already a quarter gone (*How had that happened?* I thought). There was also a half-empty bowl of chickpeas and two discarded ice-cream wrappers on the table – the not-very-guilty evidence of our end-of-holiday 'rewards'.

Carrie was seated on her wooden stool. I suppose we'd created a little Scandinavian dreamscape really – her shocking red bunches, freckles (she gets those from Eddie) and brightly-coloured clothing were Leamington's answer to Pippi Longstocking. She had just finished the last book of her holiday set reading and was illustrating a page from a favourite Moomins storybook. The third person in the kitchen that evening was Penny Dore; Penny is a lovely girl, a close family friend, and now, impressively, a police detective constable. She had abandoned the search for criminals for the week and was standing by the AGA, stirring a saucepan. She helps me once or twice a week in the evenings, as she has done ever since she was a teenager, and was finishing up preparations for our evening meal. Carrie and I had had a really busy day – it was the last Friday of the summer holidays before school restarted and it had been the usual rush to find things, buy things and get all of Carrie's school clothes ready and labelled for the new term – so I was glad for Penny's help that evening.

'I hope I get Miss Burley this year, Mum,' said Carrie.

'Yes, she's really nice,' I replied absently, thinking back over our mad day.

By tradition, the local mums organise a party for our children in the nearby Dell Park on the last Friday before the autumn term. We had spent an enjoyable couple of hours there that afternoon, meeting up with some of Carrie's school friends and their mums before heading into town to get the last bits and pieces for the new term. In the park we had also bumped into another friend, Isobel, or Izzie, who works in the nursing home across the square and had recently been taking music lessons from Eddie. Izzie is a slightly other-worldly Irish nurse with striking, long, light-blonde hair, a gentle voice and an infectious laugh. Her voice is the sort of voice that could melt even the most cynical heart.

When we met her that afternoon, she was taking one of her long-term patients for a walk around the gardens. Unfortunately that turned out to be the only time I ever met Winnie. Izzie had explained that this lady was once a famous actress, Winifred Norbury. I remembered at once that I had actually seen her playing Cleopatra at the RSC. She was in her prime then, long before she succumbed to early-onset dementia that had put her in the nursing home. In the play, I remembered that she had had beautiful shoulder-length blonde hair, disappointingly un-Egyptian, more Greek goddess really. I'd marvelled as an impressionable teenager at the way she switched effortlessly from vulnerability to aggression, with serenity and swagger that left no one in any doubt that she was the most important character on the stage.

I switched off the radio and put on one of my all-time favourite records before opening up the book for Carrie. We had borrowed both *The Little Prince* and a battered Kate Bush CD from the town library that afternoon. I remembered how I had loved that book's illustrations when I was the same age as Carrie. In fact, I was always reading then and had grown up quite the little bookworm. Later at senior school, I was mildly bullied for being a swot, but it didn't bother me too much. I had been happy to while away the hours with my nose in a book, almost any book. To encourage Carrie in her reading, I began to sing along to the record – but I soon realised that I hadn't listened to it for years and the words came out all jumbled. I could still remember vividly the first time I had heard its opening whale calls; now, like then, it made me think of swimming.

When I was a girl, the present library building had been a swimming pool. I learnt to swim there and can still recall the evening that we all had to jump into the pool in pyjamas to collect bricks from the bottom of the deep end for our life-saving certificates. Gosh, that was a long time ago.

I also remember that at one stage, I kept a whole collection of disembodied bugs and beetles in little tins in my bedside cupboard, before my mother threw them all out. They were carefully wrapped up in cotton wool. Maybe it was this early interest in amateur dissection that had translated into such a strong ambition to be a doctor. My hard work at school enabled me to win a place at Bristol to study medicine, the first in my family to go to university. After I graduated I trained as a junior doctor in Birmingham. That was also hard work, and at the time I could not see myself continuing to slog down that road forever. It was also around then that I first met Eddie and the serendipity joker played its part. I was chosen to participate in an experimental mobile forensics unit. The work completely fascinated me. However, unplanned motherhood meant that I could not immediately pursue this new career. It did whet my interest in pathology, however, and so, after I returned from maternity leave, I spent two years studying histopathology. I have now advanced to an 'apprenticeship' in forensic pathology.

After Carice, or Carrie as we soon called her, arrived in our lives, Eddie and I had argued for months about whether we should get married. Eddie was quite happy for us to continue to live as partners. 'I am an artist and God is against art so why do we need to get some priest's blessing?' was his stock response. But to me this seemed to be more a convenient reflection of his general attitude to anything like a commitment rather than a fundamental philosophical position. Basically, he hated anything that constrained his own free actions; no doubt influenced by the stubborn rejection of his Catholic upbringing. In the end, my persistence and determination won through against his apathy. I insisted that Carrie needed 'proper' married parents and we eventually had the pretty church wedding that my mother and I had always wanted.

My daydreams were interrupted by Penny's voice reminding me that she had to go soon. She asked if I'd mind if she ate her supper before the rest of us; of course I agreed. Penny's very competent vegetable curry was simmering away on the AGA, smelling glorious but getting drier by the minute. Eddie, the love of my life, the man with the child in his eyes, my *romantic and delicate inspiration* and my very own Peter Pan, was still not back. I had no idea where he was, maybe coaching at the (real) tennis club or more likely drinking (real) ale in the club bar with his (real) mates. Wherever he was, he was now very late for dinner but that was hardly unusual. If he wasn't playing tennis or rehearsing with his band he was usually working on some recording project, or occasionally giving violin lessons in the evening to supplement his meagre sound engineer's salary.

Yes, life with Eddie has its moments. As I approach the dreaded 'four zero', I am beginning also to reappraise my own ambitions and have even become somewhat broody again. Our weekends are always so busy and holidays tend to be a few days grabbed here and there in North Devon or Wales, surfing or walking. We never travel abroad, no long sunny days for me luxuriously tanning by the pool like most of my girlfriends. Probably the most exotic thing we do during the year is jam along at the Leamington Peace Festival with the beatniks, spiritualists and organic food zealots.

During the week it is worse; we seem to spend less and less time together as a family, there is so much going on. I guess at heart I am happy enough but I would love to be able to buy a home of our own, rather than rent the flat, nice as it is. But money is *the* issue. I wish I didn't have to care, but it is corrosive; we both work so hard to keep our heads above water. Money is such a robber of time; if you aren't careful you can work your whole life to earn it but never enjoy it. I am pretty determined that this will not be our fate, but looking around I can see that it won't be so easy to avoid.

When I first met Eddie, he was a DJ, five years younger than me and with his own reasonably popular band playing local gigs. He was gorgeous and had an obvious talent for music but had lacked confidence somewhat in his own ability. Although he was younger than me, I was charmed and then bowled over by him. Later he worked for a spell at an event management company but found that frustrating as it allowed no time for his own music. He went back to study for an audio engineering diploma and then got his present job at the Woodbine Street recording studio. The studio was well-known in earlier years for recording big names like The Specials and Paul Weller but now has a more eclectic clientele.

More recently he has become interested in video and film, helping his director friend Jack with the soundtracks to the art films he makes in his spare time. He also works a shift in the local music store where he can meet other artists and musicians, including composers and amateur filmmakers, some of whom he has also helped with music for their short films. But of course that does not pay particularly well. Most of the work has been pro bono to get his name out there. He has had more joy doing some background music for friends in the local games industry. It is a long and slow process and he is still a long, long way from hitting the big time. As a result we have little cash for luxuries.

Totally endearing as he is, Eddie tends to struggle with the concept of deadlines and fixed appointments. With the patience of a saint, I have encouraged him to make entries in the family diary, but they are always somewhat vague and quite often plain wrong. If I were the jealous type, I might be forgiven for wondering if he gives some of his music students a few 'extra' bits of tuition in these unexplained gaps in his life. But I'm not and although he is a flirt, I am quite sure he isn't the type to initiate anything as serious as an affair. In fact, I doubt he is even capable of organising such a thing. I confess I'm not quite as confident that some of the young ladies he teaches (and probably some of the older ones too) wouldn't be more than happy to lead him astray if they got the chance. I am well aware that he has more than his fair share of female admirers. I guess the simple problem is that he is just too beautiful.

At home he is attentive, just frustratingly unreliable, hardly ever there and too easily distracted. He is certainly not interested in adding to our family, despite the loud and persistent ticking of my biological clock, but I am working on him.

I glanced over to the washing line above the sink, where half a dozen pieces of Eddie's clothing, including his beloved Wolves football strip, were drying. That reminds me of another bugbear: his clothing. His fashion sense leaves a lot to be desired – in the ten years I've known him he hasn't really progressed much from college student grunge. I've concluded that this aspect of his character is probably irredeemable and have almost given up attempting to sort him out. He tends to treat any notion of 'designer' with disdain and is colour blind to boot, preferring his battered old T-shirt and jeans to the nice clothes I patiently buy for him in the boutique shops in Park Street.

That morning I was sure he had gone out (again) in a moth-eaten tweed jacket he'd bought at the Spot for Value gentlemen's clothing shop, a bowtie, Levi's and Converse shoes. All this rather than one of the smart Ben Sherman shirts and chinos I had freshly ironed for the interview he was attending that day. He had been invited to pitch for a games advert soundtrack and with the advice of Jack, he had written what I thought was a really great piece for the brief. But that morning, when it came to the moment of truth, he did not seem to have the confidence or even the motivation to carry through with it.

Despite all of this, I continue to believe in him and hate to see him disheartened by the many inevitable rejections he gets in the entertainment business. That morning, as usual, I read him the riot act and hoped on this occasion he might actually get his act together, but I wasn't too confident.

'Surely you are doing something that has never been done before?' I had suggested encouragingly.

He just shrugged and turned away.

At last the phone began to ring; I let it go to voicemail so that I could hear the voice on the loudspeaker. Thankfully it was Eddie calling from the Tennis Club saying he was just leaving.

'I guess that's nice of him,' I said to Penny ironically. At least he'd called to let me know this time, but he had not given any hint to how the interview had gone earlier.

'OK, well I'm off now then, see you next week,' said Penny as she cleared her plate.

'Thanks Penny, it really makes a difference, you know; there's so little time. Make sure you enjoy yourself before you have kids is my best advice.'

'Kids will never happen.'

'We'll see. Anyway, are you going anywhere nice tonight?'

'Sort of, just meeting up with a few girlfriends, we're going to the flicks and then I hope it won't be too late a night, I could do with catching up with my sleep. See you soon.'

'Well have an amazing night.'

Penny is an attractive, sensible and courteous girl with an endearing hesitation in her speech. She is still in her early twenties. I remember when we first met, Penny had a stutter so debilitating that she could barely hold a conversation, let alone elbow her way into the limelight. She was certainly a smart kid and had a lot to say, but just couldn't say it. Her father worked for a church charity and left her mother to bring her up alone in England for long periods while he travelled to remote trouble-spots around the globe. Tragically, her mother died of a tropical infection carried back by her husband and after that, because I knew the family, I went out of my way to befriend Penny, spending a lot of time with her and arranging for her to see a speech therapist I knew. That's when she started helping me out at home.

No one was more surprised than me when this talented girl left the local college and went straight into the police force instead of going on to university. At that time, she was sharing a flat with a girlfriend, but was planning to move into the attic flat of the main house above us following the remarriage of her father. Penny is great with Carrie, but we can't pay her much for the hours she gives us. So Eddie makes up for the stingy wages with the occasional music lesson free of charge.

Penny paused before closing the door. It appeared that she had been reading my thoughts. 'Don't give up on him,' she said. 'He's got a heart of gold really and there'll be a long queue.'

I smiled, knowing that she was right on both counts. I glanced up at the picture of me surfing on the beach at Croyde on the mantelpiece. It was nearly a decade ago now but I didn't look so different, except of course for the much less violent shade of red in my hair. The photograph next to it was one of Eddie, manipulating baby, pram and changing gear, like a real involved modern father, not the slightly detached one he had become. He had more stubble then, wisps across his chin, his curly hair even more untidy and his clothes even more grunge. Maybe I had been able to make a difference after all; maybe I was wearing him down a bit. He was worth the effort, a project that still had some way to go to complete, innocent but knowing, my own man-child.

As soon as Penny left, I turned the saucepan down to simmer and cleared a space on the table for our three rush placemats, laying out the brightly-coloured plates and cutlery and lighting a scented candle. I prepared the rest of the rice ready to boil and poured a glass of wine for Eddie and mineral water for myself. *I still just have time for a run* I thought, taking a large gulp of water to steady my resolve. Thinking of all the reading I still had ahead of me, I could have done with Eddie putting Carrie to bed for once.

I caught a glance of myself in the mirror. My face was still girlish and attractive, but probably no longer quite teenage daydream material. I take care to exercise and am proud that I still have a toned and slim body. In my twenties, I appeared near-naked covered in mud as an extra in the *Sweet Things* video with Mick Jagger. It was filmed in The Pump Rooms and I got the part by chance as a stand-in – it was absolutely amazing but it took a long time to live down that notoriety with my friends.

*

My ancestor Caroline Alice Elgar, nee Roberts, was a genuine nineteenth century superwoman. She was born into a distinguished family: her mother's side founded the

Sunday school movement; her father's served in the army in India. She studied geology with the Rev. William Samuel Symonds before girls did such things and went fossil-hunting with him on the banks of the Severn. She played the piano well; spoke fluent German, Italian, French and Spanish – basically an all-round Victorian goddess. Apparently, she had met her own Edward, or Eduard, as she called him, when she took piano accompaniment lessons from him – a spooky coincidence? Like me, she was quite a bit older than he was. Eddie found me a great *Look and Learn* giclée print on e-bay: 'One of Edward Elgar's pupils was the attractive Caroline Alice Roberts'. You can just imagine what went on in those lessons, can't you?

So anyway, when her mother died, Caroline went abroad for a while before returning to settle down. She got engaged to Edward, the young violin teacher, much to the disapproval of the rest of her family. He was seen as a gold digger, just a poor tradesman's son. Besides, her family were Anglican and his Catholic, and that mattered a lot in those days. So not only did she marry beneath her class, but she also rebelled in religion through her choice of partner. He described her as his 'romantic and delicate inspiration'. I've adopted that for Eddie. But it sounds as though Alice was no wallflower; she was full of steel, determined and pretty dogged in her own belief in Edward – real girl power. When they married, his music took wing and he began to compose on a much more ambitious scale. Personally, my favourite is the cello concerto, especially the Jacqueline du Pré version and of course the Enigma Variations. I recently copied out one of the poems that Caroline wrote for Edward as a love gift and pasted it on our notice board to encourage my own Eddie:

And the wind, the wind went out to meet with the sun
At the dawn when the night was done,

And he racked the clouds in lofty disdain
As they flocked in his airy train.
And the earth was grey, and grey was the sky,
In the hour when the stars must die;
And the moon had fled with her sad, wan light,
For her kingdom was gone with night.
Then the sun up leapt in might and in power,
And the worlds woke to hail the hour,
And the sea stream'd red from the kiss of his brow,
There was glory and light enow.
To his tawny mane and tangle of flush
Leapt the wind with a blast and a rush;
In his strength unseen, in triumph upborne,
Rode he out to meet with the morn!

Caroline Alice Roberts, *The Wind at Dawn*

Our daughter, Carice, has the same name as Caroline and Edward Elgar's daughter. That was Eddie's silly idea not mine. She has red hair like me too, but hers is naturally curly like a pre-Raphaelite watercolour. Because of her hair, Eddie gave me a spectacular amber bracelet when she was born. We both share the same soft gentle singing voice, he says.

★

At last, around 8pm, I heard Eddie's key in the door and then his footsteps in the hall. I shut down the lid of the laptop. Whenever Eddie arrived home at night he usually whistled the same four note melody, something from a musical he once took me to, but there was no whistle that night; he clearly wasn't very happy. I immediately assumed the pitch had gone badly. I waited to see the face of my genius appear through the lace curtain, my red-cross knight, my lionheart.

As soon as he came in through the door, Carrie ran up

to give him a big hug but his expression already told me all I needed to know.

'Hullo, fishface!' he said to Carrie and then turned to me. He gave me a light kiss and then said *it went OK* but then added that he thought they were looking for something completely different.

'We'll see,' he said. I took that as a doubtful, but perhaps not a complete write-off, not yet anyway.

'So where were you that made you so late?' I asked.

'Sorry, I was playing a club doubles match with Hugh. There's a ladies' tournament on all weekend, so it was the only slot we could get. Sorry I forgot to tell you again.'

I examined his face intently; he seemed genuine, although it was a pretty lame excuse. From the odours emanating from his sports bag, his tennis kit certainly seemed like it could do with a wash and he knew that I could check on him later if I wanted to. At least Hugh, a champion of justice in my mind, would be a reliable witness if I bothered to ask him.

As soon as I had dished out their food, I left Eddie in charge of Carrie (knowing that I would probably regret this later) and quickly pulled on my running gear. I had just enough time while it was still light. I told him I would eat later and asked him to get Carrie ready for bed.

As I climbed the steps up from the basement flat to street level I pinched myself again to feel how incredibly lucky I was to live here. Because of its largely intact character, the eastern side of the square directly opposite our flat is frequently used as an historical film set, most recently to replicate Belgravia for a BBC production of *Sherlock Holmes*. The film crew were busy packing up for the day with large vehicles blocking the road, so I decided to avoid them and head south down towards the river, one of my regular circuits. As I left the house I shouted 'Hello' to Dottie, the lady who often visits the university professor in the corner house. She was emerging from a taxi with her bags. I like her, she is the one who had encouraged me to enter a half-marathon for a children's charity later in the year. She is one of those practical, Christian women who has unlimited wells of kindness to share with others, self-sacrificing, a sister of Charity, and who unlike me already possesses a certainty and all that is necessary for salvation.

I jogged down past the fire station and then turned left into Dormer Place just before I got to the bridge at the bottom of the hill. From there I ran past the Catholic church and then diagonally across the Pump Room Gardens, over the main river bridge, past the Post Office and then left into Priory Terrace. I continued past the entrance to the elephant wash and on to Mill Road Park. There I turned back north over the river, watching the water cascading over the weir as I crossed it and shortly arrived at the new Aviary building, where I took a breather. I do love what they have done with it, its mix of glass and steel and exotic planting bringing a small taste of the thrill of the jungle into our suburban lives.

It was one of my New Year's resolutions to get fit and as usual I had overdone it – cycling, jogging *and* yoga. This was all part of my training for the half-marathon. I was probably in the best condition of my life, maybe not quite Paula Radcliffe, but I could kick ass and take names with the best of them. I had been gathering sponsors and had the target to collect £1000 to help the starving children in Africa. Eddie's view on that had not impressed me. 'What's the point?' he asked. 'It's a drop in the ocean, and we've got enough problems back home.' Although I clearly disagreed, it was not worth a fight with him. In any case it was my business, not his.

I continued on along the riverbank and passed the spot where we had gone swimming together as a family in the mini heat wave of the last bank holiday weekend; secret swimming, wild swimming, bathing in the deep pool made downstream by the weir, where they used to wash the circus elephants all those years ago.

I felt powerful and strong, fully in my stride. I continued into the main part of Jephson Gardens, up to the Corinthian temple that honoured Dr Henry Jephson; past the obelisk to Edward Willes, the Hitchman fountain, the Davis clock tower, the statue of the three elephants and a boy and, most poignant of all, the Czech war memorial dedicated to the seven parachutists who successfully assassinated SS General Reinhard Heydrich after being dropped by the RAF. On these evening runs, these landmarks were no longer just lonely monuments to forgotten history but newly familiar way marks, each with their own story that illuminate the past in remarkable ways and keep me on track.

I continued on past the small lakes and fountain, where the ducks were still making a racket in the late evening air, out of the park and crossed the Parade back into the Pump Room gardens on the other side of the road. I loved being alone in the outdoors where there was hardly anyone around and I was enjoying the feeling of lightness in my legs in the evening air. As I reached the bandstand, I took the opportunity to take my place on the stage and sing (a little out of breath and certainly out of key) at the top of my voice. I remember it was the song about running up a hill to make a deal with God. Different album but as usual Kate had captured just about perfectly how I felt; deal or no deal.

My attention was caught by a poster for an open-air show tied to a lamppost and I paused to catch my breath and read it.

Enter a dreamlike world full of colour, song and rhyme ruled by a crazy, croquet-playing Queen with very little heart and a very short temper!

That could be me, I thought. An Asian businessman approached me, walking very fast. He was talking intently on his mobile, not looking where he was going and nearly knocked me over as he passed too close. All I could hear was 'Very good, very good.'

'*So, don't be late, and don't lose your head!*' I shouted after him. It was the phrase I'd just read on the poster. Later on, when I knew better who he was, I would see that this was somewhat prophetic.

I calculated that I just had time for one more circuit before it got dark, so turned and crossed the road again in front of the Spa rooms, retracing my earlier route down the path to the river by the Mill Bridge weir. Normally, I would have continued across the bridge and run back through the old town, but it was past 8.30pm and nearly dusk, which was when they locked the park, and I still hadn't eaten. Instead, I decided to take the underpass towards the town that ran under the main park promenade. On approaching the tunnel, I saw immediately that there were two men sheltering within. They appeared to be sleeping rough; they'd built a small camp fire and one of them was bending over a few sheets of newspaper.

Despite their harmless appearance I still paused for a second before entering the tunnel. I couldn't see very much of the detail of their features in the gloom, apart from the brightness of their eyes. I imagined they might be Tamils or from southern India at least. The way they were singing in unison made me think oddly of the funny elephants in a TV wildlife film that Carrie had been watching earlier that week, flapping their ears in perfect synchronisation. I had passed the elephant memorial moments earlier – three bronze beasts and a boy sitting on one of them, connected by crescent shaped concrete benches. Carrie had recently done a project on them; I had helped her to find this piece from a local history website and of course it has taken on a new significance for us now:

Leamington has had a long association with elephants. Hegler's Equestrian Circus, a permanent circus building, opened in the town in 1849. Sam Lockhart (1851-1933), the world-famous elephant trainer, was born in Leamington to a circus family. He travelled to Ceylon to work on a tea plantation, and while there learned how to train elephants, decided to form an elephant act and so brought back to Leamington three elephants named Haddie, Trilby and Wilhelmina – also known as the Three Graces. These elephants appeared in Lockhart's Circus in the town. The Circus was a permanent structure, and the elephants had their own elephant house. They would bring the elephants to bathe in the river, which also helped promote the Circus as well as providing quite a spectacle.

There was a sudden sharp glint of a knife. My mind shifted back from the elephants and focused firmly on the Tamils. One of them was using the knife to gut the fish and it unsettled me, despite their cheery song. Since an incident the year before in the park when a young girl was accosted walking back from the station, I had been much more careful about personal safety. However, they seemed occupied with their cooking so I decided to proceed through the subway. I did speed up though, running past them as quickly as I could. They smiled at me and nodded as I passed and I nodded back, feeling somewhat foolish at being afraid, but none of us spoke.

I emerged from the other side of the underpass but my adventures were not over; now there was a stray dog chasing me, which scared me more than the Tamils. It yapped at my heels and my heart pounded as I left it behind.

I had now met a wolf but no rabbit and was late but with no pocket watch. A modern-day Alice; I ran pretty well straight up the wide sweep of The Parade in a sprint, so by the time I reached the top of the hill I was really panting. It felt good and then I jogged the rest of the way home to cool down.

When I got to the flat, I discovered to my frustration that it had been invaded. Even before I descended the steps I could hear the impromptu jam session going on below. I opened the door and went to find the source of the noise. The kitchen table was now covered with Chinese takeaway in addition to the food I had left for my own supper. Eddie had been joined by two of his fellow 'band' members and Carrie was still up, singing along merrily with them in her pyjamas, food all down her top, the four of them jamming to some random pop song. Despite my glares, they started anew on Carrie's current favourite song, the one she had been singing all day, words that are totally inappropriate for a seven-year-old, but what could I do? It was something about a girl crashing her car into a bridge. Clearly Carrie loved it even if I didn't.

The noise was horrendous, and they were not exactly playing like guitar heroes: Hugh, as usual, was all over the place on the keyboards; Bas was in another world seemingly playing a different song on bass and Eddie, well Eddie was just playing guitar on Bas's borrowed Fender. I gave them an earful and headed off in disgust for a shower.

'But we've left you the bamboo shoots,' was the pathetic excuse they shouted after me.

I went to shower and then returned to the kitchen wrapped in my dressing gown. It was still a mess despite my earlier protestations. I had to laugh in despair at the comic scene before me. I issued a set of stern instructions to 'the band' and after a few contrite minutes, in which the boys made a pathetic and incompetent attempt to clear up the kitchen, shooed them all out of the flat and they skulked off to the pub

I ate the bamboo shoots with a bit of goat's cheese, the curry and the rest of the bottle of Sancerre. Wine solved a lot of things nowadays. I was half in despair, and half relieved to get them out of the house. I was thinking about Hugh. There was history there after all.

★

Hugh is a bit older than Eddie – and in fact he is also an old crush. My elder sister knew him from the Anglo-French society at school, which was generally an excuse for the boys' and girls' schools to get together for a not-so-innocent social under the vague supervision of a certain Miss Wainwright. Hugh used to live in the house at the corner of the street, No. 10 Clarendon Square, where Dottie's university professor partner now lives. A group of my sister's friends regularly met up there before going on to Wildes Wine Bar. I was too young for Wildes but remembered being invited as a trailing sister to listen to the first ever radio episode of *Hitchhiker* in the darkened sitting room on the first floor of No. 10. I sat next to Hugh and loved the way he laughed and joked and had a girlie crush on him after that. My sister probably got fed up at the way I flirted with him continuously, although for some inexplicable reason he continued to resist my charms. Even when I was older and wiser we never officially went out together, although we did enjoy a 'moment' or two.

I've never actually told Eddie this, but the only time I've ever seen Hugh really drunk was at his twenty-first party, and it was there that we had the nicest last dance snog in the basement of No. 10. I often smile at the thought when I walk past the house. I still fancy him a bit; he is always incredibly kind and considerate, although physically he has turned into a bit of a greying rugger bugger. He recently divorced after a difficult marriage but in my view he is the one that disproves the theory that all the best men are taken. I am now working on that too – and am determined to get him paired off soon.

Basil, or Bas, on the other hand, is quite another matter. More Eddie's age, dentist, not much hair left and what he has is closely cropped. Nice eyebrows and well-built but in his case I'd definitely recommend leaving first 'base' to his guitar. I hear that he parties hard.

Of course, after my puppy-love crush on Hugh, there were other more serious boyfriends. The most significant of which was my relationship with Seb, also long before Eddie's time. That was a bit more than a teenage crush; in fact it had gotten close to an engagement, before he died of a fractured skull in a motorbike accident in Germany whilst touring with friends. The true story of that accident is still drowned in the alcoholic haze of his comrades. I was devastated of course but am still friends with his mother, Lady Mary, and with Julia and Cordelia, his sisters, who semi-adopted me after the accident and whose basement flat Eddie and I now occupy. It was through them that I met Penny, who has since become their stepsister when her father recently married Lady Mary.

As for Hugh, we lost touch for a while when he went off to join the army. Years later when he returned to Leamington, we met again at a party held by Julia and Delia's father, who had now moved into No. 6. I still remember Julia's sweet excitement when she saw Hugh in the mirror in her father's hallway. We had been playing a silly game where the first person you saw in the mirror was the man you'd have to try to seduce that evening. He was wearing full dress uniform for the soirée and he looked magnificent. Julia was unable to keep her eyes off him for the rest of the evening, but as far as I know nothing really happened. Since then he has been through a difficult marriage and a messy divorce. I have wondered recently if I can get Julia and Hugh together again, but I also have a couple of other potential ladies lined up for him. It is all getting very complicated. Sometimes I feel I need to write it all out on a bit of paper to avoid getting into a muddle with the Jane Austen-like complexities of these interrelationships and my own amateur match-making.

Will you embrace the time we share brave soul,
And seek release, forgive my foolishness?
Will you now slay the doubt that clouds your goal?
Allow my truth to break your deep darkness.
No roar of war or traitorous caress,
Will douse this flame of pure fidelity.
Afresh I bring to you such holiness,
In hope lie down again and sing to thee
As I worship in faith, without contingency.

CHAPTER TWO

The Newly Polychromatic Hugh – (Allegro) 'H.D.S.-P.'

It's in every man's destiny to rise up against the tight binding chains of female tyranny at least once in his life. This isn't a call to arms, but rather a call to party. A single man doesn't have to think about the consequences, unless it involves where he's going to sleep that night. On the other hand, a good father always thinks about his kids first and foremost. But should you decide to go the untamed way, be wary of long-lasting proof. Don't be reckless; evaluate your chances first and be careful eyeballing the all-night buffet.

Curt Smith, *Getting Away With a Boys' Night Out*

Bas, Eddie and I escaped the wrath of Alice and decided to continue our evening with a quick pint in the Benjamin Satchwell, a pub on the Parade. The beer in the Satch was pleasant enough, but that night the bar was full of old timers venting about the day's political events. The music there was almost as dated as the decor.

'So when are we going to get you fixed up with a decent woman, Hugh?' Eddie asked me, teasing again.

'All the good women are already taken,' I replied philosophically.

'Well I think we need to do something about that,' replied Eddie. 'What do you think Bas, where can we find Hugh a good woman?'

'I don't know about a good woman, he just needs to get laid,' Bas added helpfully.

Bas looked around the bar and commented that there was a distinct lack of talent, so Eddie suggested we move on to the Tennis Club, where there was a ladies' tournament that weekend. I thought this was a great plan. Bas, however, had other ideas for the rest of the evening; he said there was a Quentin Tarantino theme night at The Willes Arms with a guest DJ – billed as Jack Rabbit Slim's Twist Contest. He figured there were sure to be some hot girls there. Eddie quickly vetoed this idea on the grounds of bad taste so, much to Bas's disappointment, we compromised instead on one of the busier town pubs. I tended to think of Bas as Eddie's faithless friend; he had a reputation for partying hard. I'm not sure what that meant exactly, but I'd seen enough of his behaviour around women to know that Quentin Tarantino was not a role model to encourage. Anyway the women in question would turn out to be a bunch of Uma Thurman lookalikes. I was therefore also not confident that Bas's idea of a suitable attachment for me (suitable generally specified as far as I could see in terms of the shorter the skirt and the smuttier the behaviour) would match my own romantic standards.

We got to The Red Lion just as things were beginning to really kick off. It was on the corner of one of the main crossroads opposite a couple of popular shot bars. The place was heaving with people, the Friday night crowds spilling out onto the street in the late summer evening. As we forced ourselves past the packed bodies, the shouting and laughter increased in intensity, drowning out any chance of a normal conversation. A group of girls were dancing to a Rihanna song (one that even I recognised) under the coloured lights that strobed from rotating lasers suspended from the ceiling. Bas pushed his way through the crowd and leaned over the bar. Like most places, he knew the barman there well. He caught his eye and ordered three beers and tequila chasers using a mixture of shouts and hand signals.

'Well, Eddie, Alice certainly seemed upset with you,' I shouted loud enough that Eddie had a chance of hearing.

'Yeah you really got the death stare, bro,' added Bas, helpfully again.

'Yeah, well thanks guys, thanks for all the support. I guess I'll have to sort it out with her later. Anyway I'll take her out tomorrow, she'll calm down soon enough,' replied Eddie. 'While I think about it, why don't you guys come along too, we could invite some of Alice's girlfriends as well and make a night of it?'

'Ah, that does sounds romantic, but don't you think she'd prefer something a little cosier?' I suggested somewhat ironically.

'No worries, I'm sure she'll be cool if there's a crowd of us,' he replied without taking the bait.

'Anyway, does she know anything about you-know-what yet?' I asked.

'Nope, she hasn't a clue. It's all going to plan so far; we're all set for next month.'

We found a few inches on the edge of a bar table to lean on and looked around the crowd, searching for likely pick-up prospects. Although we were relatively regular midweek visitors, Fridays took on a completely different complexion in that pub. It was one of several frequented mainly by townies rather than students. It was already busy; the crowd seemed ten years younger than the mid-week regulars. Girls wore oversized heels and skirts six inches too short; some looked distinctly underage. Many of them were drinking cocktails before hitting the clubs; ogled in turn by groups of sixteen- to eighteen-year-old lads with tattoos, abs and fake tans hanging around the bar. I have to say that I felt distinctly queasy about being in such teenybopper company; there were very few women anywhere near my age.

'Look at those idiots over there,' Bas said, pointing to a group of smirking lads with gleaming white baseball boots and leather jackets. They were drinking Jägerbombs, their hair gelled back like reality-TV stars.

'I just wish I was their age again.'

'No you don't, just look at them. They haven't got a clue how to talk to birds, unlike yours truly...' Bas flexed his shoulder muscles, cracked his knuckles and opened another button on his shirt to reveal more chest hair and a thick gold chain. 'Look at those three girls over there, for instance, they look bored as hell with those idiots,' he added, pointing to a group of twenty-somethings in the corner. 'I bet even you could show them a move or two, Hugh.'

'I doubt it Braggadocio – I'm old enough to be their father.'

We continued to watch, half-amused and half-appalled at the increasingly boisterous and noisy drinking games performed by the group of Y-chromosomes standing around the bar. Outside, one of the boys had pulled up his top to show off his steroid-induced abs to another bunch of passing girls on the street. His friend poured a drink on his stomach and he rubbed the liquid in like baby oil.

'Fancy a feel then, later?' the boy shouted at the passing girls as they threw him an admiring glance.

'Heh Wayne, just get lost before I end you!' the lead girl replied sharply, seeming to recognise him. Her mates giggled and his mates sniggered back. She threw a little more than a play punch towards his stomach from which he pretended to recoil in shock with a pained expression.

'Heh, she *really* fancies you,' her mates jeered.

'Come on then, we're off to the V bar if you're men enough,' she said, pouting her lips as she stroked back her hair and adjusted her skirt higher up on her hips. I had to turn away to avoid laughing.

'For heaven's sake, chill out guys, the night's still young. *Save the fight 'til it's over,*' said Bas, but he was careful not to say it too loudly in case the lads heard him.

'OK, so tonight is the night to find Hugh a soul mate; is it to be Spice or Sahara then, boys?' Eddie shouted over to us.

'I think I'm a bit past both of those,' I laughed and added, only half-jokingly, 'Is Rimini still going, or maybe Wildes?' They rolled their eyes at me.

'Actually yes, they both are, but they're full of sad relics like you, replaying their youth and listening to Frankie and Abba, looking forward to a good mug of cocoa when they get home,' said Bas, not quite getting my subtle irony.

'OK, OK, don't rub it in. At least I act my age.'

Clearly Bas had other ideas and was already sizing up a different group of girls in their early thirties who had just arrived and taken a free table in the corner.

'This lot look more your age,' he said, despite the fact that I was a good ten years older than any of them. It did not take him long to make his move.

'Hey girls, I'm sorry to interrupt but would you mind if we joined you? We've got something to celebrate – my friend over here's going to be in the movies. Let me get you some shots?'

I watched, amused as the slim pretty one amongst them, dressed to kill in a very tight pair of trousers, looked on in disdain and some alarm at the thought of being hit on by this bald, middle-aged man. To my surprise, Bas's words were apparently not completely lost on her because she looked Eddie up and down, seemingly intrigued by his comment. I heard her mutter to her two friends.

'What a loser, but his friend's fit.'

I was of course more than aware that she was not referring to me and noticed with interest that Bas had already moved on from her and was in fact now deliberately ignoring her and concentrating instead on her two plainer but curvier friends, one of whom had mousey brown hair, the other bleach blonde brushed back locks. They were both plastered with heavy make-up.

'Stop staring, you're acting like a creep,' Bas whispered to me, somewhat harshly I felt. 'Relax and tell them about something you like doing.'

I felt myself flush and wondered what these girls would possibly want to know about army signals, rugby, security systems or even playing the keyboard badly.

*

I confess that I still find this middle-aged dating business a torture. I spent eighteen years in the army, the last ten of which I was married to a manipulative accountant I met on a tour of the Gulf. I belatedly realised that my own fidelity and devotion were not being reciprocated. In fact I was being routinely lied to and cheated on. I never found her in bed with another man like some of my soldier mates had with their wives but there were enough stories going round the mess that I should have been forewarned. In retrospect, the signs were probably obvious to everyone but me, I had just been too trusting, even naïve. Now divorced at last, I've had a series of short relationships but haven't yet found anyone more permanent.

I am rapidly reaching my mid-forties and am somewhat at a loss on how to move forward in the love stakes. There are no children from my marriage, but a divorcée's freedom is not quite the fun ride that everyone expects and I'm distinctly rusty at the dating game. All my old girlfriends are in long-term relationships. I've tried speed-dating, internet-dating and singles bars but I'm beginning to think that it is all too much like hard work.

★

Plucking up courage, I coughed and rehearsed my next line a couple of times in my head. Fortunately, before I had time to open my mouth, Eddie came over and joined us and, to my great relief, he, as usual, immediately became the centre of attention.

A tall red-headed girl dressed in black designer jeans, classy jewellery and a *Peace* top joined the group and greeted her girlfriends. She was in a completely different league from the others with a stunning figure. I didn't see her face until she turned to talk with Eddie, who clearly knew her. Then it hit me that this amazing girl was none other than Alice's friend Penny.

'Hey Eddie,' she said with confident eye contact and a broad smile that masked the slight hesitation in her speech. The other pretty girl with blonde curls frowned, realising Eddie knew her and that her attempts to get Eddie's undivided attention had temporarily been thwarted.

'Come on girls,' the pretty one said rather shortly, ushering the other girls towards the ladies' room. 'I think we need to freshen up.'

'Stay here and get some more drinks in, we'll be back in a few minutes,' the mousey one said, breathlessly touching Bas on the arm with a little too much familiarity.

'He's bloody hilarious,' she whispered to her pretty friend as they walked away. Her friend just rolled her eyes at her. Fortunately Penny stayed with us.

'Why do women always go to the bathroom together?' I sighed.

'To talk about you lot of course,' said Penny, still smiling at Eddie, who now had her perching on his knee.

The other girls returned and we all drank another round of shots and then agreed it was time to hit the clubs. No one wanted to go to Sahara, 'the music is just too cheesy' the girls said. In any case, they added, it was normally full of acne-faced teenagers and had the most obnoxious bouncers in town. So we started off in the Cloud Bar across the street with Birds Nest cocktails and the DJ playing a selection of what I was informed by Eddie to be hip hop. Bas complained before long that the place was too full of students; this was true as there were a whole crowd of them gathered in a last fling before they returned to uni, so we decided to move on to one of the dance clubs.

There wasn't much choice, having rejected Sahara and Rimini's. It was a short walk up the hill to the club that had been rebranded Spice in its latest incarnation. The combination of the giggling girls' heels, alcohol-unsteady legs, parked cars and other inebriated pedestrians meant that we made slow progress. There were many groups of youngsters marauding through the streets, watched over by bouncers and policemen at the main venues.

We walked around the back of some shops and through the multi-storey car park that backed onto the supermarket. There were only a few cars in the car park and the orange safety lighting there was far too dim to light all the shadows, creating a somewhat menacing atmosphere that dampened our high spirits. Of course, with my security training, I was naturally concerned and suggested we go back and stick to the street. But Bas said that seven of us, four of whom he knew were policewomen, should be enough to see anyone off. The girls' heels clicked on the concrete as they giggled away. Bas and Eddie laughed with them, arms tight around the girls' waists to steady the effects of the shots.

The pretty blonde had now regained the initiative vis-à-vis Penny and had Eddie to herself again, while Bas guided the other two girls through the parked cars. I wasn't too impressed to see that the blonde girl now had her hands around Eddie's waist. Penny dropped back a little to talk to me. I continued to be circumspect: that place had a reputation for drug-pushers and addicts. We followed a yard or two behind the rest of the group, with me nervously looking around for any threat.

I heard the ricochet echo of a car door slam at the far end of the car park. I turned and saw a man walk towards the boot of the black cab that was parked there. I could just make out the registration number in the gloom and made a mental note of it. He was short and tanned, with thick silver hair and gold-rimmed glasses, dressed in an expensive looking business suit and raincoat. He was speaking into his mobile. Another man got out of the driver's seat of the cab and opened the boot of the vehicle. A turbaned Sikh – the minicab driver, I assumed at the time.

Two more figures emerged from the shadows by the pay machines, both short and poorly dressed, very dark-skinned and swarthy. Our friend the businessman passed them a parcel from the back of the car, which they opened and inspected wordlessly as far as I could tell. Whatever it was, it seemed to pass muster; they nodded to each other but did not shake hands. The man and his driver got back quickly into the cab which sped rapidly towards the exit and off into the night. By now the two darker figures had also disappeared into the shadows. It was all over in a matter of seconds. Of course I did not realise the real significance at the time.

'Did you see that?' I asked Penny but she shook her head. She had been busily tapping away at her phone looking through her contacts list and had not noticed anything. I told her exactly what I had just seen. We discussed for a second what kind of seedy transaction I might have just witnessed but didn't wait around longer, hurrying on quickly to catch up with the rest of the group.

When we got to the club there was a queue and we had to negotiate our way past some fearsome bouncers before paying the exorbitant entrance fee. There seemed to be a random process of selection to determine which clubbers the bouncers would let in. For whatever reason, we seemed to pass the inspection. After I'd got over the shocking size of the entrance fee, Spice proved as far from a cup of cocoa as I had expected. It was pitch black inside, packed and sweaty with only a few red lights, like a devil's lair. The DJ was playing more hip hop downstairs and you could hear hardcore dance music playing at several decibels above the human pain threshold upstairs.

The cheap vinyl seating did not encourage sitting around to talk. Even I had to get onto the dance floor. The beat drilled through my body like continuous electric shocks. I tried to make conversation by remarking to Penny about the marbles set into the floor and walls, presumably to prevent the dancers from hurting themselves in the dark. She couldn't hear me. Having given up on that, I tried my best to enjoy myself in my own private cocoon of sound, watching the strobe lighting flash across the dancers, catching their movement in staccato bursts, keeping as close to Penny as I could. She proved to be an amazing dancer and soon attracted a posse of admirers. It was impossible to talk to anybody in the crush. When Eddie eventually signalled to me that it was time to leave I have to say I was glad to go.

When we got out, it was as if my normal hearing had been replaced by a dull ringing pulse. It was probably over twenty years since I'd done anything like that. It was a long way from Earth, Wind and Fire at a 90s student disco.

★

'So, did you two pull?' I asked when Eddie and Hugh eventually got back to our flat past 1.30am, looking drained

32

and even more sheepish than usual. I was still working away at the court papers at the kitchen table. The bottle in front of me was empty, and Eddie could probably see from my smudged mascara that I'd been crying. I was absolutely shattered. He put his arms round me and attempted rather pathetically to give me a hug before kissing me on the back of the neck.

'Sorry we're so late.'

I shied away from him. I had no intention of letting him get around me that easily. Hugh wisely seemed to decide that discretion was required and went off to use the bathroom leaving us alone in an awkward silence. While Hugh was out of the room, Eddie clearly decided his best course of action was to confess all, well nearly all as it turned out. He told me that after visiting a couple of pubs and bars, they had gone on to Spice to dance, just for a couple of hours (he mentioned bumping into Penny but not the other girls they had met and gone to the club with). Understandably my response became somewhat emotional and tearful.

'For heaven's sake, when will you grow up, Eddie? You know how much pressure I'm under, I could have done with some more help this evening. You realise you and your mates are probably old enough to be the fathers of most of the girls who hang around that place. I told you before I don't trust Bas, but Hugh should have known better,' I sobbed. I admit a little theatrically to make the point.

'Yes, well, don't worry. Hugh kept us out of trouble. Look, love, I'll make it up to you tomorrow. I'll book a table at the Regency, I'll invite some friends and we can get a babysitter. Penny said she'd be up for it.' I decided to ignore the sop that was being offered to me.

'I've a good mind to make you sleep on the sofa, Eddie.'

'But I can't, Hugh's got that. Come on; let me give you a cuddle.'

'And what happened to Bas?'

'Hmm. I think he had other plans,' he winked.

'Honestly Eddie, I told you I don't trust him,' I said quietly, but this time I relented and accepted his embrace, kissing him back.

When Hugh returned he seemed pleased to see that I had relented. I offered them both cocoa, to which they laughed and smirked at each other; there was obviously some private 'cocoa' joke going on between them. I made up the couch for Hugh. He looked like he would fall asleep on his feet if he didn't lie down straight away.

Your lover's doubt written a world ago,
A dragon slain blatant and still forlorn,
Endured, enjoyed in persistent shadow.
Man's tame pleasures guiltless but newly torn,
Love's precious gift seen through blue cautious dawn.
Ambitious, audacious, clouds rise with light,
Burning schism, from sad silence still born.
Blown away by the sweet breath of your might,
New veiled by simple faith, becalmed, becalmed till night.

That night I slept fitfully though. It wasn't so much that I objected to their little bit of fun. I could forgive them that and was fairly sure it was all perfectly innocent. After all, I had my own girls' nights out occasionally where we probably got up to far worse than the boys. It was just so inconsiderate of Eddie; I had so much to do and he never seemed to notice how tired I was. All I wanted was a bit more support, that was all. *Was it too much to ask?*

The next morning, despite the lack of sleep, I rose at my usual time and prepared breakfast for Carrie and myself; muesli with almond milk and scrambled tofu. Eddie and Hugh were still sleeping off the previous night. Hugh was half-wrapped in a sleeping bag on the sofa; he looked ten years younger asleep. He was still an attractive man and would be a really good catch for the right woman. I was more determined than ever that I would find a suitable partner for him and had been hatching my own plans overnight. I thought about making them tea but decided to leave them to sleep it off instead – it gave me a chance to get out of the house for a while. I switched on the TV for Carrie and donned my cycling kit, emerging from the front door with my bike and climbing awkwardly up the steps from the flat.

It was a cool but bright morning outside but I could smell something odd immediately. There was blue, oily smoke in the air. As I got to the top step, I could see the same two dark-skinned guys from the subway again, skulking with a scooter a little further down the road by the post box. I looked around. There was a taxi with its engine running a little further down the square but apart from that, and the guys with the scooter, the street seemed deserted. It was still too early for the Saturday traffic to have started.

I put on my cycle helmet and then swung open the little wrought iron gate, hearing at the same time the door of the big house next door being opened. The Napoleon House they call it, on account of the blue plaque on the wall honouring Louis-Napoléon Bonaparte who lived there once. I saw an unfamiliar man step out with two yelping dogs by his side. He nodded politely at me; I noticed immediately from his somewhat colonial clothes and demeanour that he was foreign and smart, grand even. I didn't think I had seen him before so he couldn't have been staying there that long. Perhaps he was a weekend houseguest of Sir William Flyte, our next door neighbour. That was not unusual as there were always lots of visitors to that house.

Before I could get on my bike, one of the Tamils began

to walk up the road toward me and the other started his scooter. I saw again the glint of the fish knife from the night before in his hand as he started to run.

Suddenly this became threatening. I flinched instinctively to avoid him, but he ran straight past me and lunged instead at the poor businessman on the steps. It was all over before I even realised what was happening. I heard the businessman gasp softly and then he went down, silently to his knees.

The dogs went wild, snarling at the attacker, who swung his knife in their faces. Without thinking, I dropped the bike and ran at the Tamil, kicking the knife out of his hand, using my ten-year-old remembered Taekwondo. Yes, I know it was a stupid thing to do, but the attacker was so shocked that it worked. His accomplice had already mounted the pavement behind me, revving the engine of his scooter; back tyre screeching as he came up the kerb. The other man did not tackle me further. Instead he abandoned the knife and jumped on the rear seat, the two of them racing off down the pavement with the dogs giving chase. My heart was pumping; I was unsure whether to give chase and hesitated as they sped off down the street. I decided against this and instead turned to the man bleeding at my feet.

As I knelt by the man's side, I heard a loud bang and looked over my shoulder to capture the image of the body of one of the Tamils flying through the air. The black vehicle that had hit them paused for a couple of minutes and then raced off. I thought I heard a shout and a man running. My mind couldn't compute what I had just seen but luckily my triage training cut in and I slipped effortlessly into work mode. I realised that I couldn't deal with the RTA right away, the man in front of me was too badly hurt. His blood was already seeping on to the pavement through his rapidly reddening white shirt. I asked him his name, but there was no response.

He had a Roman sort of face, aquiline features with yellow-olive skin creased into deep ridges, maybe slightly Arabic or Iranian in appearance. He was in his late 60s or 70s but despite his age he was still quite handsome; his silvering hair swept back into a ponytail, bushy eyebrows shadowing eyelids, which were already closing. He wore an old-fashioned tiepin, a smart silk handkerchief in his suit pocket and a single gold ring, with three letters picked out in scarlet red – *APX*.

I spoke to him again but he still didn't reply. I proceeded straight into first-aid 101: airway, breathing, circulation. There was no obstruction and he was still breathing, but I could hear something hissing in his breath. I put my ear to his mouth and felt his chest. I opened his eyelids – the pupils were turned up towards the sky. I continued to talk to him, unable to tell if he was aware at all of what I was saying. I opened his shirt quickly to see the wound better, a neat slit but evidently deep into his chest. Alongside the cut there was a tattoo, and another older scar carved into the surface of his skin, rapidly being obliterated by the new blood. All this took no more than seconds.

I shouted to a passer-by to phone for an ambulance. By now, the man's dogs had returned from their chase and were barking loudly by my side, stopping me from thinking properly. Without the knife in the wound, he was already losing a lot of blood. From somewhere deep in my training, however, I remembered a trick I had been taught. You could use a credit card to seal the wound. I did not have one but instead felt for the library card in the pocket of my cycling shorts. I used the rest of his shirt to pad the open wound.

By then, Eddie and Hugh had heard me shouting to them for assistance and were alongside me.

'Alice, what happened?' they both asked at the same time as they hunched over me, beside the bleeding man.

I quickly told them about the knife attack and then asked Hugh to go over and help the motorcyclists, while I got Eddie to help me pull the businessman up the step a little, so that his heart would lie above the puncture wound. I reminded Eddie about his first aid training, how to apply pressure to the wound, telling him to be careful to keep clear of the fluids.

Once I'd sorted Eddie, I decided there was not much more I could do for this one but wait for the ambulance. I ran over to where Hugh was checking the motorcyclists. Dottie was already there with him.

In his wakeful inebriation, Eddie apparently did not immediately notice the red dot on the man's forehead. But as it caught his eye, he was entranced by the way it began to move and dance, caressing the man's brow. The explosion of the old man's temple into his face as the bullet hit home surprised him even more.

I had already reached the motorcycle accident, so I heard nothing of the shot except Eddie's surprised cry. The silencer reduced the sound of the bullet to that of a bird gliding through the air. Hugh was with one of the Tamils who was lying across the central reservation in the recovery position; the other was spread-eagled across the road, hit full on by the car. *Probably already dead* I thought, but I checked him over first to be sure. Out of the corner of my eye I could see Hugh pulling at something. That taxi was back, pausing for a second while someone got in.

*

Hugh was fiddling with the strap of the helmet of the man, trying to remember his army training. Although the man was clearly struggling to breathe, he was unsure whether he should release the strap or not. The answer came not from me but from another more authoritative source.

'Stop!' Dottie shouted as she ran over, seeing what he was about to do.

'But he can't breathe,' he replied.

'Don't release the strap; you could break his neck.'

We were joined by another man; an off-duty Sikh policeman. Hugh knew him. He used to shoot skeet with him at the Wedgnock shooting range, a very spiritual man, another ex-soldier, who observed all the articles and prohibitions of his religion and was an excellent marksman.

After a couple of minutes, I joined them and freed the scarf from around the motorcyclist's mouth. I was sure he was one of the Tamils from the subway in the park I'd seen the night before.

The man was still breathing but I could tell that he was near the end of his life. I quickly looked over his body and we both saw a new flood of blood escaping from an artery that had been severed below his groin. There was little that we could do for him apart from apply pressure and hope the ambulance would arrive before it was too late. The man opened his eyes for a second and stared at me. He smiled and whispered something very faint before closing his eyes for the last time.

'What did he say?' I asked.

'I don't know. It sounded like *ningma*,' Dottie said.

I continued to fight for the man's life to the end. I was almost in tears with the concentrated effort.

'You're wonderful,' Hugh said under his breath.

It was only then that we heard Eddie's plaintiff calls for help.

CHAPTER THREE

THE LONELY PINE – (ALLEGRETTO) 'R.B.T.'

On the day they were going to kill him, Santiago Nasar got up at five-thirty in the morning to wait for the boat the bishop was coming on.

Gabriel García Márquez, *Chronicle of a Death Foretold*

The long-case clock in the hall struck eight (yes, I know it probably should have been thirteen). Something caught my eye outside as it flashed past and I got up quickly to peer out onto the corner of the street through the yellowing net curtains that lay limply in the sash windows.

I saw the black cab hit the two men on the scooter, sending one of them cartwheeling ridiculously across the bonnet. He landed prone, already neatly curled in the recovery position, on the kerb between the two bollards that had been placed there a few weeks ago to protect pedestrians crossing the busy street. The other motorcyclist lay alongside the spinning wheels of his scooter in the middle of the road.

It was hard to see well what was happening because of the angle from the window but I recollect the cab waited a minute or so whilst a man got out of the far door, checked the bodies and then ran down the road, after which the cab sped off. I moved to the side window to see better and noticed a lady staring down at the same scene from the upstairs window of the nursing home opposite; our eyes met for a second before she turned away.

In the peaceful ambiance of my study, this carnage

seemed unreal, like an unfolding dreamscape. In the corner of my eye I saw a couple of people run past the front window towards the scene of the accident. The gunshot, when it came, was largely silent and did not disturb my private reflections further, but I did notice the black cab now driving the other way and pausing for a second down the street. I crossed out the sentence on the pad before me, paced round the room for a few moments and then sat back down heavily at my desk, taking up my pen with new enthusiasm and writing out a second line.

Hale knew, before he had been in Brighton three hours that they meant to murder him.

Graham Green, *Brighton Rock*

I was in the middle of preparing my weekly seminar for my regular creative writing classes that were scheduled that afternoon. My chosen theme was 'the best first line of a novel'. I had the radio tuned to a local music station, having tired of the inspiration of my usual jazz that morning. Some soporific singer whose name was new to me was explaining her personal connection to her muse. The dead poet she mentioned was someone whose writings I knew well and whose poetry I had actually taught on a course at Harvard years earlier. Her version of his lines sent a cringe down my spine.

'Really, you have to be joking,' I muttered aloud, *singing the body electric*.

*

I poured myself a cup of tea from the tray that my partner Dottie had brought me earlier and then stood and peered through the window again. Outside on the pavement, I could see a small crowd gathering. I heard the front door open and saw Dottie run out onto the pavement towards the accident scene. There was a man I didn't know already kneeling over one of the two bodies. I assumed the guy on the ground was the driver of the scooter as he was still wearing a helmet. Dottie and this man were joined by another woman, whose face I did know. This woman went immediately to the side of the second motorcyclist who moments earlier had been catapulted from the back of the scooter by the massive car and who wasn't wearing a helmet. She was one of our neighbours. Her face was one of those pretty faces, which ought to have a name in my memory bank but that I struggled at that time to connect to a name. Her head was close to the young man's face and her hair fell over him like a veil.

'*Betwixt the stirrup and the ground, mercy I ask'd; mercy I found*' I whispered under my breath.

I wondered whether I should phone for an ambulance or join Dottie but I could see that there were already several more bystanders at the scene, any of whom could have already made that call. Maybe I should have gone out to help as well but I generally do not like to get involved in those kinds of situations and possess no medical skills; Dottie would have known much better exactly what to do. The woman on the radio was still insisting that '*Whitman was my daddy*'. Just too much, I thought, some people have no class. Indecisive, I considered again if I should go out and help but thought better of it; *no*, there were already too many people there, I'd just be in the way. In any case I did not have much time left to finish my tutorial. On reflection, I wonder if I was being pragmatic or just plain callous.

★

On the desk, I noticed the folded newspaper I'd brought

back with me the night before from my trip up to town. I'd picked it up off an empty train seat, where it had lain, discarded by one of the many faceless passengers on the rail journey back from Marylebone. The front page had tickled my interest. I studied again the photograph of a thirty-something woman staring out from the page, above her the headline *Thirteen Years of Solitude*. Was this the *Evening Standard*'s attempt at magical realism but 87 years short-changed? I chuckled at the conceit, at the coincidence of authorship with my original choice of text for the afternoon tutorials. Term was over of course, but I liked to keep my brain ticking over during the summer months with a series of private seminars that I ran for local writers and those who did not write. It was a book club of sorts for the deeply committed, for those who loved literature. The events unfolding before me on the street and the words rolling from my pen on to the paper appeared to be linked, through coincidence or intent, in a fatalistic dance.

*

Coincidence, if you'll permit the indulgence, is God appearing at each step that humankind takes, I jotted down on the paper.

In anticipation of such coincidences, my parents conceived of my existence more than fifty years ago on a dirty weekend in Tenby. There is an earthiness to that South Wales origination that I cherish, even if most of my subsequent life has been lived in the elite world of literature and music. Both my parents were academics. My father died a peaceful death some time ago and my mother sold off our inherited London house and retired to a splendid home in the Worcestershire countryside. She won a prize for a novel when she was young and still writes poetry for pleasure. I remember the excitement of that earlier time. I've never been as successful a writer as my mother, but I'm still hopeful and supplement my professorial income with various articles and editorial pieces. In fact I've published two novels and had been planning a third for some time before this new opportunity presented itself to me on a plate.

I have both an elder brother and a younger sister, but none of us have yet produced grandchildren for our mother. That is clearly a matter of regret to her. My brother was an analyst at a London stockbroker and made a lot of money but has now retired to the Caribbean. My younger sister, Claudia, with whom I now share the house, is both extremely beautiful and extremely difficult to know; a psychologist and now a sculptress, with a gleaming but rather cold intelligence. Despite her talents, she eschews fame and fortune and has totally dismissed the attention of numerous suitors, seeming to prefer the company of other women to that of men. She always reminds me of the heroine in that Keats poem, *La Belle Dame sans Merci*.

> *See a lily on thy brow,*
> *With anguish moist and fever-dew,*
> *And on thy cheeks a fading rose*
> *Fast withereth too.*

Keats, *La Belle Dame sans Merci*

★

In the 1970s, my father invented a theory, a 'coincidence theory' we jokingly called it within the family. In reality it had had a more abstruse mathematical name; something called 'cusp bifurcation'. I was never too clear on the detail. My father lectured in mathematics at the same local university where I now teach and achieved a modicum of fame for a time in the 70s and early 80s; his lectures were apparently generally 'standing room only'. For me, this interface with university academia sparked an unfortunate adolescent interest in unachievable women, a string of twenty-something student babysitters – girls with IQs of 160 and impossibly beautiful figures. They too often left me aching with lust and even more bored with my spotty teenage peers.

*

Richard Baxter was sent to the local public school. At first as a newcomer, he was disliked by the other boys, who found his interest in art and classical music discomfiting. They wondered whether he was 'queer', a word that was still in common usage at the time, sniggered when he approached and avoided standing too near to him in the changing rooms, as young boys do. He was smart and tough though, a decent cricketer and an amateur actor. These attributes soon broke down the barriers, especially when his less-able classmates needed help with their homework. He was generous with his time, so attitudes amongst his peers moved on quite rapidly. It quickly became apparent from his reputation for daring behaviour at parties and the minor fame of his parents that he was a magnet to attract the more desirable girls from the neighbouring school.

In turn, it was these girls' parents who now became wary of his liberal upbringing and warned their daughters to be careful of this perceived predator. There was no boasting but it was clear that he was already intimately familiar with the fairer sex in a way that the other boys only dreamed of. His openness about his experiences intrigued his peers and his experimentation with smoking weed, permitted at home by his parents, created a tension and a reputation that meant he was able to maintain some covetous respect from the prevailing schoolboy cliques. Still, he never tried too hard; if some girl wanted to go to bed with him, he would indulge her, but sex was never a compulsion of his and he did not have a long-term girlfriend till much later in life.

He went up to Cambridge with a scholarship and received the affectionate name of 'Cherub' because of his curly hair, blue eyes and pink cheeks. He both studied and partied, achieving a first in the first year of tripos, but in his second year he began to drift steadily into less desirable fringe behaviour. His looks received attention from both men and women at the Sidgwick arts site and although he continued to be popular, he never engaged totally with either his peers or his studies again. Despite this social and academic ambivalence, he somehow repeated his excellent results in finals, gaining a double-first and a further scholarship to study at an Ivy League college in the US.

After three brilliant years at Cambridge, Baxter moved across the Atlantic to Harvard and taught history and literature for a while, pandering to precocious freshmen and sophomores, many of whom also tried to bed him, entranced by his golden locks and seductive English accent. He was hesitant about their advances for ethical reasons but found their connections and fathers' money useful and their willing, athletic bodies a worthwhile distraction from the deep study required of him for his doctorate. Hawthorne, Melville, Hemingway and Henry James became his staple fodder but Kerouac and Ginsberg were increasingly his spiritual inspiration.

*

I glanced out of the window again and noticed how the woman in the street was becoming more agitated. Maybe I really should have phoned 999. What was her name? Annie, Alice maybe? Yes, that was it, Alice. Yes, I had placed her, I knew her a little: she was a friend of one of my relatives, a nice enough lady whom I had said good morning to once or twice in the street and who, from all appearances, seemed to be on good terms with just about everyone. Now that I had remembered who she was, I also recalled reading something about her in the local newspaper. It was something about forensics, I think.

They seemed to be coping well with the situation outside. It was only then that I became aware of the other incident further down the road, in the direction of the town. I could see that another crowd had gathered there. But even standing on my chair, I was unable to get a clear view from the window. The first ambulance had arrived. I noticed how the pigeons in the trees were making a mess of the roof of the electrical sub-station opposite. I would soon have to ring someone at the council about that.

*

After teaching diligently through the first few semesters at Harvard, Baxter spent the first long summer vacation in the more lucrative and urgent pursuit of cash. He had heard of a scam where men were able to double or triple their investments by bringing contraband in crates from the maquiladoras south of the border and selling it up north. No narcotics just spare parts and machinery. Baxter, as the younger son of a writer and an academic, was not one of the wealthier speculators, but he did have some money saved from teaching to invest. It was the start of a new adventure when he stepped off an Amtrak train with $300 in his pocket and headed straight towards the Mexican border, into the exciting drama of the south west in 1985.

Being an educated public school boy, drilled in the grammatical precision of Cambridge Latin, he quickly assimilated the Spanish language and enjoyed the challenge of becoming a native speaker. This period also heightened his interest in the new wave of Latin-American writers that were now exploding on the world literary scene and caused him to adapt his own narrative style to reproduce the idiomatic Spanish that he heard all around him.

In the fall, he returned to Harvard a much wealthier man. After further tedious periods of teaching, Baxter was determined the next summer to fulfil a growing ambition. He would journey south again, this time by foot, hitchhiking along the eastern slope of the Rockies, down towards Arkansas and Kansas before tracing the Okie trail. He would follow the legendary Route 66 through Amarillo to Arizona on the way to the golden promise of California. He was planning to teach his own course on the relationship between Steinbeck and Kerouac and as a 'tenderfoot' he knew that the best way to get into the soul of those 'dust-bowl' writers was to experience the landscape first hand.

'Jack Kerouac is overrated, Steinbeck was my god.'

Along the route, he planned to take a detour up into Colorado to pursue a research project he had taken on to fund his trip. A century ago, prospectors had discovered gold on the Ute Indian lands in south-western Colorado. The miners had ignored the reservation boundaries and swarmed over the native hunting grounds. The Utes threatened war. Baxter had agreed to research the history of the federal commission that went to the reservation to preserve peace – an interesting historical event that had never before been documented in detail by any other writer.

While travelling in this mountain land, he also developed an increasing interest in the role of guns in the American frontier story and throughout this time met many men who still considered a gun part of their everyday apparel. Jake Chisholm taught him how to shoot after rescuing him from two men preparing to skin him at poker. Wild Bill taught him the meaning of 'the drop' and warned him against wearing a gun in town unless he wanted trouble. Shooting was the source of his later deafness. He brought quite a collection of hunting rifles and handguns back with him to England, most of them still working. He had never bothered much with gun licenses but they made a nice display now on his study walls.

After finishing this project and in the weeks left before returning to Harvard, Baxter stopped at Jemez Pueblo, New Mexico, a village west of Santa Fe. He took a room in the pueblo where his blue eyes and rosy English cheeks earned him the name of 'Poshizmo', or 'Dawn God'. He was inspired and writing prose again. After one morning session, with nothing to do *except wait for the shadows of ladders to the flat roofs creep along the smooth walls,* he wrote the following:

A moon just past its first quarter was shining on the Indian pueblo of Santiago, so that one side of the main street (it only boasted four) was in deep shadow, while on the other the mud-built houses were made almost beautiful by the silver light. The walls on the bright side were curiously barred with the slanting shadows cast by low, broad ladders, which led from storey to storey of the terrace-like buildings, and by the projecting ends of the beams that supported their flat roofs. Outside each house, clear away from the wall, stood a great clay oven, in shape exactly like a gigantic beehive as tall as a man. In the deepest shadow on the dark side of the street, between one of these ovens and the wall, something was crouching. There was no one to disturb him, however, and the bright moon of New Mexican skies sank lower and lower in the west, and yet he remained there motionless, except when now and again the night air, growing colder, caused the blanket to be gathered more closely to the body it was protecting.

Richard Baxter Townshend, *Lone Pine*

It was at that time that he learnt belatedly of his father's death. The distressed letters from England soon convinced him that after a three-year absence he should go home directly to his widowed mother. So instead of returning to Massachusetts, he boarded a cheap flight bound for London from Denver.

As soon as he set foot back in England, Baxter found the mellowness of an English autumn oppressively muggy compared to the Rockies' bracing air. Moreover, he felt like a stranger in his native land having become accustomed to the expansiveness of the desert landscape for so long. His heart was soon longing for escape and adventure again.

Returning to England, he had also immediately realised that most of his friends were already well established in their various situations, most in stable relationships, many married, nearly all with professional jobs. He found it difficult to break into a social circle again, feeling excluded by these mature relationships, frustrated that few listened to his stories of the Wild West with any degree of interest or conviction. Fortunately, he was introduced by his mother to a sweet girl, Lettice Dorothy, or Dottie as she preferred to be known, a cousin of the famous Lygon family. She wrote poetry and read English history – she was later to become the biographer of Endymion Porter and an expert on the Long Parliament. Baxter wasted no time in falling for her and decided almost at once that he wanted to marry her but without a steady job this was deemed impossible by her father.

Baxter was obviously frustrated by this rejection, but set about trying to find work at a publisher to please his prospective father-in-law. He moved to a village near Dottie's home and then in 1997 settled in rooms at Oxford. Through influential friends he became a member of the Common Room at Wadham where he could sip tea on the emerald lawn and dream of the desert light. He spent many hours in the Pitt Rivers Museum studying old photos and shamans from the Ute reservations. Through this research into the traditions and beliefs of the Indians he began to form and write about his own version of secular humanism; a belief in an ethical life, morality without religion, about coming to terms with the consequences of human decisions while being at ease with nature. Maybe it was the mathematical genes within him but his adversity to religious thought could sometimes boil into stridency. He became interested in the works of E. F. Schumacher: *'Any intelligent fool can invent further complications, but it takes a genius to retain, or recapture, simplicity.'*

In 1998, Baxter saw his first novel published. It was a Pueblo Indian story with his own blue-eyed, curly-haired self as an important character complete with a fictional meeting with Billy the Kid. A story told through his eyes that contained a maze of contemporary detail and silvered prose.

A year later, he made a nostalgic return visit to Colorado. Armed with a camera this time, he visited the Great Plains, the Sangre de Cristo Mountains, the Grand Canyon of the Colorado and the pueblo at Jemez. The open-range life he had known for a time in his youth was rapidly giving way to asphalt, casinos and second-home developments. The old friends he sought out no longer possessed the energy and youthful glamour that he remembered, and he returned to Oxford with a portfolio of photography, yet feeling somewhat disillusioned, wondering why these toothless middle-aged rednecks had ever seemed as appealing as compatriots. *Where have all the cowboys gone?* he lamented. The photos were made into a nice coffee-table book.

> *A lone pine stands in the Northland*
> *On a bald and barren height.*
> *He sleeps, by the snows enfolded*

Richard Baxter Townshend, *Lone Pine*

After he returned to England, Dottie and Baxter lived together for a while but never married; for a while they appeared to be slowly drifting apart as sweethearts but still saw each other frequently as friends. She was by necessity increasingly devoted to her elderly father and became his constant nurse during his later years. With Baxter's literary connections, she was able to get her father's book of memoirs published. In the manuscript of one diary entry, written shortly before his death, she had recorded his personal annotations consisting of these consoling words: *Life has not been a disappointment, and there is a good deal of truth in the line: 'And for His chosen, pours His best wine last.'*

Released from this constant caring, she had travelled for a while both alone and sometimes with Baxter and then returned to Oxford where she found a new desire and mission to help the underprivileged. Rather than make a permanent move to Leamington, she instead visited Baxter and his sister most weekends. During these regular visitations she was the tender homemaker, taking his sister's place in the kitchen and he was the detached writer, hurtling now towards sixty, unable to put on the brakes.

★

Breaking my daydreams, my sister Claudia, dressed still in her dressing gown, came up alongside me in my study and put her arm around my waist, self-consciously moving her hand away from the line of my trouser belt.

'Do you think I should go out and help them?' I asked.

'I think it's too late now. Dottie's out there; best let sleeping dogs lie.'

There was almost immediately a ring at the front door. Claudia went out into the hall to answer it.

'Who is it?' I shouted after her.

'It's Dottie with Penny,' she shouted back, letting Dottie and the policewoman in.

'Do you need some help?' I asked, coming out of my study into the hall.

CHAPTER FOUR

Et In Arcadia Ego – (Allegro di molto) 'W.M.B.'

The king doth keep his revels here to-night:
Take heed the queen come not within his sight;
For Oberon is passing fell and wrath,
Because that she as her attendant hath
A lovely boy, stolen from an Indian king;

Shakespeare, *A Midsummer Night's Dream*

On the day they were going to kill him, Arish Nariman got up at five-thirty in the morning, far too early to wait for the train his friend the American architect was arriving on. He'd dreamed again of the lush tea plantations of his boyhood and he had been happy in his dream, a dream of an arcadia built by his ancestors on the coconut oil trade of the nineteenth century. There were elephants then, and tigers and monkeys and he had been treated like a little prince as a boy, with a hundred servants at his beck and call and a blue and silver Rolls-Royce to drive him to school everyday. Exiled now from his beloved Sri Lanka to this new Arcadia-Arden, he felt the sweat of the early morning in his sheets. Like his mother had once said, 'Arish, you always dream of trees.'

The Regency pleasure dome, in which he now resided, was the home of his granddaughter, who had recently married the owner, Sir William Flyte. It was both a house of escape and a house of correction. A place of self-exile for sins that he had committed but never confessed. He was revered by name in a hundred towns and villages in his native land but he knew deep in his heart the canker of his own thoughts, the obstinacy of his own will and the measure of both the right and the wrong he had done. Fortune favours the brave. He had been brave and he had amassed a fortune. He always tried to do this in an ethical way but of course this was not always possible in business.

For years he spoke out against corruption and avoided any association with the scams and government bribery that plagued his country. But late the previous year he had been caught up in a scandal involving a former associate that threatened to blacken even his good name. It was a sordid affair. He was grilled for hours by the parliamentary investigations committee about allegations of fraud during a privatisation deal and all through this painful experience he grew increasingly weary and tired of the commercial world. Towards the end of the hearings, he built up an irresistible longing to escape from the family business, to regain the freedom of his academic youth, to enjoy again the solitude and loneliness of his own thoughts, away from the concerns of money, princes and empires. In short, he'd had enough of making money. Finally he had acted upon that impulse.

For him, it was an unexpected but welcome discovery that the future King of France had lived here too. On learning about this connection, Arish had thought that maybe he too would live here for two years, he liked both the irony and the symmetry; but the restrictions of being Sir William Flyte's houseguest soon became an increasingly tiresome burden to him. Of course, he was grateful for the immediate sanctuary he had been offered as he needed to recover physically from his courtroom ordeals. He was also plagued now by a raft of minor ills and sleep loss. He had soon begun to resent the interference and loss of privacy that being part of his this man's household imposed on him. Therefore, although he had arrived with no specific plan, he became increasingly anxious to move on, to see what came his way, preferring serendipity to grand plans or any notion of destiny.

During the past few weeks, he had largely kept himself to himself, taking long walks in the town parks with his newly-acquired dogs, avoiding the tedium of social intercourse with Sir William's endless list of houseguests. Like his French predecessor, his ancestry was an adopted one, uncertain, born of the necessity of family dynasties and maternal infertility. Like Louis he was the jewel in the family crown, the last pretender. He felt that burden keenly, and had always tried to succeed through merit, but the powers of family cronyism were intense. The brutal and often cruel behavior of his business lieutenants was now a source of regret to him and in some cases guilt, so he had banished himself into self-exile, his chosen retirement to this foreign wooded Arden, amidst a countryside of rolling hills and fields, rather than further pollute the luxurious thick jungle of his Ceylonese youth.

He had been thinking a lot during this time. His mind had always been a battleground; he was smart, talented at design, visionary sometimes but fundamentally his gift had turned out to be making money. He believed that good could come from such creative tension, but his own weaknesses and temptations had equally become continuous sources of regret. Unable to quell the cynical manipulation of his cronies, who were thoroughly corrupted by his reflected power; order and truth, falsehood and disorder had all become jumbled. His was a mind that had become increasingly filled with a sense of shame. And as he neared the end of his days, he was evermore mindful of his approaching appointment with the old woman who would lead him down the bridge that narrows until the departed fall off into the abyss of hell.

All that is necessary for the triumph of evil is that good men do nothing.

He was haunted most in these thoughts by the little people who lived in the shadow of his wealth, exploited, poorly educated and often hungry; exposed to poor safety conditions in his factories. Their downtrodden lives starkly contrasting with the fabulous wealth and privilege of his family and business associates. He felt dishonoured by the extreme poverty and despair that was still on view night and day on the streets of his native city of Colombo.

The ten richest men in his home country owned more wealth than the 20 million poorest and he was certainly one of, if not, the richest. But he was also too weak to resist the self-serving flattery of his counsellors and advisors, the ugly sycophants, the venomous toads that surrounded him. Sometimes he dreamt of flying his little tin airplane over those slums, showering money over them, flying through the despairing prayers of the little people, the poor villagers trying to find gold in the downtrodden streets. But in the reality of those streets, he would still seek to avoid them, fearful of bumping into anything that was too nasty, that might stain his smart tailored suits. The auguries were clear: in the dreams that filled the darkest hours, on the nights before his predetermined death, in this godless foreign forest.

Of course he had not acknowledged the portents, or else he might have taken a different course of action that day. Compared to Colombo, where he was under the constant watch of bodyguards and security cameras, Leamington was safe, a fabulous peace, just him and his dogs and his granddaughter; believing his enemies and so-called friends to be half a world away.

Although he had a large extended family, he counted only his granddaughter as close blood now. His parents were

57

dead and he had no siblings or wife. He had nearly married once and he had fallen in love secretly many more times. His college days in the US were a history complicated by both male and female affairs. His adopted daughter had been an accident of one of those romantic interludes. Her mother was a renowned cellist who had played like an angel but had taken fright at the thought of marrying into a dynasty. She had, instead, run off with one of his friends, even though she was already carrying Arish's child. She died only a few days after the girl, his daughter, was born. On hearing the news, he had punished himself by carving a small letter *A* into his chest, the initial of his lover's and his own name, a symbol that would remind him forever of his lost love. All he had of those days of romance now were her recordings – her Elgar cello concerto was still his favourite. At the time of her death, he had been broken hearted but on this one occasion had taken responsibility for the product of his loins and arranged for the child to join him in Colombo, rather than become a long-term burden on his friend. This same architect friend was the man of molten wax who was to visit him today.

His daughter possessed courage, wit, and penetration. She had read much, and had an admirable memory; she never forgot anything she had read. At home, she had successfully applied herself to philosophy, medicine, history, and the liberal arts; and her poetry excelled the compositions of the best writers of her generation. Besides this, she was a perfect beauty, and all her accomplishments were crowned by solid virtue.

Anon, *The Arabian Nights Entertainments*

In a bitter repeat of the earlier tragedy, his adopted daughter had also died in childbirth after an affair with an unknown employee. The sad cycle had continued as he had taken on the responsibility now of caring for her child, his granddaughter Nadia. This was no chore, he had watched with delight as Nadia grew up to be a precociously talented girl, clever and well-read as well as beautiful. But her ambition soon outgrew what she could find in her native city. Arish had therefore supported Nadia's desire to study overseas and although she was certainly good enough in her own right to claim a place at any US grad school, he had made sure of her place at this lesser known English business school with a little endowment just to be sure. England was safer for a young girl than the US; he knew that from his own bitter experience. However, he had definitely not bargained for her falling in love with an English knight while she was studying here.

The two of them had met first at a university event; Sir William Flyte, the guest of honour, Nadia invited to attend as a student representative to demonstrate the university's commitment to diversity. This political knight was apparently bewitched by her right from the start as she held the whole table in her thrall with her eloquent arguments and rhetoric; she in turn was flattered by the close attention of one so powerful in this ennobled land. There had been a return invitation to his home and soon the relationship had become official, despite their considerable age difference.

As soon as he found out about it, Arish had objected to this new association. He agreed however to meet her chosen suitor at his London club for dinner but took an instant dislike to him, finding him arrogant and far too old for her. He had his assistant do some research and was soon presented with a dismaying collection of distinctly seedy stories and articles about the former MP's previous relationships. But something had clearly turned the girl's head and before he had had time to intervene, he was informed that she had travelled with Sir William to the Caribbean where they had married on the beach. Furious, Arish refused to accept the situation at first but after several long months of venting saw that his granddaughter was immovable and seemingly happy. He relented and become reconciled to the situation rather than fall out forever with the remaining love of his life. But he would get his revenge one day.

Quoth the Caliph, 'Say me, wilt thou return with us to Tigris' bank and cast thy net on my luck, and whatsoever turneth up I will buy of thee for a hundred gold pieces?' The man rejoiced when he heard these words and said, 'On my head be it! I will go back with you,' and, returning with them river-wards, made a cast and waited a while; then he hauled in the rope and dragged the net ashore and there appeared in it a chest padlocked and heavy. The Caliph examined it and lifted it finding it weighty; so he gave the fisherman two hundred dinars and sent him about his business; whilst Masrur, aided by the Caliph, carried the chest to the palace and set it down and lighted the candles. Ja'afar and Masrur then broke it open and found therein a basket of palm-leaves corded with red worsted. This they cut open and saw within it a piece of carpet which they lifted out, and under it was a woman's mantilla folded in four, which they pulled out; and at the bottom of the chest they came upon a young lady, fair as a silver ingot, slain and cut into nineteen pieces. When the Caliph looked upon her he cried, 'Alas!' and tears ran down his cheeks and turning to Ja'afar he said, 'O dog of Wazirs, shall folk be murdered in our reign and be cast into the river to be a burden and a responsibility for us on the Day of Doom? By Allah, we must avenge this woman on her murderer and he shall be made to die the worst of deaths!'

Richard Burton, *The Three Apples* from *The Book of the Thousand Nights and a Night*

This be-knighted husband was undeniably a charismatic and successful man, an engineer from an illustrious family background, who had worked in various industrial companies in the Midlands and built up a personal fortune that outshone even the huge fortune squandered by previous generations of his once ennobled family. Small, brash and wiry, his ancestors had apparently enjoyed dalliances with royalty and could trace themselves back to Edward Hyde, the First Earl of Clarendon. His father, Frederick, had been a younger brother of a previous Earl, but through a series of missteps had lost huge amounts in gambling and misplaced land deals and had died before the title passed down to him. This meant that the Earldom was now forever lost to Sir William's family line. Wherever Sir William's new money had come from, and this was by no means clear despite all Arish's assistant's research (there were rumours of a mining venture in New South Wales as well as tea plantations in Sri Lanka), it had been his ticket to influence and political intrigue.

Arish could see at once that Sir William was an inveterate self-publicist and chameleon, a ruthless man who was expert at tailoring his views to be supportive of the right part of the political elite at any one time and even more expert at getting those views published in the press without ever being directly attributed. His mastery of these black arts had even earned him the nickname 'The black dog of Arden' within the party, a reference to Guy, Earl of Warwick, who was Piers Gaveston's executioner. The knighthood had been a political reward from the grateful new Prime Minister, along with his selection as the local MP in a by-election following his predecessor's death. During his short time as a legislator, he had narrowly avoided censure over parliamentary expenses and undeclared consultancy contracts and had run into trouble with red-top stories about a series of mistresses around the country. These colourful adventures however appeared not to be major obstacles for a man of his ambition.

More problematic however was the unexpected loss of his safe seat, one that had been Tory since Eden (and before) in a particularly bitter general election fight. Despite this setback, he fully expected to be promoted to the Upper House in the course of time, regaining the peerage that his foreshortened ancestry had narrowly denied. For now he was playing the role of a party grandee, remodelling himself as the country squire, gentleman and fixer, and this is why his Leamington townhouse was usually full of houseguests at the weekends.

Sir William had been married twice before he married Nadia. The first time to a society debutante, Lady Mary Lygon, the daughter of the late Earl Beauchamp, with whom he had fathered three children, Julia, Cordelia and Sebastian. Sebastian had died young and tragically and Sir William was now estranged from Lady Mary and on increasingly poor terms with his two daughters. Although strangely, and to his frustration, the women all insisted on living in the adjoining townhouse to him, which was now dangerously close to becoming a witches' coven in his eyes.

Just before he met Nadia, he had also been involved in a strange scandal that had kept the press happy for weeks with a shotgun marriage to a blonde Australian heiress, a scion of a famous newspaper dynasty. After less than a month of marriage she had packed his suitcase for him and sent him back to Britain, describing her ex-husband to the local papers as 'the perfect liar' and claiming that their marriage was never consummated. He denied all of this of course, typically blagging it out with the papers through his PR. The publicity had further strained relations with next-door however, and this was exacerbated when he had altered his will to cut them out of their inheritance in favour of Nadia. This brought upon all of them the prospect of years of litigation to follow.

Despite the unhappiness surrounding her marriage, Nadia was devoted to her grandfather and since his arrival in England she had begun to see evermore clearly her own situation. As a result, she had started to suffer her husband for the sake of form rather than love, having worked out his modus operandi far too late to regret her decision to marry him. She had also now secretly renewed her acquaintance with a younger former lover, Rohit, who once worked for her father as his assistant but was now estranged from him. He was the son of a famous cricketer, who had moved to England to be close to her and now worked for a local translation company, studying part-time as a writer. Her grandfather didn't know and didn't need to know about the renaissance of their relationship. They were discreet and although they met frequently and clandestinely, Rohit never visited her while her grandfather (or indeed her husband) were in the house. She was careful to keep everything above board.

With the arrival of her grandfather in Leamington, Nadia's earlier devotion to him had been reinvigorated. He suffered greatly from insomnia and increasingly from memory loss and tremors in his hands. She listened all night from her adjacent room as he tossed and turned, waiting for his call or for the bump if he fell out of bed in his disturbed dreams. In the early hours, even before the first rays of dawn were appearing on the horizon, she rose to make him sweet tea with the little spirit stove she kept in her room, so that the first thing he tasted in the morning was the product of her own hands, not the sediment of old age on his palate.

Despite these disturbed nights, when he awoke that Saturday morning, Arish felt in good humour, if a little sleepy. The day was already bright outside and his granddaughter had left his customary tea by his bedside. This was to be an auspicious day when his friend would arrive to visit them, having travelled all the way from America to speak at an architects' symposium. It would be the first time he had seen him in many years, although they kept in touch irregularly. His friend was a two-time widower now, did not trust hotels nor had he travelled much outside his native Michigan. He accepted Arish's offer to stay with him only after lengthy persuasion. At his request, in order to get out of the indebtedness of staying with Sir William, Arish's former company had arranged for the lease of a small villa in the town and hired a housekeeper. His granddaughter was to help him move in that day and his American visitor would be the first guest in his new home. Outside the open window of his bedroom, the bells of the local church chimed the hour. As his granddaughter put her head through his door, he remarked how happy he was, and she said she was pleased, in return, to see him in such good spirits.

From the east to western Inde,
No jewel is like Rosalinde…

Shakespeare, *As You Like It*

He dressed in his normal careful manner, shaving with brush and cream and cut throat razor; put on a smart shirt and tie and one of his trademark Savile Row suits, tailored in an old-fashioned colonial style, tucking a smart pink silk handkerchief in his pocket. This was a special occasion and he would dress the part.

'Any dream about flying means good health,' she said.

At breakfast, Sir William announced loudly his plans for the day, laying down the law in his usual energetic and expressive style and enquired if Arish would need transportation to the train station. Arish respectfully declined this unwelcome attempt to interfere, he preferred to walk to the station and was not one for breakfast. But he was persuaded by Nadia to take a fig from the bowl of fruit in the music room. As he put it in his pocket, he admired one last time the Poussin that hung on the wall over an exquisite Carlton House desk. He re-read the card underneath the painting: *Shepherds wandering out in a morning of the spring, and coming to a tomb with the quotation, 'I also was an Arcadian'.* Satisfied he went to collect his dogs from their kennel in the scullery.

The last time Nadia heard his voice was as he called out his plans for the morning to her. He would walk, sinless, down to the train station with the dogs and take his friend back to the villa in a taxi; he would meet up with her there later. Then she heard the uncharacteristic slam of the door as if a moment of impetuosity had taken over from his normal controlled reserve; as if he was slamming the door decisively on the past.

He's as excited as a little boy, she thought.

CHAPTER FIVE

LOVE, LET US BE TRUE – (MODERATO) 'R.P.A.'

Ah, love, let us be true
To one another! for the world, which seems
To lie before us like a land of dreams,
So various, so beautiful, so new,
Hath really neither joy, nor love, nor light,
Nor certitude, nor peace, nor help for pain;
And we are here as on a darkling plain
Swept with confused alarms of struggle and flight,
Where ignorant armies clash by night.

Matthew Arnold, *Dover Beach*

I know now that the Dell Park holds a special sort of magic for Izzie. Like an urban Miranda she is able to summon the sprites that live in the undergrowth and command them to weave their spells. She walks through the park each evening in the gathering dusk on her way back to the care home from her bedsit. My darling, darling Izzie loves this little sunken pleasure ground, surrounded by its high, flowered banks, overlooked by the lights from the balconies of the sparkling mansions across the road. It is her bejewelled island in the storm of the town.

Once the course of a small brook, the Dell Park was originally created when a stream was culverted and the road to Warwick built up to avoid the muddy ground on either side. The sunken hollow that remained was improved with formal gardens and a 'pepper pot' summerhouse but it later fell into decay, becoming grassed over between the wars. By the 1970s, it had become infamous for gangs and drug users but in recent years, dedicated volunteers have returned it to a place of safety.

By day, it is a quiet refuge for mothers and nannies with their young charges, protected by the steep banks from the traffic noise above, a place to run and play safely on the swings and roundabouts. By night, it takes upon itself a more subtle mantle, a more delicious place of intrigue, of lovers' trysts, where benches, thronging with children by day, give host to softer pleasures, bats and foxes roam and the calming balm of night scents hang like a fragrant mist over the promenade and entrance steps. It was and is her special place.

*

The afternoon before they met had seen the annual children's party take place there with the local mums bringing picnics and games. There was a local band playing folk songs, a tea tent and traditional games and tombola stalls. Although she was not on duty, Izzie had taken one of the ladies from the home where she worked for a walk there to enjoy the afternoon sun. Now, immediately before their first meeting, she was returning to the home again for her night shift. All signs of the party had been cleared away, the gazebo had gone, the Punch and Judy man had been returned to his local rest home and not a sign of the staging remained apart from the slight depressions on the grass.

As Izzie peered over the iron railings from the north entrance, she began to make out the sound of the playing of a lone guitarist and single clear male voice singing down below amongst the shadows. Intrigued, she opened the little iron gate carefully so that it did not squeak and walked down the steep unlit path towards the source of the music below, moving quietly so as not to disturb the musician in his performance; in case there was any danger there.

As she moved past the scented drifts of mallows and veronica, she saw a young man seated on one of the benches, a can of beer by his side and a battered acoustic guitar in his hands. He was a little older than her, with close-cropped blonde hair and a little goatee beard. He was wearing grey cargo pants and an old U of M college T-shirt and playing with the precision of someone classically trained, using his finger as a bar and plucking the strings expertly, This contrasted with the few borrowed chords strummed with a plectrum that she could manage on the guitar. He finished the Rodrigo 'Adagio' and started on a new song, this time playing a popular standard with a full body and chorus. She recognised the introduction immediately and then the chords and familiar words as he started gently onto the first line of Simon and Garfunkel's 'America'.

From her hidden viewpoint, Izzie fingered these same chords in her mind, remembering her first guitar lessons with her tutor Eddie – C, Bm, Am, G, F. Later Eddie had set her more taxing études as she progressed to the viola. One of them involved a tricky little exercise in crossing from the fourth to the second string without accidentally catching the third, something that she had never quite managed to master. Although she enjoyed playing, she was not particularly musical herself although many said that she had a nice singing voice, if slightly unusual in its lilting cadence.

She hesitated in the shadows, her curiosity for once beginning to get the better of her normally cautious nature. She did not make a habit of approaching strange men drinking beer in parks but this one was cute and played exquisitely. She watched while he continued to sing through the first few lines of the song. He stopped at the end of the first verse to take another swig of beer from the can.

This was her chance. She was now determined and could no longer resist the temptation, even though it meant revealing that she had been watching him. Softly, she returned his words with the familiar next line in her own fey Irish voice.

★

There was a slight pause while I considered this newcomer's intervention. Gently at first, I returned the next line back to her. The line hung like a question in the sweet night air, before I increased the tempo and volume of my playing towards a crescendo. Our solos met in a duet as we followed the words of the song. We both went to look for America.

In full flow now, I finished off the riff with a flourish and turned, eager to see who it was singing along with me. I watched breathlessly as her heavenly figure emerged from the shadows of the bushes. She smiled and I smiled back encouragingly, noticing immediately the unusual length of her linen-white hair and the capricious brightness of her eyes. Two piercings on her face glinted in the park lights. She was wearing an overcoat over a nurse's tunic and sensible flat shoes.

'Your voice is amazing. Maybe I've found my next co-singer?' I ventured to her half-joking, half-flattering, eager to break the silence.

'Hardly,' she said somewhat pensively but then walked more decisively up to the bench where I was sitting. Her long part-braided hair was tied back with floral bands, almost reaching down to her waist.

'Hi, my name's Penn,' I said, with disappointing lack of originality, holding out my hand in greeting. 'Tristan Penrose Arnold to be exact.'

'My, that's a very distinguished sounding name,' she said,

shaking my hand demurely, her eyes not quite meeting mine.

'Yeah maybe, I also go by Tris but Penn works too. And, may I ask the name of my anonymous seraph?'

'You may. It's Isobel, but everyone calls me Izzie,' she said and I received the full gift of her smile as her face came alive.

'Well, come here and sit beside me Lady Isobel aka Izzie, I promise I won't bite and there's plenty of room on this bench.'

> *Guiltless I gaz'd; heav'n listen'd while you sung;*
> *And truths divine came mended from that tongue.*

Alexander Pope, *Eloisa to Abelard*

'Oh, I think I'd prefer to stand,' she said, staring away from me again, twiddling her hair with her fingers.

'Whatever,' I replied, somewhat disappointed but not discouraged.

'So, are you some sort of professional musician?' she asked, becoming a little more engaged as she turned back to face me.

'No, I just play to relax and busk for a few pennies here and there, that's all.'

'But you're very good, you know, that was really beautifully played,' she replied softly. *But nowhere near as beautiful as you*, I thought.

Instinctively, I jumped up onto the bench and opened out my arms to the sky, pointing up at a bright evening star as it emerged from the clouds above the park. To prove my point I started into an improvised thing that rapidly transformed into a rambling speech, playing both lovers' parts with alternate deep male and falsetto female voices:

*'I swear to thee, youth, by the white hand of Rosalinde, I
am that he, that unfortunate he.'
'But are you so much in love as your rhymes speak?'
'Neither rhyme nor reason can express how much.'*

Shakespeare, *As You Like It*

My fooling about had the desired effect. She laughed,
seemingly delighted, and applauded.

'You're mad,' she said. 'So if you're not a musician are
you in rep?' She was clearly beginning to warm to my
charm. The air was turning chilly now and she held her coat
close to her body. In the distance, I could just hear the
sounds of the traffic above the earth banks that protected the
park. Hopefully she no longer felt any sense of threat from
me. I continued to play the amiable clown.

'Not at the moment, dearest Lady Isobel aka Izzie. At the
moment I am an actor of film, no less,' I replied with a deep
bow, in the most pompous Shakespearean character voice
that I could muster. She told me later that there was such
intensity to my voice and eyes at that moment that it made
her feel almost naked before me as if I was conjuring her
soul with my words.

'Wow, really, you're a serious actor? That's amazing,' she
stumbled, but her shy face betrayed immediately that she
realised this may have sounded somewhat gushing, if not a
little credulous.

'Well a temporarily-not-out-of-work actor would be
more accurate. I was in class when this audition came up
and nobody was more freaked than me when I got the
part. But yes indeed, my fair lady, we have been filming
all day over in the square. A great costume drama… well
actually an episode of *Sherlock* for the BBC,' I added, half-
covering my mouth with the back of my hand as if
speaking to a hidden audience off-stage. 'My part's a

minor character in possession of one of the clues to the mystery that Mr Holmes has to solve but I am also the understudy to the well-known actor who plays Dr Watson, no less.'

'Really? *Sherlock*? I love that programme, I'm a huge fan,' she replied.

'Well, yes it certainly has a cult following.'

'So tell me then, did Sherlock Holmes really jump in that last episode?' she asked, somewhat over enthusiastic again but getting back ahead on points in whatever game we were now playing.

'I'm afraid you know that if I told you the answer to that, I and the rest of the cast would probably have to shoot you. But anyway fair maiden, enough of those other lesser mortals, more importantly I am afraid I was not planning to entertain a lady this evening – by chance do you have anything to drink in that bag?' I asked, pointing down at the shopping bag she was holding and shaking the beer can to prove that it was empty.

'Actually I do, but it's really meant for someone else, someone special, you know.'

'Ah then my lady, I sense you have another assignation planned? I am undone. Can't you renege on that contract?' I asked pleadingly.

She teased me by poking the screw-cap bottle of cheap Italian white wine over the top of the bag.

'I suppose I could always get another bottle if you pay me for this one with your takings,' she answered, holding out her hand. 'But as for the other assignation…'

I dropped five one pound coins from my hat into her hand and she passed the bottle over to me. I unscrewed the cap and passed it back to her, indicating that she should take the first sip, which she did, before taking it back from her and swallowing a much larger gulp. I wiped my mouth with the sweatband on my wrist.

'So come fair Lady Isobel, now that I have entertained you, may I accompany you to your steed?'

I took her by the hand and led her over to the kiddies' swings, where she sat as directed, giggling, as I began to push her backwards and forwards, higher and higher. Her hair was floating in the night air as she looked up at the rushing clouds and the glint of the park lights on my face. She stopped the swing suddenly with her feet and turned to me.

'Is something wrong?' I asked, worried.

'You know what?'

'What?'

'Nothing, I really shouldn't!'

'Come on, you can do better than that,' I said.

But she thought better of whatever she was going to say, and instead blew me a kiss that hung in the air for a second before she spoke again.

'Sorry must be the wine, you'd better not give me another swig,' she said, giggling. 'And I'm afraid I really do have to get to work soon.'

I placed a finger over her lips to signal that she should say no more as we stood silently for a while, looking up at the stars and counting the meteors flashing across the sky. At that point, she looked at her watch and realised that she definitely had to go or she would be late for her shift.

'Reluctantly, Mr Penn, although I wish I could stay here all night, I do have to go to work now.'

I shrugged and we left the swings and began to walk up the path to the road, passing the remains of the little summerhouse at the corner of the garden. I stopped and this time pretended to hide behind the wall, growling like a lion before starting my next recital:

> *'O wall, full often hast thou heard my moans,*
> *For parting my fair Pyramus and me!*

My cherry lips have often kiss'd thy stones,
Thy stones with lime and hair knit up in thee.'

Shakespeare, *A Midsummer Night's Dream*

'You're crazy; you really are a clown aren't you? But a sweet, clever clown I think,' she said.

'It works for me every time.'

'I bet it does.'

'And you are now my *Angell from her bowre of blis.'*

'Come on, you daft idiot,' she said. 'Before I do something I'll regret later. I do have to get to work and you look like you could do with getting some sleep if you're acting on set tomorrow.'

CHAPTER SIX

Tristan and Iseult – (Andantino) 'Ysobel'

*Take me to that happy place of which you told me long ago.
The fields whence none return, but where great singers sing
their songs forever.*

Joseph Bedier – *The Romance of Tristan and Iseult*

Penn and I walked up to the main road and headed into town, towards the traffic lights by the fire station. We were holding hands, brushing each other's bodies deliberately as we walked. A night bus rushed past us on its way towards Warwick, faces laughing in the windows. He sang that the man with the bowtie and gabardine suit was really a spy. You know the score.

We turned north onto the road that led up towards Clarendon Square, past the estate agent and up to the row of long-term residential homes on the left where I worked.

'Well, this is me,' I said as we reached my work place. Penn peered at the sign.

'Sherridge House, rest home for the gentry,' he read. 'You really work here?'

'Sort of, it's money while I study. Don't sound so surprised. It's OK you know.'

'No, it's just that I can see the building from the set where I am working. Which one is your bedroom?' I was a bit taken aback by his forwardness.

'Sorry, they're day rooms only and no male admirers

allowed either, much as I'd love to invite you up of course,' I said with a slight reprimand in my voice.

'What you mean if I were in your neighbourhood?'

'Smoothy, I really love that movie,' I laughed.

'Yes, it's kind of cool, if a little dated now.' He kissed me courteously, creating a lovely feeling in my tummy, and we exchanged phone numbers. The street lamps lit up our faces with an amber glow as we stared at each other. Neither of us dared to lose the moment and say goodbye. I wanted him to kiss me again.

'No moon tonight though,' I said.

'It'll be out the other side of midnight, I'll wait for you here if you want?'

'Sorry, but I'm on an all-night shift so it would be a very long wait for you.'

'No matter, I can still wait, I'm cultivating a career as a frustrated romantic hero. But are you sure I can't divert you, *I'm a sure thing!*' he said, winking. He pushed up my chin lightly and then brushed my lips softly with his fingertips, as if to indicate I should not utter another word, that I should not break the silence.

'Sorry, I appreciate the seduction thing, but you've chosen the wrong movie again, I'm afraid, I've really got to go.'

'Breakfast then?'

'At Tiffany's I suppose?'

'Where else?'

'Wait for me, after all, nothing bad could happen to you here, could it?'

*

I watched Izzie for a few moments while she rang the bell and went inside. Then I walked reluctantly back down the short drive to the wall along the pavement and sat on it, drinking the rest of the wine from the bottle, watching up at the windows above. A smartly dressed old man passed me with two dogs and I noticed how serene he looked. He was foreign. I caught on his face the expression of one who could see the approaching of his own end but seemed reconciled to it. In the distance, towards the centre of the town I could hear police sirens, dealing with some trouble presumably at the town pubs. Further down the road, there was a black cab crawling slowly alongside the kerb as if following the old man home. I thought I could hear a nightingale, bringing sanity and peace, or it might have been the first sleepy lark.

Thinking back over my sweet encounter, I began to sing to myself but was disturbed from those thoughts by a loud sound above. As I hoped, I was rewarded by a further glimpse of Izzie as she opened the sash window and popped her head out of the opening to blow me down a final kiss.

'*Did my heart love till now? Forswear it, sight! For I ne'er saw true beauty till this night.*' I shouted up at the window.

'Be quiet, you idiot,' she hissed back. 'You'll wake the patients.'

'*O, wilt thou leave me so unsatisfied?*'

She threw something down at me. I picked it up. It was a little plastic juice bottle with a scribbled note and directions to her flat stuffed inside. *I'll be home about 9.00am, meet me there if you can, with breakfast and jewelled favours,* I read.

CHAPTER SEVEN

Pearl's a Singer – (Presto) 'Troyte'

*Leamington is a very new and neat town. It is more difficult
to give a person who hasn't seen England an idea of it than
of such a place as Chester. It is very characteristic of England
too. The prevalent hue of houses, sidewalks, road &
everything is a cheerful drab or buff. The bricks are buff. The
stucco with which the neat plain houses are mostly covered
is buff. The stone of the nice sidewalks is the same color, and
so are the smooth & clean roads. The houses are singularly
devoid of all attempts at ornament or where there is any it is
of a super-chaste description. The whole has that trim & trig
aspect which belongs to everything English. We are living at
a ruinous rate at the Regent Hotel here. We have a bed room,
a large dressing room big enough for a single bed room and
a parlor 7 breadths of Brussels carpet wide and as long as 11
breadths. The parlor has a wide window in the middle of its
length (All English windows are very wide, which is a great
beauty) & another at one end. An open grate with a fire at
the end, bronzes on the mantle piece & a mirror over it. On
the long side opposite the window is a long mahogany
sideboard inlaid with a white wood. On this sideboard is a
gilt and alabaster clock & two gilt vases all under glass bells
and a mirror runs the length of the sideboard & over it hangs
one of those round diminishing mirrors. There is another
mahogany sideboard with a marble top and mirror over it at
one end of the room. There is an oblong mahogany table with
a cloth in the middle of the room supported on a sort of claw.
At each window there is a little mahogany stand. At the end*

of the room is a chess & backgammon table. There are two
fauteuils before the fire. There are two ladies sewing chairs
& six common chairs. One large screen & two fire screens
complete the furniture of the room. The bed room measures
6 breadths by 7½. The furniture is all mahogany. There is
a four post bedstead and canopy. Marble topped wash stand.
High bureau, cheval glass, lace covered toilet table with
mirror, bed side table, chairs, etc. The dressing room is just
half the size of the bed room & contains a similar wash-
stand, toilet table, bath tub, bureau, etc. The house is so quiet
that no one would imagine there was another soul in it but
ourselves.

Charles Sanders Peirce, *Letter from Leamington to his family*
in America (1875)

Pearl Detroit Taylor knew before she stepped off the train that she probably would not harm him too much. She had far subtler ways planned to exact her revenge. The illegitimate daughter of a black Detroit seamstress, she was a star. She was feted across Europe as a blues and jazz singer – the woman with the honeyed voice. She had carefully built a career and a reputation as the complete entertainer; a reputation that she was not about to give up in a fit of recklessness. However, despite all this hard earned prosperity and indeed adulation, she still bore the scars of the past. Amongst them, the complex currents of her mixed race, her own troubled history and the mystery concerning the identity of her real father. She also had a diva's reputation for being 'difficult'.

Her mother's family were of Creole descent, slaves escaped from the south on the Underground Railroad into the rural villages around Windsor, Ontario. Gradually they had been pulled towards the new economic slavery of Carnegie's steel mills and Henry Ford's giant car plants. Her mother's legal husband was a sea captain, a difficult man who alternately ignored and abused his wife during his brief sojourns on dry land. Pearl herself was the offspring not of that marriage but of an adulterous affair. Her mother had looked to blues bar punters for comfort after her husband was reported lost at sea near Suriname. For years she did not know the name of her real father. She had been given the name Pearl by her grandmother, after the slave steamboat that was captured at Point Lookout in Maryland. The one celebrated in *Uncle Tom's Cabin*. The family story was that her mother had added the name both of the city of her birth, 'Detroit' and the town of Pearl's conception, 'Taylor' on the forms that she completed to register her birth.

An older man in a sports jacket was sitting across from her in the First Class compartment, deep in thought, reading the morning papers. She had followed him discreetly onto the train at Marylebone an hour and a half ago. She noticed that the headlines of his paper were all about the UK government's defeat in a parliamentary debate on Syria. Pearl found this recent British squeamishness about war rather out of character; *their ancestors were certainly not so fastidious*, she thought. Pearl herself was no stranger to trouble. Indeed, she felt she was now closer than ever to a settling of scores with the gentleman opposite. His fate was certainly a fitting subject for divine judgement, a just war, which she would now help along in its execution. The next few days would be about her own amusement and satisfaction, if not retribution.

As the man stepped off the train at Leamington, Pearl followed discreetly at a distance. Well, as discreetly as a black diva dressed in a fur stole and fishnet stockings could in this small Midlands town. She followed her quarry down the concrete steps onto the station forecourt. The man was looking around impatiently, checking his watch, pacing up and down underneath the art deco clock that hung above the station entrance. After twenty minutes, he appeared to give up waiting and got into a cab with his suitcases. Pearl followed, enjoying the cinematic thrill of asking the taxi driver to 'follow that cab'. After less than five minutes, they pulled up at the old man's apparent destination, a pretty villa called 'Hawthorne House' in a quiet cul-de-sac called 'Lansdowne Crescent'. The old man paid the cab driver, rattled the brass doorknocker and was let in by a young woman. Pearl asked her cabbie to circle round the little circus once more and, satisfied for the moment that he would not re-emerge, revised her instructions. 'Take me to the Holly Hotel.' This proved to be a second short journey of not more than 100 yards from Hawthorne House.

*

Pearl's mother, Esther, was a strong-willed and impetuous woman in her youth, frequently in trouble for her rebellious behaviour. By day she was a seamstress, but by night she transformed into a soul singer. She continued to belt out numbers in *The Soup Kitchen* with the stage name Ella, even after her lover had left her pregnant and moneyless. Under threat of exposure as an adulterer, this unnamed man had paid her off but she was too afraid to use the backstreet abortionists and so she had carried his child full term.

When the baby finally arrived and its mixed race became obvious to everybody, many in the Afro-American community of her hometown of Taylor were incensed and pilloried her for bearing a nameless white man's child. This was a blue-collar town, with a majority white population, many of whom worked in the car plants along the river. Such interracial liaisons were not uncommon but were still frowned upon. Despite the name-calling and worse, she steadfastly gave out no clue to the father's identity. As a result, Esther was progressively ostracised within her own community. She had no choice but to sing in white men's clubs at night and clean tables for hours in the local diner by day, to earn enough money to live. This came to a head when one night she was attacked and raped by a group of drunken steel workers. After this experience, she was much more circumspect. She wore her hair short to avoid attention. Although she was exposed to possible shame and humiliation on every street corner, she bore it all with a quiet dignity. She continued to resist the cajoling to reveal the name of her child's father, even when she became near destitute herself. Despite her poverty, she always dressed her daughter in the best crimson pinafores she could afford.

Esther's original husband, the supposedly lost sea captain Ishmael Chilling, returned unexpectedly to the town to reclaim his family inheritance. Small and misshapen, he soon regained his former notoriety as he trawled round the town bars haphazardly trying to find Esther. The first time he entered the bar where she worked, Esther recognised him at once. She ran out in distress to the kitchens, making an excuse of illness to leave her shift. Of course she had to return the next night or lose her job permanently, so she was careful to disguise her face as best she could. She feared what this man would do to an adulteress and her daughter when he discovered them, as she knew he surely would. She began to make plans to visit a distant relative, but that very night she was unlucky; he was back there again and she could not escape a second time.

Noticing something strange in the way she moved and avoided showing her face, the sea dog asked a local who the pretty girl who served behind the bar was. The local readily told him Esther's story. He quickly realised, that it was the story of own wife and her infidelity. He reacted angrily, exclaiming loudly to all the other drunks that he would punish her and that the child's father, the partner in the adulterous act, should be punished too. He set about immediately to reclaim his ready-made family. He dragged Esther outside and beat her in an attempt to make her reveal the name of the father of the child. She was later found sobbing, beaten black and blue, in the park. Her face bore the scars of his vicious attack for all to see.

Her story attracted the attention and protection of the local Baptist minister, who took her into his care. Fortunately for Esther, the sailor soon tired of pursuing this ungrateful and penniless woman. With his inheritance nearly spent, he gave up his fruitless quest and returned to sea to seek his fortune. He was never seen in the neighbourhood again.

The Baptist minister, now somewhat attracted to Esther himself, helped her resettle in the margins of the town. But with her disfiguring facial scars she was no longer able to go out to work in the clubs; instead she scraped a living doing needlework and chores, refusing nearly all contact with the outside world. She refused even to go to church, despite the minister's constant urging.

Her daughter, Pearl, grew up fast; she was Esther's precious treasure *plucked from a bush of wild roses* but without a father the child's behaviour became increasingly troubled. Like her mother before her, she was a capricious and unruly girl and became wilder and wilder. She chased off other children with stones when they tried to taunt her about Esther's moral lapses. The other members of the local Baptist congregation began to talk openly about having to take her into their care and decided to 'examine' the child.

On that occasion, the elders questioned Pearl closely about her religious faith. She refused to answer their questions directly, instead responding with pointed questions of her own. She questioned their own probity; they were questions of such perception and bravado that the minister and elders had to relent. In lieu of being taken away from her mother, the girl was encouraged instead to join the church choir. This released in her a precocious talent. As her singing grew more and more confident, her range expanded beyond that typical of a gospel singer and she began to imitate the soul and blues artists that she heard on the jukebox in the soda store down the street. By the age of seven, her mother knew she too would become a singer, destined to follow in her footsteps, but hopefully this time with the potential to be a star.

As she blossomed into a young woman, Pearl sang with energetic rhythm for the diners in local restaurants and began to attract her own, mostly male, following. She taught herself to play the piano, entertaining in the slots between the strippers at late night clubs. Although she was no great musician, in fact she later described herself as enthusiastically incompetent at the piano; she developed a reputation for singing with a soul and pathos well beyond her tender years. She entered and won a talent contest sponsored by a local radio station; the prize was to cut a record. It sold enough to keep them going for a while but her mother knew from experience that she was never going to make it that way.

She continued to work the clubs around the river, like her mother before her, from the age of fifteen onwards. But she was still unsure whether she could make is as a soloist. With the encouragement of the minister, she entered college instead to study for a diploma in pharmacy, but she was soon bored and dropped out after a year. She met an agent who took an unhealthy interest in her. But at least he was good at his job and found her work. She began to pursue her singing career again, touring for a while with a minor Motown group around the Midwest. It was at this time that she made her first professional recordings, initially as a backing singer and then in her own right.

About that time, Pearl also developed a strong desire to find out more about her natural father. Her mother was still completely silent on the subject and refused all pleas for information. But with the money she was now earning, Pearl could afford to hire a private detective. He was only too glad to spend her money trawling the clubs where Esther used to sing, looking for information. Eventually he identified the names of two or three possible candidates. The most promising lead was a well-educated architect, a man of some local renown, who now practised in the suburbs. In his youth, he had spent a few too many evenings with his college friends in the blues clubs where Esther sang along the Detroit River. Apparently he had enjoyed many a dalliance with the singers there and was still remembered less than fondly by them; he had earned the nickname 'Ninepin' amongst the girls on account of his multiple conquests and premature lack of hair.

The man the detective had identified, a certain Arthur Hathorne Troyte, had an obedient wife, lived in a nice home in Ann Arbor, ran a classic 1960s Lincoln Continental, and had two beautiful all-American kids at high school. He was to all intents and purposes a pillar of the local community. The detective had also found out that his family had heritage. In fact he was from deep New England roots – the Hathornes who had reputedly crossed with the puritans to Boston. One of his ancestors was the only Salem judge to have never repented of his actions in the famous witch trials; another was the better known Nathaniel Hawthorne, the great American novelist, who had added a 'w' to his name to escape the embarrassing infamy of his forefathers. Here was the uncanny link to Hawthorne House.

However, now that she had this much information Pearl was no longer satisfied just with an investigation. She felt there was a settling of scores required, but how could she be sure that they had tracked down the right man? She became even more determined not to let this go now she that had a target in sight. However, the detective advised her against a direct approach given Troyte's senior position in society, her mother's long silence and the lack of any previous attempt to make contact. So instead, she and the detective devised a strategy to put him off his guard and try and establish through a sting whether he really was her father or not. They found out that Arthur was suffering from a debilitating skin disease as a result of his earlier sexual exploits and to get close to him, the detective would trick him into believing that he was a consultant specialising in such cases.

It worked. After a few sessions, the private detective let slip that he knew something of Troyte's previous background. Arthur at first reacted with fury and denied knowing anything about Esther and her daughter and even when shown a photograph genuinely did not seem to recognise Esther at all. But the detective was persistent and clever and with the heavy threat of revelations to his family, Arthur finally reluctantly agreed to meet Pearl.

Pearl knew that she needed to get her mother to come along to this meeting as well if she was going to be sure. But she equally knew that if she told Esther who she was about to meet, she would not agree to go. So she made up a story about getting her mother to come with her to meet a potential sponsor for a record deal. The meeting place was a popular lunch stop in Greek Street in downtown Detroit.

As soon as she saw Troyte, Esther recognised him at once and reacted hysterically, starting to abuse and then scream at him across the table. She tore herself away from Pearl's hold and started to land blows on his shocked face, before storming out of the restaurant cursing. In a state of shock at this violent outburst, but still not being clear himself that he knew who this woman or her daughter was, Troyte continued to deny vehemently to Pearl and the detective that he had anything to do with them. The detective started to argue with him loudly.

To avoid an even bigger scene in front of the amazed and

prosperous lunch crowd, Troyte suddenly changed his tune. He blurted out a rash promise to pay them a substantial sum to keep silent and leave him alone, before hurriedly walking out of the restaurant himself. Pearl looked at the detective in amazement; she had not really been after money, it was really about finding her father, but given the turn of events she quickly began to recalculate her next move.

Even after this dramatic meeting, her mother continued to deny that this man was Pearl's father but equally would not explain her amazing behaviour or how she knew him. After a week or so of arguments, Pearl decided belatedly that she had better drop the whole thing. In any case, she had now decided that she really wanted nothing to do with this man. Despite what her mother said, he had now confirmed in her mind by his actions, if not his words, that he was the love cheat. Still, money was money and with the sum he agreed to pay them for their silence, Pearl was able to move to New York with her mother. She agreed as part of that settlement to make no further attempts to contact him. To her dying day, her mother would never speak about the incident again.

Now thrown into a whole new world of possibility, Pearl soon began to get jobs singing at off-Broadway venues and jazz clubs like the Blue Morocco. Her mother spent her time in contemplation and charitable work with the poor and the lonely of SoHo. Pearl was noticed by Randy Benjamin at the Blue Chord club in Greenwich Village. After a trial period, the club booked Pearl on a semi-permanent basis, singing four nights a week to the post-theatre dinner crowds. At first, the money was not enough to live on and she had to supplement her income by working in a pharmacy during the day. But her reputation spread rapidly and soon she was playing for playwrights and presidents, ambassadors and bankers and further record deals beckoned. She got herself a proper agent. Cool and strong, singer and storyteller, happy black courage in a white man's world, she rapidly became the darling of every Kubla Khan and pleasure seeker along the entertainment venues that lined 42nd Street. Within a few years, she had made enough money to set her mother up in a nice brownstone apartment overlooking Central Park while she prepared for a grand tour of Europe. Once across the Atlantic, she repeated and built further on her success and quickly gained a new following in the capitals of the old continent, feted as the new Anita Baker, a blues and jazz sensation. There were television appearances on French and German TV, recording several albums of soulful songs. A new transatlantic star was born

*

Now approaching fifty, Pearl is still physically striking and a mature and brilliant singer. She has the face to rival the most beautiful of women and the mind of the most resolute of men. A mulatto Amazon of weird and haunting beauty, with deep black locks and a powerful body customarily encrusted with scarlet and gold, she is given to wearing flamboyant native African clothing on stage and designer couture off-stage. On her fingers she wears rings of every shape and colour, but the one she still values the most is the simple ring on her middle finger. It is solid gold, with a great scarlet *E* picked out with rubies in a field of diamonds, in honour of her mother who had died the previous year. Tipped off out of the blue by an informer about Troyte's planned trip to Europe, she had come up with a scheme, now that her mother was dead, to exact further revenge on him. Importantly, she now has the money and means to make her mother's former lover suffer a whole lot more for his past sins.

Pearl had to admit that she found The Holly Hotel a little

disappointing compared to her normal standard of accommodation at the George V or Claridges – the *lodgings were fashionable enough, but rather limited in point of space and conveniences*. She spent the afternoon wandering round the town's boutique shops and pleasure gardens, which were amusing enough, if provincial in range and ambition. She also sought the assistance of a very knowledgeable young man in the computer store and bought a trunk appropriate for a travelling lady, as well as a number of other specific items on her growing shopping list.

On her tour, she inspected the statue of Queen Victoria, who apparently enjoyed her visit to the town so much that she had granted it the right to use the prefix 'Royal'. She read on a plaque that the queen's statue had been moved an inch on its plinth by a German bomb in 1940, but her expression had reportedly remained steadfastly unamused by this indignity. Pearl visited the Pump Rooms and sampled the saline brew 'rediscovered' by Benjamin Satchwell in 1784, apparently a mild laxative and cure for rabies, which had made the town's fortune in the early nineteenth century. In her view, it could hardly now pass for ditch water, let alone spa water. She admired the restored Hammam with its striking red and black tiles, the frigidarium and tepidarium, there were separate facilities of course for ladies and gentlemen.

She asked at the information bureau next to the library about which excursions were available from the town. The agent recommended to her a rather overwritten flyer that described a guided tour over a landscape of *'smooth undulations, windmills, corn-grass, bean fields, wild-flowers, farmyards, hayricks,'* visiting Warwick Castle where *'grim knights and warriors looked scowling on,'* with further stops at *'several admired points of view in the neighbourhood,'* to take in the views and then *'a stroll amongst the haunted ruins of Kenilworth,'* that once hosted the Faerie Queene.

It all sounds very nice, she thought, *but perhaps this is all for future, more relaxed visits*. Before that she had more urgent business to attend to. The information booklet on the art gallery at Compton Verney was however one that caught her eye and a little more relevant to her own immediate proposed agenda. To finish her afternoon of exploration she took a tourist's carriage ride to the beacon at Newbold Comyn to admire the views from this local highpoint.

> *The rule of law or law of the ruler,*
> *Natural harmony or invention*
> *Of man. What is fair is often crueller,*
> *Revenge, sexual orientation,*
> *Colour, gender the pursuit of ration-*
> *ality. Fate or divine providence?*
> *I am she who will bring retribution,*
> *An eye for an eye to maintain balance.*
> *Justice always proper, will regret my absence.*

CHAPTER EIGHT

QUEEN MAB – (ALLEGRETTO) 'W.N.'

[Enter Nurse, to the chamber]
Nurse: Madam!
Juliet: Nurse?
Nurse: Your lady mother is coming to your chamber:
The day is broke; be wary, look about.
[Exit]
Juliet: Then, window, let day in, and let life out.

Shakespeare, *Romeo and Juliet*

'MAB, MAB, busy old MAB!' I heard Winnie crying.

'Winnie, what is it? Calm down love,' I shouted at her down the corridor of the nursing home.

'MAB! MAB, busy old MAB!'

'OK, OK, Winnie, I'm coming!' I called.

'I don't know what's come over her – she's just this minute started screaming her head off,' shouted the bemused Czech nurse as I ran down the corridor towards Winnie's bedroom. It was nearly the end of my shift, what had seemed like the longest shift ever and I was looking forward to meeting Penn at my bedsit in less than an hour.

'MAB!' something in her cry curdled my blood.

When I reached Winnie's room, she was standing at the window, her white nightdress billowing insanely in the wind, as if trapped in a tragic scream. For a second, I marvelled at this vision of innocent sensuality, her creamy white shoulders and svelte figure; her face glowing with the same luminosity that once made her a star. But I quickly began to worry that she might be trying to jump, her hair was entangled in the net curtains, blown about through the half-open frame of the sash window. Luckily, the window had been fitted with blocks as a precaution, so that it could open no higher than six inches. But all the same, in this state anything could happen. Winnie was laughing dementedly, a merry little trilly laugh, while shaking uncontrollably.

'Please, Winnie – come away from that window, you silly girl…' She jumped away in surprise at my voice.

The initial crisis over, I calmed down and tried to speak more soothingly as I approached her. There were tears streaming down the actress's cheeks, her eyes fixed intently on something in the street. Her face was aflame with passion.

She turned to me and began to recite as if back on the stage again with the same intensity of delivery and focus as when she was a twenty year old straight out of the National Youth Theatre. Her normally gentle voice was projected with power, both intimate and rapturous. It was somewhat scary.

> *Her whip of cricket's bone; the lash of film;*
> *Her waggoner a small grey-coated gnat,*
> *Not half so big as a round little worm*
> *Pricked from the lazy finger of a maid:*

Shakespeare, *Romeo and Juliet*

'Sshh Winnie, come on please calm yourself, what's happened? Has something given you a shock?'

Although I was relatively new to this nursing home I was already terribly fond of this remarkable woman. I looked quickly around the room to see what might have caused this sudden change in Winnie's temperament. Her room was a real treasure trove, drawers bulging with letters, shelves of diaries and theatrical programmes, piles of crochet lying patient and unworked on the bedside cabinet. There was a mahogany bureau covered with photographs of Winnie with her leading men, captured in scenes from the plays that she had starred in. The walls of peeling plaster were set with yellowing alcoves filled with objects of chintzy cheeriness. It was a mess and I loved it but I couldn't see anything out of place.

I still couldn't fathom this sudden change in Winnie's behaviour; she was normally so sedate and gentle. I scanned the medicine chart on the shelf; nothing unusual there that I could see. Winnie was one of our long-term patients with advanced early-onset dementia. The home was always extra careful with anti-depressants for such patients because of the risk of a fall. The chart showed that she has been given no more than her normal dosage that morning, yet her actions suggested that she was having some sort of paranoid hallucination. Although I was a fully qualified SRN, studying to be an Admiral Nurse, I'd never seen anything like this during my training or care of dementia patients.

> *Her chariot is an empty hazelnut*
> *Made by the joiner squirrel or old grub,*
> *Time out o' mind the fairies' coachmakers.*
> *And in this state she gallops night by night*
> *Through lovers' brains, and then they dream of love.*

Shakespeare, *Romeo and Juliet*

I searched again, but still I could see nothing out of place in the room. Winnie now began to point resolutely towards the open window again. I walked over and looked out at the road below, and immediately saw the cause of Winnie's anxiety. There had been some sort of an accident. A motorcyclist lay across the central reservation and another man was on the ground, people gathering around them.

'Winnie, did you see it happen? Did you see the accident?'

'MAB,' Winnie said again, this time much more calmly. 'All in black.'

'Come on, come and sit on the bed and let me get you some tea,' I said, trying to get her away from the window while looking out of it myself. I had no idea what this MAB business meant, however.

Eventually I managed to calm Winnie enough that I could leave her in the care of the Czech nurse while I reported what the actress had seen to the manager of the nursing home. Fortunately, the young policewoman that arrived a few minutes after 9am was none other than my good friend Penny; she was immediately very kind and reassuring with the actress.

'So what do you think she saw, Izzie?' asked Penny.

'I can't be sure, but I suspect she saw whatever hit those poor young lads. Are they going to be OK?' I asked, but Penny shook her head.

'No, and they are not so poor or innocent either. We believe they may have committed a murder on Clarendon Square a few minutes before the accident.'

'A murder on the square? Oh my God, Penny, who was it?' I replied, quite shocked.

'Nobody we know. The victim was one of Sir William's guests. He was stabbed then shot. Do you think Winnie will be able to remember anything else? We had a report of someone getting out of and maybe back into the car that hit them before it raced off.'

I hesitated, truthfully more concerned for Winnie's welfare than answering Penny's questions right then, but equally I still had something else on my mind.

'I don't know, she's really behaving quite oddly and is certainly not herself at all. Maybe I can ask her when she's calmed down a bit more. She is normally so lucid and calm. It's really sad; she still has a fantastic long-term memory but forgets things that have happened only a few minutes earlier.'

'Dementia?'

'Sort of, she was quite famous in her time, you know. She played Ophelia, Lady M and of course Juliet, all the classic roles. Look at all these photographs. She must have been quite a heartthrob, she was even considered for the part of Juliet in the film by Zeffirelli, but she lost out to Olivia Hussey. To think, she used to learn all those lines off by heart and now...'

Mirrour of grace and majestie divine... whose light like phoebus lampe throughout the world doth shine.

Spenser, *The Faerie Queene*

'Does she have any family?'

'Oh yes, her daughter and her niece come to see her regularly. They've told me the stories. She lived in a wonderful house in Cheltenham, very musical as well, played the violin beautifully and was always entertaining. Her husband was also a famous actor, but he died many years ago. I think it was suicide. There was something wrong with him, burnt down their house after a long argument and then accidentally set himself on fire – trying to gain notoriety apparently.'

'How awful.'

'Yes and it's so sad to see the effects of dementia in someone so relatively young.'

'And you say she was quoting Shakespeare, when you found her?'

'Queen Mab I think, word perfect, as precisely as if she was still on stage.'

'How strange.'

'Look, Penny, I know this is really awkward, but it's the end of my shift and I'm afraid I've got someone waiting for me at home. Is it OK if I go now? The other nurses will look after Winnie. I'll be back later to see if she is ready to answer your questions.'

Penny raised her eyebrows and I could tell what she was thinking. But I already had five texts from Penn in addition to those that had arrived at regular intervals during the night. Before hearing the scream I had been counting down the minutes and seconds to our meeting. I had even wondered briefly whether Penn might be interested in meeting Winnie, given they were both actors.

★

Do you want me?
If you do there's something you've got to get for me.
Well you do want me don't you?
Well what is it you have to give me then?
A stable full of big racing stallions?
Oh no, no, no.
A great big lilac Cadillac?
No no.
Or lots of tiny pink babies?
Don't be silly of course not.
A slinky snake-skin parasol with two knobs?
No no no, oh.
Anybody who really wants me will have to buy me.
Orators orange rubber gloves,
Smooth on the inside they're absolutely leak-proof,
Use them for all your dirty work.

Helen Mirren's speech from Don Levy's *Herostratus (1967)*

Izzie got back to her bedsit around 10am, an hour later than her nightshift had been due to finish. Reluctantly, she had left Winnie with the other nursing staff and police, sedated and calm but as yet not up to talking more about the accident. I could tell as soon as I saw her that she was stressed about something, but assumed it was just the effects of the long night shift.

I had been waiting for her by her front door, leaning against the wall, reading a copy of Robert Frost's *Mountain Interval*, a bunch of Michaelmas daisies lying by my side. They had been relieved from a neighbour's garden, but I wouldn't tell her that.

'Sorry, I know I'm late.'

'I'm still here. What kept you?'

'Don't ask.'

I offered her the flowers and showed her the contents of the shopping bag in my hand. She smiled and turned the book to look at the cover.

'What's this?'

'*The road not taken*,' I quoted. 'My inspiration, Robert Frost, he was a resident of Ann Arbor, Michigan just like me,'

'Sounds great, but I still prefer my Emily Dickinson,' she said, laughing. I was pleased to see a smile return to her face. Apparently she had a good memory for song lyrics as well.

I had bought oranges, maple syrup and all the ingredients for pancakes and muffins to cook in her bedsit. I calculated that this would be an unexpected bonus, a man who could cook as well as play the guitar. I'd been up all night as she probably suspected from the frequency of my texts. No really, I'm not a stalker, but something about her had enchanted me and I couldn't sleep.

She opened the door and settled down at the small table in the kitchen while I started to prepare breakfast. Her flat was tiny, but she had clearly done her best to cheer it up with plants and art objects, mainly 60s and 70s stuff. In the corner of the room was a music stand and propped against it her viola. The kitchenette held only the bare essentials, the walls covered with turquoise post-it notes listing things she had to do: she told me she was a vegetarian and bought fresh food daily, but admitted she was not a particularly great cook. I scanned the photos on the fridge for any sign of another half, but they were mainly girlfriends. There was no separate bedroom and her clothes hung on a rail on the far side of the room. It revealed an eclectic collection of high street and vintage.

'It's amazing what rich people throw out,' she explained defensively as she saw me assessing the clothing. 'No really, such a waste,' she added.

'Don't worry, I like them. You have a great sense of style. You could set up your own theatrical costume shop,' I joked. She scowled.

As she recounted the morning's events to me I soon understood why she had looked so stressed earlier. But before she had finished describing Winnie's experience, I stopped her. 'You've reminded me, I saw something strange myself going on last night after you left. There was a cab following an old guy slowly down the street as he walked his dogs. It seemed almost like the car was following him. I wonder if there is a connection.'

Izzie suggested I give her policewoman friend Penny a call, but I decided that could wait; I'd got plenty of time as I'd already received a text to say that filming was cancelled for the rest of the day. Now I could understand exactly why.

'Anyway I've been waiting to see you again, all night,' I said keenly, trying not to sound obsessive.

'Then you're mad, but I'm really glad you're here,' she said. 'But I'm afraid you can't stay long, I'm going to have to get some sleep after breakfast. I'm really whacked.'

Something in her voice told me that sleep was not foremost on *her* mind *either*.

After we'd eaten, I decided it was time to make a move and shifted round to her side of the table. Kneeling beside her, I took her hands and gently kissed first her collarbone, then brushed my lips along the furrow at the back of her neck and finally up behind her ear. There was absolutely no resistance from her only a sweet groaning.

'You don't look tired at all to me,' I said hopefully.

'Well I think I can probably hold out for a while longer, you know,' she said breathlessly.

I cradled her face in both my hands and kissed her fully on the lips. I could feel the warmth of her breath on my cheeks as I moved my hands slowly down her back and began to unbutton her uniform, slipping the collar carefully over her shoulders, checking her eyes for permission as I went. She kissed me with a passionate intensity that I certainly was not expecting and then withdrew again, seemingly waiting for me to make the next move.

★

Normally Penn's forwardness would have been far too fast for me, but after the morning's events I wasn't anywhere near the mood for normality. This was just what I needed. I felt myself really beginning to get into this guy. God and he was *so* cute.

'Hey, what about you,' I said determinedly and began to pull at his shirt until he raised his arms and it was released over his head. He had a boyish, smooth chest, nicely formed but not muscular, unlike most film actors these days. In any case I didn't mind, I didn't need a muscle-bound action hero right then; this one would do just fine. Things were moving very quickly and I had absolutely no intention of slowing things down. I felt the excitement welling up inside my body. I sensed where we were going, first date as well. I reached into my bag just in case to find what I wanted.

'Are you sure you're OK with this?' he said, sensing my excitement, beginning to kiss my neck again. I couldn't believe he was actually seeking my consent and felt another tingle inside at this sensitivity. *Is this one for real?* Now I was really getting nervous.

'Absolutely sure, it's only the thought of this that has kept me going through the night shift,' I whispered, barely able to speak. Suddenly he stopped kissing me and stared into my eyes as if he'd thought of something. I wondered what was wrong.

'I have dubious morals you know.'

'What do you call having dubious morals?' I groaned. *Where did that come from?*

'Largely being dubious about other people's morals,' he replied. 'I have the wrong genes, all inherited, a tendency towards being a waster.' I shook my head.

'Given what I've seen of the quality of your acting, I find that hard to believe,' I said, now pulling his ear lobes with my lips to encourage him to continue undressing me.

'No really, I'm afraid it started with my grandfather on my mother's side. He was a total philanderer, one of the lesser-known beatniks, but possibly the best poet amongst all of them.'

'OK, so what's a beatnik?' I asked, now getting somewhat exasperated. *Was he just teasing me?*

'You know, Kerouac – *On the Road*. He knew all of them, Burroughs, Snyder, Holmes. Alan Ginsberg was apparently infatuated with my grandfather. Bob Dylan even used a line from his prose in one of his Vietnam songs.'

'Wow that's cool.' I wasn't sure where he was going with this but I changed tack and decided to engage in the dangling conversation for the time being, waiting for the right moment to resume our earlier intimacy.

'My mother was the product of one of my grandfather's many affairs. Her own mother was a Native American and like my mother was apparently very beautiful. My mother got married to another man after she had me, but died when I was still very young.'

'Really? That's so sad, I'm really sorry. What about your father?'

'I've not much idea about him; I'm a bastard son of a bastard daughter. Arnold was my adoptive parents' family name. The only thing I know about my father is that he was English, a writer, with the nickname 'Poshizmo'. Unfortunately, I am just the wasted product of a whole series of lusty affairs from a family of serious dropouts. Not a great bloodline, is it?'

'I don't know.' *Poshizmo… I think I've heard that name before somewhere* I thought. 'Anyway your family actually sound quite exciting, especially compared to endless generations of Irish labourers.'

'I just wanted you to know what you're letting yourself in for, that's all.'

O and yet when it's asked of you 'What happened to him?'
I say, 'What happened to America has happened to him…'

Gregory Corso, *Elegiac Feelings American*

'That's OK, thanks for the health warning, but right now Mr Penn a waster, with or without a checked flannel shirt and ankle boots, suits me fine. All these years I've been looking for the perfect man and now I've suddenly found myself an impossible *lover*,' I said ironically, hoping he'd get the hint.

'All these years? OK, so how old exactly are you?'

'Twenty-three.'

'*Twenty-three?* Jeepers, wait until you're at least thirty before you say 'all these years'. Look at me for heaven's sake!'

'You look fine to me.'

'Yes but I'm an extra, not exactly James Dean taking the world by storm.'

Now James Dean happened to be my pet subject and I had just the right rebuttal ready from the hero himself: '*Dream as if you'll live forever. Live as if you'll die today.*'

'That's really nice, and well-remembered. Anyway I really don't know who I would be even if I could be someone else. *Do what you've got to do* works for me.'

'Well, Mr Confused, whoever you could be, I am really getting to like who you are right now,' I ran my finger down his chest, stopping suggestively just above his belt loop.

'You may not like me when you know my politics, I know you English girls are so restrained...'

'What?'

'You know, conservative.'

'OK, Mr Penn, I really sense we are getting the confessions out of the way early here.' By now we were sitting on the floor half undressed, him seemingly earnest in his questions, me getting increasingly frustrated the longer that this verbal foreplay continued.

'So, confession, you get the full works with me. I aspire to be a hobo songwriter, a modern day Jack London, anti-war, anti-fascist, anti–'

'Well I hope that doesn't extend to anti-women,' I interrupted.

'Sure, animal rights are cool with me too.' I threw my bag at him, narrowly missing his head. He ducked and then dived to tickle me, but I was too quick and turned him onto his back, pinning his arms to the carpet, my thighs astride him.

'OK great, so are we finished now, or is there something else you want to get off your chest? Some other deep philosophical point before you get laid, because you are going to get laid, Mr Penn, whether you like it or not.' *God, I never normally talk like that* I wasn't sure exactly what had come over me.

'Sometimes we just have to avoid thinking about the problems life presents. Otherwise we'd suffocate,' he said, feigning inability to breathe. I sighed, bent down to kiss his chest and then had an idea how to get this back on track again. I rolled off him and took the empty water bottle from the kitchen table, spinning it. It stopped, pointing toward him.

'So, are you religious then by any chance?' I asked, guessing the answer already.

'I'm a non-practising atheist. *I believe that when I am dead, I am dead. I believe that with my death I am just as much obliterated as the last mosquito you and I squashed.*'

'Now don't make me laugh, that sounds like a cop-out.'

'It's the only way to go. Are there any more difficult questions?'

'I don't know. Well yes, in fact. Tell me right now, just how many lovers have you had?'

'Now you are making assumptions. I'm not like other guys. They say sex is the quickest way to ruin a friendship. I've been celibate for years you know. By the way men or women?' I pointed down at his socks, which he removed.

'Well I'm hardly surprised, if you've put all your girlfriends through this kind of nonsense.'

'Well, I guess I do more or less.' I span the bottle again and it pointed towards me this time. He was silent.

'OK, this is supposed to be truth or dare; so it's your turn to ask me a question.'

'That's easy, so where's the most unusual place you've ever made love?'

'Now who's making assumptions, you rat? So you don't think I'm a good Catholic virgin?'

'Heh, don't get so uptight. I wasn't implying anything, but the evidence is to the contrary,' he said, pointing at the unopened packet on the floor by my side.

'Well it's probably none of your business then,' I blushed and hid the offending item behind my back.

'OK, so I guess if you're not going to tell me, I'd better tell you.'

I put my finger to his lips and removed my own vest and then span the bottle again. It pointed towards him this time.

'OK then so what about you, which exotic beach with which sun-kissed babe?'

'There were a bunch of them but actually it was probably Times Square in the rain after the New Year celebrations. At the time it seemed romantic, now I'm not quite sure about getting my name up in lights like that.'

'Yes, you'd probably best not advertise that one, I agree. Your turn, it looks like it's going to have to be those cargo pants next.' He picked up the bottle and looked at the label.

'Evian is naïve spelled backwards,' he said.

'So you're into the philosophy of advertising now?'

'They make advertisements for soap, why not for peace?'

'OK, this is ridiculous. That's enough talk.'

But a sudden wave of tiredness had come over me and I abandoned my earlier amorous thoughts, instead snuggling up to him and lying quietly in his arms. He let me sleep in the shadows cast by the blinds across the room. While I slept he began to compose the verses of a poem for me that he would later set to music. He sang it to me later that afternoon, sang that I looked like beauty personified, like a little angel curled like a cat amongst the pillows. I slept right through to 2pm when he woke me with a cup of tea and finally we made love.

'By the way, I was planning spaghetti bolognese for dinner?'

'I thought I told you, I'm a vegetarian.'
'Well that will now be tofu spaghetti then.'
'It sounds delicious; very *Lady and the Tramp*.'
'I told you I was a vagrant at heart.'

CHAPTER NINE

An Inspector Calls – (Adagio) 'Nimrod'

Let man and beast appear before him,
And magnify his name together.
Let Nimrod, the mighty hunter,
Bind a leopard to the altar
And consecrate his spear to the Lord.

Benjamin Britten, *Rejoice in the Lamb*

Detective Inspector Hunter arrived early at the new Justice Centre in Newbold Terrace first thing on Saturday morning. He had a postponed appointment with the CPS in preparation for the next stage of a case. It seemed to him to have dragged on forever in the magistrates' court. Now he was required to take the stand again in the Crown Court on Monday. It had been a long week and he was tired; he much preferred being in the field on active investigations, but everything was remarkably quiet on that front. He speculated to himself about whether Leamington's criminals had found better things to be doing over the summer holidays. All the same, at least this meant he would be able to spend the rest of the weekend at home, quietly, with his music. He had a ticket for a concert that afternoon, and an invitation for dinner with friends in the town's best restaurant, but he was in two minds whether to attend either event. A good cognac, a little jazz or maybe Beethoven, seemed more in keeping with his somewhat reflective mood.

He poured himself a coffee from the machine, thumbed rapidly through the local newspaper he had bought on the way in and waited impatiently for the brief to arrive.

★

DI Hunter was a man commonly acknowledged as a prodigious talent for the future. He was held somewhat in awe by his colleagues. He was meticulous and always carefully dressed, courteous, with a clipped, precise way of speaking that slightly betrayed his mixed nationality. He also had an enviable track record of getting results through endless questions and careful observation. In fact, he seemed to have the miraculous ability to extract new evidence in cases that others would file in the 'hopeless' category. Despite this growing reputation he was a private man. Although friendly enough at work, he did not tend to socialise with the rest of the team. For instance, he had never been one for drinking with the lads, he was a lifelong non-smoker and partial to fine dining and expensive wines – none of these attributes fitted well with typical detective inspector material.

As a result, although respected, he was regarded as somewhat aloof and a bit of a loner by the team. Formally he was known around the station as DI Hunter, hardly anybody addressed him by his first name; in fact few actually knew what that name was. He had recently collected a nickname though, which was commonly used when he was not present – Amadeus – on account of his well-known interest in classical music and his half-Austrian ancestry. His paternal grandparents were early political refugees from the Nazis but although they had changed their name from Jaeger to Hunter, they had not managed to escape British internment during the war.

Hunter was still a bachelor; tall, skinny and blonde with

chiselled, somewhat Aryan features and a lean, athletic figure. He'd had no shortage of female admirers over the years, with a number of shorter and a few longer-term relationships, mostly platonic. However, the inescapable truth was that, charming as he was, his expectations in a partner were so unrealistically high that no woman ever quite managed to penetrate through the polite formality of his external persona deep enough to capture his heart. He was quite comfortable with his single status, jealously guarding his continued independence and privately polishing his aura of existential angst.

Earlier in his life, he had thought about going into the church, but his continued religious circumspection had made a priestly future improbable. For him the basic narrative of Christianity was a myth, a delightful and decorative myth, but a myth all the same. In his view, even its basic ethical teaching was more a product of the inhibitions and complexes of modern, domesticated man than of some eternal truth. The received conventions of morality were for him boundaries to be tested. Elements of behaviour that some treated as gospel truth and others treated as a hobby to be paraded on Sunday and ignored for the rest of the week. He was quite cynical about this in a way. He believed in the man, the Servant King, but all the rest of it he regarded as invention, quaint superstition. They were appealing ideas, but not a coherent philosophy. Unable to reconcile these views with a 'divine calling' he eventually rejected the priesthood and instead joined the police force. But in some ways he still retained some of his monk-like spirituality. Joining the police and its world of drug addicts and hoodlums was a life choice even he would now struggle to explain.

★

It was now 8.15am, the brief was definitely late and Hunter hated lateness. He noticed the sudden increased level of noise leaking through the thin walls of the stuffy briefing room, signalling unusual activity in the corridors outside. When the brief finally entered the room, Hunter made a quick apology and stuck his head outside to see what was going on. He was made aware immediately of the events in Clarendon Square and barked a few instructions to the duty sergeant, asking him to get the whole team in from weekend leave, before returning to the conference room. He then sat in increasing frustration for an hour while the CPS lawyer went methodically through the evidence with him yet again.

By the time he finally escaped and arrived at the incident scene, it was nearly 10am. His capable team was already in full operations mode. They had been keeping him updated during the morning and he was pleased to see that they had sealed off most of the gleaming Regency streets in the immediate vicinity of the attack. Uniformed officers were preventing traffic from passing along the southern, eastern and northern sides of Clarendon Square and had blocked Clarendon Place to the west; a major thoroughfare. There were therefore extensive diversions in operation around the Beauchamp Avenue, Warwick Street and Parade areas. He had to use his blue light to get through all the traffic.

Satisfied that the immediate crime scene was locked down, he went over to talk to the forensics team, who were already working in their specialist gear at the two separate crime sites. Other uniformed search teams were combing the square for evidence of a sniper. There was a calm urgency to their work, which contrasted with the mêlée around the police cordons; a combination of irritated motorists, residents and the gathering mix of spectators and press corps.

As a consequence of the morning's incidents, all filming had of course been cancelled for the day and the actors and crew were now looking on at the crime scene in morbid fascination at the modern parallel to their own historic set.

After a brief inspection of the murder scene, he received a preliminary debrief from his detective sergeant, learning for the first time about his friends', Alice and Eddie's, involvement as witnesses of the murder scene. The DI bypassed the front doorstep of No. 6, where the murder took place. The forensics team were busy taking photographs and tagging samples. He headed instead down the side drive to the tradesman's entrance to meet with the occupants inside. He heard shouts and questions from the press who were already congregating around the police lines further down the street. He had no intention of speaking to them before he had made an assessment of the situation.

No. 6, or the 'Napoleon House', was one of the best-known houses in Leamington, on account not only of its history but also of its present occupant. He had met the owner, Sir William Flyte, a few times before at formal civic functions. He had taken an instant dislike to him, which had not been helped by the politician's racy reputation in the red-tops. The man appeared to Hunter to be a fake, a somewhat seedy political opportunist who had gained position through money rather than talent. Hunter had a natural aversion to such men. Added to this, he knew Flyte's first wife, Lady Mary, and her daughters, socially; they were in his opinion the most charming of ladies, and active like him in the local music scene. For this reason, he had felt even more aggrieved when he learnt that they had been so badly treated by Sir William following his divorce and most recent marriage.

He had not met Sir William's third wife, Lady Nadia Flyte, although he'd heard with interest that she was a cultured and kind person. He considered it so much more a tragedy that she had become involved in the machinery and household of such an unpleasant man.

In any case, he knew that all these personal feelings had to be put to one side. He needed to deal with this tragic and potentially highly political situation in the most professional way he could, whatever his own personal prejudices. He was already prepared to be at his most courteous as he rang the bell. Surprisingly, Sir William himself answered the door, a thin, wiry man dressed like a country squire.

'Ah, Hunter, at last. I wondered when you'd get here, please come in and join your colleagues,' Sir William said in his normal, authoritative, slightly bullying way. Hunter sensed a note of irritation in his words, maybe because he had arrived so late.

Two female members of Hunter's team were already in the building talking to and consoling Sir William's wife, whose grandfather had been killed on the doorstep just two hours earlier. A couple of uniformed officers were talking with Sir William. Hunter looked around the hall, noticing immediately with disdain that the lanterns hanging from the ceiling were of the wrong period and that the Carlton House desk was too early for the house. He also noticed that Sir William was looking remarkably relaxed for someone whose doorstep was now a murder scene.

'First of all, Sir William, please let me offer my sincere condolences on behalf of the whole force on the death of your wife's grandfather. This really is a most distressing incident, and you can be assured my team will do their very utmost night and day to resolve what has happened here as soon as we possibly can.'

'Thank you, Inspector; of course, as you can imagine we are all in a state of complete shock. Nadia, my poor dear wife, is just inconsolable and for this terrible thing to have happened here on our very doorstep, in such a brutal way, is just unimaginably painful for her. It's just too bad.'

'I do understand completely, Sir William and you have my utmost sympathies. We've already got a full forensics

111

team in place and we are searching the local area extensively. There are several good leads to follow already and of course with the death of the two assailants nearby we will have some hard evidence that we can gather quickly. I know how difficult this must be for you, but I do have a few initial questions; in these cases it's most important that we quickly build up a picture of what's occurred without losing any time.' Hunter paused for a second and Sir William nodded for him to continue.

'First, Sir, are you able to give me any idea of the context of what may have happened here? I understand that the victim was your houseguest, indeed as you have just confirmed Lady Flyte's grandfather, and that he was a very senior figure in the Sri Lankan business community? Were there any signs of trouble leading up to this?'

'No, Inspector, I cannot recall anything of any particular significance. Of course we all know that senior business people have their enemies, but I have no inkling what could have caused such a brutal and unforeseen attack.'

'May I ask, had Mr Nariman been staying with you for very long?'

'No. He'd been with us only a matter of a few weeks. In fact he was due to move out today to a villa that he had rented in Lansdowne Circus. Nadia had arranged all that for him through his company. He was exhausted, you know, after all those years of running his family business and had only officially retired a few months ago. That's the tragedy of this. It was just him and his beloved dogs staying with us and he was looking forward to living a quiet life here for a while, keeping himself to himself. Inspector, this is just so terrible, how can such a thing happen in our lovely town?'

Hunter studied Sir William's face carefully.

'Were there any threats, anything he was worried about? Especially concerning his personal security? Have you or any of your household noticed any strangers hanging around?'

'No, nothing at all, certainly nothing that I'm aware of. In fact, although he was tired and quite ill physically, mentally he already seemed renewed, free at last of all the day-to-day cares and burdens of his business. I'm sure Nadia would say the same, but as you can understand she is in a state of shock at the moment and I really don't want to disturb her with such difficult questions.'

'Yes of course, we won't disturb her yet, but obviously if either of you have any information that would speed up our investigations, please let me know immediately. You can phone me any time of day or night on these numbers.'

He gave Sir William his card.

'And what about the men with the knife, have you found out who they are yet? They're, not your typical muggers, are they?' Sir William asked somewhat impatiently.

'Not yet. Unfortunately they were not carrying any identifying documentation but I am sure we will track them down pretty quickly.'

Hunter was interested to note that in asking about the knife attack, Sir William had omitted to mention or ask about the rifle shot that had killed Mr Nariman. Did he really believe this was just a mugging? He assumed Sir William must be aware of the gunshot, but made a mental note to check later.

'Well, Sir William, I think that's all for the moment. I will need to speak to you a little later, when we have made a preliminary assessment of all the evidence. Will you be around later in the day?'

'Yes of course, Inspector, I'm not going anywhere with Nadia in this state and am at your disposal any time. The sooner we have cleared up what happened here the better. Might I ask though, what we should do about the press? The party is already on to me to make a statement.'

'Yes of course they would be, well for now please say nothing other than a straightforward, *this is a personal tragedy;*

you have full confidence in the police investigation; you are asking for privacy for your family etc. Please don't make any comment on evidence or events or speculate on motives as we don't want anything to compromise our investigation or any subsequent prosecution.'

Hunter noted that, given his wife's obvious distress in the room next door, dealing with the press seemed to be surprisingly high on Sir William's agenda. For the moment he put this down to the career politician in him.

Before Hunter left the crime scene to return to the station, he decided to take a few minutes to visit the other half of the Flyte family in No. 5, the house next door. But he soon discovered from their housekeeper that Lady Mary was away on a honeymoon cruise with her new husband and that her daughters were staying with friends overnight. The girls were expected to return later in the day. He discovered that they had planned to attend the same concert as Hunter that afternoon, although of course his own attendance at that event was now impossible.

He had not been in Lady Mary's house before, but he catalogued with pleasure the Empire period furniture, Persian carpets and paintings that decorated the hall. He also noticed that Lady Mary had the *right* period lanterns in contrast to the ugly Florentine lamps in Sir William's house next door. *More than enough proof of her superior taste* he thought. Although he must formally treat them as possible suspects until he confirmed their movements, he felt he knew them well enough to discount immediately any involvement in these dreadful events. He decided not to try to contact them further during the morning, but wait until they returned.

He thanked the housekeeper and walked down the steps to the pavement, opening the little gate that led to the steps to the basement flat below. He descended the steps and then rang the bell and saw an eye staring at him through the uncovered spyhole. Immediately the door opened a few inches and he was greeted by his friend Eddie's worried face. Eddie removed the chain and invited him in, apparently relieved to see him

'Sorry, I thought it might have been the press again. Come in, Gus.'

'Thank you, Eddie, I won't stay long.'

He entered the hallway and Eddie led him into the kitchen, offering him a cup of tea, which Hunter declined.

'So Eddie, how are you doing? This must have been a huge shock for both of you.'

'Yes, it's been insane; we've certainly had better days. Alice is fine though, I guess she's getting used to this sort of gruesome stuff with the forensics, although having it happen on your doorstep is a bit weird to say the least. She's already gone over to the hospital to get ready for the autopsy. As for Carrie, fortunately she didn't see too much. She's in her bedroom, probably Instagramming it as we speak.' Hunter frowned; social media had its drawbacks in this sort of situation.

'And you, Eddie, how are you doing?' He looked at his friend, who was unshaven, dishevelled and pale, his red eyes suggesting he could do with a good night's sleep.

'I'll admit I'm still shaking, Gus. I feel a bit of a wuss now. I'm afraid I was a bit hung over this morning after a late night. I was still in bed when it happened. The first I knew about the whole thing was when I heard Alice shouting for help from the street. I woke my friend Hugh, who was sleeping on the couch, and we both ran up the outside steps to find out what was going on. I thought she was being attacked or something, but realised at once when I got up the steps that she was trying to save this guy's life. We dragged him up on to the doorstep of No. 6 and she told me to check his breathing and pulse and apply pressure to the knife wound until the ambulance arrived. She thought he'd been mugged.'

'You did exactly the right thing; it could have saved his life.'

'I have to admit I was struggling to remember my old Red Cross training, but Alice was amazing; she knew exactly what to do, told me to shout if I needed help and then ran off down to the street corner with Hugh to where those guys had been knocked off their scooter. I was concentrating so hard on what she told me to do that the weird thing is I didn't hear anything until suddenly my face was covered well, covered with all sorts of foul stuff when his head exploded. God, the bullet must have been so close to hitting me as well. Then I saw Lady Flyte's face when she opened the door... her face... she said something to him and then screamed before she fainted. I think that's why I'm still shaking.'

'Yes, I'm sorry you had to go through that kind of horrific experience. I've never seen or heard of anything like this; it appears there was a double murder attempt on the same person at the same time. Is there anything you can tell me about him or the attackers for that matter?'

'No, not really. I had seen him a couple of times recently out late walking his dogs; Alice can't remember seeing him at all. I assumed he was a houseguest of Sir William's; so many people come and go from that house. He looked Iranian, maybe, clearly very wealthy given his suit and the gold rings on his fingers.'

'Apparently he's a Parsi rather than Iranian – from Sri Lanka – there's a small but wealthy population of them around Colombo. He's Sir William's wife's grandfather. Of course, she's in shock at the moment; my officers are with her right now.'

'Oh my God, he was her grandfather. I had no idea, that's dreadful. She was talking to him in her own language so I couldn't understand a word, no wonder she screamed and fainted. God, how is she?'

'Well, still in severe distress as you'd expect and probably not helped by the fact that there are police all over her house, reporters with TV cameras and crowds outside given the connection to Sir William.'

'Yes, one of the reporters phoned our number earlier. A young woman. But I didn't tell her anything and put down the phone as soon as I realised who she was.'

'That's probably Lucy Fleming. She's OK but best not to speak to any of them; leave that to us. Eddie, did you happen to notice anything about the assailants?'

'No nothing, I didn't really get a good look at them. Alice already told your officers that she thinks she saw them the previous evening in the park while she was out running, but she can't be sure. Hugh has a theory also that he saw them in the car park last night, we were out drinking late I'm afraid – Penny was with us so she'll know. How's she doing by the way? She's a good kid.'

'She's doing just fine. OK Eddie, well that's all for now, let me leave you in peace, thank you again for all you and Alice did, you were both terrific in the circumstances. Look after your family, they need you to be strong now. I'll get one of the lads to come and take a more detailed statement later, but let me know if you or Alice think of anything more or get bothered again by those reporters.'

'So I suppose we won't see you tonight, I'm in two minds whether to just cancel?'

'No, I'll definitely have to give tonight a miss. Let me know if you're still going though and I'll see if I can pop in just to say hello.'

Hunter noticed a photograph on the mantelpiece.

'My, is that Alice?' he asked, pointing to the picture of a young, long-haired girl sitting cross-legged on a beach in cargo pants and black vest top, carefully tending her little baby. She was smiling up at the camera; behind her there was a row of surfers holding their boards.

'Yes, that was before we were married, just after Carrie arrived. We were winging it then, happy new parents.'

'She could have been a model, couldn't she? You're a lucky man, Eddie,' Hunter said, looking again at the pretty eager face staring back at the photographer.

Hunter turned to go but noticed the audio equipment Eddie was working with on the kitchen table.

'By the way, I was going to ask you this evening but I guess I won't have a chance now. I realise this might not be top of your mind either but didn't you have that big interview with the video company yesterday? How did the pitch go?'

'Not good. It seems like a long time ago now. I don't think Alice is too pleased with me about that, either. They were obviously looking for something else entirely. I did push myself. You know when something's outside your comfort zone, and you're living on the edge a bit. I thought I had the brief nailed, but I obviously got it wrong. After this, I think I might as well take up kite-flying instead.' Hunter laughed.

'Oh no Eddie, please don't give up. I know a lot about music and although your style isn't exactly my thing, I know that you've got talent. You mustn't give up yet; maybe I could help you work on the composition?'

'Has Alice been working on you as well?'

'Well, maybe a little. Just a hint, look at what Elgar was doing in his Nimrod variation. He wrote about something that happened, *not* about the *man*, most people don't see that, they think it's a portrait. When you know that, it lets you get underneath the whole piece, there's something in there you could emulate.'

A day's attack of the blues… will not drive away your desire,

118

your necessity, which is to exercise those creative faculties,
which a kind providence has given you. Your time of
universal recognition will come.

Augustus Jaeger to Edward Elgar

★

It was now about 10.30am. The housekeeper brought
morning coffee to Arthur Troyte in the beautifully furnished
formal drawing room of the Lansdowne Circus villa, around
a mile from the incidents in Clarendon Square. Like No. 6,
this house also once had a famous resident, commemorated
by another blue plaque. Nathaniel Hawthorne, ancestor of
Arthur and the author of *The Scarlet Letter,* stayed here for
several years with his family.

The house itself was a William Thomas designed, two-
storey stucco villa, with a pretty garden and balconies,
looking out onto the central circus. Thomas was trained by
Pugin but went bankrupt trying to develop housing in
Leamington too quickly. In 1843, he emigrated and left
England for Toronto. He went on to design many famous
gothic-revival buildings across Ontario. The circular road
called Lansdowne Circus was constructed in the 1830s; it
had eight pairs of semi-detached villas, each in a Regency
style, grouped around a private central garden. The land was
leased by a Squire Willes for two thousand years. The villas
and another unusual gothic house at one end of the circus
are largely pristine, one of the lesser-known but practically
perfect architectural gems in our delightful Leamington
town.

Troyte had spent a couple of hours unpacking and settling
in. In complete contrast to his own modernist house in Ann
Arbor, he realised this house had breeding. Although neither
grand nor particularly spacious, it was a very pleasant size, in

a quiet backwater away from the town centre. He had been admiring the detailing of the marble fireplaces, cornices and mouldings that decorated most of the main rooms. As well as the architectural details, he was of course also fascinated by the house's connection to his literary ancestor, a completely unexpected coincidence. The peace of the circus, however, had been broken ever since he arrived. Indeed, Leamington seemed a much livelier place than he had ever expected; there had been sirens sounding in far off streets all morning and a police helicopter circling overhead. Worryingly, he had still heard nothing at all from his friend Arish, whose mobile number was just going to voicemail.

This was all beginning to concern him a little. Although it had been twenty-five years since they had last met, he was very eager to see his old friend again. He was sure Arish must be busy with the moving arrangements in some way or another but he was very surprised not to have heard anything from him. The housekeeper had called Sir William Flyte's house a couple of times on his behalf, but nobody was answering the phone there either. He was beginning to think that he ought to stretch his legs and walk over to the address in Clarendon Square himself to find out what had happened. He consulted the housekeeper, it did not sound like a great distance to walk.

Along with his coffee, the housekeeper brought him an unstamped letter that had just been put through the letterbox, addressed to him personally in beautifully crafted handwriting. Maybe this was a message from Arish. Arthur opened the envelope immediately. Inside he found an equally carefully handwritten invitation, on a fine vintage *carte de visite* with elegant gold edging.

> *I heard that you are in England and wondered if we might meet up for old times' sake. I will be in the bar at The Holly Hotel around noon. P. xxx*

Troyte was puzzled. He was a somewhat vain man with an over-inflated view of his rapidly waning attractiveness to women. He was balding, had poor skin and still suffered somewhat from the embarrassing physical complaint that had bothered him in his younger days. He had been a widower for a number of years, but he was also wealthy, with little to spend his considerable wealth on, now that his children were all married. But he certainly wasn't expecting an invitation from an admirer.

After his second wife died, the absence of a visible partner had the potential to cause him some difficulties in his chosen career. For a period there were even rumours about him being gay. He had felt his masculinity somewhat under threat. That, combined with his underlying homophobia, a hangover from student encounters, had driven him to set out on a determined campaign to take advantage of his new found freedom. He had used a variety of escorts in public for female company at outward facing and company events and to fulfil the conventions of his professional persona. In private, he increasingly used recreational drugs and indulged in ever wilder opportunistic sexual encounters. He was both manipulative and smart, satisfying his sex drive by running through all the usual suspects of divorcees, frustrated married women and a selection of vulnerable, young, single women from the office. He was therefore more than intrigued by this invitation and started to rack his brains to remember who, from a long list of female acquaintances, had a name beginning with *P* who would be inclined to add three kisses and more importantly who would know his whereabouts and be currently present in Europe.

'*P*… who on earth could that be?' he said aloud to the housekeeper, trying to give the impression to her that he had a whole crowd of lady friends who might be addressing him so.

The housekeeper was already wise to his nature after a couple of inappropriate touches and told him in a no-nonsense and slightly uninterested way that the Holly Hotel was just around the corner; he could be there in a couple of minutes. She further suggested that he could easily continue on to Sir William's house afterwards to investigate what was delaying Mr Nariman (rather than continuing to bother her around the house). Accepting this advice, Troyte asked the housekeeper to prepare lunch for him and put it in the fridge with some champagne. Secretly he wanted to be prepared in case this mysterious acquaintance turned out to be an attractive woman and a return invitation to lunch was accepted.

After the housekeeper had prepared the requested lunch of cold cuts and smoked salmon, she explained to him all the other delights that she had stocked in the fridge, made sure he had all the towels and linen he needed, demonstrated the workings of the various electronic gadgets in the house, showed him the book of instructions she had carefully written out – including contact numbers – and then, seeing her chance to escape his wandering hands, finally added that although she did not usually work weekends, she could always pop over if he needed her. She then asked him if there was anything else he needed for now. In other words she had done her job and had no intention of hanging around all weekend at his beck and call unless he was paying overtime.

He was blind to her messaging but all the same thanked her for her diligence. He told her his plans for the weekend and that he was sure he could now manage by himself. He would see her first thing Monday morning. He had been unusually polite in this discussion, quite against his normal sharpness. He could not fail to notice that she too had her own womanly attractions and was somewhat disappointed, but not without hope, to learn that she was newly married.

Still, she may be a good back up later, he thought, he was sure she could do with some extra cash.

★

By now it was 11am on Saturday – a little more than three hours after the fatal shooting. Detective Inspector Hunter was irritated. His train of thought had just been interrupted by a totally predictable phone call from the chief constable. He hated this kind of political interference, especially with such a complex and dynamic situation. He looked out over the neat files and empty coffee cups grouped on the desk in his office. Unlike most DI's offices, his was decorated with artwork and books. The crime squad was based in the oldest part of the Justice Centre complex – the original 1970s police buildings that overlooked the park. The chief constable had been short with him:

'Hunter, this is already getting out of hand in the press… a knife attack, a drive by shooting, the involvement of a senior politician… you need to get a grip and take drastic action,' all rendered in a raised and directive voice. Hunter was polite but had no intention of being browbeaten by such pressure.

His new assistant recently assigned from uniform branch, Penny or DC Penny Dore as he should more properly refer to her, sat opposite the entrance to his office, typing reports into her computer. Hunter called her in and asked her to collect the squad together in the major incident room. Before he finally released her, he said one further thing:

'Look, Penny, err DC Dore, I really want you on this case but I realise that you have pretty close connections with the witnesses as well as family connections. If you ever feel compromised you must let me know. I will monitor the situation carefully of course, do you understand?'

'Of course, Sir, but you can absolutely count on me. There won't be a problem. And please call me Penny, guv.'

The team crammed into the constrained space of the incident room, where other officers were busy pinning photos on maps and filling the situation whiteboards with the information that was flowing in from the field.

'So what do we have now?' Hunter asked Detective Sergeant Jones, his deputy, who immediately began to summarise the situation. Hunter had a gold Crossman pen in his hand that he tapped against the desk rhythmically but impatiently, as if he were a conductor marking time for the Welshman. Jones proceeded with his exposition.

'At approximately 8am this morning, there was a knife attack by two assailants outside No. 6 Clarendon Square. One assailant had a large hunting weapon and approached and stabbed the victim, the other was backing him up with a scooter a few yards down the street. The attack was aborted following the intervention of a neighbour, but was followed by a single rifle shot to the same victim's head from range a few minutes later. We believe this shot killed him outright. The victim was Mr Arish Nariman, a respected, retired foreign businessman and houseguest of Sir William Flyte.'

'Thank you, Detective Sergeant, but maybe we could have a few more details?'

'Yes Sir, of course. Mr Nariman emerged from and then shut the front door to No. 6 accompanied only by his two dogs. He apparently intended to walk to meet an American visitor at the station. He was struck in the chest with a knife by the first assailant. Seconds after this initial attack, this first assailant, still holding the knife, was approached, tackled and then frightened off by a neighbour, Ms Alice Roberts, who of course we all know well as one of the forensics team. As they were escaping, the two assailants were knocked off their motorcycle by a black car. Ms Roberts applied immediate first aid to arrest the victim's bleeding while an ambulance was called by a passer-by. Her assessment at that time was that the wound was severe but probably not life-threatening. She assumed she'd witnessed a mugging. She left the victim in the care of her husband while she went to attend the RTA involving the assailants down the street.' He paused but the inspector indicated for him to continue.

'A few seconds later, while Ms Robert's husband Eddie Peters was tending to the man, there was a shot to Mr Nariman's forehead that appears to have killed him instantly. It looks like it came from a high velocity rifle. Mr Peters mentioned a red laser spot appearing on the man's head in the instant before the shot. He did not hear anything so we are assuming the shot was from long range, maybe with a silencer.' Hunter scowled as he heard about the red spot and interrupted his sergeant's account.

'Sergeant, are you sure about the red spot? Eddie didn't mention that to me when I saw him earlier. Nobody round here would use laser sights for a robbery, that's just for the films.'

'Mr Peters was pretty sure about it, Sir.'

'Then that indicates to me that this was an assassination and someone was probably shooting from a moving platform, maybe at shorter range. Was it a pistol or something like an assault rifle? Did we find any rounds?'

'There's nothing yet, Sir.'

'OK that must certainly be one of our priorities. Do we know anything about these men with the knife and scooter yet?'

'No identification yet, Sir. They had absolutely no paperwork on them. They both seem to be of Indian sub-continent extraction, very dark skinned. Ms Roberts told me that she had seen men similar to the two assailants the night before in the tunnel under Jephson Gardens, cooking fish and using a similar knife. She noticed them again with the scooter as she wheeled her bicycle up the steps from her basement flat. The attack occurred while she was getting the bicycle through the gate. Uniformed officers are being asked to look urgently for any sightings of these two men around the town in the last few days, but we've got nothing more yet.'

'And tell me more about the RTA.'

'After Ms Roberts frightened them off, the two men made to escape on the scooter but were hit at the corner of Clarendon Square and Clarendon Place by an unknown black car or cab. This part is still a bit confused. It appears to have then halted for a few seconds and subsequently been driven off again at speed. There is one report of a man getting out of the car, possibly the sniper. There was also a report of a black cab a few minutes later down the street doing a pickup, which may or may not be the same vehicle we don't know. One of the assailants, the pillion passenger who had the knife, was killed instantly by the impact of the car hitting their bike, the other, who was wearing a helmet, died from severe internal wounds and a severed artery before the ambulance arrived. Ms Roberts, a friend – a Mr Hugh Powell – and one of our off-duty uniformed officers tended to the surviving assailant while waiting for the ambulance. They thought they heard him saying something like *ningma* just before he died.'

'Ningma?'

'Yes, Sir.'

'Which officer was it?'

'Sergeant Singh, Sir.'

'I see. What about the sniper, did our man see him?'

'No, he was down by the fire station when it happened and ran up to help. There are no other accounts, nothing more than I just mentioned, Sir. We are searching the square for evidence, but nothing yet and no other witnesses to the shooting.'

'Ok well our second priority is to find that car. It sounds like it quite possibly may be linked to the sniper.'

'Yes, as I said, we do have a report from the resident of No. 10, the corner house, who was working in his study at the front of the building. Mr Richard Baxter. He thinks that the vehicle was a black cab and he was the one that reported that another man with a turban got out of the car before it sped off. He thought he saw the same cab pick someone up down the street a few minutes later. DC Dore also spoke later to a witness in the top floor of the care home opposite – a former actress who now suffers with dementia I'm afraid. It seems she got a good look and referred to a black vehicle. She was heard shouting 'Busy Mab' just after the incident happened. However we have not been able to get anything else out of her yet.'

''Busy Mab', as in a registration number maybe?' said Hunter, as sharp as a whistle. Jones looked at him as if he had just spoiled his party piece.

'Yes, Sir, we thought the same; based on other evidence it could well be a reference to the registration number of the cab. We have not been able to get anything more specific, but we have specialists there, seeing what they can coax out of her. There are no cabs with the registration 'BU51 MAB' or anything close to it locally, in fact DVLA have just confirmed there are no vehicles nationwide with that registration number so, if our assumption is correct, they may be false plates. Of course you know, I assume, that there are no licensed black cabs in Warwick District, but we are also checking in Coventry and Birmingham to see if any black cabs have been reported stolen there recently.'

'Good work, sergeant, and a nice summary of a serious and perplexing situation, but remember we have to keep looking at every detail, that's where the clues will be.'

'There's one more thing, Sir,' added DC Dore. 'I was off duty on Friday night and by chance met up with Eddie

Peters and his friend Hugh Powell. Hugh said at the time that he saw something strange as we were passing through the Covent Garden car park on the way to 'Spice'. He was walking a few yards behind us, so he was the only witness but I made some notes at the time about what he told me he saw, just in case. He said there was a car with a similar sounding registration, he mentioned it ended in 'MAB'. He saw four men talking and exchanging a parcel. Two of the men match the description of the assailants; another was a Sikh wearing a turban. Hugh believes he was the driver of the black car, and there was another man, short and stocky with a heavy tan, silver hair and gold glasses.'

'OK, well that's very helpful Dore, yes Eddie Peters mentioned that to me also. Two Sikhs, although I guess that's not so unusual in Leamington, is there anything else, anybody?' he asked, looking round the room. He was already gathering a picture in his mind, and some of the missing parts to that picture and the coincidences were disturbing him. This was clearly no drive-by hit and run or attempted mugging.

'Yes, two things,' said one of the other junior detectives. 'It appears the landlines to Sir William's house were cut some time during the early morning, which also suggests it was a professional job. Secondly, one of our uniformed officers interviewed the members of the film crew that have been working in the square. The director told us he has heard from one of the actors, a Mr Tristan Arnold, who saw a man outside the nursing home walking dogs opposite the square late the night before. We have not been able to interview him directly yet as he is not answering his mobile, but the description matches that of the victim. Apparently the actor mentioned that he had thought it curious at the time that the man seemed to be being followed by a large black car moving slowly.'

'So it seems as though we may be looking at a contract

killing, we definitely need to find that cab and this Sikh fellow,' murmured the inspector. 'But I'm perplexed why there were two methods of execution. Was the sniper the backup if the knife attack failed? What more do we know about this businessman, Mr Nariman? I'm going to need to know chapter and verse on him as soon as we can. And get hold of that actor, we need a better description of the driver of that cab. Meanwhile, DC Dore, you and I will go and talk to Sir William again. And by the way, has anyone tracked down Mr Nariman's friend yet?'

There were blank stares around the room; this was something they had all overlooked. Trust Amadeus to pick up straight away on some detail like that.

CHAPTER TEN

PENNY'S CIPHER – (INTERMEZZO, ALLEGRETTO) 'DORABELLA.'

The repeated changes of electrical path through an Enigma scrambler implemented a polyalphabetic substitution cipher, which provided Enigma's high security. By itself, a rotor will perform only a very simple type of encryption – a simple substitution cipher. The Enigma's complexity and cryptographic security came from using several rotors in series (usually three or four) and the regular stepping movement of the rotors, thus implementing a polyalphabetic substitution cipher.

Wikipedia, *Enigma Machine*

I was over the moon when they offered me the opportunity for a reassignment from uniformed branch to work with DI Hunter. It was exactly what I had been hoping for. I joined the police force straight from college. I guess I surprised everyone when I said that I wanted to be a policewoman. As a teenager I suffered from a stammer and wore braces. For some girls my age that combination might have resulted in a lack of confidence, but I'm not one to hide behind something like that. I'm kind of a tough girl at heart. I worked incredibly hard to get over my speech impediment. I also trained every day to gain my judo black belt while still in sixth form.

On joining the police, I spent the first two years doing

standard beat policing, but Hunter's reputation was already growing fast and I was desperate to get into his crime squad, sure that I was going to learn a lot from him. I'm twenty-two, single but not unattractive, with long reddish hair that I tie into a topknot for work and ice-blue eyes; the sort of girl-next-door look that grows on you, they say.

My friends often tease me about my weird resemblance to Ginny Weasley, Harry Potter's love interest in the films and secretly I enjoy the comparison. But what everyone seems to notice straight away about me, and I think the thing that marked me out from the crowd in the selection process, is my sheer determination. Apparently I'm pretty scary. Somehow, I give the air of being organised and knowing exactly what I'm doing on pretty well any task. It's probably lucky they can't see how untidy and disorganised my room is! I'm also quite creative and learn quickly. And I always try to be courteous and professional. I like to think Hunter knew exactly what he was doing when he selected me to be his assistant from the pick of the new recruits in Warwickshire. By the way, I hate that nickname 'Amadeus' that everyone uses. He was mad wasn't he, Hunter certainly isn't mad.

★

With Hunter's encouragement, I quickly set about researching the background of both of the two assailants and Arish Nariman himself, I trawled the police computer as well as searching the Internet. Mr Nariman was easy enough: he was a very well-known figure in his home country having run a large multinational organisation for many years. I printed out details about his career to make a little summary for Hunter and then neatly added some information about Nariman's company. The surprising thing for me, given all the business information that was available, was that there was very little on his personal life. It was really only a handful of formulaic interviews about his recent retirement. The contrast was surreal; there was basically almost no tittle-tattle about him on the Internet. But it appeared that he was a very private man who had never been married.

Given this fact, I was really perplexed for a while about the stated paternity of his 'daughter' and 'granddaughter' Nadia Flyte. It appeared that he had adopted the 'daughter', Nadia's mother, as a young girl after the death of her parents and at the request of her guardian. Apart from this somewhat odd detail, it all seemed very neat and tidy, even the newspaper stories about his most recent interrogation at a parliamentary committee appeared to be very respectful. It seemed he was only an incidental player in that particular corruption scandal and no mud had stuck on him.

When I googled for any other scandal or enemies I also found very little, apart from the usual corporate intrigues and some past misdemeanours by overzealous affiliates that appeared to have been put right years ago. The most satisfying part of my investigation was probably my discovery about the ring he was wearing. I was able to quickly identify it as a ring of the APX fraternity, founded at about the time of the First World War at the University of Michigan: the only US architects' fraternity. It appeared that he had had ambitions as a young man to practise architecture and had studied at U of M in Ann Arbor, but all of that had been put aside when his father had died suddenly. He had been called back to take up the reins of the family enterprise. That was kind of interesting.

This and the snippet about the adopted daughter were all that I could find that cast any light on the human side of the man. It was weird, almost as if someone had wiped the slate clean of any other details of his life outside the company itself. I wondered about this as he had clearly been forced to abandon his earlier dreams in order to become a company man; maybe he had sacrificed more than ambition as he did that.

I continued to research the fraternity connection further and found out that one of the fraternity's most famous members was a certain Eliel Saarinen, a Finnish architect who became famous for his art nouveau buildings in the early years of the twentieth century. Incredibly, this was a name I already knew from my own fine art studies in sixth form. Not the father, but the son. Eero Saarinen, who was on the jury that had selected the designs for the Sydney Opera House – a project that I had studied for A level. But that Saarinen was probably better known in our household for his Tulip kitchen chairs that had been ripped off by a host of 1990s furniture stores. My father had a set in our breakfast room.

I was sure Hunter would be very interested in these fragments of information, given his interest in almost anything about the art world. When I had got all that I could from the Internet, I put in calls to the appropriate contacts in both New Scotland Yard and Colombo to find out if there was anything more they could tell me about Nariman's business arrangements and any other contacts or leads that might be relevant to our investigation. All in all it was a very pleasing couple of hour's work. I was sure the governor would be pleased.

The picture became much more difficult when I started on the assailants. There was really nothing to go on, no identifying documents or marks, nothing very unusual about their faces that I could see. Initial checks with the Sri Lankan, Indian and Pakistani embassies in London brought up nothing about any relevant wanted persons. We might of course be able to check the dental records later with various agencies once the autopsy was available, but for now I was at a dead end. Checks with New Scotland Yard on flights out of the sub-continent over the last few weeks into Britain also drew a blank; there was nothing unusual at all that we should be aware of, no suspicious arrivals. I added all this information neatly into my growing folder and eagerly awaited my chance to show off my diligent work to Hunter on his return.

★

About the same time Penny had been doing this research, Hugh Powell had returned to his own flat in the Old Town. His recovery from his hangover had been made more challenging than normal by the stress of attending a murder scene, a motorcyclist dying in his arms and his best friend being covered with the brains of an elderly Asian businessman. Of course he had seen some pretty terrible things over the years during his various tours of duty in the army, but then he had been prepared and trained to deal with such situations. The shock of these events occurring before his eyes in his comfortable hometown, and the feeling of helplessness as he struggled to work out what exactly he should do, had left him shaken. In contrast, Alice had been absolutely superb. She was in full professional mode and control from the start. After the initial assistance he gave her, he had soon realised that he was really not needed and probably getting in her way.

After the ambulance arrived, he had gone back to help Eddie, who was shaking uncontrollably; assisting him back down to the flat to help him clean up. He had also helped to deal with a hyper-excited Carrie. Hugh was Carrie's godfather and she adored him but it was all he could do to keep her in her bedroom and stop her running out on to the street to watch. Both he and Eddie were still shaking an hour later. He had left the two of them about 10am when he was sure they were OK and gone back home to shower and change. As he emerged from the shower, Penny called to ask him to come into the station to make a statement. He just had time before meeting up with Bas. They were both due to travel to watch a rugby match that afternoon.

★

Rohit Dhawan, Arish Nariman's former assistant, was already on the way to his weekly composition tutorial with Richard Baxter, when Nadia texted him with the news of her grandfather's death. He heard the bleep from his phone and pulled up in a lay-by on the road to read the message that flashed up on his screen. He had idolised Nariman; for three years he had helped him with just about everything he did. That made their enforced separation so much more distressing. It was not just about losing a job, it was more like losing a father. As for Nadia, he had had to create a shield around their love affair to keep it secret. And now Nariman was dead. Despite his male pride, he felt tears welling up inside.

After waiting for fifteen minutes to calm himself, he got back on his bike. He had cycled all the way from his digs as he didn't own a car, and in any case had not taken a UK driving test yet. As he arrived in the square he could see the police cordon; it looked like there was no way he would be able to get anywhere near to No. 6 to see Nadia. He texted her back to ask her to call him if she could, afraid that if he called her, she might be discovered speaking to him. They had developed a system of code using their native Sinhalese language to avoid any chance discovery from any of Sir William's household, but of course that had been made more risky by the arrival of her grandfather. Given the contents of the text message, this was clearly no longer a risk. He looked at his watch and continued on, getting as close as he could to the corner house on Clarendon Square where Baxter lived, where he was allowed through the cordon as far as No. 10.

> *Tell me about the dream where we pull the bodies out of the lake*
> *and dress them in warm clothes again.*
> *How it was late, and no one could sleep, the horses running*
> *until they forget that they are horses.*
> *It's not like a tree where the roots have to end somewhere,*
> *it's more like a song on a policeman's radio,*
> *how we rolled up the carpet so we could dance, and the days*
> *were bright red, and every time we kissed there was another apple*
> *to slice into pieces.*
> *Look at the light through the windowpane. That means it's*
>   *noon, that means*
> *we're inconsolable.*
> *Tell me how all this, and love too, will ruin us.*
> *These, our bodies, possessed by light.*
> *Tell me we'll never get used to it.*

Richard Siken, *Scheherazade*

★

As Baxter held his weekly composition class in the first floor drawing room, he noticed how the young Sri Lankan writer seemed more distracted and nervous than usual. He knew that he was somehow connected with Sir William's murdered guest, but even so he still expected his full attention. After all, he, Baxter had spent the whole morning preparing for this seminar, and he'd had to witness the whole gruesome thing out of the window as well.

Baxter had asked the group the week before to look at the *Three Apples* story from the Arabian Nights, one of the earliest, if not *the* earliest known detective story. Rohit's latest essay was of the usual high standard; he had produced an excellent analysis of the symbolism of death within the Arabian Nights stories. In Baxter's view, there was no doubt that the lad had talent, but his verbal synopsis that day appeared almost morbid in its focus on violence and revenge within the story. He chose to question why Scheherazade allowed the game to go on so long, and didn't just use her smartness to kill Shahryar, her captor. Rohit argued that she could have avoided her own probable fate and escaped with her lover if she had wanted to by taking things into her own hands and killing him, but that she was constrained from doing this by some misplaced loyalty to her lord.

After the seminar was over and most of the others had left, Rohit began to ask Baxter about the guns on the wall that he collected during his American sojourns. Baxter knew from earlier sessions that Rohit was a committed pacifist and answered his questions cautiously, concerned that he might report the firearms to the police. Baxter did not have the licenses he needed and he knew that Rohit often worked with the police as a translator. He left the room for a few minutes to go to the bathroom. When he got back, he was determined to get reassurance from Rohit on this, but found that Rohit was already oddly more relaxed. He managed to quickly get him focused back on the next week's assignment, the one he had prepared an introduction for that morning – the 'greatest first sentence of a novel'.

After attending Baxter's writing class, Rohit decided to stay in the town and walked over to a local internet café, where he could monitor the news reports of the incident. During the next few hours, he and Nadia exchanged several more texts, Nadia explaining that she wanted to speak with him desperately but couldn't get privacy at the moment. Her texts became progressively more distraught during the day, and by late afternoon she said that she really needed to see him. She asked him to try and get to her bedroom window later under the cover of darkness.

After a quick trip to the station to give a statement, Hugh found Bas in the bar of the Benjamin Satchwell. He seemed oblivious to what had been going on in the town. In fact, he seemed more interested in recounting the results of his 'chav-hunting' the night before. Apparently, his subsequent late night attempts at conquest had been at least partially successful, although Hugh was never quite sure whether to believe Bas's boastings or not. His friends had a fitting name for him – Braggadocio – on account of his frequent tall stories of sexual exploits. In any case, Bas shut up quickly when Hugh recounted the tragic events he had witnessed that morning.

'That's really heavy stuff. Alice is such a great girl. Damn Eddie for nailing that franchise. However, you'll get over it. Life goes on. You still up for the rugby?'

Hugh sighed.

'Bas, you really are a jerk. But you're right, maybe it will do me good to shout at a bunch of grown up children throwing leather balls around rather than mull on all this gory stuff I've been through this morning.'

'Great, that's my man. If we hurry we'll be able to get a pie and a couple of pints in first.'

★

At Warwick Hospital, Alice had by early afternoon already finished the first steps of the autopsy under the close direction of her boss, the senior consultant pathologist. She had of course been with the scenes of crime officer while he was taking photographs of Nariman's corpse, and had helped in the measurement of the head and abdominal wounds in situ immediately after death. Now, in the lab, she marked out the entrance wounds under post-mortem conditions.

She also measured the bullet wounds again in order to gauge the closeness of the assailant to the victim and also to try and establish what kind of gun was used in the attack. The exit wound of course was huge; the bullet had shattered the whole side of Nariman's skull. In terms of weapons, they already had the knife, and had found the remains of a .22 calibre bullet that was now with ballistics for rifling analysis. Other officers were still searching the areas for more clues, but had not yet identified any spent shell casings in the vicinity.

Throughout the process she made audio notes and photographs with the help of an assistant, as well as written notes for the detailed autopsy report. Once the external examination was complete she moved on to the internal organs.

Before she even started the important Y-incision, she noted again the details both of the knife wound and the previous scarring on the victim's chest. The shape was distinctive; it was almost as if someone has carved a red letter *A* into his skin sometime in the past. She proceeded to cut from the shoulders to the lower end of the sternum and then downwards in a straight line across the abdomen to the pubis in order to gain access to Nariman's major organs.

Next, she removed the organs and her assistant weighed each of them while Alice took additional blood samples. It was standard practice to test for signs of poisoning using toxicology, even when there were obvious physical injuries manifesting themselves. She then checked the abdomen and took tissue samples for analysis before examining the contents of the stomach; these were consistent with the reports that he had not eaten breakfast. She had seen the ripe fig he had taken from the breakfast table drop from his hand and splatter on the pavement uneaten as he fell to the ground. She also took further samples of bile, eye fluid, liver tissue and urine; again for toxicology.

After this was complete, she turned her attention to his head, which showed the small entrance wound in his forehead and the massive exit wound behind. She removed what was left of the brain for a more thorough inspection. This seemed pretty straightforward, all the more so having witnessed the attack herself. Within an hour she had reported her preliminary findings back to the police team and was moving on to the examination of the two assailants. It would be a long day and she would be more than glad to see her bed at the end of it. It was all in the pursuit of truth, one version of the truth, the virtue of unity.

Truth: the Una was the first feminist periodical that was owned, written, and edited entirely by women, launched in Providence, Rhode Island in February 1853. 'Out of great heart of nature seek we truth,' was the quote in Vol. No.1.

Wikipedia, *The Una*

*

Like Hugh, Eddie had also decided that a sporting distraction might be the best plan to get the events of the morning out of his mind. Alice was at the hospital and he didn't expect her back anytime soon. Instead he decided to do the father-daughter thing and take Carrie to watch the women's tournament at the local tennis club. During a break between matches, one of the lady professionals gave Carrie some basic tuition on how to hold the racket and showed her the slicing action required to serve the ball onto the court's hazard roofs. 'She's very good, Eddie but watch you don't take anybody's head off with that racket, young lady!' Carrie seemed to have a real feel for it and more importantly for Eddie she seemed to be quite taken by the game. So much so that Eddie promised her he would take her down to the beginners' session the following weekend, to give it a try for real. 'And by the way,' said Carrie, 'I'll need my own racket please and a proper tennis outfit.' He was cool with that; actually he was rather keen on the idea.

★

Returning to the investigation, another member of Detective Sergeant Jones' team had managed to track down the possible location of the cab they had been looking for. It turned out that a black cab usually driven by one of the Sikh community in Coventry had been loaned out to another driver for the summer. The owner usually did airport runs, but was due to be off work for several weeks with a broken leg, and had rented his cab out. From this information, they quickly tracked the other driver down, also a Sikh, but this time living in South Leamington.

The address they were given was in an area of insalubrious terraced housing that was renowned as being quite dodgy after dark. When Detective Sergeant Jones and two armed uniformed officers arrived outside the driver's house in a marked police car, they were immediately conscious of the inquisitive faces appearing at the windows of the houses opposite. They signalled to these neighbourly observers to keep away. The road had a dejected feel to it, with rubbish piled up in a couple of the gardens and dogs barking behind fenced cages. There was a car with Warwick District taxi plates on the road outside the house.

The turbaned man who answered the bell at the address they were given looked nervously through the chained half-open door at the two burly officers standing in front of him. The hallway was untidy and there was a strong smell of Asian cooking coming from within. After a moment's pause to clear his throat, Sergeant Jones wasted no time in beginning to question him. The man unchained the door and stepped forward onto the doorstep, carefully closing the door behind him.

'Good afternoon sir, would you be Mr Gurvinder Singh?'

The man nodded without saying a word.

'And is this your taxi cab sitting on the drive?'

He nodded again, Jones noticed that his eyes appeared bloodshot as if he has been up all night.

'Mr Singh, we are investigating an incident earlier this morning in the centre of town involving a black taxi cab and we have reports that you may be using such a vehicle,' he pointed across the lawn to the saloon car standing on the driveway. 'Is it correct that you are using a black cab at the moment instead of your normal car?' The man shrugged as if he did not understand, however Jones noticed a slight twitch of his neck as if involuntarily he was acknowledging the factual accuracy of the question.

'Is that a yes or a no, sir?'

'Yes, it's in the garage, I haven't used it for a few days.' The man replied. He looked behind him into the house; there was an energised woman's voice coming from inside. He shouted something to her in his native language and she quietened down.

'I'd really like to see that other vehicle, sir.'

The man shrugged again and went back into the house to fetch a bunch of keys. He shouted something else to the woman inside, who yelled back and then stepped out and closed the front door behind him. He walked across to the door of his garage and undid two large padlocks with the set of keys that he now had hanging around his neck. As he opened the door he mumbled something about using the black cab to do a number of minicab jobs for local businessmen. He explained that he was only using it to put off doing some expensive repairs that were needed on his own car until he had saved enough money to pay for them.

The police officers understood immediately from this that he had probably been moonlighting as a minicab driver, something strictly outside the conditions of his license. That could be useful. On inspecting the cab, it became clear that there were some dents and some very recent repairs to the front end, as if he had hit something and tried to hide the evidence.

'You had an accident or something?' asked one of the constables who had accompanied Jones.

'Just hit a lamppost, I'm not used to the turning circle,' the man replied unconvincingly.

'Mmm, just a lamppost you say, you sure?' asked Jones.

'Of course sir, please I am a poor man, I'm only trying to make enough money to keep my family, please don't report me. I don't make any trouble.'

'Look at these, Sir.' The constable had been looking around the back of the car. He pointed to a sack propped up against the back wall and opened one of them, 'Number plates.' The man's face looked crestfallen, like he had tasted a particularly strong lemon.

'What's this about, Mr Singh?'

'They're just old plates; I meant to throw them away.'

'They don't look particularly old sir, if you don't mind my saying – 'BU51 MAB',' he read. 'Now that is a very interesting plate isn't it, and practically brand new?'

'I think you'd better come with us to the station, Sir, and we are going to need to take the car away for a while,' said Sergeant Jones. As they left the house in the police car, the constable alerted the sergeant to the renewed shrieking in the house as they left. 'That seems to have given her indoors something to think about, Sir.'

CHAPTER ELEVEN

DAN THE BULLDOG – (ALLEGRO DI MOLTO) 'G.R.S.'

Have we imprisoned ourselves in three dimensions? Is reality, (the world we live in) just what our minds tell us is real, or could there be multiple alternative realities existing simultaneously? Quantum physicists believe there could, and that parallel universes could exist less than one millimetre away from us. In fact they suggest that our gravity is just a weak signal leaking out of another universe into ours! We normally think of ourselves as living in a three-dimensional world where we can move in three ways: left or right, up or down, forwards or backwards, but now we are told there may be eleven dimensions – hidden worlds beyond our human senses – a multiverse full of unexplained happenings and strange visions. Imagination is limitless – it doesn't have to make sense.

Paul Windridge, experimental film maker, from his website

Jack the director walked past the police lines at the corner of Clarendon Square, the scene of the horrendous accident and murder earlier in the day. He had been working on an episode of *Sherlock* with the crew all week, his bulldog Dan keeping them amused with his antics between takes, but the incidents that morning had forced them to abandon filming. He had therefore spent some time in his own studio that afternoon, working on one of his personal short film projects but now was free for their regular early evening stroll. He took the road down towards the river, turning right just before they reached the bridge; past the Sea Scout hut 'T.S. Satyrane' and then walked directly along the river path. The river was lit perfectly by the late afternoon sun. Dan, now off his lead, was in and out of bushes, chasing ghosts of ducks and other wildlife, in his own mysterious doggy world.

Jack Sinclair, or 'Mad Jack' as he is affectionately known, is renowned in the film world for being as nutty as a fruitcake but a seriously good indie filmmaker. He lives in a large penthouse flat near the town centre, in the building where Sir Malcolm Sayer, inventor of the E-type Jaguar used to live. He shares Sir Malcolm's enthusiasm for fast cars but that is not his main love. He is a movie man. In his spare time, he experiments with video and music, making films with few words but memorable imagery. He also keeps his collection of Wurlitzer organs and even more prized collection of taxidermy cases there, many of them from the celebrated Leamington firm of Peter Spicer & Sons that was situated on the corner of Victoria Terrace near the post office.

Jack knew Eddie from the Woodbine music studio, they had worked together to produce videos for a local rock/Kerala-fusion band and recently Eddie had also been helping him out with some of the music for his film projects. Jack had inherited great wealth and an old hall house out near the Long Mynd in the Shropshire hills, remote from anything, where he often disappeared for weeks on end. Eddie, Alice and Carrie had spent weekends with him there, and had the disconcerting experience of wandering the rooms and corridors of the Elizabethan mansion at the dead of night, alone with no other sounds apart from the hooting of owls and Mad Jack's gothic music-making rasping below in his studio.

In Jack's younger days, he had indulged in all sorts of stupid pranks and drunk far too much port. For a bet, he had once ridden his motorbike up the stairs of the hotel opposite the Town Hall, out on to the balcony. Then, still seated on the bike, he had accelerated and leapt through the glass plate window of the restaurant, onto the Parade below. He'd survived the bike hadn't. He was also a fanatical soccer supporter and player. In his twenties he had allegedly been sent off several times for fighting with rival players and twice for biting opponent's ears, fortunately he was a little calmer now. His early life had been described by one friend as 'a series of failed suicide attempts'.

Although he has matured since his younger days, in some ways his antics have not grown any more normal. With Dan his constant companion, he often goes out at night into the countryside around Leamington or on to the Staffordshire moors to hunt ducks and rodents, often in the middle of cold winter nights, reputedly sometimes dressed only in a deerstalker, coat and boots. In fact, the students at one of the local universities, the one that he had attended before he was thrown out, now run an annual mixed streaking event in his honour on the first day of class following Easter, despite the best attempts of campus security to stop it. The irony is that he was recently awarded an honorary doctorate by the same university in recognition of his avant-garde filmmaking. He suspects that no one had put two and two together.

The Leam is a tributary of the River Avon that flows through rural Warwickshire and Leamington Spa on its way to meet up with its big sister near Warwick. It is usually slow flowing, meandering through low lying farm land, however there have been occasions in the past when it has flooded; achieving particularly high water levels in 1998 and 2007. That day, it was relatively quiet and low after a dry summer and Jack remarked on the peaceful state of the riverbank compared to the din from the emergency service sirens and hectic police helicopter activity that had filled the town all morning.

There was a loud splash in the reeds and Jack turned to see that Dan had slipped down the mud of the steep bank into the river and was now paddling back towards him upstream to find a landing place. After a few minutes, Jack heard his rejoicing bark on landing and thought to himself, *Echo Bravo Golf, I challenge anyone to make a short film of that!*

As Dan approached, Jack saw that he was carrying something man-made in his mouth.

'What have you got there, boy?'

> *Then first of all forth came Sir Satyrane,*
> *Bearing that precious relicke in an arke*
> *Of gold, that bad eyes might it not prophane:*
> *Which drawing softly forth out of the darke,*

Spenser, *The Faerie Queene*

The dog dropped the package at his feet. It was a plastic bag, tightly sealed with gaffer tape, with an envelope inside. Jack could see it was stuffed with fifty-pound notes, but realised at once that he should not open it for fear of contaminating evidence.

He got on his mobile to the local police straight away.

★

When the call came in, Hunter and I were already on our way to see Sir William, but hearing the news on the radio, decided to divert to the riverbank instead. When we got there, the uniformed officers were already at the scene.

As Hunter gingerly inspected the bag, I was really hoping that in his enthusiasm, he would not open it until the forensics team had had a chance to take a proper look. It might of course have had nothing to do with this murder, but if it did it could turn out to be a critical breakthrough.

'It doesn't look like it's been in the river very long. I wonder if there's any connection to the two lads Alice saw last night down by the river?' I asked, anxiously keeping an eye on what my boss was up to.

'My thoughts exactly, Penny, especially given that your friend Hugh saw a package changing hands in the car park that night. I can't see any marking on the banknotes from outside, however,' he said.

'Well, let me get it checked out as soon as possible,' I replied, quickly taking the bag back off him before he attempted to open it, already convinced that we would find something inside, a chance to prove myself in his eyes.

As we left the scene, Hunter saw Lucy Fleming, the reporter from the local paper, who clearly must have been monitoring our radio traffic to get there so quickly. Hunter murmured that he had forgotten to follow up with her; we had been so busy during the day. He went over to her and gave her a briefing on the general situation without getting too specific on evidence. He thought she might be useful later, and was still keen to keep her onside as someone he could trust.

'Thanks, Inspector, we never did have that drink did we?' she said, flirting with him just a little.

★

> *She bolted the big round window,*
> *She let the blinds unroll,*
> *She set a match to the mantle,*
> *She covered the fire with coal.*

Betjeman, *Death in Leamington*

In the early evening, Izzie and Penn returned to Sherridge House to visit Winnie before the home shut to visitors. Winnie was not in her room. Izzie inspected the bottles on the tray and looked quizzical.

'They seem to have significantly increased her medication during the afternoon.'

She read the chart and frowned, checking the words on her iPhone.

'Wow, Moban, I haven't seen that drug before, it seems to be very powerful stuff. It's certainly not something we would normally use, and this dosage just doesn't seem right, the bottle's half-empty.'

As she said the words she heard a sudden scream from along the corridor and set off immediately towards the bathrooms. A nurse rushed out from one of them and called to her for help. Izzie pushed past her then halted suddenly in shock. Underneath the foaming waters of a tepid bath, lay Winnie's body, still, blue and quite motionless.

Izzie pulled the emergency cord and together, they pulled her out of the water to attempt resuscitation although it seemed like it might already be too late. Izzie could feel no pulse and her skin felt deathly cold.

'How on earth did she get in here by herself?' said Izzie.

'I don't know,' the other nurse said defensively. 'One of the consultants was here and I left him to it while I went and helped with the tea.'

'Was he male or female?'

'Male.'

'You're kidding me? You left her alone with a man? And how often do we see a consultant here on a Saturday?'

★

Downstairs, in the laundry room, a dark-skinned slightly portly man with gold-rimmed glasses pulled off the white coat he had been wearing and dumped it into the laundry basket. He exited the building unseen through the side entrance and over the fence into the back lane.

> *Nurse looked at the silent bedstead,*
> *At the gray, decaying face,*
> *As the calm of a Leamington ev'ning*
> *Drifted into the place.*

Betjeman, *Death in Leamington*

★

It was now getting on for 6pm and at Hunter's orders I had reconvened the crime squad in the incident room in Police HQ. During the afternoon, Detective Sergeant Jones had been directing most of the manpower in following up our various leads. I had been trying to get more answers from Asia before it was too late and chasing forensics on the autopsies, ballistics and now the package salvaged by Dan from the river.

As Sergeant Jones was about to start the briefing, he took a call and scowled.

'Well now we have another body, Sir. Winifred Norbury, the actress, our witness, has just been found dead in a bath at the care home. There is nothing to indicate foul play but all the same.'

I gasped at the news; I had only seen her with Izzie a few hours earlier and although unbalanced she certainly did not seem to be near death's door.

'Please go on, Sergeant,' urged Hunter, a little callously perhaps but keen to avoid the briefing getting derailed before they had more facts.

Jones summarised what we had found out so far from the autopsies and the search for the black cab. Although we did not yet have the full reports from the various bodies, the picture continued to build of a botched attempt to knife Nariman followed by a calculated assassination, probably from a moving car. Hunter whispered to me that he was also already wondering whether the Tamils were then run over deliberately to silence them.

'DC Dore, anything yet on the bag we found in the river?'

'There are no trace marks, Sir, the lab is taking a closer look but they are not hopeful – they look like random used notes. But they did find something else in the bag which is more promising.' I pointed to a photo on the table of a small leather pouch that had been found inside the envelope contained with the money.

'There are three newspaper cuttings in a Sinhalese script inside the pouch.' I handed the photographs to Hunter. 'We got Transtec to come in and help with a quick translation; apparently they are all about a factory accident in Tamil Nadu that killed a load of workers. I've done some more research: take a look, Sir.'

I had followed up immediately on the incident reported in the newspaper cuttings with further questions to the local authorities. However, given the time difference, I did not expect any answers until the following morning. A brief Internet search had revealed that several men of similar facial features to the assailants were wanted by the police as members of a terrorist organisation connected with these incidents. This organisation also had links to K-Company, a mafia ring that ran a large swathe of the underworld in Colombo. They had been responsible for one or two bombings and attacks on the property of a chemical company that was part of Arish Nariman's empire. Further investigation had revealed that there were three sisters and a number of child workers that had been killed following an explosion in a local factory. The factory had poor safety and environmental standards but the company, with the involvement of the local police, had covered up the incident initially. The men's involvement in the terrorist group dated from that time. They were brothers and uncles of the women and children who had died.

'Forensics are analysing the fingerprints we found on the knife. If we can confirm that connection, then I think we might be quite close to a motive for the knife attack at least then, Sir?' I volunteered.

'This is excellent work, Dore. But I am not sure that retribution can be the only motive, where for instance did they get the money from to fly over here, and why did they do that rather than make an attempt on his life in Sri Lanka?' pondered Hunter. I agreed that there must be more to this than a revenge attack by some embittered relatives but still thought this lead was important. He must have seen this on my face.

'What are you thinking, Dore?' he asked me in front of the whole squad. I was somewhat embarrassed that he had singled me out in front of a number of more senior officers.

'Maybe they did it here because there was less security around him, Sir?' I ventured.

'True, but even so someone must have paid for it. These two weren't exactly dressed like international travellers and the money to finance this had to come from somewhere. I wonder if there is a connection to the gentlemen from the car park. And if there is a connection, where does that leave us with our sniper?'

'I'll get on that straight away, Sir,' I said somewhat too enthusiastically, which elicited a ripple of amusement from my colleagues. I would definitely be getting a ribbing for this later.

'Well, we can't do so much more on this tonight, I think we had better get back to seeing Sir William to see if he can give us any insights to what is going on here,' said Hunter. Like him, I was now convinced that we were going to have to get deeper into Sir William's affairs if we were going to understand this case. He was right; someone with a lot of money must have bankrolled this assassination. The question was who, and why?

★

Dottie was just finishing preparing supper for herself and Baxter. They usually spent Saturdays quietly at home together in Leamington and she had travelled up the previous evening, bringing provisions for the weekend. Claudia would normally have joined them as well, but she was out for the evening, so they had the luxury of the whole place to themselves for once. Of course the events of the morning had been very upsetting; to have such things happen right outside their house was unsettling and there were still a lot of police and reporters milling about outside.

Baxter and Dottie had provided statements on what little they saw to the police. The rest of the day had gone remarkably calmly given the storm outside and Baxter continued to give his composition classes intermittently to groups of students during the afternoon. Dottie had supplied them with tea and scones as each new batch arrived.

She began to serve up supper in the drawing room upstairs. They did not usually bother with a formal dinner setting unless they had guests, preferring supper on their knees on the nice padded trays she had found in the pound shop in town. She was just about to open a bottle of elderberry wine when she noticed something different about the wall. There was a space amidst Baxter's cherished collection of Wild West artefacts, the ones that he never allowed her to clean.

'Something is missing, Richard.' A note of alarm crept into her voice as she pointed to the dusty space where a Browning revolver had once rested.

CHAPTER TWELVE

SWEET BASIL – (ANDANTE) 'B.G.N.'

We found a roaring fire, an elegant dinner, a snug room, and capital beds all ready for us at Leamington, after a very agreeable (but very cold) ride. We started in a post chaise next morning for Kenilworth, with which we were both enraptured, and where I really think we MUST have lodgings next summer, please God that we are in good health and all goes well. You cannot conceive how delightful it is. To read among the ruins in fine weather would be perfect luxury. From here we went on to Warwick Castle, which is an ancient building, newly restored, and possessing no very great attraction beyond a fine view and some beautiful pictures; and thence to Stratford-upon-Avon, where we sat down in the room where Shakespeare was born, and left our autographs and read those of other people and so forth.

Charles Dickens, *Dombey and Son*

It was early evening and Pearl had dressed up properly for dinner. She sat on a bar stool in The Regency Brasserie in the old Regent Hotel building, by common consent the town's premier meeting place. Pearl was chatting to the rather handsome young Italian barman and sipping Manhattans. Sam the pianist was playing 'It Had To Be You'. It could have been a set straight out of a movie.

Pure diva and radiant, she looked about a million dollars more sophisticated than the townies that were spread lazily around the settees in the lounge. Pearl was wearing a black sequin and sparkle cocktail dress with sheer panelled sleeves. The outfit coordinated beautifully with her glowing ebony skin, sophisticated jewellery and beautifully manicured nails. The contrast with the other women in the room was stark, making them appear rather shabby in their high-street cocktail dresses, fake tans and rip-off designer shoes.

After a very successful afternoon, she was now contemplating the next stage of her plan and looking for her next victim. Her interest was piqued immediately when two men in their mid-thirties entered the bar, unattached but clearly in search of company. She did not react to them openly. Instead she continued to sip her Manhattan coolly, smiling to herself, wondering if either of them would dare to make a move or whether she would have to make the running herself. She felt like a black widow spider marking out her prey. In this respect, she was immediately surprised. The elder and uglier of the two came up beside her at the bar and ordered from the barman, then turned to her with a fawning smile, delivering one of the least original pick-up lines she had ever heard – and she'd heard a lot.

'What are you drinking?'

'Manhattans,' she replied. From his blank expression, the name obviously meant nothing to him. 'Whiskey, sweet vermouth and bitters,' she explained.

'Sounds interesting, can I order you another?'

'Well, that would be most kind,' she answered and gave him her most gracious smile. 'But before I accept, do I know you from somewhere?' she asked, intent on making him work a little bit harder.

'No, but I always make a point of talking to the most beautiful woman in the room,' he answered. The sheer cheesiness of this line made her want to laugh out loud at him, but she maintained her poise.

'Well I'm truly flattered, young man, but I think some

of the pretty ladies in here tonight just might take issue with that appraisal.'

'They bear no comparison to a real woman like you,' he rebutted, seeming quite genuine.

'Well, on age at least, I'm guessing I could be the mother of most of them.'

'I can assure you that neither they nor their mothers ever looked anywhere near as good as you do. You're a picture of sophistication and what's more you're gorgeous. Frankly, you're in a different league from them. Anyway, I'm forgetting my manners, I should introduce myself properly, my name's Basil, Basil Nevinson to be exact.'

'Pearl Taylor,' she said offering him her hand, allowing herself to be somewhat flattered despite the lounge lizard act. From his lack of reaction, she realised that he clearly did not recognise her name. She was going to have to make the running here. The pianist had moved on to 'As Time Goes By'. She stared intently at her admirer, painting his face with her eyes.

'Here's looking at you, kid,' she said and clinked his glass against her own in a reversal of roles that her admirer also seemed to completely miss the meaning of.

'I love your outfit and that divine scent you're wearing, Miss Taylor – Chanel?'

She rolled her eyes – *is this guy for real?* This was too easy; he was just perfect for her plan.

'Actually, it's my own brand, and very originally it's called 'Pearl's'.'

This time she had scored easily, his mouth dropped and his eyes nearly popped out of his head exactly as she had intended. His expression was precisely that of a man who had just realised he was hitting on a woman that had her own perfume brand. The pianist in the corner continued to play the 160-year-old Collard & Collard grand piano, moving on now to 'Perfidia'.

How appropriate, she thought. *Maybe I should just tell him now that I'm a singer*, she wondered before adding seductively, 'Maybe with your evident good taste this could be the beginning of a beautiful friendship…'

★

We left the police station and drove the mile or so back up to the murder scene in Hunter's battered old Volvo. We got out of the unmarked car and crossed the police lines again. I noticed Lucy Fleming again, evidently now one of Hunter's more enthusiastic fans. She had clearly spotted him getting out of the car. She ran over to him and asked him breathlessly for an update, flashing her eyelids and touching his arm. To my annoyance he caved immediately and promised that he would talk to her again later. She'd clearly already partly got her claws into him. A case like this could make her career if she got the inside story. I'd have to watch this one like a hawk.

We approached the front door of No. 6, knocked and were let in by one of Sir William's servants. Hunter remarked approving on the stained glass fleur-de-lys set into the door as we passed into the hall. We had apparently just missed my stepsister Julia, who had been there consoling Nadia. She had left ten minutes earlier. Hunter was disappointed but as it turned out we would later have an opportunity to catch up with her in the brasserie. We were shown straight into the library.

I had not been inside No. 6 before; my relationship with Sir William's ex-wife meant that I was now even less likely to get a social invitation. The library had the feel of a well lived in room, with a fire roaring in a massive marble fireplace. The walls were well stocked with formal looking leather-bound volumes, probably bought by the yard Hunter said, including a practically complete set of Wisden.

Every nook and cranny not taken up by the books was filled with dubious oil paintings, mainly nudes and valuable-looking but again, in Hunter's opinion, poorly-chosen erotic bronzes and artefacts. Hunter was clearly already making an inventory in his mind. He studied an Edward Ward engraving of the Disgrace and Fall of Clarendon (Edward Hyde, 1st Earl of Clarendon) above the fireplace.

'Possibly very prescient,' he said authoritatively.

The floor was covered with a patterned Wilton carpet on which were scattered a variety of button armchairs and small card tables. It all had the smell and feel of what I imagined one of those more archaic London clubs was like. All had been transported wholesale to this provincial town house, complete with the overpowering smell of leather and stale tobacco mixed with the warm smoke from the hearth. The combination made my stomach turn slightly. The butler brought each of us a glass of sparkling water, as we had requested. I gulped mine down. When Sir William came in he looked slightly flustered to see us and clutched a glass containing something a great deal stronger. I could tell he was already half-cut. He looked at Hunter but did not acknowledge my presence.

'Good evening, Inspector, do you have an update for us?' he said, his voice somewhat slurred. I noticed at once the use of the regal 'us'.

'I'm sorry to disturb you again, Sir William, but yes, there have been some developments this afternoon and I wanted to see if you could cast any light on a couple of things for me,' replied Hunter. I was watching Sir William's face closely and thought I could detect signs of nervousness in the lack of eye contact from one usually so forceful and full of bluster.

'Of course, well, please fire away – so to speak,' Sir William winced and appeared to immediately regret his poor choice of words. Hunter had asked me already to check on gun licenses for the property. I was certainly aware that Lady Mary kept a fine set of hunting rifles next door and the news about Baxter's missing revolver was worrying.

'We now have suspicions that the two assailants could have been associated with a Tamil terrorist group that is known to have made attacks and threats on Mr Nariman's company. Do you know if he was aware of any such threats being made recently?' Hunter asked.

'My goodness, are you serious, terrorists here in Leamington? No, I certainly wasn't aware of that and as I told you he was always very relaxed about security, too relaxed in my view. But I'm sure he would have said something to Nadia or me if there had been a recent terrorist threat. In fact, even before he arrived I had offered to organise some personal protection for him and he said there was really no need in a country as peaceful as England. Does the Home Office know about this?' Sir William did seem to be genuinely surprised by this information.

'Well, at the moment it is only a suspicion. We are hoping to have more information on this in the morning, but I suggest we do take some additional precautions, just in case. We don't know exactly what the motivations are for this attack and it is possible there is still an extant threat to your family. If you don't mind I am going to recommend we station a couple of armed police officers on duty outside the premises for the night.'

'Of course, Inspector, if you think that is needed. I certainly won't object.'

'Now, I know that you and Mr Nariman had a variety of business interests, Sir William, but is there anything that you could think of that could have triggered this attack, especially something that could have caused it to have occurred here rather than in Asia? Are there any arrangements or deals that you might have been discussing with Mr Nariman that would affect the UK?'

'Well, I'm really not sure what you might mean, Inspector, I don't and never have represented his company, it's purely a family relationship resulting from my marriage. There are absolutely no business connections between us.'

I noticed now that although Sir William's voice was raised and firm, his body language was showing signs of nervousness. He had raised his hand to his mouth and he was now definitely avoiding direct eye contact with Hunter. I saw my chance to insert myself into the conversation.

'But you do have financial interests in Sri Lanka, don't you, Sir William?' I asked sweetly. He turned his head towards me and stared somewhat witheringly with the expression of someone who was not used to being questioned closely by a young woman. He turned his body away and back towards Hunter. Gosh, he was a piece of work. I guessed that he must be aware that I was his first wife's stepdaughter and was therefore even more on his guard.

'I think you'll find that all my business interests are fully on the public record, young lady,' he muttered without looking at me.

The forced smile on Sir William's face and the repetition of my phrasing both seemed false, as if he was hiding something. I could tell that Hunter was also already beginning to suspect he knew more about the background to the attack than he was letting on; however he signalled to me surreptitiously with his hand that a less direct approach might be needed. Understandably, having spoken up, I felt slightly deflated by both men's put-downs.

'I'm sorry, Sir William, maybe there is a misunderstanding here,' Hunter said apologetically. 'We are not questioning your business interests themselves, we are just trying to understand possible motives here, especially given this potential terrorist connection. Can you think of any other avenues we might need to explore to get to the bottom of this, indeed, most importantly, anything that might continue to pose a threat to you and your family?' This made me feel better as I could see now how Hunter was playing on the tension created by my earlier question and adding in the security of Sir William's family as a leverage point.

'No, really there's nothing. Look, old man, I'm sorry if I seemed a bit short a moment ago, but I am keen to get an early night tonight, I'm very tired and Nadia is still too upset to see anyone. Do you think we could leave any further questions to tomorrow?'

'Yes of course, and by then it's possible we may have heard something more concrete from Sri Lanka. One last thing, do you know of a Rohit Dhawan?' Sir William paused for a moment; his face betrayed some surprise at the question.

'Yes, of course, he used to work for Nariman.'

'Do you know of his whereabouts?'

'No idea, Inspector, but I never liked him, I'm afraid. He's a troublemaker. What's he got to do with this?'

'Nothing specific, just a missing person report we have.' Sir William shook his head and looked annoyed.

We left, but as soon as we were outside the property Hunter turned to me and I was relieved, in fact elated, by what he said.

'You're a clever woman, Penny. He's definitely hiding something; your question about financial interests really unnerved him. Well done. Come on, let's get back to the office and find out what Sir William has been up to over the last few months that might have a bearing on this. And we need to track down this Rohit character as well. No, but wait, I almost forgot. Before we do that, I have a quick social call to make; you're welcome to join me as I think the Flyte sisters and some of your friends should be there too. It's just along from the station. It will save time in the morning if we can talk to them now.'

★

As soon as they were gone, Sir William returned to his study, closed the door and was careful to use the prepay mobile phone that he and his contact had agreed to use in such circumstances.

'I'm worried Khand, that damned inspector has started asking questions about my business arrangements.'

'Don't worry, Sir William, everything is under control, it's all going to plan. It's natural the police will ask questions about your relationship with Nariman – you're clean on that right? You sorted everything out in advance?'

'Yes of course, but under control you say? You could have fooled me. You said you were only going to scare him. Well, what on earth was that about this morning if everything is under control? You never said you'd kill him or that you'd do it on my doorstep for God's sake. My wife's close to a nervous breakdown and I've had all sorts of bother today from the party about this. If you intended to kill him, why on earth did you use those bunglers and not do it properly the first time? What's more, Julia told Nadia that someone at the care home over the road apparently saw the whole thing and so did my friend Baxter in the corner house. And the police were asking me about that nuisance Rohit Dhawan just now. I don't like it. The whole thing's a dog's breakfast.'

The voice on the other end of the phone turned cool and menacing.

'Please calm down, Sir William. It's no surprise that there would be witnesses in a residential area. I have that situation completely under control. I need you to keep your cool. Remember you've done very well out of these business arrangements. You owe everything to us. We set you up, your house, your business, your knighthood, everything, including the peerage that's in the works if you keep your nose clean. If Nariman's dirty little boyfriend hadn't got nosy, everything would be fine, but he did and Nariman started asking too many questions and now's he paid for it. So I suggest you just pull yourself together and do exactly what I tell you to do. I'll take care of Rohit.'

'You can't talk to me like that!' Sir William spluttered. 'I'm not one of your lackeys.'

'I think I can. You know perfectly well who you're dealing with here and *he* won't be crossed. So for your own sake, just calm down and follow the plan otherwise you might get some of Nariman's medicine coming your way as well.'

'Are you threatening *me* now?'

'Look, calm down, I say, we've covered all our tracks so far, there's nothing to link you to the murder and we don't need you going wobbly. The Tamils have got credible motive and they're not going to be talking, are they?'

'OK, but what about that woman in the care home and Baxter, if you say you have everything under control?'

'I repeat, I know what I'm doing. We've got all the murder weapons and as for the woman at the care home, unfortunately it appears she got her dosage mixed up, took too many pills and then took a bath alone which you should never do with those drugs. They found her a few hours ago with goose skin and a bar of soap in her hand. A sad death, in fact all these things are very sad but accidents will happen. So you see it's all under control and all in the plan. I think you can look after Mr Baxter for me, can't you, or do I need to find a little accident for him as well?'

'What? There's another body? Christ, how many more will there be? I just don't like it, this inspector and his clever clogs assistant, who by the way is related to my ex-wife, they look like they're going to be trouble to me.'

'Don't worry; I will take care of Hunter and his pretty little assistant as well if needs be.'

★

The next call Sir William made was to one of his pet press poodles – Robin Duffie, a sleazy freelance journalist who had been trawling the West Midlands for wrecking stories. He was generally avoided by everyone with any sense, but Sir William had courted him, finding he had his uses, feeding him gossip from his sources in Whitehall about the local business community.

'I've spoken to Dom Laurence at *The Standard* and they will run a comment piece on Nariman's murder, but I need you to write something a bit sharper, a bit critical, that also distances him from me.

'OK, I think I know what sort of thing you mean. When do you need it to appear?'

'Is there time to get it into the Sunday editions?'

'It's tight but I'm sure I can swing the late edition for you.'

CHAPTER THIRTEEN

ROMANZA – (MODERATO) '***'

How the gentle Chibiabos, he the sweetest of musicians, sang his songs of love and longing. How Iagoo, the great boaster, he the marvellous story-teller, tells his tales of strange adventure. That the feast might be more joyous, that the time might pass more gaily, and the guests be more contented. Sumptuous was the feast Nokomis made at Hiawatha's wedding.

Samuel Coleridge-Taylor, *Hiawatha's Wedding Feast*

Eddie was completely fascinated by the way that the pianist in the bar next door was improvising a playful, syncopated narrative around a selection of show-tunes from the 1930s. He sipped his scotch and tapped his fingers, looking on increasingly amused at Bas's persistence in attempting to chat up the beautiful black woman at the bar. He could hear Bas boasting to her about some skiing escapade or other in the Swiss Alps. He was hoping that some of their other guests would arrive soon, otherwise he would have to interrupt his friend's little tête-à-tête.

Both Eddie and Bas had dressed up uncharacteristically smartly for the occasion – Eddie was wearing the second-hand Paul Smith jacket and open-necked shirt that Alice had selected for him before she collapsed exhausted into bed. The restaurant had an open-mic policy in the piano bar and there had already been a few takers. Even the devilishly good-looking waiter interrupted his table service to croon a moody number to get things started. The bar was rapidly filling up with locals who were enjoying the relaxed atmosphere and Eddie was beginning to worry that he would have to give up their table if his guests didn't arrive soon.

Someone touched his arm and kissed his cheek in greeting, breaking his concentration on the music.

'Hi gorgeous, I really wasn't sure if you'd still turn up here tonight,' the girl said with an affected Bugsy-style voice, which contained a little too much of a hint of American musical theatre for his liking.

'But of course, it had to be you that walked into my gin joint!' he replied.

It was Delia, the younger and flirtier of the Flyte sisters. She was just eighteen and wearing a red satin cocktail dress that was cut to reveal as much flesh as she could decently get away with. Eddie could smell the spiced scent wafting around her body and noticed the new piercings in her nose. Her raven black hair had been styled into a razored bob. Gone were the curls and the appealing sweetness of her early teenage years, she was clearly trying hard now to be an adult. Eddie was unsure whether to be impressed or not. Despite the sophisticated makeover, she still managed to give the somewhat awkward impression of a young Lolita destined to break a thousand hearts but not quite ready to be a player. Devout innocence mixed with a still slightly off-track teenage mind palace. He noticed the red rose tattoo on her shoulder and wondered what else she had done to her body.

'Well Delia, it's been just another amazing day in Babylon today. In fact after the really weird day we've all had, I suspect eating out with loopy-you and your sister is just what I need to take my mind off things.'

'You're such a tart, Eddie. I've told you before I'm your one and only, we just need to get darling Julia to fulfil her destiny and run away with Alice, then we can disappear together into the sunset.'

'I thought you were supposed to be a good little convent girl?'

'Of course I am, all the time,' she said, touching his arm. He got another strong whiff of her scent. *She must have poured it on*, he thought.

'Well I can't say I've noticed that recently.'

'Would it make any difference to you if I was?'

'Maybe not, but aren't you supposed to be saving yourself for a nice young Catholic boy?'

'Oh God, Eddie, it's so difficult being a Catholic,' she laughed; now running her finger along his thigh. *She has certainly learnt a trick or two* he thought. He laughed in turn, somewhat embarrassedly, and removed her hand. She feigned disappointment.

'OK I'll admit defeat for now,' she said. 'Seriously though, isn't it such a terrible business with that man next door? We've only been away a couple of days and the world turns upside down. It must have been so exciting. Tell me everything, all the gory details.'

'Sshh, have you quite finished? A man died for heaven's sake,' he said somewhat annoyed but also somewhat flattered to be the focus of her adulation.

'Come on,' she wheedled. 'Don't be boring, I hear the guy was killed and died in your arms. That's so cool. Did you hear the bullet whizz past your ear?'

She was firing off questions with the velocity of a machine gun, without a pause for breath or the remotest pretence at hesitation. She sounded more than slightly disappointed that she had not witnessed all this herself.

'No I didn't, and yes it took me ages to get the various bits of him out of my hair, thank you,' he said, brushing his hair slightly dramatically to emphasise the point.

'OK, no need to be disgusting,' she frowned. 'Where's

Alice tonight then, I thought she was coming too?'

'She's just too exhausted – I told her to stay at home and get some rest. She's had a right old day of it.'

'Ah, so now I know your agenda, any excuse to get me on my own.'

'I think we've been down that road already once this evening, haven't we?'

'True. Anyway, just as well that she's getting some rest. She's been a bit of a hero today, and we love heroes don't we? Don't worry, I'll keep you company, oh gorgeous one,' she said, winking at him in a way that only Delia could and continuing. 'Just like in Paris.' She was referring to a holiday that they had all spent together, where her precocious fantasy pursuit of him had first started. Eddie shook his head in mock despair.

'She's been more than a hero, she was a real superhero this morning, and then she had to work all day on the autopsies. She's only just got back home.'

'Poor love,' she said, stroking the stubble on his cheek with the back of her hand.

'So, OK, Matahari, where have you been all dolled up like that?' he said, changing the subject and removing her hand again.

'We were at a hen night last night and then a friend's wedding this morning and then sneaked back in time for the afternoon concert in the parish church.'

'All dressed like that?'

'No silly, this is all for you.' She said running her hand down her fishnet stockings. She opened her bag and showed him the programme – Elgar, Delius and Mendelssohn. 'I'd rather have been here though, whilst all this murder most horrid stuff was going on.'

'Delius? I thought you liked edgier stuff, Chali from Jurassic, Slightly Stoopid etc.?' he teased.

'Now, don't be petulant, it doesn't suit you.'

'A calm sea and a prosperous voyage,' he read. 'That's certainly a nice contrast from today. I suppose you know the Elgar connection, being a clarinettist yourself?' he asked.

He was now somewhat pleased with himself. Following the hint from Hunter that morning, Eddie had been reading up all day about the Enigma Variations to try and put the other events out of his mind. It was amazing what he had found out.

'What on earth are you babbling on about?' she answered, bemused.

'Variation 13, 'Romanza',' he replied. 'He quotes the Mendelssohn piece musically – it's a reference to the initials of an unnamed lady denoted by three asterisks in the score – some commentators have speculated that it was a Lady Mary Lygon who was undertaking a long sea voyage at the time, some love interest that he had an attachment to. Very appropriate, maybe one of your mother's ancestors?' he teased.

'Now, that's getting more interesting. Eddie, you're always such a dime piece,' she said, smiling adoringly at him.

'Anyway where's the lovely Julia, and just as importantly how's young Betjeman?'

This was his standard tease at her expense, referring to the teddy bear that she had kept since she was a young child. Eddie knew the bear in question well, having frequently baby-sat for her when she was younger.

'Betjeman is absolutely fine, thank you and boring old Julia will be joining us soon; she said she had something else to do first. I suspect she was going next door to see if they needed any help. Waste of time if you ask me, that silly horrible man will never ask for our help.'

'Would you be talking about your father by any chance?'

'Whatever,' she said, changing the subject herself this time. 'I see your sleazy friend Basil has been busy already; he seems to have made a new acquaintance.' She pointed over to the bar at Bas and the amazing woman he was chatting with.

'It's certainly a vast improvement over the girl he ended up with in Spice last night,' he said.

'You went to Spice without me? I do think you might have taken me with you.'

'I thought you were at a hen night? Anyway I don't think you're old enough, the bouncers wouldn't let jailbait like you in,' he joked. 'Anyway, as for Bas, this one looks a bit out of his league, I think I may need to help him out,' remarked Eddie, somewhat conceitedly.

They continue chatting. Delia told Eddie that she had been successful in getting a place to study modern dance with the Birmingham ballet.

'I played the veiled hidden theme in my audition just to confuse them,' she joked. He doubted there was anything veiled or hidden about Delia's performance.

There's one thing I'll say to my credit. Just one: I'm not intellectual or artistic or anything of that sort, but I'm jolly human. It is being human that counts, isn't it? Being real. Now, are you real?

Virginia Woolf, *The Voyage Out*

A few minutes later Julia joined them. She was also dressed to melt, but much more elegantly than her sister with considerably less flesh on show. She was clad like a bohemian waif in a flame and gold sequined top, taffeta skirt and ankle-strap heels. Unlike Delia, she was wearing very little make-up, her blonde tresses floating loose and free around her shoulders. To Eddie's eyes she looked radiant; any imperfections she had only serving to increase her allure, half-way between 1930s screen goddess and doe-eyed innocence.

'Sorry I'm late, Eddie, but with Mother away I had to go and see William and Nadia,' she said in her delicate and serene voice. 'Nadia is really cut up, devastated in fact, but Father obviously didn't want me to stay, so I gave my condolences and then made my excuses. But what about you? I can't believe her grandfather died in your arms.'

'Yes. It's been a pretty strange day all round. By the way, Alice decided she was just too tired to come out though, I hope you don't mind putting up with me for company?'

'Of course not, I understand completely, but are you sure you shouldn't be back with your family? We won't mind, really.'

'No, Alice was insistent I still come and I could do with something to take my mind off things, tonight. Anyway, thank *you* for coming out. You look beautiful this evening, as always. Now there are truly two and a half divine creatures in the house,' he swooned, nodding at Pearl standing at the bar to Delia's clear annoyance at her 'half' valuation in his appraisal. 'Did your father happen to say whether the police are making any progress on the investigation? I saw Hunter earlier today but haven't heard anything since.'

'They arrived just after I left; I saw Hunter's car pull up from my bedroom window as I was getting dressed, it's a very nasty business. I hadn't even realised that Nadia's grandfather was staying there or I would have paid them a visit earlier. I'll see if I can go round tomorrow when things have calmed down a bit, she must be feeling completely lost without any family members around her.'

At this moment, they were interrupted by Bas and his new friend walking over to their table. Both girls looked at this beautiful woman in admiration, dressed as if she had just stepped off a Paris catwalk. Despite being many years older, she could only be described as dazzling: flawless skin, impeccably dressed and with a gorgeous, winning smile.

'This is Pearl Taylor; she's over from the States,' said Bas. The others nodded at her curiously.

'Pearl's a singer. Pearl, this is Eddie, my rather charming companion and the delightful Flyte sisters – Julia and Cordelia, aka Delia,' he continued.

'Nice to meet you all,' Pearl said in a deeply sexy American drawl.

'Ladies, if you don't mind, I've asked Pearl if she'd join us for dinner, she's alone in town and it'd be a shame for her to eat by herself.'

'Of course, that would be lovely,' they both said almost in unison, giving each other knowing looks.

'And Pearl, this is Basil, a fine bassist, a serious and devoted friend and an utter sleaze-bag. But as he often tells us, probably the most eligible bachelor in this part of Leamington. So with that consider yourself warned, Miss Taylor,' Eddie chipped in.

'Oh, I think I can look after myself but he's certainly a charmer,' she chuckled, deepening her honeyed transatlantic voice further.

Delia wasted no time in asking her how much she knew about the day's events. When Pearl expressed ignorance of them, she set about a little précis, asking Eddie to fill in the details at appropriate points. Pearl was wide-eyed and expressed genuine shock that such a thing could have happened in 'this quiet, peaceful town'. She explained to them who she was and of course they immediately forgot about the murder and fell under her spell, urging her to take to the microphone herself.

'Later maybe,' she said. 'I think I'd better let the local talent have a go first. I liked the waiter earlier, a real opera voice. Anyway I need to get into the mood and I'm starving after walking all over your pretty little town today, notwithstanding the worry of your rapidly increasing crime rate! Really, I thought I'd left New York behind me.'

Bas ordered champagne and they tucked in to their seafood starters. During the meal, the girls noticed that Pearl had an incredible appetite, demolishing the biggest steak on the menu as if it were a burger.

'Where I come from, you eat before it disappears from the table or you starve,' she said in a surprisingly matter-of-fact way for an international superstar.

★

Pearl was enjoying herself and had almost forgotten about the dirty little secret locked away in her hotel room. When they finished desert and ordered coffee, she was as good as her word. She walked over to the piano, took the microphone and whispered a few words to the pianist. He could barely conceal his excitement on learning who she was, but to his credit he accompanied her faultlessly through one of her better known songs, and one of his own jazz standard covers, without missing a note. After enthusiastic applause from the gathering crowd, they performed a mini-encore with a song from her latest album *This Bacchic Crime*.

When she was through, she returned to join her hosts at the table.

'Champagne does it every time.' said Bas, rather obsequiously.

While she had been singing, four further guests had joined the party. Hugh was standing next to Claudia from the corner house, one of the names high up on Alice's 'attractive and available for Hugh' list. Alice had suggested to Eddie that he invite Claudia in her place. *The other two are obviously police officers*, thought Pearl, *although neither is in uniform.*

★

'Pearl, let me introduce you to Hugh Powell, Claudia Baxter, Detective Inspector Hunter and his beautiful assistant, one of my very best pupils, Detective Constable Penny Dore,' said Eddie, rather grandly.

'Delighted to meet you all,' she replied charmingly.

'The Inspector is leading the investigation into this terrible murder and he was due to join us for dinner this evening, but I fear he seems to have allowed himself to be distracted from our idle pleasures in favour of working all through the night. Forgive his Germanic correctness; he's really a lot of fun when you get him off-duty,' added Eddie.

Pearl looked approvingly at Hunter. I was beginning to realise that my boss was a bit of a hit with the ladies. He was after all undeniably a rather handsome man. Hunter took her hand gently and raised it to his lips in an old-fashioned greeting. He appeared surprisingly nervous and I was amused to see him bow to her and click his heels ever so slightly; she replied with a smile and a sympathetic curtsy, also nodding a greeting to me and then in turn to Hugh and Claudia. Out of the corner of my eye I was looking at Hugh questioningly as he took his seat between Julia and Claudia, wondering whether this juxtaposition was Alice's doing.

'Inspector Hunter you say? What a good name for a policeman, but a case of poacher turned gamekeeper, maybe?' she joked.

Hunter smiled. 'There's an element of truth to that indeed, Miss Taylor. It is truly an honour to meet you; I am really a very big fan of yours.'

'I'm sure the honour is mine, Inspector, my friends here have already been telling me about you, your reputation goes before you, Leamington's own star detective, no less,' she laughed.

'Please, Miss Taylor, that's too kind. Indeed, I know that there may be some idle gossip in that vein about me, but my results are simply down to following correct procedure.'

'And are you close to solving the case?'

'Unfortunately at this stage in this case, we have more mystery than leads, so I'm afraid we cannot stay long. I just wanted to drop by and make my apologies to my friends and now I find I must also apologise to you Miss Taylor for not staying with you tonight.'

'That's quite alright, I fully understand. Off to round up the usual suspects I suppose.'

'If only it were that simple,' he said. 'Before we go, however, I wonder if I could persuade you to sing once more; you are someone I have long admired. It would be such a great pleasure for me.'

'Of course I will sing for you, Inspector, do you have a special request in mind?'

He thought for a moment and then said, 'Well, I am rather partial to one of the numbers from your last album – 'Nobody Loves Me' I think it's called.'

'Yes of course, a good choice, and I'm sure that sentiment's not personally applicable, Inspector – such a handsome man like you.' This love-in was getting comical; I'd have to physically separate them soon. 'It would be a great pleasure to sing for you. And with a clever young assistant like Penny here I'm sure this mystery you are struggling with should not prove too big a problem to wrap up.'

At the mention of my name I looked away from Hugh and stared back at her again. She smiled at me, and I had to smile back somewhat grudgingly. I felt that in some subtle way I had just been patronised by this larger-than-life woman.

'Yes Penny, 'bright as a new penny', don't you Brits say? So with that name in particular, you should be able to help the inspector solve his little old enigma quickly,' she added cryptically. I could feel the hackles on my neck rising and decided that there was something about her I did not like, despite the fact that Hunter seemed to be drooling at her like a school kid.

She got up, moved back over to the pianist and whispered to him. He smiled broadly back at her, presumably still not quite believing he was accompanying an international star.

As she sang one of the lines from the song she gestured at me as if inviting me to sing along with her. *'I don't take clues from horoscope hounds,'* were her words. They would become etched onto my mind, but at the time the significance was lost on me.

When she returned to the table, I was anxious to ask her a final question but in my annoyance stuttered over some of my words.

'Miss Taylor, you were saying the mystery should not be too difficult to solve, do you have any information or thoughts on the case, anything you saw while you were walking around town today perhaps?' I asked, my female suspicions now more than aroused by this mysterious and exotic visitor to our little town. *What on earth is she doing here?* I thought.

'No, my dear, it was a jest, nothing specific, just my silly old dark sayings, and I'm sorry if I made a little joke at your expense. Please, excuse my odd sense of humour.'

'Well, let me give you my card, in any case,' I said, puzzled by her words. 'If you happen to think of anything, here's my email.'

'That may well come in very useful, my dear, thank you,' she replied.

I was baffled and somewhat irritated by the singer's mysterious comments and indeed her unexplained presence in our town. I stared defiantly at Hunter, expecting his support with some further questioning. But the DI seemed completely besotted with this woman and merely smiled and signalled to me with his hand to calm down for the second time that evening. On the other side of the table, Bas was also scowling noticeably at the conversation. I guessed that he was more worried that his own later plans for the evening might be slipping away from him. Hugh, meanwhile, having seemingly made little progress with Julia, was now staring into Claudia's blue eyes, she looked away embarrassed, perhaps already regretting accepting the last minute invitation. Apparently she'd only done it to help Alice out. Bas was obviously also quite taken with her, I knew from her reputation however that she could be difficult when she wanted to be. Julia was a far better bet for Hugh if I could get them together properly.

'One last thing, Miss Taylor, if you are staying in Leamington for a while, there is something I would love to discuss with you, a revival of Coleridge-Taylor's 'Hiawatha's Wedding' I am planning. I wonder if I could tempt you to make a guest appearance, perhaps?' Hunter asked.

'Oh my dear lord, that sounds adorable but I'm afraid I have such a long list of engagements to fulfil, Inspector. I'd love to do something like that, especially given that Coleridge-Taylor is a personal hero of mine. Unfortunately my schedule is determined months, sometimes years in advance. I will, however, look for a gap and maybe I could join you another time if I am passing through?'

> Gentle politeness and courtly manners,
> Maintaining decorum ever righteous.
> Cleanliness next to godliness, letters
> That speak of chivalry, almost famous.
> 'Il libro del cortegiano', zealous
> Troubadour, now you are my life and your
> soul will possess my heart. It's dangerous
> To defy this sudden passion. Abhor
> Romantic courtesy, love conquers all no more!

★

177

'What was that all about, Sir? I don't like that woman; I thought we went to talk to the Flyte sisters?' I whispered to Hunter as we left. Somehow, Pearl had really brushed me up the wrong way.

'Don't worry, Dore, we'll catch up with them tomorrow, the occasion wasn't right. As for Miss Taylor, she's certainly a smart lady.' Hunter said a little formally, he stood aside to let me past and I caught him looking back, somewhat wistfully at Pearl. *I'm not going to let this happen*, I thought, *the journalist maybe, but definitely not this one*.

★

As the meal came to an end, Bas turned to Eddie and whispered into his ear.

'Do you and Hugh mind walking the ladies home? I'd like to ask Pearl to stay behind with me for another drink in the bar.' Eddie rolled his eyes. *He's at it again*, he thought, but nodded and indicated to their other guests that they were about to leave.

'Are your friends leaving already, Basil?' asked Pearl, pretending surprise at the party splitting up so early. 'I hope it isn't something I've said? If so, please forgive me for my clumsy American ways.'

'Not at all, Miss Taylor, it's been a real delight to meet you but it's just been an incredibly long day for everybody. We'd better get these young ladies home and tucked up in bed. Basil will make sure you get safely back to your hotel,' replied Eddie, with a mischievous glint in his eye.

'Do you want to stay a while longer and dance a little?' Hugh asked Claudia, who was already gathering her coat and bag.

'It's a bit late for that now, isn't it?' she said somewhat sharply.

'Yes of course, well at least let me walk you home as well then.'

Eddie left with a Flyte sister on each arm and Hugh accompanied Claudia, the two of them walking behind the others in a somewhat awkward silence. Hugh was working hard to establish common ground with Claudia; he did better when they started to talk about sport. Her studied indifference broke down and her voice began to become more animated. As they passed the Catholic church, he asked her if she was religious. She laughed and shook her head.

'*No, religion exists only to lull men to their sleep.*'

'I don't understand.'

'The lady Acrasia from Keat's *La Belle Dame sans Merci* – she who now has you in her thrall!'

★

'Another drink maybe, Pearl?' asked Bas, after the others had gone.

'Really, I'd better not, I have something to prepare for tomorrow, I'm afraid. A diva's work is never done.'

'Of course, then I'll call you a taxi,' he said, with obvious disappointment.

'No need, it's a nice evening, I'll walk back. It's really not far to my hotel. But I think I'd appreciate an escort with the sort of crime wave you have going on in this town.'

Bas accepted this invitation eagerly, paid the bill and left with Pearl a few minutes later. Conscious that he did not want to bump into Hunter again, and with a further plan in his mind, Bas selected a rather longer route rather than the road that ran straight past the police station. They took the Parade south past the Town Hall, walked along estate agents' row and then turned left along Newbold Terrace up towards

179

Holly Walk. The road that runs along the park.

'This is my surgery just up here on the left,' he said when they had left behind the main lights and noise of the town centre. He pointed to a brass plate next to the door of one of the town houses.

'The Pearl Dental Clinic: Mr Nevinson and Mr Hyde,' she read. 'Somewhat of a coincidence, but at least you're not Dr Jekyll.' she joked.

'No, I'm still very much Mr Nevinson; and my partner is Mr Hyde, Mr Edward Hyde, in fact.'

'Well, Mr Nevinson, as it happens I've been having some problems with a wisdom tooth recently; maybe you could take a look for me while I'm in town?'

'I'd love to, but actually I've been specialising recently as an implantologist.'

'And what is that exactly?'

'An implantologist is a dentist who specialises in placing dental implants using titanium rods; they are used to replace teeth that have been lost to decay or trauma, fairly new to the UK market.

'It sounds like it might be lucrative, but really I wasn't planning a whole course of implants, I just need a simple check over,' she laughed.

'Of course, anyway I can take a quick look but I'm afraid there won't be anyone in the surgery till Monday as tomorrow's Sunday. Unless...'

'Well I'm not exactly going to go in there alone with you tonight,' she said, interrupting in a half-joking voice, 'and I'm afraid I won't be here on Monday.'

'Oh,' he said, realising his mistake. 'Well I could grab my bag out of the car if you'd like and take a quick look now at your hotel to see if anything needs doing urgently.' He pointed to a Porsche that was poorly parked at an angle to the kerb just along the street from the surgery. She nodded in agreement.

Bas fetched his bag and they continued along the pavement that ran along the other side of the road from Jephson Gardens. They walked along to the end of the street and then turned left up the hill towards Holly Walk. Bas linked his arm with Pearl's as they walked up the road, putting his hand on the small of her back to lead her across the road. She smiled and he was encouraged that she did not object to this semi-intimacy. He was getting excited and she was leading him on just enough. Pearl's hotel was just across the road. As they entered the foyer, she indicated towards the bar, the next stage of her plan already forming in her mind.

'Sorry, but if you're going to examine me, I could do with a brandy, I am a little nervous about dentists. How about you?' she asked and called over to the barman, fortunately not the same one who was on duty at lunchtime. Neither Bas nor the barman saw the pill she dropped into his drink when it was served.

'To your good health and thank you for a wonderful evening so far,' said Bas, now hopeful of his chances of taking this further.

'Yes, bottoms up as you Limeys say,' she joked and gulped down her own glass in one shot. Bas was somewhat amazed and returned the toast, indicating to the barman to fill the glasses up again.

'No, no thanks, one's enough; OK, so I think I'm ready for my examination now Mr Nevinson. I'm going to take a chance and trust you, we'll go up to the privacy of my suite quickly and do what you need to do, but no funny business, do you understand?' she said, a twinkle in her eye.

'Of course not,' he said. 'You can trust me completely.'

By now, Bas was really up for this, funny business or not. He wasn't too sure about the ethics of going to a patient's hotel bedroom, but he argued that this was more of a social kind of errand in any case. They climbed the stairs, Bas's heart beginning to beat more quickly as he followed her up, watching the alluring movement her curves made as she ascended the stairs in her sequinned dress. She inserted her key and opened the door to her suite.

They entered inside into a sort of living room, but as the room door clicked behind them he suddenly began to feel light on his feet. He sat down heavily on a sofa, wondering at this odd sensation. He hadn't had that much to drink and he could normally handle just about anything without feeling its effects. Maybe this woman was driving him a little crazy; she was after all probably the most gorgeous woman he had ever met. He wondered whether this was really going to happen. Had he really gotten this lucky two nights in a row? He grabbed her leg to steady himself.

'Hey, steady on, I thought I was clear on the no funny business?' she said, leaning over him, deliberately torturing him a little with a flash of her bosom.

'I'm sorry, I came over all dizzy for a second,' he said in an already slurred voice, taking her hand and standing up again unsteadily, eager not to rush things with her and spoil his chances.

★

'Let's have some music then to take both our minds off it,' Pearl replied and she moved over to the radio on the sideboard, slowly beginning to tune the reception, playing for time; but even before she had finished her sentence, Bas was flat out unconscious on the floor.

After that she wasted no more time. She dragged him quickly into the bedroom onto a rug by the fireplace. She then pulled Arthur Troyte's limp body out of the wardrobe and placed it alongside Bas. This was the secret she had been hiding all evening, the product of her earlier meeting with him at the bar that lunchtime and all had gone exactly as planned. He was still bound, gagged and out like a light. As a precaution, however, she administered a further dose to him orally as she had calculated that the effects should by then normally have begun to wear off.

Working quickly, she stripped them both naked and arranged their bodies in the most compromising pose she could imagine. She was not sure if this was exactly what men did when they did it together, but a couple of oranges and some gold body spray rapidly enhanced the effect. She took great delight in drawing the biggest scarlet 'A's she could manage with her lipstick all over their bodies. Then she suddenly had another idea and opened Bas's dentist bag to find exactly what she wanted: a surgical scalpel.

With the precision of a surgeon, she started to delicately carve the letters $AZ\Omega$ into Troyte's skin, filling the wounds with red nail varnish, in a place on his perineum he would not be able to see very easily. She took out her camera and recorded the whole comic scene to her satisfaction. Within another fifteen minutes she had cleaned them both up and tucked her new aspirant lover-boy, Bas, under a blanket in the bedroom with a kiss.

Dealing with Troyte's inert body proved more difficult. She had his house keys and the trunk she had bought earlier that day in the living room of her suite. Fortunately his wiry frame was not too heavy and after she had deposited him in the trunk, she dragged it into the living room and closed the bedroom door behind her. She called the concierge. Flirting madly with the young man on the phone, she persuaded him and one of the kitchen staff to carry the trunk down to a waiting taxi for her. For £25 the taxi driver they called was only too happy to take her the relatively short distance to Hawthorne House where he helped her into the house with the trunk.

'What have you got in there, lady, the dismembered torso of your lover?' he joked.

'If only it were that easy,' she joked back.

Once he had gone, she opened the trunk and dragged the sleeping body out, setting about the next stage of her plan. The computer stuff was easy, he didn't use passwords as she had expected. She synced his laptop to the Wi-Fi using the code she found written on the router in the study. She then downloaded the necessary software fonts in the way that the young man in the shop had shown her, set up a series of timed messages to go from his email account and made the necessary alterations to his PowerPoint presentation, including downloading the photos from the bedroom that she had just orchestrated. She then made some more prints of the bedroom shots with a mini colour printer and finally relaxed back in the chair with a smile. She was finished inside an hour, drank two glasses of his expensive champagne, being careful to leave her lipstick on the rim of one of them, and left another *carte de visite* with him, thanking him for the wonderful evening, before slipping out of the house and back to her hotel room.

*

Nobody was more surprised than Troyte the next morning, when he awoke naked at Hawthorne House to see the evidence of his obvious conquest; the expended condom, the cryptic note of thanks from 'P' beside his pillow and a strange sore feeling below his groin, where it felt like someone had scratched his skin. He had a vague recollection of meeting a beautiful black woman at the bar of a local hotel, but could not remember anything after that or anything about her. His meeting had obviously been highly productive. Unfortunately, there was no contact number on the card; he assumed he would have to wait for her to get in touch with him again. In any case, the birds were singing delightfully in the garden outside and the sun was already warming up the late summer air. *It's going to be a good day*, he thought.

Now that the day had arrived, he was at last looking forward to giving his little talk, buoyed up by his surprise assignation. His only worry was whether his friend Arish, who had still not contacted him, would be there to help him. The bell rang and he saw a driver who had been sent to take him to the gallery waiting for him, so he quickly went back into the house to get ready and quickly collect his laptop and notes.

★

When Bas awoke in the hotel room at the Holly Hotel about the same time, he was also surprised to see the naked and beautiful shape of Pearl seated on the window seat looking out over the park.

'Did you enjoy last night?' she asked. She pointed to the champagne glasses and strawberries by the side of the bed. 'I thought you might like some morning refreshment.'

He searched his memory, a vague recollection of the singer in a bar the night before beginning to surface. He was naked, she was naked, they were in a plush hotel room, she'd ordered champagne and there were two empty condom packets by the side of the bed. *Is this a dream?* he asked himself.

'That was the best night ever,' he replied cautiously but with recovering bravado. He could remember meeting her in the bar and having dinner with his friends, but try as he might, he strangely couldn't remember a single thing about what had happened in this bedroom. But by the evidence it must have been good. He began to feel aroused again at the sight of her body.

She noticed and laughed, throwing a dressing gown at

185

him. 'Before you get too carried away, I'm afraid I've got a lot to do today. Take your time while I have a shower and get dressed. You can help yourself to some breakfast when I'm gone.' He enjoyed watching her dress and then closed his eyes pleasantly as she planted a kiss on his lips before leaving the room.

CHAPTER FOURTEEN

ENIGMATIC EDDIE – (ALLEGRO PRESTO) 'E.D.U.'

So furiously she strook in her first Heat,
Whiles with long Fight on foot he breathless was,
That she him forced backward to retreat,
And yield unto her weapon way to pass.

Spenser, *The Faerie Queene.*

Hugh and Claudia followed Eddie and the two Flyte sisters at a short distance and reached Claudia's house on the corner of the square. They talked a little about rugby and other sports but the conversation was still stilted and he sensed it was going nowhere. So when they stopped at her door, she surprised him by giving him a peck on the cheek. She whispered into his ear that she'd like to see him again, before climbing the steps to No. 10. He was left standing somewhat bemused on the street corner, wondering whether he should have been more forward, blaming his own temperance for the earlier lack of chemistry between the two of them.

*

Meanwhile, Eddie and the Flyte sisters continued further along the road. There were two policemen guarding the entrance to No. 6, Sir William's house. No. 5 next door, where they lived, was mid-terrace rather than end-terrace like Sir William's so there was no option of going round the side entrance to avoid the policemen's stares. Delia in her playful mood couldn't resist blowing a kiss at them; they frowned back, staring steadfastly ahead. She pulled her skirt further up her leg and shouted something about men in uniform before Julia pulled her away.

'Do you want to come in for coffee, Eddie?' asked Delia in a raised and slightly slurred voice as Julia opened the door and reached in to cancel the alarm. Delia had consumed rather more wine than he would have expected for an eighteen-year-old convent girl. Julia shot her younger sister a dark glance and Delia shut up immediately with a hiccup.

'Why not?' said Eddie. 'I expect they're fast asleep downstairs, anyway.'

They entered the darkened hall, which was lit by a single table lamp. There was no one else at home. Delia tripped over the entrance step and fell over in the hall, landing in a most undignified manner.

'Delia, I really think you ought to go to bed,' said her sister unsympathetically.

'Oh dear, yes my head does hurt,' said Delia. Eddie pulled her up off the floor. She hung on to him for support.

'Eddie, I'm so sorry, but if you don't mind I think Julia's right for once, I might have to get off to bed.'

He put his hands rather suggestively on her hips while giving her a kiss on each cheek, which caused her to blush, and then lowered his hands around her thighs to lift her into the air with a big bear hug, making her blush even more.

'Give Betjeman a big hug for me.' He watched while Delia walked up the stairs unsteadily and somewhat reluctantly.

Eddie returned to the kitchen where Julia had put the kettle on the hotplate of the Aga to heat. He noticed how the fine golden hairs on her forearms were picked out by the halo of the kitchen spotlights. In the amber light, the deeply cut back of her dress showed off her strong shoulder blades and his eyes were drawn to the beautifully formed ladder of her spine as it proceeded from the nape of her neck downwards. He had to try hard to resist the temptation to pass his hands around her midriff, to flirt for old times' sake. She had lost none of her *magical sadness* he thought.

'I was hoping for something a little stronger than coffee,' he said, his voice somewhat slurred. She smelt gorgeous. The only sound in the kitchen was the ticking of the wall clock.

'Eddie, please don't tell me you're drunk as well, like my silly sister,' she said sharply, elbowing him in the stomach.

'Nowhere near, it's just what you do to me, Julia.'

'Eddie, behave!'

'OK, OK but what have you got to drink then, apart from coffee?'

'If you mean spirits, there's some scotch in the cabinet in the red room and ice in the fridge,' she said efficiently but sternly, passing him a pair of cut-glass tumblers.

'After all the fun we've had today, you can pour me one as well. I'll bring the coffee through in a second,' she added more gently, relaxing a little. She supposed his flirting was harmless really.

Eddie passed into the little snug that they called the 'red room' next to the kitchen. Because of the layout of the house, the formal drawing room was at the back, looking out over a small but pretty garden. Lady Mary's private rooms and a second formal sitting room were up one flight of stairs on the first floor. This upper room was rarely used; the ground floor snug was the room where they usually entertained family and friends. Across the hall was Lady Mary's study, where she did the family accounts and planned her own busy life. Julia and Delia both had large rooms with en-suite bathrooms on the second floor and Eddie knew from his baby-sitting days there were some guest bedrooms in the attic above, originally meant for servants. Apparently, Penny had recently decided to take one of those rooms, but had not yet moved in.

He half-filled the cut-glass tumblers with Lady Mary's best ten-year-old malt whiskey so that the ice broke free and floated on the top of the liquid, then sat down against a batch of cushions on the sofa. He was feeling a little light-headed but pleasantly so; he hoped she would chill a little when she returned to the room. Julia appeared in a couple of minutes and put the tray on the table before them. She had made the coffee properly in a stylish pewter coffee pot.

'This is nice,' she said. She went over to the CD player and the sound of Anna Calvi's 'Desire' emerged. Julia recognised the track as one that Delia had been playing constantly, and quickly found something less dangerous – Carole King, an old favourite, that would do. She sat down primly at the opposite end of the sofa, her long legs closed together but turned toward him. Again he could not help noticing the way her stockings disappeared shyly into the sequinned taffeta folds of her dress. How long had it been since he touched those gorgeous legs? She was wearing a set of amber stones in a chain across her neck and a matching bracelet, setting off the flame colour of her top and echoing the depth of her brown eyes.

She really is gorgeous, he thought, a flawless beauty. She had a grace and lightness about her movement that was magnetic – unhurried, exquisite, unrepentant. She poured the coffee and took a swig of the scotch as a chaser. He noticed how her lower lip stuck for a moment to the rim of the glass where it has been cooled by the ice, before returning to its natural curves.

'So is our Braggadocio well away with this new woman by now do you think?' she grinned, rather too knowingly, he thought.

'I'm sure he's getting his just desserts,' he laughed. 'But with Pearl Taylor I think it may be a case of biting off more than he can chew.

Suddenly, there was a noise upstairs. 'Damn, it's Delia again.' There was a hint of a tear in her eye. A black cat strolled into the room, stretching.

Eddie just laughed. 'Oscar!' he exclaimed. But he was also relieved that it was not her sister.

'God, why are all the best men taken?' she uttered to herself somewhat breathlessly. 'OK, last chance Eddie. I've got something to show you upstairs, but only if you're prepared to behave. Look, if we're going to do this play-acting stuff, let's get organised and do it properly,' she said as she moved toward the door. He shook his head but got up and followed her out into the hall. She led him upstairs, up the thick red carpets, past her mother's bedroom, past the locked rack of beautiful hand-engraved Holland and Holland shotguns with polished walnut stocks on the right-hand side of the landing.

Eddie knew well that Lady Mary was a keen shooter, and might have noticed that one of her favourite rook guns was missing if he had not been so intent on another course of action. They tiptoed past Delia's bedroom, listening in precaution to the shallow breathing in the bed, climbing another flight up to the attic rooms above, where Penny's door-to-be was also closed. They entered the spare room where the manufacture of their secret plan was ready, spread out eagerly like so much evidence across the floor.

Agnus Dei, qui tollis peccata mundi, miserere nobis.

191

CHAPTER FIFTEEN

Toposcope Hounds – (Allegro con molto fuoco)

Mr Hilton Cubitt of Ridling Thorpe Manor in Norfolk visits Sherlock Holmes and gives him a piece of paper with this mysterious sequence of stick figures.

The little dancing men are at the heart of a mystery, which seems to be driving his young wife Elsie to distraction. He married her about a year ago, and until recently, everything was well. She is American, and before the wedding, she had asked her husband-to-be to promise her never to ask about her past, as she had had some 'very disagreeable associations' in her life, although she said that there was nothing that she was personally ashamed of. Mr. Cubitt swore the promise and, being an honourable English gentleman, insisted on living by it, which was one of the things causing difficulty at Ridling Thorpe Manor.

Précis of Arthur Conan Doyle's, *The Adventure of the Dancing Men*

It was early on Sunday when I bumped into Izzie and her new friend Penn in the Costa on the Parade. Like me, they were picking up coffee and muffins for breakfast. The break in Penn's filming was likely to last a few days and Izzie had also been given a couple of days off to recover from the shock of Winnie's death. Izzie is one of my oldest friends and had originally introduced me to Alice and Eddie a long time ago. Life and connections have become ever more complicated. After my mother's death, it's good at least to have an adoptive extended family in the area. The context of this meeting was slightly embarrassing, as it turned out.

I opened the door to the coffee shop and noticed immediately the young man standing in the coffee queue. He was dressed in hobo ankle boots, cargo pants and a rough checked shirt. I was not normally keen on facial hair, but this guy's smart little goatee really suited him. I was intrigued and joined the queue behind him and on some pretext started up a conversation with him. He was American with a sort of cool way of speaking. I soon caught myself in the reflection of the counter, preening back my hair around my ears. He seemed interested too and offered to buy my drink for me, which of course I declined with a flirty little giggle. That wouldn't do, accepting drinks from a complete stranger.

Unfortunately, this nascent romance was nipped firmly in the bud when Izzie emerged from the ladies and stared uncomprehendingly at me, realising at once that I was hitting on her new boyfriend. The penny dropped with me too and I understood at once why she had been so keen to get away on Saturday morning. Anyway I had to accept that she deserved to find a decent bloke and this one certainly seemed more her type than her last public school idiot boyfriend. Of course, after the embarrassment had passed, I immediately commiserated with her about Winnie's death, before turning expectantly again to look at her friend, awaiting from her a full explanation.

'Penn's an actor, he's shooting the new *Sherlock* across the square,' explained Izzie in her 'thoughtful' voice, her hands now entwined generously around her new beau.

'It's very nice to meet you,' I smiled back and looked again at this 'actor'. Izzie might have seen this one first, but I subconsciously thought that I'd at least keep him in play just in case.

'And Penn, this is Penny,' laughed Izzie, realising for the first time the similarity of our names. 'Penny's a policewoman and yeah, some sort of very complicated relative of mine – I can't remember the relationship exactly. She's a proper detective now, probably already investigating that murder that happened yesterday. How weird is that?'

'A detective? Cool, I might get a few clues from you then if we ever get back to filming,' he joked. 'I love your hair; you're a dead ringer for that Harry Potter actress. Have you ever done any acting yourself?' he added, flirting with me a little again. I could tell by his eyes that he was trying to see if he could get a rise from Izzie. He had obviously already noticed that there was an undercurrent of competitive rivalry between us.

'Well yes, you know, I had a few minor parts at school,' I answered, playing bashful.

'Oh yes, just tell him about Dorothy and Sally Bowles, you old show-off,' said Izzie, looking somewhat annoyed with Penn for asking me this particular question. We had a history of 'sharing' boyfriends and rivalry over leading roles in school plays, but I guessed she was thinking that she wasn't about to let this one wander my way that easily.

'So, which book are they filming this time?' I asked, changing the subject and by the look of Izzie's face, smiling at him a little too flirtatiously for her liking.

'*The Adventure of the Dancing Men*,' he said. And at my request, he began to briefly explain the outline of the story.

When he was done, Penn re-joined the queue to pick up skinny lattes for himself and Izzie. I took Izzie aside to chat conspiratorially on a group of sofas in the corner while we waited.

'God, Izzie, where did you find him? He's drop dead gorgeous.' I said, leaning over the table to speak to her in confidence.

'He was in the Dell Park, playing his guitar, singing 'Let us be lovers' if you believe it. It was amazing.'

'No kidding? He's a musician as well as an actor? God, you're so jammy.'

'Something like that, his father was a writer and his grandfather was a famous poet so there's more than a fair bullshit quotient mind you, but I like him all the same.'

'Who wouldn't? So, should I assume you two are an item?'

'Let's just say you'd better knock next time you call round,' she answered, grinning from ear to ear.

'OK – spare me the details.'

'You asked.'

'So the obvious question is does he have any more actor friends, preferably tall ones?' I asked.

'I don't know but feel free to ask,' she replied laughing and then suddenly looked concerned as if she had remembered something. 'Penny, there's something I need to ask you about.'

'Fire away, but I thought you knew what you were doing in that arena, you've had enough practice,' I replied.

'Don't be coarse. No, seriously it's about Winnie. You know that we found her unconscious in the bath. Well I for one don't think it was an accident,' she was whispering now and went on to explain the circumstances in which they had found her. 'The owners of the home seem to want to brush it under the carpet as an accident, but there's something just not right about it. She didn't have access to her own drugs so there's no way she could have deliberately taken an overdose like they said. And the drugs she took, Moban, are not available in the UK for regular usage.'

'Moban, that's interesting, I'll check that out? In any

case, don't worry; we're definitely getting an autopsy arranged. We'll soon sort out what happened. She was a prime witness after all.'

'Thanks so much, Penny. I was really fond of her. Oh, and by the way, Penn's got something else to tell you about that man that was killed as well.'

★

Back in their basement flat, Alice turned over in bed and fumbled for the alarm clock. It was 9am already; shafts of light from the window shutters were spreading a zebra pattern of shadows across the covers of the bed. She glanced around the room but the tentative forms of furniture and discarded clothing remained out of focus. She had removed her contact lenses the previous evening. *Is it really time to get up already?* she wondered, groaning.

The weather had turned warmer again overnight and the early morning chill was giving way rapidly to pleasant warmth as the sun's rays spread across her face. She loved this time on a Sunday morning, the moments before the day had started; the most peaceful time of the week. Eddie was curled up in his duvet, the sound of his breathing heavy and reassuring in the room. Alice slipped her hand inside the duvet and found the patch of small fine hair that she loved at the base of his neck, stroking him gently with the back of her hand before beginning to run her fingers slowly up and down the muscles of his back. She felt his body respond sleepily to her touch and knew that he was awake but she didn't speak to him and he didn't turn over, content to feel her hand massaging him. She pulled her whole body in under the duvet so she was coupled around his back, like a small glove stretched over the bent length of his torso, feeling the warmth of his body on hers. Then she slipped her hand around his hips, already sensing his skin shiver at the amorous progress of her fingertips.

He still said nothing, but she knew from experience how to break this code of silence; she banished her dark doubts from the previous evening and was eager to re-establish her claim on his affections after his pleasure-seeking and foolishness last Friday. Like freshly squeezed juice, he was easy to forgive, despite his unreliable sermons, and even easier to arouse. Eddie turned over and rolled on top of her, pulling the straps of her nightdress over her shoulders so that he could kiss her neck and chest, rubbing his nose gently over her like a puppy. She giggled, but let him continue, while she caressed his hair and then pulled him closer toward her.

'I love you,' he said. That was what she had been waiting to hear all week.

'I will always love you, Eddie.'

'And do you believe in me again, oh faithless one?'

'Of course, although to be truthful, you do have your moments.'

★

When I finally got to the office with my takeaway coffee, it was around 9am. The first email, when it arrived an hour later, was perplexing.

'It's just a bunch of dancing stick men with flags,' I said to one of my colleagues as we stared together at the screen. Given our earlier conversation about the *Sherlock Holmes* story, I wondered if Izzie and Penn were playing some kind of a practical joke on me, so I gave Izzie a call to check, but this drew a blank. Still, remembering what Penn had told me about the subject of the story they were filming, I tried simple semaphore to decode the message, but that did not seem to work. I then decided to call in some specialist help from computer forensics and had the message traced to an email account registered to an Arthur Troyte, an architect who lived in Ann Arbor, Michigan. This was a place I had never heard of before my research into Nariman's background the previous day, so it was certainly a weird coincidence. If they were really connected to Nariman, these messages might be important clues to the murder.

By the end of the morning I had received three more similar looking messages, all in the same stick man code, but I was none the wiser about their meaning. Then I had a brainwave and called my cousin who worked at Codehunters, a local computer games company to see if he had any ideas on how to crack the code. I was already impatient for Hunter to arrive to show him my discoveries. I knew that he was planning to call on the Flyte household again that morning and texted to him to say there was something I needed to show him as soon as possible.

*

Hunter was on his way up to the sitting room of No. 5 Clarendon Square with Julia when he received the first text message from Penny. He replied that he would be back as soon as possible. He was intrigued by this new development but also had some important and sensitive work to complete first. When they were seated and despite their previous social acquaintance, Hunter proceeded quite formally, asking Julia a series of very direct questions.

'Miss Flyte, I understand there's very bad blood between Lady Mary and Sir William following their separation?'

'Yes you could say that, but that's not exactly a secret. And please call me Julia, Inspector.'

'And your mother, I mean Lady Mary, is away for a while?'

'Yes, Inspector, she and Reverend Dore are on their

honeymoon. In fact, they're on a cruise ship at the moment, sailing between Antibes and the Amalfi coast. It all seems very romantic; she's certainly not hurrying back any time soon. We're lucky if we get a postcard from them from time to time.'

'So you're saying there's no way that she could have been here over the last couple of days.'

'No Inspector, of course not. As I've just said she's on a cruise ship in the middle of the Mediterranean.'

'Yes of course, that's certainly a very convincing alibi, um, explanation, but you understand why I have to ask given the situation?'

'Not really, Mother is hardly a likely candidate for a murderer, is she? But I guess if you must, you must.'

'It's my job to look at every possibility seriously. And what about yourself and Delia, can I ask what you were doing yesterday morning about 8am?'

Julia looked at him with an air of disbelief. She lifted up her hands and proffered them to the inspector as if inviting him to put a pair of imaginary handcuffs on her.

'OK, sorry Miss Flyte, but I have to ask you this. You know that, especially given your relationship to Sir William.'

'Well, you never know, I might just enjoy being a suspect, Inspector. But in all fairness, I should warn you that if we were going to bump off anybody next door, it certainly wouldn't have been Nadia's grandfather.'

'Quite, I suppose you do have a good point there on motivation. In any case, I was told that you were both away at a wedding on Friday night anyway, would that be correct?'

'Yes, in Malvern with about a hundred other people. Mind you, I suppose it wouldn't be that hard finding hit men to do us a favour in that town,' she laughed to try and defuse the formality of the situation. 'There's a lot of that sort of stuff goes on in Malvern, you know. A girl can get a Malvern man to do almost anything for a show of leg.'

'OK, OK I get the message,' he was silent for a moment, considering further what to ask her next.

'So did you find out anything more about those men with the knife?' she asked him, breaking the silence.

'We're still pursuing those enquiries,' he replied without giving anything away, thoughtfully shaking his head. 'Had you seen them or any other strangers hanging around the house at all recently, anything suspicious?' She shook her head.

'And did you know this Mr Nariman, at all?'

'No, I did not know him at all; in fact I didn't know that he was staying there. Of course I suppose it would have been more than a bit embarrassing for my father to have to introduce us, you understand, with us living next door, skeletons in the cupboard so to speak.'

'Yes I can see the difficulty. There's one last thing I need to ask. When I went to use the bathroom just now I noticed that one of your mother's rifles was missing from the guncase on the landing.'

'Really?' she paused. 'Well yes, she probably did take a hunting rifle with her. They had a few days at a Scottish castle that her friend owns before flying to the Med.'

'OK, it's just that we haven't found the murder weapon yet and we have to look at all possibilities.'

'Oh my God? How exciting, mother's ancient rifle is an assassin's weapon of choice. Will we be having one of those group sessions in the breakfast room, you know where everything is finally revealed and we find out that the butler did it and which murder weapon he used?'

*

As Hunter left Lady Mary's house, he saw Eddie, Alice and Carrie coming up the steps from their flat with their bicycles. Alice and Carrie were both wearing pretty pinafore-style dresses and Eddie had made the effort to dress up in imitation of an Edwardian gentleman.

'We're going on a Snark hunt, beyond the ocean right to the source of the river, Mr Hunter!' said Carrie in her best-behaved, prim and proper voice. 'Do you want to come with us?'

'Carrie, you shouldn't bother the inspector, he's very busy,' warned Alice.

'Well, do you at least know what a Snark looks like?' asked Carrie, ignoring her mother's warnings. 'Daddy won't let on at all.'

'Well, Miss Carice, I have to admit I've never actually met one. I tend to deal only in sharks and alligators round here, and I'm certainly up to my neck in them. But from what I've heard they are all meagre and hollow and crisp to taste, with a habit of rising late and taking breakfast during five o'clock tea!'

Carrie giggled, clapping her hands in delight. 'More!'

'Well I have also heard that they have a fondness for bathing machines as well as an inordinate amount of ambition. So I wish you well in your hunting, young lady, your expedition sounds quite delightful. Let me know if you find any, so that maybe I can join in with you the next time. Have fun, but beware of the Bandersnatch!'

'Dad, what's a Bandersnatch?' asked Carrie, excited to hear about this new danger.

'It's just a fig-mint,' said Eddie, amused at seeing the softer side of Hunter for once. He wondered what had brought this on. 'Nothing to worry about, come on now you two or we'll all be late!'

★

Eddie led off on his old Sunbeam and they cycled down the road toward the riverside park. When they reached the boat centre they couldn't agree at first on whether to hire kayaks or one of the traditional rowing skiffs. Eddie said that the kayaks would be just the thing for hunting Snarks in the reed beds, but Alice persuaded him that the skiff might be just a little more appropriate for two ladies dressed up in their Sunday best.

They hired the skiff for two hours and progressed up the river slowly, zigzagging back and forth, skirting the banks, looking up every creek, skimming through the dangling willow branches. Alice had made a vegetarian picnic, which they munched on happily, whilst Eddie rowed and Carrie dangled her fingers in the wake behind the boat. When Carrie was distracted feeding the ducks, Eddie bent over and planted a kiss on Alice's lips.

'You look beautiful in that dress,' he said.

*

Two compliments in a day, she was beginning to feel spoiled by Eddie's attention. She stared at his face, searching for confirmation of the sincerity of his intentions. She was suddenly feeling very happy again. Despite all his flaws, there was no denying that Eddie was both a darling and beautiful. But her need for love was more than physical; it was about an amalgamation with another person's thoughts and behaviours. And in Carrie they had certainly also given the world something new and wonderful: a legacy.

At birth, a child receives its genes from its parents but more importantly as it is growing up it develops something of each parent's personality, good or bad. Lately she had begun to feel the anxiety of age as she approached forty. Despite all her achievements, was she really happy? Sometimes she just wanted the world to slow down so that they could enjoy the moment, like today, like there and now in that boat on that river, with her beloved husband and her beautiful daughter, in the calm and the peacefulness. It was a picture of love, not romantic love, but something much deeper, agape love, a love of being. These were mixed up thoughts but ones that made her feel glad to be alive. She felt ever so fortunate to have both of them to herself for once, after all their free time was so limited.

Strangely, the memory of her teenage sweetheart, Sebastian, came back into her mind for the second time that weekend. They used to walk along this riverbank together as teenagers, holding hands, telling each other stories about the mundane things of life as well as their dreams. Now that had been romantic love, innocent love, intense with the first flush of passion and discovery. She had taken a long time to recover from his death, cried for weeks in private and sometimes in public. She still had a frozen image of him in her mind that would never grow up, forever nineteen. In contrast, her image of Eddie had evolved and constantly changed, so that she could not quite remember what he looked like when they had first met but the intricacies of their relationship continued to grow. She realised her memory of Sebastian was an idealised sort of love, a sweetheart, a teenage crush, not the realism of real life. If he were still alive, there was a chance that they would not have gotten on at all anymore. And if they'd married, they would more than likely have split up by now.

She thought how strange it would be to meet him again, not just an old flame, but one preserved now in aspic. What would they have to talk about? Old friends, places they had been, but all without a point, without any consequence or outcome or possible future. It probably would not be that long a conversation, unlike those with his sisters with whom she could quite happily talk for hours. She looked across again at Eddie, now concentrating hard, looking over his shoulder as they rounded a little island in the river. Yes, although imperfect he was real and worth the effort. She hadn't chosen so badly.

Suddenly there was a shout and a whelp and a bark and a splash. Carrie spotted the diving board in the reed banks.

'Look, a real bathing machine.' she shouted. 'We must be close!'

They rounded the corner and spotted a man and a dog in the river, paddling furiously toward the bank.

'It's Jack and Dan,' shouted Eddie laughing at the spectacle.

'Mummy, why is Uncle Jack swimming without any costume on?'

'Don't look, Carrie,' said Alice, realising that he really was naked. She covered Carrie's eyes with her hands. 'Brrr, it must be freezing, silly man.'

Jack pulled himself onto the riverbank, trying desperately to reach his clothing before the ladies looked round again. Dan was pulling at his trousers with his teeth, making it more difficult for him to get dressed, so that he fell into the rushes with a roar.

'Have you seen a Snark?' called Carrie from the boat, almost splitting her sides with laughter at Mad Jack's antics and the sight of his bare bottom in the reeds.

'Not as far as I can tell,' he replied reluctantly.

> *She will carry your life like your mother*
> *Before, hope filled in her tender eyes.*
> *She will hold you again and again her*
> *Very holding extinguishing your cries.*
> *Her fingers will stroke you with breathless sighs,*
> *Shaping the cliffs and caverns of your heart.*
> *While you love and worship her, fall and rise*
> *The timid delicate and straightened signs*
> *That dare to curve and dive, fluid innocent lines.*

Back in the office, I was showing Hunter the various coded messages I had received that morning. I was somewhat annoyed that he'd been to see Julia by himself.

'You're right, it's a code of some sort,' said Hunter decisively when he showed up just before eleven. *No kidding, Sherlock* I thought. 'Probably just a simple substitution code, it shouldn't be too difficult to crack, but there's not enough material here for a decent frequency analysis, we need something longer or a key to decode it,' he added.

'My cousin works at Codehunters in Banbury, he's been working on their *Hobbits of the Shire* online game. I wondered if he could help. He's into all that sort of stuff, elf language and things. I hope you don't mind, Sir?'

'Go on,' he said, cautiously.

'He thinks the flags might denote the end of each word, but like you he said he can't get to specific letters from the amount of material we have.'

'Well it's strictly against procedure, but nevertheless quite a good idea,' said Hunter. 'Who is this Troyte that the emails came from anyway? Is he the friend of Nariman from the station by any chance?' *Damn*, I realised that I had still overlooked assigning one of the team to track him down, despite Hunter's exhortations yesterday.

'Sorry Sir, I still haven't had the chance to follow up on that one yet, but yes it could be. He lives in Michigan according to his email address. Isn't Pearl Taylor from there too?'

'Troyte, Detroit, De-Troyte, I wonder,' he said, the cogs in his brain almost visibly whirring. 'We'd better find him as quickly as we can,' he added.

After making some basic enquiries I found out that there was no one called Troyte staying in any of the local hotels, but that there was a Mr Troyte who was scheduled to speak that day at an architect's symposium at the Compton Verney gallery. I contacted them immediately and they gave me some more details. The man was already there and was about to start his lecture. Given Hunter's instructions, I considered asking one of the local rural PCs to go along to see if there is anything unusual to report, but decided against it. Sitting through a talk on architecture probably wouldn't go down very well with the local uniformed lads. Instead I gave strict instructions to the gallery receptionist to let me know as soon as he had finished his talk so that I could speak with him on the phone, a decision I would later bitterly regret.

*

In the gallery's imposing Adam Hall, Arthur Troyte stood up to make his presentation to the assembled US-UK architects' convention. He was conscious that the attention of the whole room was upon him. He was not used to such events, and had only accepted the invitation at the insistence of his old friend. The venue had slightly overawed him, a beautiful eighteenth century Georgian mansion set in Capability Brown parkland, deep in the Warwickshire countryside. It had been the home first of the Verney and then the Willoughby de Broke family for almost 500 years but had fallen into ruin during the last century. It had recently been transformed from a derelict mansion into a gallery of international standing. He had still not heard any news from his friend and half-expected to see him when he arrived at the venue. Without his support, this lecture seemed like a big mistake.

Troyte was feeling more and more troubled by the soreness he felt below his groin and hoped he had not caught a dose of anything, given his total memory loss from the day before. He wondered if he should have cancelled the talk altogether, but the organisers had sent round a car to collect him and he had scrambled to get ready in time when the driver rang the doorbell that morning. The driver told him about the terrible murder the day before, that spurred all the police activity Troyte had heard, but of course without a name he had not made the connection to his friend.

He took a deep breath and clicked the button to bring up the first slide of his PowerPoint presentation. His chosen theme was the architecture of Eliel and Eero Saarinen and their influence on city planning in the Midwest – the first couple of slides seemed to go fine and he felt himself relaxing into the task, even beginning to enjoy himself a little, with a little joke or two. The bit where he began to explain how as a young student he had persuaded the great Eero Saarinen to reinstate Jorn Utzon's designs for the Sydney Opera House was probably a little bit of a stretch.

'You must remember they did not know him as I did,' he said, but why not boast – as Barnum (never) said, 'There's a sucker born every minute'.

He became a little more concerned however, when the polite mirth at his little jokes began to turn first into an awkward silence, followed by ominous mumblings. By the end of his sixth slide, ripples of laughter moved throughout the crowded room. Arthur put down his paper notes and reading glasses and turned to look at the projector screen. Instead of his carefully prepared slides, the screen was now full of several near-naked dancing girls, performing what could only be described as physically challenging activities on the screen behind him. In addition, the carefully worked words of his script were spinning and reforming randomly into a whole series of increasingly profane words. At the bottom of the screen, large plump 'stick men' in the shape of red letter 'A's, were bouncing up and down, some waving flags while they danced. This was followed by slides showing two middle-aged men photographed in increasingly compromising positions. As Troyte recognised his image on the screen his heart began to race and his mind searched for some logical explanation for the inexplicable images before him. The terrifying effect on Troyte was so absolute that his face lost all colour and he began to feel the onset of pains in his chest, collapsing on the floor, gasping for breath.

The beautiful late-registered Afro-American 'architecture student', a certain Miss D Troyte, 'a distant relation', who sat in the back row of his audience, was enjoying herself immensely. She slipped out at the end and returned to Leamington in the car that had been waiting for Mr Troyte, making some excuse that he had asked her to go ahead and would make his own way later.

> *But all those pleasaunt bowers and palace brave*
> *Guyon brake down with rigour pitilesse.*

Spenser, *The Faerie Queene*

★

There were four players on the two tennis courts where Hugh and Bas were warming up. They had decamped from their normal Sunday real tennis game because of the ladies' tournament and switched to play the modern game on the public courts. These courts were situated close to where lawn tennis was first played in the Manor House Hotel down the road. On the court next to them, two older gentlemen were playing a brisk and competitive game of singles. Hugh recognised Sir William Flyte and his near neighbour Richard Baxter – virtual brothers-in-law on account of Baxter's long-term relationship with Sir William's cousin Dottie. As they came to the net to spin for first serve, Bas pointed to the next court.

'Isn't that Claudia's brother on the court next door with Sir William?' asked Bas.

Hugh nodded. 'Yes, and I'm amazed that Sir William's here playing tennis given yesterday's events.'

'Indeed, amazed but not surprised. He's a cool customer. Anyway, talking about cool, how did you get on with the ice maiden after you left the restaurant last night?

'You really do have a one-track mind, don't you? OK thanks but she is certainly hard work. Psychology and sculpture are a bit out of my league.'

'What a waste with a body like that.'

'It's not all bad; she's into sport as well.'

'So are you seeing her again?'

'She did say she wants to meet up again but I wasn't convinced. I thought I might challenge her to a game of squash as she said she plays regularly.'

'She's certainly fit; if she'd warm up a little, she'd be perfect for you,' he joked. 'Sounds like you'd better do a bit of sculpture research though as well.'

Hugh smiled, he had been thinking about her all morning. During the next game he heard his mobile beep – unexpectedly it was a text from Claudia. He had sent a message earlier but was somewhat surprised that she had replied so quickly, and even more surprised that she had suggested he come over to the gallery where she worked that very afternoon. Her text mentioned she was preparing an upcoming exhibition there and could do with some male help.

'Blimey, I think I've got a date,' he said to Bas, showing him the phone.

'Maybe but make sure you go prepared if she's that keen,' said Bas, 'you know what these artists are like.' Hugh screwed up his face at the comment.

'Anyway, you've been unusually quiet about your own evening. How did you get on with Miss Taylor last night?'

'Glad you asked. My, we had one hell of a hot party. After I got her on her own, she was all over me. Strange thing is I can only remember the half of it. I must have had more to drink than I thought. You know I'm normally a one-night stand sort of guy, but this time I can't wait to see her again. I think I'll call her hotel later and see if she's up for a second round.'

During the succeeding points, Bas related the sordid details to Hugh in a staccato narrative, embellishing wherever his memory was strangely dimmed. For a big man, Hugh was very nimble around the courts, and with Bas strangely unable to move quickly himself, Hugh was soon serving for match point. His serve was returned by a wild volley from Bas that went soaring over the fence into the next court. Hugh opened the gate between the courts to ask the two older men if they could return the ball. As he collected it and closed the door, his interest was tweaked by the subject of their conversation.

'You know that rogue Rohit that used to work for Nadia's grandfather?' Baxter was saying.

'Only too well, he's been bothering Nadia with texts for some time,' replied Sir William.

'Well, he's one of my regular literature students. But on top of all the stuff going on in the street yesterday, he only went and half-inched one of my pistols. I've had to report it to the police: apparently he's gone missing now as well.'

'I've never trusted him so I'm not in the least surprised. That type is basically unreliable. That's the kind of thanks you get for teaching him to write in your spare time.'

So that's what Hunter was on about, he thought.

As Hugh and Bas played out the second set, the two older men left the courts and were replaced ten minutes later by Delia and Julia. Bas suggested they abandon their singles game, which he was, in any case, losing badly and instead play a game of mixed doubles together. He partnered with Julia, while Hugh played with Delia.

'Watch out,' whispered Delia to Hugh, 'Julia never misses a backhand with that enchanted lance of hers; the secret is to return on her forehand.'

The first set went to service until they reached the tie-break. The points then followed serve again until Hugh smashed another loose lob return from Bas, a backhand right down the baseline onto Julia's forehand. Her hurried return landed out and so Hugh and Delia won the set. Bas indicated he'd had enough. Delia hugged Hugh, while Julia took off her tennis cap and came to the net to shake his hand. The sweat was pouring off his face and she wiped his brow with her hand towel. Hugh realised again how pretty she was, the filaments of her golden curls forming a halo around her face against the bright September sunlight. He had seemingly not made any impression on her the previous night. Maybe he should have tried harder to make it work all those years ago when he had the chance. Remarkably, he had a sense that she was thinking exactly the same. Now he realised he really had a dilemma, in thrall to two beautiful women in one weekend.

★

After they got back from Snark hunting, Alice found a message on the answering machine. She had been called back to the hospital to help with an autopsy on the actress from the nursing home across the road. There were now suspicions about how she had come to be found dead in the bath last night and whether she did take an overdose or if she could have been drugged. She had been asked to go back in to the hospital to help out with the toxicology analysis.

★

Back in the police station, we did not have to wait too much longer for the next message to arrive on my computer. At about 1pm, I called Hunter over from his office to look at my screen.

'Sir, take a look at this.'

'Good, now that's getting much more interesting. It's a lot longer and might be enough to start a frequency analysis, but it would still be much quicker if we could find the key to read it.' He rubbed his hand over his brow, as if trying to come up with a key for the code with his own intellect and concentration.

'Sir, have you seen the message header? The wording is very strange: "WSW. Don't take clues from Toposcope hounds, blessings and Glory to God!"'

'Toposcope hounds?' He paused thoughtfully. 'My God, I hope this isn't all about Miss Taylor playing some elaborate practical joke on us. Don't you remember the words of that song she sang for me last night, the phrase that she drew your attention to?'

'Not really sir.'

'Well I remember it clearly as it's one of my favourites from her last album; it includes the phrase 'Horoscope Hounds'. 'Toposcope Hounds' is so close it's got to be connected to what these messages mean. Get on to the hotel; we need to interview her as soon as possible.'

I called straightaway and spoke briefly to the receptionist before turning back to Hunter.

'Sir, she's not in, they think she'll be out until late afternoon. Is she a suspect now?'

'I don't know, that's a bit strong but get a message out to the patrols to pick her up and ask her to come into the station if they see her, it can't be that difficult to find a woman like that in Leamington. The more I think about it the more I think we need take this seriously.'

'But why would a suspect deliberately give us a clue like that?' I asked and he pondered on this question for a minute.

'Do you know, you're right, Penny, but then again she may be trying to tell us something. Do you possess walking boots?'

'No, but I have some wellies in my locker, Sir.'

'Well fetch them and meet me in the car park, we're going for a quick hike up to the Beacon on Newbold Comyn.' I raised my eyebrows in puzzlement, but seeing how fixed his expression was did not question his instructions.

★

'Here we are,' he said as we reached the top of the hill. He rested his hands on the newly installed plinth with its perspex cover protecting a metal plaque against the elements. 'This plate is a representation of all the views that can be seen from the beacon,' he said. 'It's a replica of an original, which was stolen and recently discovered in a car boot sale.'

'But why are we here, what's this got to do with the murders? I can only see a few hills in the distance.'

'A hunch maybe,' he said. 'Look, read this,' he added, pointing out the inscription affixed to the plinth.

'This Toposcope is after the design of an original by Arthur Troyte Griffith, an architect from Malvern and a close friend of Edward Elgar,' I read. 'Arthur Troyte, isn't that a bit of a coincidence?' I asked

'It's a very big one. The original Arthur Troyte Griffith was indeed a close friend of Elgar's – in fact he was variation number seven I think. His nickname was Ninepin.'

'So is that why we're here, a British architect with the same name as the American architect?'

'Not intentionally, but it's certainly adding to the puzzle. No, we've come here to search for the key to your code, Penny. Can you read the inscription for me?' He was looking up at the sky as if waiting for inspiration. I found the words

213

a little hard to read through the condensation under the perspex, but eventually made out most of the letters and filled in the gaps.

'The Earth is the Lord's and the fullness thereof,' I read.

'Ah yes of course, that's Psalm 24, King James Version I believe – the first part of our key perhaps – I believe it continues something like 'the world and they that dwell therein' doesn't it?'

'Yes, it does, Sir. So do I just match the flag men up with the letters in the inscription?'

'Hopefully it might be as simple as that.'

After a few minutes transcribing the inscription onto my notepad, I had matched up the letters from the Psalm on the Toposcope in order to the symbols of the dancing men on the longer message.

'There are far more symbols than letters in the quotation from the Psalm.'

'OK, let me look – ah I see the problem. Then let's try adding something else, perhaps the last phrase in the message header: "Blessings and Glory to God" might help, it looks about the right length?' I wrote the extra phrase down.

'Yes Sir that works exactly now, it's just the right number of symbols.'

'OK, so now try transcribing the letters that match the dancing men in the emails to the letters on the key you just wrote down.' I worked away at this for a few minutes and then turned back towards Hunter to read out the result.

'LIDR THIAB FOWDRG DGULTARAR,' I said, somewhat crestfallen. 'That's gibberish isn't it? It doesn't make any sense at all.' Hunter scratched his head and stared first at my pad and then one by one at the various hills we could see on the horizon, turning slowly through 360 degrees. I could see that he was hunting around for a further clue.

'What's she up to?' he asked someone in the clouds.

CHAPTER SIXTEEN

A Case of Misidentity – (Allegro molto)

Sir Bernard Henry Spilsbury, the father of forensics, was born in Leamington. The case that brought Spilsbury to public attention was that of Hawley Harvey Crippen in 1910, where he gave forensic evidence as to the likely identity of the human remains found in Crippen's house. The case that consolidated Spilsbury's reputation as Britain's foremost forensic pathologist was the 'Brides in the Bath' murder trial in 1915. Three women had died mysteriously in their baths; in each case, the death appeared to be an accident. George Joseph Smith was brought to trial for the murder of Bessie Mundy, one of these women. Spilsbury testified that since Mundy's thigh showed evidence of goose skin and, since she was, in death, clutching a bar of soap, it was certain that she had died a violent death – in other words, had been murdered. Spilsbury was also involved in the Brighton trunk murder cases. Although the man accused of the second murder, Tony Mancini, was acquitted, he confessed to the killing just before his own death, many years later, and vindicating Spilsbury's evidence.

Based on Wikipedia, *Bernard Spilsbury*

Following our little ramble, Hunter and I returned quickly to the office. We had already enquired by phone with the Holly Hotel about whether Miss Taylor had returned. The concierge told us that she had not but that that he expected her back shortly. He also confirmed that she had not as yet checked out although she had a taxi booked for 6pm and was due to check out that evening. The patrols had also had no luck finding her. Similarly the story from the gallery was that Mr Troyte had not yet finished his talk and certainly couldn't be interrupted. I reminded the receptionist that I really needed to speak to him as soon as he was finished. It was proving remarkably difficult to track these two down.

While we waited, Hunter asked me to try and trace Pearl's recent movements and conduct some further research into Troyte and Pearl's background. I found that the Internet was full of reviews of Pearl's musical appearances and there was quite a bit about her life history. It was therefore not too difficult to construct a timeline for her recent engagements. As regards to her personal life, despite a number of well-publicised relationships, she was steadfastly single and appeared to be itinerant with no permanent home, spending time in London and Zurich as well as at a holiday home in the South of France on the Cap d'Antibes. In fact, it did not sound like she was home too often; she seemed to spend most of her life travelling between engagements, permanently in demand at festivals, concerts and celebrity events. The details of her origins and earlier life were much sketchier. She had emerged as a young blues singer from a poor background in the States, propelled to fame by talent, beauty and a wondrous soulful voice. There was an intriguing piece in a magazine interview from the time her mother died, where she told the story for the first time about her search for her natural father.

As for Troyte, there seemed little remarkable about him. I found only the most basic details of his career on the Internet. An architect and a keen amateur chess player, he was still a partner in a Midwest firm although he seemed to have retired some years ago from active contract work. Twice married, he led a respectable but unexciting life, enlivened briefly by his earlier marriage to a famous cellist, the name of whom Hunter also recognised from a recording in his collection. She had died early and he had later remarried and had two grown-up children but he had been widowed again a few years ago. Before he finished his training as an architect he was drafted into the navy, working as a signalman during Vietnam, nothing really remarkable in that. The signalman piece piqued Hunter's interest though.

When I phoned the gallery again after twenty minutes to ask if Mr Troyte had finished his lecture and if he might be available to talk to me, the administrator answered me circumspectly.

'I'm terribly sorry, officer, but I'm afraid I can't let you talk to him. Unfortunately he took quite a turn during his talk and the doctor has told him to rest. We're to put him in a taxi later, so maybe you can talk with him when he gets back to Leamington?' I pushed her, sensing that I had not been told the whole story and eventually got a reluctant account of what had happened during the presentation. I instructed the receptionist to let me know immediately when he was ready to speak again and certainly before he got back in the taxi.

'It seems like our architect has some enemies,' grimaced Hunter when I told him this story. 'We'd better check this out properly. Even if it turns out to be a practical joke, we really can't let someone's little bit of fun confuse the investigation of the Nariman case.'

*

On the way back from his tennis match to his flat in the Old Town, Hugh called in at the bookshop on Warwick Street. He was looking for a basic book on sculpture so that he did not come over as a total ignoramus when he met up with

217

Claudia after lunch. He just had time to shower before he drove over.

When he got to the gallery, he asked for Claudia by name and was directed up a rather grand staircase toward a screened off exhibition room. He had to move one of the screens aside to enter the room. Sunlight flooded the gallery space from two great windows and he saw Claudia standing at the far end of the room. The light was shining through her clothes at such an angle that he couldn't avoid noticing the closely defined silhouette of her body within. Bas was right about that aspect of her at least – for a woman in her late forties, she had a just about perfect, athletic physique. She called him over and he embraced her politely with an air kiss on each cheek. He noticed she wore little make up – but equally there was not so much as a blotch or wrinkle on her skin, just a few rather charming freckles and a prominent mole on her cheek. Her ash blonde hair had been swept up into a rough knot so that wisps of it delicately framed her face. She was wearing a silky pale blue top and a billowy darker blue skirt. He could smell her perfume, a very distinct rather musky scent, not at all flowery. He approved. She looked gorgeous.

'Thank you for coming,' she said with an engaging friendliness. 'I enjoyed last night.' Hugh wondered about this change in her mood. Was she just feeling unwell last night?

'So did I,' he said. 'Sorry I was such a lousy companion though. You must have been so bored all night, listening to us all chatter on.'

'No I had a good time, really, especially listening to Pearl Taylor singing, that was truly amazing,' she smiled. There was an inner radiance to her face that Hugh found irresistible.

'Yes, she's quite a woman isn't she?'

He realised his eagerness to compliment Pearl could be

misinterpreted and added quickly, 'Of course nothing like as pretty as you.' She blushed and brushed his arm with her hand in a reassuring gesture. In truth, her face was ageless; it could still be the face of a nineteen-year-old girl. How could a complexion like hers be described merely as beauty? *Surely it is something deeper than that*, he thought.

> *I made a garland for her head,*
> *And bracelets too, and fragrant zone;*
> *She looked at me as she did love*
> *And made sweet moan.*

Keats, *La Belle Dame sans Merci*

'You'll do well if you keep that sort of flattery up. *And sure in language strange she said – I love thee true,*' she then quoted and then seeing his blank face added, 'Sorry, it's from a Keats poem.'

The reference still went straight over Hugh's head. Furthermore, he had become so enamoured with her that he felt awkward in her company and struggled with what to say next; his eventual question was only slightly less original than making a comment about the weather.

'So this is where you work then? It's quite a setting.'

'Well yes, thank you. This is the room where we're going to set up our next exhibition. It's going to be built around a comparison of two works, one by Henry Moore and one by Auguste Rodin, trying to give fresh angles on familiar subjects.'

He smiled to himself, realising that he might need to finish the book if this relationship was ever going to happen.

'Anyway, come on, let me show you round. I've got a small studio out the back, my 'Elfin grot' so to speak.' Hugh wondered whether she was playing some elaborate game with him, teasing him with this new easiness, a game that he doubted he knew the rules of. He was unsure now whether her earlier coolness to him was just camouflage for shyness, or if she had indeed just been unwell. He was sensing a new openness to develop the chemistry between them. He found her intensely attractive but at the same time intimidating. He had never met such an intellectually superior woman before. What did Bas always say? Always talk to the most beautiful woman in the room, you may be surprised by the result – well this time it looked like he might have hit the jackpot.

They descended the staircase and Claudia talked for a few minutes to one of the women at the reception desk. They giggled together at something, the other woman making strange shapes with her fingers. Hugh wondered what their private joke could be.

'Apparently we had a bit of excitement here this morning,' Claudia explained. 'We've got a convention of architects using the conference centre and one of the guest speakers was taken badly ill during his lecture. He's still around the back in the medical office; he really took quite a turn. Apparently someone had doctored his presentation, and the result was both very funny and very rude. Unfortunately it seems he didn't take the joke well and he collapsed towards the end of it. Luckily it appears it wasn't too serious but the doctor has ordered him to rest here for a few hours.'

'I didn't realise architecture was so exciting,' Hugh laughed.

They continued through several corridors to the back of the gallery. Her small studio turned out to be quite a large space leading off from some classrooms. There were unfinished projects spread haphazardly over the floor and tables – drawings, sketches, clay models and some unusual stone carvings. He was immediately impressed; even he could tell that this was much more than just an amateur's work.

'I've got a residency for a year,' she explained. 'Alongside assisting the curator with the main exhibitions I do some teaching for school kids and adult art classes as well.

'I'm really impressed,' he said. 'I had no idea that you were so talented.'

'Sorry if I'm not complying with the stereotype.'

'OK I didn't mean it to sound quite like that. So how long have you been doing this?'

'I've been planning it forever in my mind, but for years I was too busy with my work as a psychologist, I never had the time. It's always been there, trying to get out though.'

'It sounds like you have found a vocation?'

'Well yes, that's a good description. It's something I've always wanted to do full time and now I have the chance at last. In fact, the connection between psychology and sculpture is something that I am also interested in trying to capture in these pieces.' She pointed to the unfinished stone works that Hugh had noticed a few minutes ago. They reminded him of those statues from the Easter Islands you see in books, he mentioned this to her.

'Yes, you're getting good at this. Have you ever thought how much our minds are like islands? We float alone in a tide of humanity, drawn on by our own ideas but who really knows what anyone else is thinking about most of the time?'

'That's especially true if you are a shy old introvert like me.'

'You're not so shy. But then we are all flawed communicators; we connect by common experience, but only fleetingly, in between the silences between words, the transient nature of thoughts. For introverts there is a whole world going on inside their heads that most of us would never even dream of, but even extroverts, the kind we would generally say wear their hearts on their sleeves, have complex secret narratives going on inside their heads most of the time. Our bodies, on the other hand, are much more accessible. Substantial, flesh and blood, skin and muscle stretched over distorted frames of bone and cartilage. This was the subject of most sculpture for centuries, in fact right back to the Greeks. Yet, even though most of our body language is actually involuntary, programmed, instinctive and easily readable, there's still an infinite variation of form. We're all the same at the core, we have the same needs, the same basic urges, but even so, the way we express ourselves can be totally different depending on our culture and own inner thoughts and fears. I'm trying to get to the heart of that, to the heart of self-will and self-belief, the connection of the soul and the body and how that inner personality expresses itself to the world. Capturing that complexity that lies beneath us in still life form is now my daily challenge.'

'Wow, that's pretty deep. I thought sculpture was about more obvious things like love and war and a whole lot of sexual innuendo,' he said, somewhat taken aback by the forcefulness of her monologue.

'Ah, then I'm afraid you make my point for me, you've just demonstrated again the vanity of male dominance,' she said. 'There is more to life than what we have been programmed to do or consume or in other words, it's not all about the sex you know.'

'Quite, well it was just a question.'

'Don't worry, I'm not criticising. And you're not unusual in those thoughts. Men have always wanted to remake women in their gaze as objects of desire; passive and agreeable, without desires of our own, increasingly it's true the other way round as well. Remove the mask of cosmetics from most women and you get a much truer story of bad skin, freckles and blemishes. Remove the mask of language from most women, or men for that matter, and what do you get – deeply felt desires, common virtues, and common sins. That's what I'm trying to capture here in these models, what is at the heart of it all when you strip away the pretence and time and words stop. What's left, what's there, what's real, what's fake. What's alive and what's dead. It's like Schrödinger's cat really, without the cat. It's quite straightforward conceptually but horribly difficult to get right in the flesh, so to speak.'

'I don't know what to say,' he said, now beginning to feel completely out of his depth.

'Ok, don't worry, I can see I'm confusing you, it's a lot to take in at once and I've been thinking about it for years. As I said, I trained as a psychologist, but that probably doesn't surprise you.'

'Indeed, now you remind me, it doesn't.'

Erwin Schrödinger's maternal family was from Leamington and maybe his cat too? *A cat, a flask of poison, and a radioactive source are placed in a sealed box. If an internal monitor detects radioactivity (i.e. a single atom decaying), the flask is shattered, releasing the poison that kills the cat. The Copenhagen interpretation of quantum mechanics implies that after a while, the cat is simultaneously alive and dead. Yet, when one looks in the box, one sees the cat alive or dead, not both alive and dead. This poses the question of when exactly quantum superposition ends and reality collapses into one possibility or the other.* Or in other words, is the cat really dead or alive?

Based on Wikipedia – *Schrödinger's Cat*

'So maybe it's about time I got to my point in inviting you,' she said. 'To keep it simple I might have brought you here under slightly false pretences. What I probably should have told you directly rather than all that psychobabble is that I'd really like you to model for me,' she laughed, pointing to some clay life studies of male torsos, strangely distorted from the classical ideal. 'I'm going to work all these up until they are ready to create bronzes for my own show next year and I need some new models – real flesh and blood men rather than willowy art students or over-blown body-builders. I thought you'd do for starters.' He stood in silence for a moment, while she looked him up and down, sizing him up, apparently waiting for him to say something. 'In fact, I think you'd be a great subject.'

He was certainly taken aback.

'I don't really think I've got the body shape to be a model,' he said.

'Rubbish. You have a nice body and more importantly you are 100 per cent real and honest rather than manufactured like most models.'

He hesitated still, despite the clear signals she was giving him.

'OK,' he said 'What do you want me to do?'

'Well we'll start with you showing me your stuff.'

'What, here, now?'

'Yes like this.' She gently unbuttoned his shirt.

Christ, why hadn't he seen this coming? Why was he always so self-controlled; why couldn't he be more forward? Her mouth was for an instant deliciously close to his. He had hoped but had never imagined that something like this would happen. Maybe Bas was right about artists. His knees were shaking as if they wanted to sink to the floor, a place from where he felt he may never want to get up.

'I think I love you,' he whispered to himself but was then suddenly aware of another woman in the room, already beginning to take photographs as he stood there, stripped to the waist, looking up at the light playing on the ceiling.

'Who's this?' he asked, confused.

'Don't worry, Jade is a professional photographer that I work with and my partner. I need her to get some initial images so I can work out the form. She'll be quick,' said Claudia, laughing. She had heard his words. 'But I'm not

sure what she would think about your professions of love –
she might even be a little jealous.'

The new woman called Jade nodded to her. *God, she is
gorgeous as well*, thought Hugh. She offered him a cup of tea.

'You can put your shirt back on, Jade's got what I need
for now and they'll be closing up the front of the house
soon.'

> *There in contemplation of you I stood*
> *Face that tells a story of form and art.*
> *Womanly perfection, temper too good*
> *The stone you carve is fashioned by your heart*
> *All your words cut and sharpened like a dart.*
> *Take time to feel the world as we connect.*
> *Now vulnerable and modest I start,*
> *To grow in humility and accept,*
> *Imperfection in love, from lust and pride protect.*

★

The receptionist of the Holly Hotel did as they had
promised and rang me as soon as Pearl returned to the hotel
so we made our way there as quickly as we could. Pearl had
returned to her room, but frustratingly Hunter asked me to
wait at reception and went alone to meet her.

★

He knocked at her door.

'Miss Taylor, sorry to disturb you, but I wondered if you
had a minute?'

'Inspector, what a nice surprise this is. Of course I have,
but I really wasn't expecting a visitor and I'm packing up.
Sorry this room is in a bit of a mess. Please come in but can
you give me a minute to tidy up?'

He nodded and followed her into the living room of her suite discreetly after a few seconds. He noticed she had gone straight for a package on her desk.

She pushed past him, smiling as sweetly as ever, with the package in her hands, which she placed in the room safe. He heard her tap seven digits into the keypad, which interested him immediately as most people would only use four digits when they were locking a hotel safe.

'Just family jewellery,' she said. 'Anyway, Inspector, how good to see you again so soon.'

'I'm sorry to bother you but there have been some more developments this morning in our murder case, I understand you have been out and about this morning and wonder if you saw anything on your travels.' He was aware that she was watching his face carefully as he was speaking.

'Oh dear, I'm afraid not, Inspector. My purpose in visiting your town was just to meet up with an old friend. I did that this morning and although I am only too aware of the terrible incidents from our conversation last night, I am afraid I have seen nothing myself of any significance, in fact those events have not troubled me at all.'

'I see, well that's reassuring,' he said coolly. 'By any chance, would that old friend happen to be a Mr Arthur Troyte? It appears you share at least a similar sounding name, Troyte, Detroit?'

Pearl was somewhat surprised by the question. It appeared the Inspector had made a connection more quickly than she had expected. She maintained a completely straight face, however, showing no hint of recognition.

'Indeed, well, no I do not enjoy personal relations with the gentleman, I have to say.' Hunter could read nothing at all into her poker face at this point. He also wondered at the nice use of the word personal. No facial or verbal signs that she was lying. *She is very good*, he thought.

'It's just that it is such a coincidence. He's American and

so are you, you have similar sounding names, he's staying not a quarter of a mile from this hotel and apparently you both arrived on the same train yesterday morning. You understand why I would want to check that out.'

She laughed. 'Inspector, I agree those are indeed coincidences and indeed neither of our names is a common name, but although all Americans are supposedly brothers and sisters under God, I am afraid I am not intimately acquainted with all of them and certainly none that I know of in this lovely town of yours. As you may be aware, I was named by my mother after the city of my birth – Detroit; and the town of my conception – Taylor. I agree that my middle name Detroit sounds spookily similar to that of your Mr Troyte but beyond that I'm afraid we have no connection.'

'That's perfectly fine, Miss Taylor. I'm just checking all avenues, you understand. We are trying to unravel an unfortunate incident that occurred earlier today.'

'Intriguing, you must tell me more.'

'I am afraid I can't at the moment. You do understand, I hope, that I have to follow up anything unusual.' He paused and then continued. 'By any chance in your travels around our town did you happen to go up to the beacon at Newbold Comyn?' Again the Inspector had surprised her with this question.

'Well, Inspector, I believe the carriage ride I took yesterday took me there, yes but why do you ask?' she asked, looking puzzled.

'And did you happen to see the Toposcope?'

'Yes I did, it was splendid and indeed that name Toposcope is such an interesting albeit unfamiliar word. Unfortunately the view was obscured by mist yesterday, I understand on a good day you can see for miles.'

'Indeed, things were a little clearer when I was there earlier.'

'I am very glad about that, Inspector. Your powers of observation are somewhat legendary.'

'Anyway, it's no matter, but just one more question if I may. Do you have any naval connections by any chance?'

Pearl feigned puzzlement for the second time.

'Well, yes my father was a sea captain.'

'And are you familiar with semaphore, you know, the language with flags that is used to signal at sea?'

'Well I suppose I have a passing acquaintance, but no more than that.'

'That's helpful to know and regarding the naval connection, does that also explain the significance of the name Pearl, if I may enquire?'

'Good God, Inspector, does your vast knowledge even extend to the Pearl Incident?'

'You mean Pearl Harbor?'

'Ah no,' she laughed. 'Then I have you at a disadvantage. That is indeed another 'Pearl' date, which is certainly a day that will live in infamy, but it's not the one I'm referring to. No, I mean the nineteenth century Pearl Incident. It was a slave ship that was captured during the Civil War period, that's the one I'm named after. *Uncle Tom's Cabin* and all that. It's maybe another one for your pretty young researcher?'

★

She nodded at me, as I had now joined them. I indicated to Hunter that I needed to speak with him. Seeing this, Pearl checked her watch. 'Oh my, is that the time? Sorry but I must be getting on, Inspector, I have one or two further errands before I have to leave this evening and you obviously have more pressing things to attend to.'

'Of course, we won't detain you any longer, Miss Taylor, but it would be helpful if you could let us know of your whereabouts in the coming days.'

'Of course, I will leave the address with the hotel. Well I hope I've told you what you want to know. Please keep in touch, Inspector, and I would be even more delighted if you'd come to a concert I am going to give next month in London. Perhaps I can send you the details and some complimentary tickets?'

'Thank you, you have been most generous with your time, Miss Taylor. And I'd love to come to your concert – as you know I am a great fan of yours.'

'That is most kind, Inspector. Now, talking of names, you never told me your own full name for the invitation.'

'Hunter.'

'Come on you can do better than that, I was asking about your first name?'

I grinned as I watched this interchange unfold; I was quite enjoying seeing Hunter given a run for his money like this for a change.

'Well as you seem to like puzzles, maybe I'll leave you with my personal favourite clue to my first name: *in summer a golden breath of wind revolves around us.*'

'That's really not too hard,' she laughed. She paused and then turned to the inspector again. 'Then I too may have a little riddle for you, too. I don't want to cause confusion, Inspector, but it might help you to relax later. *Don't be confused, my mighty Nimrod, it's in G-minor after all, but as a rule you should always keep the major key in sight.*'

Hunter laughed along with her politely. He realised that she had just set him a cryptic clue from some of the key words she used and his mind was already trying to solve the puzzle she had posed. I scowled at him ferociously now and he noticeably reddened.

'I will certainly think that one over,' he said. 'Did you write that one down, Penny?'

'What do you think, Sir?' I asked as we left the hotel.

'I don't know,' he said. 'She's certainly a cool customer. I'm still inclined to the practical joke theory but these coded messages are a very disturbing development. It seems like I have another riddle to solve. Can you find out where she's going in London in case we need to pull her in again?'

'Yes *and* I still don't trust her,' I said. 'By the way I finally got to speak with Mr Troyte.'

'OK what did he have to say for himself?'

'Strange. He was very subdued when I asked him if he was better after his experience in the lecture. He seemed to want to brush it off quickly as being of no consequence. Then he asked me why the police were involved and that's when I mentioned Nariman. That seemed to come as a complete shock to him; he appeared to know nothing about the murder yesterday. He asked me what had happened and then just went totally silent when I told him.'

'How odd?'

'Yes it was. I spoke and then shouted down the phone but I could not get him to reply to me. Anyway the receptionist came back on the line and said that Hugh happened to be there and wanted to talk to me so they put him on the line for me. Once I had explained the situation to him, Hugh said that Troyte appeared genuinely shocked and was ashen and had needed to sit down when he got the news. All he had muttered to Hugh was that he had wondered why Nariman had not met him yesterday at the station but now he understood; he said he had thought it was a misunderstanding. Hugh said he would bring Troyte back to Leamington and make sure he's alright. I'll talk to Hugh later but I've tentatively arranged to see Mr Troyte first thing tomorrow if that's OK, after he's had a good night's sleep?'

'Yes OK, I think we could both probably do with some downtime. Get some rest Penny – I sense we have a busy week ahead of us.'

As they drove down the Roman road through the rolling countryside, Hugh and Troyte had an awkward conversation about the events of the morning. When he dropped him off at the house in Lansdowne Circus, Hugh mentioned his own security background and offered to check over his laptop and see if he could work out how someone was able to doctor his presentation. He also checked the alarm security settings and advised him to keep all the doors to the house locked in case there were any more intruders before leaving for home.

★

By now, it was late on Sunday afternoon; Eddie had taken Carrie to the Dell to play on the swings while Alice returned to the hospital to assist at Winnie's autopsy. The temperature had continued to rise during the day and the air was beginning to feel oppressively close. There were several other families in the park enjoying the last of the sun in the dog days of summer. They bumped into Izzie walking with her new friend.

'Izzie!' shouted Carrie.

'Hello, my little darling, it's so good to see you,' replied the Irish nurse a little sheepishly. She was hand in hand with her new actor friend. After their trip to the coffee shop, they had spent a quiet Sunday morning in Izzie's bedsit, most of which had been passed in bed. They had only just emerged, somewhat guiltily, to catch the last of the day's sun.

'Carrie, this is my new friend Penn. I know it's a funny name, but he's an actor, although I'm afraid not a very funny one despite that name.' Penn dug her in the ribs so that she burst out in giggles.

'I'd love to be an actress,' said Carrie.

'Well, my princess, sometimes a little fantasy is a very good thing you know.'

'Do you want to join our play?' asked Carrie, her expression studied and completely serious.

'What play would that be?'

Eddie pulled him aside and whispered to him. Penn smiled and shook Eddie's hand, nodding.

'Of course, that sounds a lot of fun. I hear you've been hunting Snarks, would you like to hear about the Jabberwocky then?' asked Penn and proceeded to quote her the opening lines.

> *Twas brillig, and the slithy toves*
> *Did gyre and gimble in the wabe;*
> *All mimsy were the borogoves,*
> *And the mome raths outgrabe.*

Lewis Carroll, *Jabberwocky*

They walked back towards the town together. As they came to the junction of Beauchamp Hill and Clarendon Place, they saw Pearl standing on the opposite corner outside Mr Baxter's house, as if she was searching for something. She saw Eddie and beckoned urgently for him to cross the road.

'Stay here a second with Izzie, Carrie, I just need to go and talk to that lady for a moment.' Eddie crossed the road, wondering what had happened.

'Hello Miss Taylor, what are you doing in our neck of the woods?' he asked. She seemed somewhat energised about something.

'Ah Eddie, I was really hoping to find you. I knew you lived around hereabouts because of the newspaper reports of the murder. There's a really big favour I would like you to do for me.'

232

'Of course, what is it, Miss Taylor, how can I help?'

'I'm afraid I might have given your friend Inspector Hunter a little bit of a run around for my own amusement this morning. I have to leave this evening and I'm afraid he is not going to be very pleased with me when he finds out about something I did earlier. There's no real harm done, nothing permanent anyway, just a wounded woman's practical joke on a rather nasty man I know. But I wonder if you could give him this letter tomorrow all the same, so he's got the real story, but not before tomorrow. I'm flying this evening, I'll be back in a month's time and I'll make my peace with him then. And when I return, perhaps you would all join me in London for a performance I'm giving.'

'Of course I'll give him this, but it all sounds very mysterious. As for the concert we'd love to do that, Alice was so disappointed she missed your singing last night,' said Eddie. 'But I wonder in that case if you might also be around on October the 9th, there is a big favour you could do for me as well.'

'Yes I'll be back in England for a couple of weeks with the concert program,' she said, checking her calendar on her Blackberry. 'And yes, remarkably I'm free that evening at the moment, although I have a matinee in London that afternoon.'

While they had been talking the sky had grown ominously dark. The storm that had been threatening all day had arrived. There was a sudden clap of thunder. Carrie called to Eddie in a concerned voice from across the road. Almost immediately the skies opened and there was a torrential downpour. Eddie grabbed Pearl and led her quickly across the road. Izzie, Penn and Carrie were already running towards the entrance door to Sherridge House. Within a few seconds they were soaked, but quickly reached the entrance to the nursing home. They all gathered in the hall while Izzie went off to find some towels. When she

233

returned she handed them out and then said to Pearl, 'Miss Taylor, I'm told you are a singer?'

'Yes I am indeed, my dear.'

'I wonder if you could sing a couple of songs for our old ladies while you are sheltering, I am sure we can offer you a cup of tea and a scone in return. They would so love that.'

'Of course, I'd be very glad to,' Pearl said but then looked at her watch. 'Although I must be gone by 5pm, I have a plane to catch and the taxi will be waiting for me at my hotel at 6pm.'

'That's fine; just a few minutes will be more than enough.'

'And I'll need to get you home too, Carrie,' added Eddie. 'It's school tomorrow, and you need to pack your bags and get a good night's sleep.'

★

Later on that afternoon, after the storm had subsided, the assassin passed from the garden onto the back veranda of Hawthorne House. Someone had made this all too easy for him. The doors to the garden were unlocked and he passed easily through the heavy curtains into the living room. He removed his shoes to avoid leaving prints on the carpet. The room was in relative darkness, but he could see the reclined form of his intended victim stretched out on a chaise longue. There was no movement and he assumed that the man was fast asleep after a heavy Sunday lunch. He did not hesitate to grab this ready-made opportunity. The Browning was not exactly a silent weapon, but it did the job. He then placed it carefully in the dead man's hands. As he did so, he noticed and inspected a scrap of paper lying under the day bed. There were strange characters written all over it. He screwed it up and put it in the victim's pocket.

'Whatever Nariman told you will remain between you

and me now, Mr Troyte,' he said coldly. He called the number that had been dialling him persistently all afternoon on his cell phone.

'Thank God you called,' Sir William said, 'Apparently Rohit has got a gun, what if he comes after me?'

'Correction, Sir William. He had a gun and now that gun is the primary evidence in the passing of our mysterious and now quiet American friend, Mr Arthur Troyte.'

'The American's dead?'

'There's a nice elegance to that don't you think, Sir William?'

'My God! Another one? What about Rohit, he can still make trouble for us, surely.'

'I don't think we need to worry too much about Rohit again,' replied Khand as he moved to press 'end call' on the phone. 'He'll have quite a bit of explaining of his own to do.'

★

The housekeeper, when she got the call from Hugh was in two minds whether she should leave her family and go straight round to the villa. The weather had turned nasty, and she was cooking Sunday dinner. The reaction of her husband when she said she would have to go out and leave them to make their own dinner was enough to make her change her mind. 'OK. He's got my number, I'm sure it can wait till morning,' she said. 'It serves him right if he had a hard time this morning, the old letch.'

★

At home at last on Sunday evening, Hunter put on one of his favourite CDs – of course, given all that was on his mind, it was natural for him to play Pearl Taylor's latest release. He had been re-running in his mind all the evidence they had gathered so far, but he knew there was something missing, something that didn't quite fit. Maybe Troyte would provide the clue they needed in the morning. He wondered whether he should go round himself that evening but it was likely to be his one night off for a while and he didn't want to undermine Penny's decision. He had been looking at the coded messages again, trying to see if he could make anything fit. Pearl Taylor had been enigmatic but the one link to her in the word 'Toposcope' had been too tenuous to take any further action that afternoon. Somehow he felt she had the upper hand with him on this. She was certainly a very smart lady. He poured himself a glass of brandy and put his feet up on the ottoman. His bachelor pad was spartan but tidy, his books, his music, a few choice pieces of furniture, chosen for their design integrity rather than comfort. 'Form follows function' was his mantra, although he would also agree with the sentiment of William Morris when he said, *Have nothing in your house that you do not know to be useful, or believe to be beautiful.*

Hunter had begun to doze off when he suddenly woke with a start. He looked at the photograph on the CD of Pearl in front of the Sydney Harbour Bridge and Opera House.

'Of course, Pearl Harbor,' he muttered to himself. 'Why didn't I think of that before? Seven digits, it works exactly.' He looked up at the nineteenth century engraving of the British Camp on the Malvern Hills on the wall and had another brainwave. He rang Penny immediately.

*

'Read me that header to the message we got at lunchtime again,' he asked.

'WSW. Don't take clues from Toposcope hounds, blessings and Glory to God!' I replied.

'God, I'm stupid, I thought WSW was an initial of some

236

sort. Have you got that iPad of yours? From the beacon, which towns would you hit if you went west southwest would you say, Penny?' he asked. It took me a minute to look up the map function.

'Alcester, Worcester, Malvern…' I replied.

'Yes of course you do, Malvern, how stupid I am. "Nimrod confused"', oh how stupid of me, yes that's clever, so very clever. I think we may need a little bit more work on this, Penny. Think back to when we met Miss Taylor in the hotel, did you happen to write down exactly that cryptic clue about Nimrod she gave us?'

On the other end of the line, I opened my notepad again and read: 'Don't be confused, my mighty Nimrod, it's in G-minor after all.'

Hunter groaned. 'Which of course also refers to me given my name is Hunter – Nimrod the mighty hunter – *confused*. OK so "confused" in a cryptic clue would normally signify an anagram. What's Nimrod an anagram of?' he asked. I started to scribble on my pad.

'Mindor, Romind, D-minor?' I answered.

'She said "G-minor after all". Think. What does she mean?' he replied. I could imagine him beating his brow with his hand. 'What else did she say?'

'But as a rule you should always keep the major key in sight.'

He gave out a gasp of discovery. 'Yes, if I remember right, Elgar's 'Nimrod' variation is in the key of G-minor not D-minor, so that works. But she also made a little joke about your name didn't she – bright Penny? And if I take that first, the letter 'd' is the old money symbol for a penny and D-major would therefore be the major key. What's the significance of D-major to Elgar?'

'The key of one of his famous pieces?' I guessed.

'Maybe, but I have another idea, what would you see on an old penny?'

'The Queen's head?'

'And on the tails side?'

'I don't know, a portcullis isn't it?'

'No, I mean on an old penny.'

'Britannia?'

'Yes, Britannia, that's right.'

'Britannia or 'Rule Britannia'?' I added in triumph.

'Yes but that's by Thomas Arne not Elgar. Oh but of course, well done Penny. Beethoven's 'Variations on Rule Britannia' are in D-major. Many people believe that's the secret theme that runs through Elgar's Variations. So we've got 'Nimrod' in G-minor and 'Rule Britannia' in D-major. What happens if you write out the scale of G-minor from 'Nimrod' and the scale of D-major from 'Rule Britannia' side by side?'

'That would be G A Bb C D Eb F and D E F# G A B C#,' I said. Scales were one thing I'd had lots of practice at over the years. I wrote out the two scales alongside each other.

'Bravo, so if you transpose all the G-minor notes that appear in your transcription with the corresponding D-major notes in the scale in the emails, what happens?' We were beginning to see how Pearl's mind worked. I worked away at the paper for a minute or two and then shouted out in triumph.

"LIAR THIEF COWARD ADULTERER'.'

'Bullseye!' he replied in triumph. 'Now we're in business, but what on earth is she up to? We'd better go and talk to her again.'

'But she's already left.'

'What?'

'She was leaving for London this evening, don't you remember?'

'Damn, OK first thing in the morning we need to get on to her.'

CHAPTER SEVENTEEN

THE RETURN OF THE DANCING MEN – (CON FUOCO)

Randolph Turpin became world middleweight champion after he beat Sugar Ray Robinson on a fifteen round decision. He shot his 4-year-old daughter Carmen twice then ended his life at Gwen's Transport Café, near Leamington, on May 17, 1966.

Based on Wikipedia, *Randolph Turpin*

When the housekeeper found Arthur Troyte sprawled dead on the daybed early on Monday morning, the blood that had dribbled from the bullet wound in his head had already dried into a sticky brown patch like a halo around his brow. An old-fashioned Browning pistol lay on the floor just out of reach of his fingers.

*

When we arrived at the scene twenty minutes later, we noticed at once the gold ring with similar markings to the one that Nariman had been wearing. The forensics team arrived shortly afterwards and their preliminary examination revealed no other signs of a wound than the gunshot to the head.

Hunter turned to the shocked housekeeper and asked, 'When precisely did you last see Mr Troyte alive?'

'I left him with his lunch on Saturday – he was very tired after the journey,' she replied. 'I had fully stocked the larder for him for the weekend but he said that he would probably be dining out that evening and away on Sunday at the convention. He was due to be speaking yesterday and he said he would see me bright and early this morning.' Her voice was nervous and still trembling from the shock of her unpleasant find. I knew she was clearly hiding something.

'And what happened last night?' I asked.

'How do you mean?'

'You were supposed to go round and check up on him last night; you got a call from Hugh Powell?' I said to the housekeeper, who looked at me guiltily, knowing that I had caught her out.

'I had something I had to take care of at home, he had my number, and he only needed to call,' she replied defensively.

'Looks like that might have been difficult in the circumstances,' I chided with my most ironic voice. Of course what she didn't know was that I was feeling even worse than her about this given that I had not insisted on seeing Troyte the previous afternoon.

'OK Penny, that's enough. We all make mistakes, don't we? What do you make of the bullet wound, Alice?' asked Hunter.

'Point blank range, I'd be very surprised if this isn't the weapon, but forensics will test it as soon as they can,' she said.

'Seems like a classic suicide, even though there's no note,' Sergeant Jones chipped in.

'Indeed, sergeant, but we also know from Mr Baxter that a Browning like this was stolen by Rohit Dhawan on Saturday evening, so we certainly can't discount foul play. Let me see the victim's hand a second,' said Hunter.

With Jones's help, Alice turned him on his back.

'No sign of any damage to the web,' Hunter said, inspecting the skin between Troyte's forefinger and thumb. 'That's not conclusive but this pistol has a tendency to 'bite' the web of the shooter's hand, between the thumb and forefinger. You'd expect to see a mark if it was a suicide.'

'But if it's not a suicide then it must be murder and Rohit's in the frame?' I asked, trying to get back into the action.

'Or an accident, we do have to keep an open mind, Penny. But equally, if you were planning to kill yourself, would you really choose a gun with such a poor reputation for reliability? I suppose it could be a coincidence but this single-action Browning Hi-Power is a very unusual handgun in the UK. On the other hand, it's unlikely to be a hit; a criminal gang would tend to prefer semi-automatics for a hit.'

'I've just found this screwed up in his pocket,' said Alice. She gave him a glove and then passed him a ball of white paper marked with the now familiar dancing men.

'Wow,' said Hunter. 'I didn't expect that. Let's see what this one says; why don't you have a go, Penny?' At last I was useful again.

He spread out the piece of paper and I brought out the earlier copy that we had made of the longer message with the quotation inscribed on the Toposcope. I got out my pencil and began to transcribe the letters corresponding to the dancing figures into my notebook.

'It's meaningless again, Sir. But then again this code is different to the other one, look: they are all holding flags, not just the men at the end of each word.'

'Of course, that's very well spotted. Maybe for this one we just need to use some simple semaphore then.'

I got out my iPad again and substituted the letters for semaphore characters read off the screen. My work quickly revealed a new but altogether more chilling message.

'TROYTE PREPARE TO MEET YOUR GOD.'

'I think suicide is beginning to look much less likely, don't you?' asked Hunter.

'And it certainly doesn't look like an accident now,' I replied.

'Yes, it looks as though we have another murder on our hands. But the nature of the message and the code is perplexing – we need to get Rohit in and track down Pearl.'

'Inspector, one more thing,' Alice said as we turned to go. 'We haven't finished our report yet, but the victim from Saturday – Mr Nariman – the indication is that he was dying already of mercury poisoning.'

'Really, could it have been something in his diet, fish, sushi, maybe?' asked the inspector.

'Unlikely. The concentrations were far too high for that unless he ate nothing else. Evidence so far suggests he was being poisoned.'

★

In the control room at the Woodbine Studio, Eddie was in the middle of mixing a track for a local indie band on the Audient Asp8024. Absentmindedly, he reached down into his sports bag for his lunch and instead pulled out a brown paper package. It was the envelope that Pearl had given him the night before to give to DI Hunter. He had forgotten to drop it off at the police station as Pearl had requested. He opened it slightly and pulled out a sheet of paper.

Room 23, The Holly Hotel – remember a day of Infamy.

He called Hunter immediately on his mobile to tell him about the letter.

★

Filming had resumed and the square had recovered its theatrical 'normality' after the disturbing events of the weekend. Jack was talking to Penn who was dressed in a towelling gown. They had been debating how Penn should leap so as to fake the fall from the balcony of the second floor window. They would need to cut to the stunt man for the real shot, but Penn needed to give them the start of the scene.

Across the square, Izzie was watching somewhat anxiously but proudly from the windows of the top floor of Sherridge House. The other nurses were looking on as well, all eagerly waiting for the action to begin as Penn removed his robe.

★

When we reached the Holly Hotel, we found that our female American friend, who had occupied Room 23 that weekend, had indeed checked out the previous evening, but she hadn't left any forwarding address as she had promised to. We hurried up the stairs with the concierge in tow. He was complaining loudly about the intrusion and the lack of a warrant. I snapped at him to be quiet.

'Get this door open quickly!' ordered Hunter when we reached the room. He seemed genuinely angry, a tone in his voice that I had not heard before. We knew we had both made mistakes here in not following up with Mr Troyte the previous evening. The concierge unlocked the door as quickly as he could, steeled by the directive tone of Hunter's commands.

We entered the room and Hunter ran straight over to the closet safe that he had seen Pearl put the package away in on his previous visit to the room.

I studied the keypad. 'It's locked with a combination,' I said, and then turned to the concierge who shrugged his shoulders.

'We'd have to get the locksmith in – we don't have codes to open the safes ourselves, it's company policy.'

Hunter studied the safe for a few seconds more and then said out of nowhere, 'Try 12, 7, 19, 41,' I tried this combination and was surprised to hear the electronic beep as the safe door opened.

The small question of how he knew the combination was left hanging as I opened the door and removed a collection of papers from the safe and a larger package. There was a signed copy of Pearl Taylor's promotional photograph with the message, *My dearest Gus, xxx*, there was also an airline ticket stub to Sydney, New South Wales and a flyer for a concert the next month in London at the Elgar Room, *An evening with Pearl Taylor, please join me, P xxx*, which I handed to Hunter with a wry smile.

I opened the larger package. There were a number of flash drives and computer disks as well as papers and photographs inside. At first, I had to turn my eyes away in disgust as I inspected the images that I pulled out one by one from the package but then quickly realised that I recognised both Troyte and the other man in the printed photographs. *Isn't this Bas?* I thought, *Eddie's friend? How could that be?*

I was soon back working my magic machine. 'Flight BA15 left on time at 21.15pm last night, do you want me to check with the airline that she got on, Sir?'

'Yes, but I suspect Miss Taylor is well on her way to Sydney by now. Can you just summarise the timeline for me, Penny?' Before I did so Hunter dismissed the concierge and warned him not to say anything about what he had just seen to anybody. I checked my notes.

'Well we saw her here at around 2pm,' I began. 'She'd been somewhere that morning and returned just after lunch. The curator at Compton Verney says Troyte arrived around 10am to give his lecture but did not leave there until around 4pm, as he was feeling unwell. Hugh was there visiting

Claudia Baxter and dropped him off back in Leamington about 4.30pm. So that's still enough time for Pearl to meet him when he got back, kill him here and then get to Heathrow to catch a 9.15pm plane.'

'That's true, but Eddie told me earlier that she was also with him and Carrie singing at the nursing home from 4 till 5pm and that she was due to catch a taxi to London at 6pm.' I frowned, I was a little annoyed that Eddie had chosen to tell this to Hunter and not me.

'But it's still just about enough time.'

'All the same, I'm pretty sure that Miss Taylor is not our murderer. Given all the clues she's left for us and your account of what the curator said went on at the conference yesterday, I rather suspect that she has already had her revenge for whatever Troyte did to her.'

'What about the photos? Maybe she was planning to blackmail him.'

'A good idea but even that's not a very likely scenario for murder, unless something went wrong. I can't imagine she needs the money either.'

'Well, whatever happened, she has certainly been wasting our time during a very serious investigation.'

'True, but I don't think we can drag her back to the UK just for that.'

'Ok, Sir, what do you want me to do next?' I said in frustration. I knew my boss was a fan of Miss Taylor's but this had begun to feel like he was getting dangerously close to protecting her for personal reasons. Hunter must have noticed this tone in my voice as his next statement was clearly designed to get me back on side.

'I'm sorry; forgive my funny little ways. The thing that's confusing me is that I can't see any connection between the Troyte and Nariman murders, have you got any thoughts on that from your research to date?'

'Well obviously they knew each other from the past.'

245

'Yes there could be something significant there, but again, it hardly gives us a motive for murder. What else, Penny, what's the connection, what are we missing? Might it be about something that happened, not about the man himself?'

'Well, as you said yesterday, the phone lines were cut and the sniper shot that killed Nariman made that killing look like a hit or professional assassination, but Troyte's death is completely different. It looks more like a domestic than a professional job.'

'I agree, they could be completely separate incidents but we also need to consider who would have wanted them both killed. Nariman I could understand, given his business interests, we just need to work out who wanted to kill him enough, but this guy is just a mildly successful Midwest architect on a personal trip to Europe as far as we know. I just don't get any possible motivation yet for the Troyte murder.'

'Maybe someone thought he knew something about Nariman's death, something that they needed to shut him up about.'

'Possible, but it seems unlikely given that he had hadn't even arrived in Leamington when Nariman was killed.'

'Perhaps he knew something about why Nariman was going to be assassinated.'

'Yes I think that's more promising. We do really need to find out exactly what Nariman knew or did that would have caused someone to want to get rid of him.'

'OK, I'll get on to it again straight away, but I'm still confused about Miss Taylor. Do you want me to get the Sydney police to question her or not?'

'No, we know where she is, and an international artist like her has fixed appointments for months to come. She hasn't exactly been covering her tracks. For now, it looks to me like we should just work out what our next steps should be here. Although I'm intrigued to know how she knew that Troyte would be here this weekend, but let's think about that more before we create an international incident.'

'OK and I'm sure you know I'm dying to ask you this. How on earth did you know the combination to the safe?' I asked, stroking his ego a little more. He laughed, but looked distinctly pleased to be asked.

'Let's say it was an informed guess – 'a day that will live in infamy'. That's the expression Miss Taylor used with me when I asked about the origin of her name, and it was on the note she left Eddie – it was originally said by Roosevelt to describe Pearl Harbor.'

'Pearl Harbor?'

'It was attacked by surprise by the Japanese fleet on December 7, Nineteen-Forty-One.'

'So, 12, 7, 19, 41, that's very clever.' I said, realising that he had even got the American date system the right way round. He was truly a genius. I reminded myself that that was why I still wanted to work for him, despite all his foibles and predilection for unsuitable women.

*

In the autopsy room, Alice removed Troyte's clothes and then rolled the body on to its side. She noticed and then pointed to a freshly tattooed scar that had been carved into the perineum below Troyte' buttocks – three Greek letters – $A Z \Omega$. She got on to the phone straight away to Hunter, who put the call on his speakerphone.

'It's the same mark as on both the rings,' said Alice.

'Are you absolutely sure, Alice, can you look closer?' asked Hunter. In the autopsy room, Alice looked again at Troyte's ring and compared the markings to the drawing in her notebook.

'As usual, you're absolutely right; both rings are marked with APX, the architect's fraternity. But this one is different, I'm afraid my Greek is not great, Sir.' She described the shape of the letters to him over the phone.

'Alpha, Zeta, Omega. Penny, can you look that up?'

'Just give me a second.' I turned on my iPad and put the new combination of letters into Google.

'Alpha, Zeta, Omega, it's a pharmaceutical fraternity,' I read and then noticed the next sentence with excitement. 'It is also known as the 'Dead Men's Club', Sir.'

Hunter turned to me and whispered, 'What more does your magic machine say about this Dead Men's Club?'

'Nothing much, Sir, they just seem to be a bunch of pharmacists doing charity stuff. What do you think it means?'

'At the moment it means we have a bit more than a practical joker on our hands – the Dead Men's Club is becoming more apt by the minute.'

'And Pearl Taylor started a pharmacy course didn't she? So what are we going to do next, Sir?' I asked.

'Well what would you suggest, if you were me?' he replied, but I was at a loss also.

'Really, Sir, I've no idea. It's a confusing picture with all these codes and secret societies. Maybe we'll get something on the identity of the Tamils from Sri Lanka.'

'Hopefully, but in the meantime we need to speak to this Rohit and let's get back on to researching Sir William's business interests. My guess is there is something there he doesn't want us to know about, something that links him and Nariman and maybe even Troyte. Meanwhile, your fraternity research has given me another little idea. Stay here, I'm going to pay Sir William another visit but it's probably best if you don't come this time.'

The initial forensics report on the Browning proved interesting; the serial number was from a batch that was produced by the Ishapore Arms Factory for Indian Army service and that had been decommissioned several years earlier. They had also now confirmed that Winnie was killed by a massive overdose of Moban or Molindrone, a drug no longer approved in the UK for psychosis and one therefore that the nursing home had no access to. Interestingly also Moban is an anagram of No MAB.

★

Hunter was seated again in the library of No. 6 Clarendon Square.

'Sir William, I wonder if you'd had any more thoughts about whether there are any business arrangements that may have triggered these events,' he asked.

'Inspector, you asked me that yesterday and my answer is unchanged. I really can't think of anything.'

'OK then this may seem a strange question, but have you ever had any dealings with US fraternities by any chance?'

Sir William laughed. 'Well that is a most surprising question, especially coming from a police officer. But no, of course not, those fraternities are really just like the Masons aren't they? They're silly games for middle managers?'

Hunter told him about the murder of Nariman's friend. Sir William responded quickly yet did not look completely surprised.

'My God, another murder? In the circumstances I had completely forgotten about that gentleman, Inspector.'

'Yes indeed, we all had to some extent. Nariman and Troyte obviously knew each other from way back, but the only real connection we can find is that they were once both architecture students at the University of Michigan in Ann Arbor and belonged to the same fraternity. That's why I asked about that aspect – I was wondering if there was anything there you could remember?'

'Well again, Hunter, nothing that I am aware of.'

'OK, thank you. Do you know anything else about their past, anything that linked them that might account for the fact that they have both been murdered?'

Sir William hesitated slightly before speaking.

'Well, yes, there is something, but it's a long time ago and very personal. Apparently Arish got Nadia's grandmother pregnant just before Troyte married her – there was some sort of three-way thing going on. The woman died in childbirth and Arish had the resultant child spirited away back to Sri Lanka and adopted her. That child, Nadia's mother, also had Nadia out of wedlock, she is dead now too but I can't believe that would have caused someone to want to murder either of them.'

'I agree, but we should not rule anything out, Sir William. On another matter, do you by any chance keep any weapons in the house, any guns for example that might be missing?'

'No, your officers have already asked, guns are my ex-wife's department; I'm a rotten shot, I've never really been interested. I certainly don't have any guns on the premises.'

'One final question if I may, Sir William. Are any of your employees ex-military, UK, Canadian maybe, Singapore or Indian Army?'

'Well I can't say for certain, possibly, we recruit widely. Do you suspect an insider now? I thought you said these Tamils were terrorists?'

'No suspicions yet, just checking all possibilities. Maybe I can get one of my officers to check over the personnel lists of your companies as a precaution.'

'Well of course, but really Inspector, we need you to

make some real progress here. You seem to be trawling about for ideas, all this secret society and secret code stuff. Do I need to speak to the chief constable to make sure you have the right resources?'

Hunter looked at Sir William intensely. 'There's no need, I have the resources I need. The secret codes are certainly a puzzling element, but I think we are making good progress. By the way I hope the press have left you alone.'

'You're not a very political animal are you, Inspector Hunter?'

'I'm just doing my job, Sir William, the best way I know how. I leave the politics to smarter people like you.'

'Yes, but you know if you solve this you'll be up for chief inspector next. I could help that along, you know.' Hunter looked at him, finding it hard to hide the look of disdain on his face. The bad taste was returning to his palate as he sensed the corruption in this man.

'Really, Sir William, as I said I am just trying to do the right thing, that's all.'

'Well you don't have long to sort all this out and you need to learn to watch your back Inspector, that's my advice to you.'

'Thank you, Sir William, I'll remember that, but I think that's all for now.'

In the study of No. 6, Sir William was on the phone to the chief constable immediately after Hunter left, demanding to know what they were doing to wrap up the case. Having heard the inspector's comments about Troyte's death, he was even more eager to make sure that nothing could possibly stick to him.

After he had finished with the chief constable, Sir William called Khand again on his special mobile.

'He's on to something, something about ex-Indian Army personnel.'

'OK let me handle this; I've got someone in his office who will let me know what's going on.'

'My God, you've got a spy on his team?'

'Of course.'

Later that morning Sir William left for London, intending to meet with friends who managed party business, to see if he could get them to calm down the noise around Whitehall that had been caused by DC Penny Dore's persistent enquiries into his business affairs.

★

After his meeting with Sir William, Hunter decided to walk back to his flat, which was around a quarter of a mile away. Sir William's guard had slipped; he had told him something very important in their meeting. Only his team knew about the *secret codes*, but Sir William had definitely used those words in addition to the *secret societies* that they had discussed. Hunter was worried; he was sure this was more than a coincidence. It meant that either Sir William was involved in the codes or he had a leak on his team. He needed to think about this one, he had been working pretty much non-stop over the last forty-eight hours and even he recognised the need for some downtime occasionally.

On the way back to his flat, he stopped off at Kang's corner store to pick up the local newspaper, a bottle of scotch and a ready meal that he could reheat in the microwave for dinner. As he walked past the Dell, he could hear voices in the playground below. After the storm of the previous night the air had cooled considerably. *Kids probably*, he could hear a guitar and a girl singing. He thought about walking through the park to see what was going on, but he was feeling very tired. He noticed the birdsong as he crossed the road toward his flat in Strathearn Road and the last flowers of summer in the window boxes of the large house on

Beauchamp Hill. He did not notice the two men that ran up behind him and forced a crowbar down on his shoulder. At least not until it was far too late.

He woke half an hour later, bound, gagged, blindfolded and tied to a chair. He could sense others in the room, could hear murmurings in a language that he did not understand. He struggled to free himself to no avail.

Suddenly the sacking was ripped from his head and his eyes were filled by a strong light source from across a table. He blinked and turned away from the brightness. He could now see the blurred shapes of three or four masked men in the room, all brandishing weapons of some sort. One of them lashed him across the face with a crude mace fitted with leather-thongs. He felt the blood running down his scalp onto his cheek. One of his arms throbbed like it was broken and each hand felt like it had been stamped on. He couldn't register any feeling from his legs apart from a shooting pain in his right knee.

'Now my friends, it's so good of the great Detective Inspector Hunter to drop in on us at last,' said a quiet voice, clearly well-educated and with a distinct Asian accent. Hunter could hear the voice and the distant sound of something that sounded like snooker balls clicking in the background, but couldn't see anything beyond the strong light that shone directly into his face.

'Who are you, what do you want?' he murmured through the gag that was bound tightly around his face. His knee was really beginning to hurt him now; he thought that they might have broken his patella.

'Oh don't worry, Inspector. This is just a little fireside chat. We are good friends of the police, who just want to help you close this case quickly and painlessly.'

'Like hell you do.'

'Please, Inspector, we are on your side, and I am sure you

understand what I mean by closing the case. You are making it far too complicated. You have your victims, you have your assailants, their motivations and in a short time you will be provided with the murder weapons and the rest of the evidence you need. As I said, it is really very simple and at the moment you are trying to make this all too complicated. It really isn't. I think you know that and I hope you'll see to it that it is wrapped up quickly.'

'I'm not going to be intimidated and diverted by a bunch of thugs. How do you know all this anyway?'

'Oh Inspector, I quite understand your point of view. But please think of this as a little guidance rather than intimidation. We are just trying to move you along a little in the right direction to the inevitable conclusion.'

'Is that why my arm feels like it's been broken and I can't feel my legs properly?'

'Oh yes I am sorry about that, some of my colleagues can get a bit carried away I'm afraid. Like you, they just want to do their job properly too. And I know of course that you yourself will bear any amount of pain, you are a proud and brave man, aren't you?'

'Don't believe anything you do will stop me from pursuing these murders until the culprits are behind bars and that includes you lot, whoever you are.'

'Inspector, I just ask you to consider this. Next time I'm afraid it won't be you in that chair and none of us want to see what my friends here would do to such a pretty colleague of yours, do we?' He pushed a photograph of Penny into Hunter's line of sight.

'You bastards! Who's been feeding all this to you?'

'We have very reliable sources, Inspector, impeccable. And by the way my parentage too is of the highest quality, but that is of no real consequence.'

'What are you planning to do with me?'

'Oh you can go now. I'm going to ask my friends to put

that mask back on and dispose of you somewhere you won't be found too quickly.' He felt strong hands drag him away and received several more blows to his head and body before he passed out again.

When he woke for the second time he could smell earth, vegetation and something worse smeared around his head. It was cold and he sensed immediately from the damp air on his exposed skin that he was in the open. He could hear the sound of running water nearby. His eyes were still masked and he was gagged. He tried to call out but his voice was muffled completely by the gag. He wriggled his hands, which were tied behind his back. He could move them a little, and strained toward the pocket where he kept his cell phone, but it was just out of reach. His legs appeared to be tied to something so that he couldn't move them at all. From the rough feel on his ankles it appeared to be the trunk of a tree.

The pain was beginning to return all round his body, so much so that he thought he might faint. He struggled again but to no avail. He realised there was nothing much he could do for the moment but wait and he settled himself as comfortably as he could to wait for a long time if necessary, gritting his teeth against the pain. Surprisingly there was already another sound, the sound of panting and sniffing in the undergrowth. Some sort of large animal was searching through the vegetation nearby; he wondered if it was a fox. He heard a bark and then a yelp as the first animal was chased away by another, larger dog – the bark was a familiar sound he recognised only too well.

'Come on Dan, come on, over here boy,' he mumbled through the gag.

★

'Are you feeling any better, Sir?' I asked as I sat alongside Detective Sergeant Jones at Hunter's bedside in Warwick Hospital. It was nearly 10pm on Monday evening and Hunter had been patched up as well as possible.

'What do you think, Penny? I've got a smashed patella, my arm is broken in two places, my fingers feel like they have been through a wringer and I've got 23 stitches around my body. It would be fair to say that I have felt better.' I could hear the pain he must be feeling strained in his voice.

'Yes Sir, I'm sorry for asking. Well at least with Dan finding you, you know there is a dog.' *That was a stupid thing to say* I thought as soon as the words left my mouth.

'A dog, you mean God? If I was sure of that, I wouldn't have joined the police force, would I?' He didn't get the joke. This was probably the first time I had really seen him lose his cool. He was grimacing in pain but appeared to regret immediately talking to me quite so sharply; I was only trying to cheer him up after all. Hunter took a few minutes to describe his experiences, leaving out the bit about the threat to me as I found out later. He asked for all known snooker and billiard halls to be searched as soon as possible, given the noise that he had heard in the background during his interrogation.

'OK, Jones, what progress are we actually making here?' he snapped.

'Well Sir, there's been quite a lot going on but maybe not a whole lot of progress. Forensics came back to us on the black cab. Nothing at all, it's as if it's been wiped completely clean by someone. They confirm that the dent was most likely caused by a lamppost, not by an impact with a body. We had to release the taxi driver as we had nothing on him, the plates were not enough, and in any case the only linkage was that actress whose statement is not admissible because of the drugs we found in her. We are still keeping a watch on where he goes. And the murder weapons, Sir, they've confirmed that the sniper shot and the spent copper cartridge we found in the square were both .22 LR calibre, the same as Lady Mary's missing rook rifle, the one that the kids found in the playground this morning. What's more, the Browning Sir?'

'Yes, what is it?'

'It matches the one that Mr Baxter reported missing from his collection: Canadian Army issue, Sir, not Indian, we got the serial numbers confused initially. There are fingerprints all over the gun that match those on the paper Mr Baxter gave us written by Rohit Dhawan. We've searched his digs, it has been turned over properly by someone and there's no sign of him anywhere. It looks like he's disappeared.'

'Damn. We need to find him. What about Troyte?'

'Toxicology found traces of Rohypnol and Scopolamine in his blood,' I said.

'Scopolamine? Are we looking for Dr Crippen now?' muttered Hunter. 'So what do they think could have caused that?'

'It's only small quantities; it can be used to cure motion sickness, Sir. It's possible he might simply have taken it to sleep on the flight over,' I suggested.

'True, but it's also popular amongst criminals as a truth drug or to drug a victim's drink; often men, targeted by young, attractive, women.'

'I didn't know that, Sir. This still doesn't make any sense at all, does it?' I added helpfully.

'You're too right, Penny. Ever thought you were at the wrong end of being given the run around, my friends?'

'What do you mean, Sir?'

'That's how I feel at the moment, that's all.' He shook his head and took a sip from a glass of water by the bedside.

'I could do with something stronger.'

'Here, don't tell the nurses,' Detective Sergeant Jones

unscrewed the top of a hip flask and passed it to Hunter, who took a long swig.

'OK Penny, what about the fingerprints on the knife, and the dental records of the two assailants, were there any results?'

'Yes Sir, we have their names now. Both of them are from Tamil Nadu, associates of a terrorist group, both arrived on an Air India flight last week.'

'And what do we know about Sir William and Nariman's business dealings?'

'There's nothing at all yet, Sir.'

'Nothing at all?'

'We have a forensic accountant looking at their companies but they have found absolutely no connections so far at all.'

'OK, I'm beginning to clutch at straws now. How about the mercury poisoning – was it a box of chocolates with holes in the base by any chance?' I knew that he was referring to a famous case tackled by Sir Ronald Spilsbury, a personal hero of his, as he had mentioned it before.

'Forensics' latest theory is that it may have been the tea, Sir.'

'The tea? Are we going back to Wonderland now? You'll tell me next he was suffering from Mad Hatter syndrome that he got from felt-making.' Hunter was sounding more and more exasperated as each answer seemed to send him down yet another blind alley.

'No Sir, the tea stove that his granddaughter had been using to prepare his morning tea – the gilding may have been contaminated with mercury, apparently that is not uncommon in village metal working.'

'That seems a bit unlikely – he hadn't been here that long. Was she using anything else alongside the tea?'

'Some herbal preparation, a bit like ginseng I think.'

'You mean rasa shastra. For heaven's sake, doesn't forensics know anything? Rasa shastra is a mixture of minerals and herbs used commonly in Ayurveda medicines – it's been tested with up to 20 per cent heavy metals.'

'OK then, let me follow that up with them, Sir.'

'I suppose you'll tell me next we have a full confession from whoever shot Troyte.'

'No Sir, but I think I've worked out the meaning of *ningma*,' I said, a little excited. I knew this one was going to cheer him up.

'You mean the word that Alice, Dottie and Hugh thought they heard the motorcyclist saying?'

'Yes, all that stuff about cryptic clues and anagrams got me thinking, I think *ningma* was probably *enigma*,' I said, now exceedingly pleased with myself.

'You're a genius Penny, have you got that wretched iPad with you?'

'Yes, Sir.'

'Put 'enigma' and 'Sir William Flyte' in there and see what you get.'

I pulled out the iPad and fired it up, entering the words into the search engine. I scanned the first couple of entries then spotted it.

'OK the third result is around a 'Project Enigma', a major government signals contract for the army. Sir, it says in the detail that Sir William Flyte's company is advising the Defence Ministry procurement team on it.'

'Bingo! Now I'm feeling a lot better Penny.'

To say I was glowing was an understatement.

★

During that same evening, the Sikh taxi driver joined his friends in the snooker club behind the railway bridge in the old town. He received high fives all round from the other members of the gang following his release without charge that afternoon.

'I told you there would be nothing to worry about, clean as a whistle: that lamppost did the trick didn't it? That bent copper did us all a favour with his report.'

'So what are we going to do about Hunter, Boss?'

'Oh I think we've scared him off for now, but let's keep a close eye on him. I want to know exactly what he does from now on, reports on the hour from our friend please.'

'It will be a pleasure, Boss.'

When the snooker club was raided by the police after hours, they found nothing except for some somewhat dubious activities involving lap dancers in the back of the club.

★

On the same Monday evening, Sir William had arrived in London from Leamington in time for dinner with his friends who managed the party business. As a result, the chief constable was woken up by a late night call from one of the special advisors at Number Ten.

'Chief Constable, I understand that one of your detectives has been asking questions around Whitehall about certain confidential government procurement programmes,' said a voice trained in the civil service, the Guards and Eton.

'I am sorry, Sir Brian, I don't know what you are referring to.'

'A Constable Dore, works for a DI Hunter, part of your CID?'

'Ah yes, well what of it, Sir Brian? Hunter's working on a serious murder investigation, you know that?'

'Of course and we would always want to provide the police with any information we can that will help you with your enquiries. However, I want you to understand that these are very sensitive projects and I would really appreciate it if you could direct any further questions through me directly rather than broadcasting them around Whitehall. Would you be good enough to ask your DI to direct any questions he may have through this channel? I think that would be better for all concerned. The Secretary of State is fully aware of the situation. Do we have an understanding?'

'Yes Sir Brian, of course, I completely understand.' He heard a click and then the telephone line went dead. The chief constable swore to himself and then rang Hunter but there was no answer, so he telephoned his PA at home where she was just getting ready for bed.

'Hilda, track Hunter down for me and get him on the line as quickly as possible.'

★

Back at Number Ten, Sir Brian turned to the gentleman standing next to him.

'OK, Bill, is that what you needed from me?'

'Yes, Brian, I am really much obliged, can I get a transcript?'

'Yes of course, all calls are recorded here. Will you be in the club tomorrow?'

'Around 4pm for tea?'

'Perfect, I'll bring it round with me.'

CHAPTER EIGHTEEN

Time for a Disappearing Act – (Allegro Marziale)

I owe you many apologies, dear Watson, but it was all-important that it should be thought I was dead, and it is quite certain that you would not have written so convincing an account of my unhappy end had you not yourself thought that it was true.

Arthur Conan Doyle, *The Empty House*

'Good Morning, Henderson. I really need to speak to Sir William again, is he here by any chance?' Hunter asked Sir William's butler politely as he opened the door to No. 6. He had discharged himself from the hospital against the objections of the ward sister and was now hobbling around on crutches.

'I'm afraid he's down in London, Inspector, he won't be back until early this evening,' said the butler. Hunter looked at his watch instinctively; this was exactly as he had hoped and would enable him to broach the next question.

'OK, well in that case would I be able to speak to Lady Flyte this morning?'

The butler looked at him doubtfully, but given his injuries he reluctantly agreed to let him wait in the morning room rather than leave him standing at the door while he asked his mistress whether she would see him or not. He added that he was really not sure that she would want to see anybody just yet. Despite Henderson's words of caution, she did in fact appear after a few minutes; her eyes still heavy and dark, her cheeks streaked with tears.

'Inspector, what on earth has happened to you?' she asked, her voice concerned and still somewhat cracked and strained.

'Nothing to worry about, I had a little accident when I was out with some friends last night,' he said, not wishing to concern her more.

'Well you must be more careful, we're depending on you. Please tell me what I can do for you, apart from offer you a cup of tea that is?'

'Well, tea would be a very welcome start,' he said. As expected, she was putting on a brave face. Even before he met her briefly on Saturday he had developed a picture of her from what others had said of a very calm and composed personality. She seemed like a remarkable woman in her own right; it was obvious to see that she had class, just from the way she dressed and the way she moved as she entered the room. He had heard that she was exceptionally bright also, with a cultured appreciation of art and music. He intended to be very careful how he proceeded with this interview, as he realised it could be pivotal. Lady Flyte signalled to the butler to bring them tea and then turned her attention fully toward Hunter.

'So Inspector?'

'Lady Flyte, I'm so terribly sorry about your loss and I really didn't want to disturb you during this period, but your husband is apparently not available this morning and there are a couple of sensitive matters I would really appreciate some help with concerning your grandfather's murder.' She nodded at him and indicated with her hands that he should continue.

'Please call me Nadia, Inspector. I'm a simple village girl really; I don't go with all this Lady Flyte nonsense.'

'Well Lady Flyte, err, Nadia then, I understand that you have a friend called Rohit Dhawan, a translator and writer?' She looked slightly taken aback by the direction of this question, as if she was expecting something else entirely.

'Well yes I do, although he is probably better described as an acquaintance than a friend. He used to work for my grandfather but I still see him occasionally.' Hunter noticed that she flushed slightly as she said this. Her answer sounded forced; she was clearly not used to this kind of direct personal examination. He already knew that the relationship was much closer than she was admitting to.

'Do you by any chance happen to know where he is?'

'No, I'm afraid not,' she answered hesitantly, catching the frown on the Inspector's face. 'My God, has something happened to him as well?'

'We're not sure at the moment. Are you certain you haven't seen him? This is really quite important.' He was being very careful, he realised he was at risk of pushing too hard and didn't want her to clam up on him. She paused for a minute or two before answering as if she was searching her memory.

'Well, now that I think about it, maybe we did speak very briefly on Saturday evening, there was so much going on that day. I wasn't thinking clearly a minute ago.'

'Of course and I'm sorry to be impertinent, Nadia, but did you say speak or meet?'

She looked at him mortified, her eyes met his and he could see the look of helplessness, almost pleading, within them. His questions had clearly disturbed her, cutting across the sensitivity of polite discourse, but he could see that she also wanted to know where this line of questioning was leading. For a few moments there was complete silence in the room, before he tried again.

'Don't worry, Nadia, I'm afraid I do know a little about your relationship and any private information will absolutely stay with me,' he said gently. 'I really do need to find Rohit. I think he and possibly you could be in some personal jeopardy.' Again, she said nothing for a minute and then sat down rather heavily on one of the armchairs. As she answered him she was looking down at the floor, rather than addressing him directly.

'OK, Inspector, well yes, he did come to see me on Saturday evening. We had been exchanging texts during the day and I had asked him to come over. We have a signal that he uses to enter from the balcony outside my room. Please understand there isn't anything physical between us, it's purely a long-standing and deep friendship. Anyway, I was nervous at first when I eventually heard his special knock, but I was also worried and desperately wanted to see him, so I took the risk and opened the shutters. He didn't stay very long as there was a lot of noise outside and people were milling about downstairs. He was scared silly as well.'

'May I enquire why he took the risk of coming to see you then, in person?'

'I needed to see him, in fact I insisted. I was afraid that he would be next in line after my grandfather and I wanted to warn him, but I couldn't risk doing that over the phone,' she delivered this line in a completely matter-of-fact way, as if she was informing him about the weather or a relative's upcoming wedding arrangements. He decided not to ask her directly yet what she meant by this statement and left the question hanging between them.

'OK, well that's most helpful but it's very important that you tell me absolutely everything you know. I too believe that both your lives may be in danger. He's been missing since Saturday afternoon, there's no sign of him at his flat but it looks like someone else has been there.' This was a minor white lie, but he needed to know exactly how much Nadia knew about Rohit's movements.

'Oh my gosh, Inspector, so do you know where he is?'

She is a smart woman, he thought, realising that she had already worked out that he knew more about the situation than he was letting on.

'Not at the moment but we are looking. We know him at the station because he occasionally does translation work for us as well. He's a good lad, but he may be in a lot of trouble and we really need to find him quickly. Mr Baxter at No. 10 told us that he turned up at his writing class on Saturday as normal, but seemed very agitated. He was asking a lot of questions about guns. Did he and your grandfather still get on? I'd really like to understand better why he left his employment so suddenly.' Again Nadia looked slightly shocked and definitely uncomfortable about this direct line of questioning.

'They were once as close as father and son, but just recently they avoided each other completely. Rohit used to work for my grandfather as a sort of Boy Friday, helping him organise his work and appointments and doing research for him. Something happened to break that relationship; neither of them would tell me exactly what. He blames my grandfather for not protecting him from getting the sack and also for not getting me out of this damned marriage.' This was the first indication from her that her marriage to Sir William had become a sham. Hunter was surprised about how open she was with him about this. 'But if you mean to ask if he might have been the murderer? No. That's impossible. He wouldn't harm my grandfather, he loved him too much, nor would he ever do anything violent, he's a complete pacifist and wouldn't harm the proverbial fly.'

'Do you have any inkling where he might be hiding then?'

'No, I don't know, he hasn't been returning any of my calls or texts since Saturday evening. He doesn't have any family here. It's possible he might be staying with one of his college friends; there is a group of them he knows in the

Spon End area of Coventry.' She wrote out the address for him. 'Inspector, please find him, I am so worried about him. I have never seen him as scared as he was on Saturday. I've been thinking about little else ever since.'

'Who or what is he so scared of?'

Nadia hesitated as if deliberating whether she should say the next words, but she took a deep breath before continuing. This time as she spoke she was looking at him very directly, as if trying to emphasise that she was revealing to him her deepest anxieties. Her speech was measured but full of controlled venom.

'There is a man called Khand. He also worked for my grandfather. He is a completely evil man, corrupt and ruthless. Rohit thinks it was Khand that had my grandfather murdered. Please don't tell my husband any of this; I'm worried how he will react, especially if he knows Rohit has been visiting me in secret. Sir William is not a good husband but he is also not a violent man. Khand on the other hand would stop at nothing to shut us up.'

'Can you tell me more about this Khand?'

'As I said, he is one of my grandfather's old lieutenants, representing a number of his business interests including those in England. He's a very nasty piece of work, out of control really, behaves almost like a gangster. I warned my grandfather about him so many times but he had a blind spot, either that or Khand had something on him.'

'Do you have any idea where I might find him?'

'None I am afraid, but I wouldn't be surprised if he is hanging around here gloating somewhere.'

'Any description you can give me?'

'Short, stocky, silver hair, likes to pass himself off as a respectable businessman, but as I said he's an utter crook. I'm sure I'll have a photograph somewhere if you can give me a few minutes.' She searched through some papers and handed him a photograph of her grandfather and other senior managers at a company function. 'That's him, there on the right.'

'OK Nadia, this is all very helpful. I'll let you know as soon as we find Rohit and in the meantime, please be extremely careful and don't go out of the house under any circumstances. Whatever you do, don't mention our conversation to anybody.'

'You can rest assured of that, Inspector.'

★

When Hunter arrived at the police station late on Tuesday morning, I was waiting for him anxiously.

'Sir, we've just found Rohit, he was hiding out in his friend's house in Coventry, exactly like Lady Flyte said,' I said as Hunter hobbled into the office. 'He's already told the boys who picked him up a bit about his relationship with Mr Nariman. He worked with him night and day for five years but then was cast aside at the advice of one of Nariman's lieutenants, someone called Khand. No redundancy, no notice, just kicked out to fend for himself. He seemed very sad about it – from the way he spoke he seemed to regard Nariman as some sort of adoptive father. He moved to England to be near Nadia when she came over. He's very scared; he didn't want to tell them much. He said he was afraid we would give him away, but we persuaded him to come back to the station in Coventry for his own protection. He's waiting for you in the interview room there.'

Hunter and I drove as quickly as we could to Coventry police station and went straight down to the room where he was being held. Rohit was there of his own volition and had not yet been cautioned so there was no brief present. Hunter clarified this with Rohit before they started and Rohit indicated that he was happy to cooperate as long as we did not give away where he was hiding.

'Rohit, I have a number of important questions for you, but before we start on those, what can you tell me about how and why you left Mr Nariman's employment?' I was surprised that Rohit hardly hesitated before answering. In fact he spoke very quickly, as if eager to share his troubles and get things off his chest.

'It wasn't his choice, that bastard Khand made him do it. I'd been looking into something that had caused Mr Nariman some concern and I got too close. I had always had my doubts about what was going on in his companies, Inspector Hunter. Khand was feeding him a line, misrepresenting completely the position of the company he controlled and at the same time poisoning our friendship and blackening my name. It was a horrible situation for me.' Hunter could sense the hatred in his voice – he certainly wasn't holding back, which seemed slightly at odds with the picture that Nadia had painted of a petrified young man. The person in front of him was clearly keen to get his story out.

'OK, can you tell me more about what you had found out then?'

'It was chaos. They'd launched a product on the market back in Asia that didn't even meet basic safety standards, there were accidents, several customers were maimed, and then there was the explosion in the plant in Tamil Nadu. They bribed the local police and investigators to cover it all up. Those poor women and children, they were horribly burned and mutilated and they didn't get a single rupee in compensation. So I did some more of my own digging. I found out that Khand had been lying about the situation to Mr Nariman for years, the business was losing loads of money, he'd been fiddling the books, and there were payments nobody could explain to politicians and stuff. It was all a web of lies. I got too close and was asking too many questions; that's why Khand forced him to get rid of me. I'm probably lucky it wasn't worse than that. That's why I had to get out, come to England, I warned Mr Nariman that it was too dangerous for him to stay but I never thought...'

'Now, look here, we have a report from Mr Baxter whose composition classes I believe you attend, saying that you expressed strong interest in his gun collection last Saturday. Do you have anything to say about that?' Hunter appeared deliberately aggressive in the no-nonsense way that he asked the question, I assumed to try and work out if he was being spun a line. In response, Rohit began to look worried and his body language became notably more defensive.

'I didn't mean anything by that. I was just wondering whether I should arm myself given what went on that morning. I don't know anything about guns and I hate any kind of violence but I suspected I might be next on the list.'

'So, did you take one of his guns?' Rohit's eyes fell to the floor. 'Well, did you?'

'Yes, Inspector,' he replied sorrowfully.

'And where is that weapon now?'

'I don't know,' he said shaking his head.

'What do you mean you don't know?'

'It's missing.'

Hunter looked at him sceptically. At this point I was beginning to wonder whether he was just a very clever liar.

'You are really trying to tell me you stole a gun from Mr Baxter three days ago and now you don't know where it is?'

'I was so worried about Nadia, her texts were becoming increasingly distraught, and so I decided to risk it on Saturday night. I had returned to my flat during the afternoon to hide the gun but then returned again in the evening when it was getting dark. I waited in the bushes in the square watching her window. When the light went out, I climbed on to the balcony of the house two doors down and then made my way across the balconies to the window outside her room and gave our normal signal on the windowpane. I had to be very careful because one of your officers was on guard at the front door just underneath.'

'Yes, he was supposed to be watching out for people like you.' Clearly irritated, Hunter made a signal to me to raise this lapse of security with the officer concerned.

'Anyway, it took a while but eventually she opened the shutters and pulled up the sash to let me in. I spent about an hour there consoling her. I would have stayed longer but we heard more voices downstairs. I crept out onto the balcony as quietly as I could and escaped down the drainpipe again. I felt really bad, unsure whether I should leave her in that state, but there were just too many police around. When I got back to my flat, it had been ransacked, every drawer pulled out, stuff all over the floor, everything upside down. Of course, I checked for the gun but it had gone. I didn't hang around, that's when I went to Coventry to stay with a friend of mine. I was really afraid by then.'

'Can anyone corroborate all this?'

'Well, Nadia of course, but I don't want her involved. You can speak to my friend in Coventry if you want.'

> *Dazzling colourful adagio,*
> *Denoting friendship, vibrant and lustrous,*
> *Vitality with rhythmic audio.*
> *The wife and her lover telling wondrous*
> *Tales to sate their sentiment, rapturous*
> *In conceit of your voice tonight.*
> *You have no idea of time, my amorous*
> *Story-teller. Writing with passion's sight*
> *Till the stars have risen, and the moon remains light.*

We left the interview room and Hunter turned to me.

'I think this is whole thing is getting very dangerous Penny. This Rohit is an innocent; I don't believe he's a murderer. On the other hand this guy Khand seems ruthless. If we could search Sir William's place I bet we'd find something, but we'll never get the chief super to get us a warrant. I fear this Khand is too clever, it looks like he's been covering his tracks every step of the way – the murder of the Tamils, the spotless car, our little interview in the billiard hall, the sudden appearance of various weapons, Rohit's involvement. I suspect also that Khand is going to be very hard to find, that's if he's even still in the country. See what you can do to get more information on him, maybe we can get an arrest warrant. Meanwhile, we need to find a way into the relationship between him and Sir William otherwise I suspect we won't break this open. The more I think about it the more I think we need something more subtle to smoke these vipers out, some sort of diversion and a sting to catch them off guard, as the jazz singers used to say, *a swift, sly suck on a skinny little joint.*

'Vipers, Sir?'

'Yes, they've been one step ahead of us so far. To catch a snake we need to set a snake trap, a dead man's trap. Something they will never expect so they relax and make a mistake.'

'You mean a trap for Sir William?'

'Indeed, and more importantly we need a trap for Khand and his accomplices. I have an idea how to do that, something I saw in a film once. It will require a little bit of play-acting though,' said Hunter. 'And that could be dangerous. I suspect strongly that we have a spy in the team and until I am sure who that is I can't afford to use anyone from the regular force for this. How about your ex-army friend, Hugh? He's in security isn't he? Do you think he'd be willing to help us?'

'I'm sure he would and I'm certainly up for it, Sir,' Already I was feeling a frisson of excitement about this plan but I knew as well as Hunter did that what he was suggesting was well outside of normal operating procedure.

'This may mean putting you in danger, I'm afraid, Penny. I'll understand completely if you say no.'

'No way, I can take care of myself better than anyone else around here,' I said in a determined voice.

★

Louis-Napoléon built the 'Jeu de Paume' in Paris to house his tennis courts. Louis X (the Quarreller), Henry I of Castile, Philip I (the Fair), Charles VIII of France, Arnaud de Montaigne, James I of Scotland and Frederick, Prince of Wales all died of tennis-related injuries. Death by tennis is obviously a much underrated crime.

Hugh had a back door key to the real tennis court in Bedford Street where he had installed the security systems earlier that year. We had decided that the overhead court lighting would be perfect for filming.

'Hey, you're hurting me you bastards,' I complained loudly as I struggled theatrically with Hugh and Eddie. They were both masked and roughly removed my uniform jacket and tie and loosened my blouse. Eddie tied my hands to the wooden pillars of the hazard while Hugh stretched gaffer tape over my mouth. If this had been for real by now it would have been very scary but I was struggling to stop myself giggling during the whole process. Penn was taking the video, Mad Jack was directing.

'Your turn, Scooby,' Eddie said to Dan, laughing. 'And look ferocious.'

'Stop laughing you lot, and Penny look scared and scream, this is supposed to be realistic isn't it? Not an Ealing comedy,' Jack shouted.

And tell the pleasant Prince this mock of his hath turn'd his balls to gun stones.

Shakespeare, *Henry V*

273

In the situation room at the police station, Hunter began the briefing he had organised at short notice. He knew he was taking a huge risk, the piece of theatre he had planned was completely against procedure, but in the circumstances of having a spy in his team, he thought the risk was worth it.

'OK, as I am sure you all know we have a serious development. DC Dore has been abducted from her flat by two unknown masked men.' There was a ripple of concern and chatter around the room. Hunter was careful to let this play for a few moments. This was all part of the subterfuge he was crafting, information that he hoped would get back quickly to Khand through the informer, whoever that was.

Next he played them the CCTV footage that appeared to show two men dragging Penny kicking and screaming into a white Transit van with no markings and obscured plates. This was another piece of Mad Jack's excellent video montage from the afternoon's filming.

'Sir, why on earth would anybody abduct a junior DC?' asked one of the more cynical older officers, somewhat perceptively. Hunter had expected and therefore anticipated this obvious question.

'DC Dore was attempting to decode some vital new information about the Nariman case that we extracted from Rohit Dhawan's laptop. We believe she was abducted. That information could hold the key to why Nariman was murdered. We have to find her as soon as possible as her life could be in danger.'

Next Hunter read out a letter he had received (a nice piece of creative cut-out newspaper montage by Penny) and played them the rest of the video footage shot in the tennis court. There was no money involved, the key demand was a face-to-face meeting, and Hunter was expressly requested to go alone with Rohit and his laptop to the old ruins at

Guy's Cliffe. There was the usual warning that nobody else, especially no other police officers, should be present or else the policewoman would be hurt.

'Sergeant Jones, I need you to come with me and drop us off near to the site and I need an observation team at a safe distance. We can't afford to spook them.'

'Sir, you know this is highly unusual. It seems like a trap to me, they just want to lure you there. Why would they be interested in you going personally if they have Constable Dore and the data? It doesn't make any sense. And using a suspect as bait...'

'In the circumstances, Sergeant, that's just a risk that I'll have to take. I'm responsible for her safety, not you.'

'Well at least let's get an armed officer in there as well. And what about your knee and broken arm, Sir? You won't be able to defend yourself if you're attacked.'

'That's exactly what crutches are for, Sergeant, and I don't want anyone else within a quarter of a mile, I'm not going to gamble with Penny's life.' He closed the meeting, but before he left to get ready, Hunter went to see Rohit, who was hiding out in Hugh's flat, to explain his plan to him. Rohit grinned and agreed readily to cooperate. Hunter then made one more call to a number in London.

*

Shortly after the meeting had been concluded a conversation was happening not far from the station.

'Our spy in the crime squad tells us that one of their team, the junior policewoman who's been sniffing around, has been abducted. They've received a video and a request for a meeting. Something to do with information downloaded from Rohit's computer. I couldn't find out who the meeting is with. That idiot Hunter is going alone to the old ruins at Guy's Cliffe with Rohit with no back-up. Do you want me to pick him up again, Mr Khand?'

'Not yet, but this is bizarre, it sounds like a complete cock-and-bull story to me. Just follow him for now; I want to find out what he's up to. I smell a rat, but I want to be really certain what game he's playing before we decide to do anything. I hope Sir William isn't playing games with us.'

From the station at Warwick we took a carriage driven by an old coachman who knew the history of the place and was glad to talk about it. He took us to Guy's Cliffe, the site of one of the famous Crusader stories of England and the home of the Percy family.

Grace King, *Memories of a Southern Woman of Letters*

Guy's Cliffe has been occupied since Saxon times and derives its name from the legendary Guy of Warwick. Guy is supposed to have retired to a hermitage on the site, this legend led to the founding of a chantry. The chantry was established in 1423 as the Chapel of St Mary Magdalene and the rock-carved stables and storehouses still remain. The house dates from 1751 and was started by Samuel Greatheed, a West Indian merchant and MP for Coventry 1747 – 1761, whose family were local landowners.

Guy's Cliffe House was sold in 1947 with the intention of converting it into a hotel, but these plans came to nothing and the house fell into disrepair. In 1955, the house was purchased by Aldwyn Porter and the chapel leased to the Freemasons, establishing a connection with the Masons that remains today. The roof had fallen in by 1966. In 1992 during the filming of The Adventures of Sherlock Holmes (The Last Vampyre) *a fire scene got out of control and seriously damaged the building…*

Based on Wikipedia, *Guy's Cliffe*

The unmarked car driven by Detective Sergeant Jones parked at the end of the long drive that led up from the Warwick–Kenilworth road on the way to the old ruined house. Hunter had only ever been there once before as part of a guided tour organised by the local historical society, but he could roughly remember the layout. He pulled his crutches out of the back seat of the Discovery and swung a rucksack onto his back, indicating to Jones that he should wait for Rohit and himself in the car park at the end of the drive, and even if a car came past toward the house he should do nothing but wait. By now it was late afternoon and the shadows were lengthening rapidly in the September sun. The heavy rain the previous day had left the ground somewhat treacherous in places. Hunter was slightly nervous but also excited to see how his plan would pan out. Although highly unusual he felt it was a risk worth taking to smoke Khand out, but if it went wrong or the chief found out prematurely he knew he would be for the high jump.

He struggled on his crutches past the remains of the picturesque ruin, past the chapel and function rooms used by the Freemasons near the sandy overgrown path that led down toward the banks of the River Avon. He had already noticed a flash of light, a telltale sign of someone watching him with binoculars from the ruins that were normally out of bounds to visitors. This was exactly what he wanted. He dropped the backpack; it was only a few seconds until he heard the sound of a Range Rover making its way up the drive into the wide courtyard.

'Bingo!' he whispered to Rohit. A wiry but smartly dressed man got out of the car and walked towards them.

'Sir William.'

'What's this all about, Hunter? Why have you dragged me back from London to this godforsaken place, and what's that no-good rogue doing here for God's sake? Are you mad?'

Hunter noticed the shadow of a man passing behind one of the ruined windows of the old house. *Yes, he's wearing a turban* he had been right about that. He signalled surreptitiously toward the door to the mason's chapel where two masked men were holding Penny. She was blindfolded and bound and they were holding a gun to her head. Hunter pulled a laptop from the rucksack and passed it to Sir William.

★

'What is all this about Hunter? I need an explanation now. NOW DAMN IT!' I heard Sir William shout.

Eddie fired and Rohit fell to the ground. 'Watch out!' I screamed from my hiding place. At this point I was still wearing the blindfold but had managed to squint through a gap in the binding.

'What on earth?' I then heard Sir William swear. But it appeared he did not wait for an answer, instead I heard his footsteps on the gravel as he ran as quickly as he could back to the car. Hearing the shot, his driver had already started the vehicle and as soon as Sir William was in the car it accelerated and swerved violently out of the car park and down the road as fast as the man could drive.

Hunter moved as quickly as he could towards me and untied the ropes binding my feet and hands, then removed the blindfold and gag. I grinned at him, but dared not say anything; everything was going to plan so far. We heard a further noise near the door and we could see the beam of a torch and then the silhouette of a second man with a gun aimed towards us. This was the bit I was most nervous about. Hugh fired, and fortunately the shot just missed Hunter's shoulder and ricocheted harmlessly off the sandstone wall. I knew Hugh was an excellent shot, but that was a bit closer than any of us would have liked.

> *Sir Calepine by chaunce more than choyce*
> *The selfe same evening fortune hither drove*
> *As he to seek Serena through the woods did rove...*

Spenser, *The Faerie Queene*

'Run, Penny, get out of here!' Hunter shouted theatrically and drew his own firearm. He fired back into the gloom of the entrance, but then Hugh ran out and brought his weapon down on Hunter's shoulder, which unbalanced him from his crutches. He fell to the ground. This was all a bit too realistic. By now I was already running away through the undergrowth onto the path that led to Guy's Cave, where I knew Alice would be waiting for me.

★

A second man joined the first next to Hunter's prone body. They were masked but speaking in whispers. He offered only token resistance while the two men quickly bound him and then pulled his and Rohit's bodies onto a wooden gardener's trolley. They proceeded to wheel them rapidly back up toward the gateway. From the trolley, Hunter scanned carefully to see if he could spot the observer again in the ruins above them as they passed through the old archway.

As they reached the drive, a white van pulled out from the cover of a stand of beech trees, dislodging the undergrowth that had previously hidden it. Hunter was bundled into the van and Rohit's body thrown in beside him. Once they were safely in the van, and the doors were closed, Rohit glanced up at him, grinning. They heard a third voice, the driver, Penn, using a somewhat exaggerated New York accent, order the two men to get in while he drove them to 'the hill'. As the van left the car park, Hunter heard the sound of a motorcycle engine starting in the distance, a noise that he continued to hear as they passed down the drive. Good, this was going exactly as he had hoped it would.

After bumping along for ten minutes or so the van stopped and a few seconds later he heard the rear doors being flung open again. Hunter was dragged bodily from the back of the van. From the road noise in the distance he could tell they were near to the motorway junction. The drive from Guy's Cliffe had been relatively short, maybe a mile or two and he had felt the van turn through two roundabouts. This was the place he had described to his team; they were exactly where he had planned.

Hugh and Eddie struggled as they carried the two bodies up the ascent, through the wet overgrown slope of the hill. The sack was still over Hunter's head and his hands were tied uncomfortably tightly behind his back. Several times the two minders had to pause for breath. While they rested, he felt the angular barrel of a gun in his back, and a low voice urging him to keep quiet. His captors spoke together in their hushed drawl. Hunter kept quiet, not wishing to give anything away. When they reached the top of the hill, Hugh and Eddie were sweating and gulping in air.

Hunter knew exactly where he was. This was after all his idea; historically speaking they were off the Earl of Warwick's lands and onto Lancastrian territory, or more relevantly off his own patch onto West Midlands CID's manor. The chief couldn't object to that, could he? He was pushed to the ground against a rough stone pediment, one he knew from his frequent rambles in the area to be the monument erected to the memory of Edward II's favourite – Piers Gaveston, murdered by the King's enemies on this spot. He knew that the monument was erected in 1823 by the squire of Guy's Cliffe – Bertie Greatheed, whose family also owned much of Leamington before the great 1830s building boom – a nice coincidence that he would remind them all of later, if he remembered. He heard the sound of spades striking and turning over the stony ground. *So my accomplices really mean to do it properly*, he thought. He heard the motorcycle again in the distance and was assuming they were still being closely observed. He needed Khand's observer to think that this was for real and report back on their meeting with Sir William.

The noise of the spades stopped and an American voice he didn't recognise but that he assumed was Penny's actor friend said simply, 'OK let's do it, guys.'

He felt one of the two heavies cut the ropes around his hands with a knife and replace them with handcuffs. The sack that was covering his head was removed but the blindfold remained. Hunter smarted as the blade of the knife dug into his skin. He winced again as it was placed against his belly, but nowhere near his heart and in a way that the flat of the blade merely scraped the surface of his skin, drawing blood but not too deeply. In contrast, the blood from the blood bag that oozed through his shirt felt exceptionally thick against his skin. This procedure happened twice. The second time the knife was scraped around his throat. He felt the blood running down his chest but knew it was not his own. He wondered if his assailants had any real clue how to kill a hostage. *Hugh was in the Army, wasn't he? He must have an idea.* Hunter continued to act his part and fell to the ground with a cry.

'That's him done,' said one of them.

'Not so quick, use the shooter too,' replied the other. 'Just to be sure, like.'

Hunter heard a shot strike the ground close to his ear but felt no pain.

'For God's sake boys that was close,' he muttered, jerking his body and biting his tongue so that the blood oozed from the side of his mouth.

'One more, take his head off this time,' laughed the voice.

They are enjoying this too much, he thought. The bullet missed his body by a few inches again but kicked up dust around him. He jerked his head this time to simulate the bullet hitting its mark, and then felt himself being kicked into the shallow grave and soil poured over his head. When he had asked them to make it look realistic, he had not meant it to be quite so much so.

There was silence. A few minutes after the three men left he felt a fourth pair of hands scrape away the loose layer of earth and check over his body. This was the most dangerous bit of his plan, the part over which he did not have much control. He heard the new man breathing heavily and muttering as he found the envelope that Hunter had carefully planted in his own inside pocket, the smell of Asian spices heavy on his breath. He realised this new man was speaking into a cell phone, first in a strange Eastern tongue and then in clear, well-spoken English. Hunter calculated all the possibilities of potential escape, in case he had to play a further variation on the plan but came up with no immediate options. *Even Harry Houdini would find these handcuffs a struggle*. He hoped Hugh had him covered as planned from the undergrowth.

'Your friend Sir William was there too but scarpered when the shooting started. I couldn't see who it was, two of them I think. Rohit was killed and Hunter was hit too. They've brought the bodies to a hill near the Warwick bypass and buried them in a shallow grave. There's no doubt it's him, Mr Khand, Hunter's not dead yet but he's in a pretty bad way. There's a document in his pocket headed 'Enigma code'. He can't have long, do you want me to finish him off?'

Despite instructions from his boss to leave Hunter be and bring the package back quickly, the man kicked him in the groin, followed by two kicks to his head. There were now other voices in the distance and Hunter heard a familiar song from his youth – *Always Look on the Bright Side of Life*. They sounded like boy scouts or hikers probably, hopefully another of Mad Jack's theatrical diversions. He heard the fourth man swear as he realised he needed to leave quickly, followed by the sound of the motorcycle restarting.

★

That evening, Lucy Fleming, the young journalist, was the first to break an exclusive story on national television about the murder of Detective Inspector Hunter on Woodloes Hill, near Warwick. She explained that the four hikers that had found his blood-stained body were alerted to its presence by the sound of his mobile phone ringing in the bushes. The TV crew cut from her to the scene of the mobile forensics team who were combing the undergrowth in the sharp glare of portable spotlights.

★

Sir William arrived back from Guy's Cliffe in a foul mood, barking at the butler as he entered the house. He washed quickly, got changed and then came down to the drawing room. Nadia was listening intently to a news programme on the television.

'William, come and see this. That poor Inspector Hunter has been murdered.'

'What on earth are you talking about?' he snapped irritably.

But he saw that she was watching the regional evening news programme, where one of the local reporters was talking about Hunter's murder. She was saying that there was already speculation about a link to the Nariman case. The reporter said she understood from police sources that Hunter was close to uncovering new information. Sir William was astounded that the reporters had got the news so quickly and began to feel a little panicky, but as he listened further and collected his thoughts his feeling of panic turned to a strange sense of relief, even euphoria. With both Rohit and Hunter gone, and seemingly no other witnesses except the policewoman who was blindfolded and whoever the masked men were, maybe this could be their lucky break.

'This is terrible, William.' Nadia said. 'That poor man, when this will ever end?'

He switched off the television.

'Indeed, my dear, but I don't want you troubling yourself further over this, you have enough to worry about already. I agree it's very unfortunate but after all, that was his job. When you've seen as much as I have in your life you come to expect these kinds of things from time to time.' She looked at him in disgust, amazed by the callousness of his words. He went to his study but decided not to ring Khand this time.

*

At the police station, the chief superintendent was going crazy with the crime squad. The station was besieged by reporters, he wanted answers and he wasn't getting them.

'Why wasn't I told about this operation? What the hell is this all about, Sergeant? What on earth was Hunter up to? This is unbelievable. It's like a sick Ealing comedy. My God, we look like a bunch of amateurs.'

CHAPTER NINETEEN

FLY SINGING BIRD – (VIVACE)

Fly, singing bird, fly,
Leave thy nest 'midst the wood, lone, unsought,
Leave the cradling boughs, spread thy wing,
And swift as my following thought,
Onward speed, and swift flying, still sing,
Come, or I die!

Edward Elgar, *Fly Singing Bird.*

Safely back in his flat after his kidnap escapade, Hunter reread the report Penny had emailed through to him. He was waiting for news from the surveillance team. Everything was ready for him to spring the last part of his trap. One report in particular provided the last clues he needed in the jigsaw puzzle to understand what was behind the Nariman murder:

K-Company generates billions of dollars in revenue from legitimate business activities such as real estate and bank overhaul transactions, as well as illegal criminal enterprises around the world, especially in Sri Lanka, India, Pakistan and the U.A.E. The organisation has a history of rivalry with the police and other underworld groups. Its operations include arms trafficking, contract killing, counterfeiting, drug trafficking, extortion, and terrorism, being responsible for a series of bombings that killed 257 people in one year. Last year, intelligence agencies linked K-Company with Sri Lanka's mobile bandwidth privatisation. In March security was tightened after it had been suggested that K-Company might launch an attack in an attempt to destroy documents relating to the ongoing probe of the spectrum scam.

★

At Sir William's residence, the light illuminated on the upstairs security control panel, signifying an intruder near the rear entrance. Outside it was dark and stormy and the house was already locked up for the night. Nadia peered in concern through the curtains of the upstairs sitting room; she couldn't see anything due to the overhang of the porch so she rang down to the butler instead.

'Henderson, can you check out the security panel? There seems to be something wandering around at the back – it's probably a fox but we had better be sure.'

At the same time as his wife was speaking, Sir William emerged from his study; he had just received a mobile phone call asking him to open up the side door. When he saw the butler coming up the stairs from his basement flat he chased him away. Instead, he himself went to unchain and unbolt the door and peered into the wind and rain outside. At first he saw nothing, but quickly a short man in a heavy dark overcoat and trilby emerged from the shadows cast by some bamboo screening. He pushed his way past him into the side hallway. Although neither man spoke, Sir William directed him quickly toward the door of his study. He attempted to shut the heavy oak door, but it did not close immediately because of an obstruction from a rug.

'Who is it William, is it the police again?' Nadia shouted down from the landing. He turned to see her standing at the top of the stairs in her dressing gown. She noticed that he appeared worried.

'No, it's a courier for me, just some urgent documents I need to attend to,' he said somewhat bluntly.

She could see that he was lying.

'What sort of business would someone need to do at this time on a Tuesday evening?' she asked suspiciously.

He was somewhat irritated that she was questioning him like this, but decided to moderate his voice to a softer, more reassuring tone. He needed to avoid her coming down the stairs and discovering the true identity of his guest.

'Really, it's nothing dearest. As I said, just some documents that need signing, I'll deal with it as quickly as I can. You look tired, my dear, why don't you take a soak in the bath and I'll be up soon,' he said patronisingly.

Sir William realised from her sight line that the door must be ajar and pulled it shut quickly. He repeated that he would be up with her again soon, his voice containing an element of exasperation. She uttered an audible tut of disgust and stormed back toward her room, slamming the door behind her, not attempting in any way to conceal her rage.

He did not know exactly why she had reacted in this way; her out of character behaviour disturbed him as much as the appearance of his unexpected visitor. He was becoming worried that she may understand more about the situation than he had realised. To make matters worse, as Sir William re-entered the library, Khand's stony face had taken on a distinctly threatening expression. The French clocks on the mantelpiece were individually sounding the hour, none of them quite synchronised to the right time. Sir William was forced to let them complete their cycle before he could speak, his face reddening to a shade that complemented the colour of the upholstery of the armchairs by the fire.

'What the hell are you doing here, Khand, are you mad? There are police crawling all over the place,' he said when the ringing of the clocks has stopped. They remained standing, with no invitation from Sir William for them to sit down in the chairs and no indication that Khand was going to explain his presence. The fire had virtually extinguished itself and only a faint glow and crackle emanated from the grate. Sir William gave it a sharp stir with a poker so that a shard of sparks flew up the chimney. Eventually, and very deliberately, Khand began to speak.

'I've come to make sure you are still on message, Sir William. Your young wife is a very pretty woman, but I can see now that she's also bright and therefore a risk. Especially now that that young writer friend of hers is involved again,' said Khand. 'Did you know he was here on Saturday evening, carrying on with her in her bedroom?'

Sir William looked at him askance, reddening further as if he might be about to strike his guest. 'What on earth are you talking about, Khand? Nadia would never carry on with someone, especially that lowlife.'

'She would and has, right here, under your very nose. He has confessed as much to the police.'

'What rubbish. It can't be,' he said, shaking his head. But seeing that Khand's expression was deadly serious he changed his tone to a more contrite voice, bottling his earlier bluster. 'Look, it must be a mistake. I'll talk to her, whatever happened I'm sure I can sort it out with her. She was grieving for her grandfather, that's probably what it was about. There's certainly some perfectly innocent explanation, she's just not capable of anything worse than that.'

'I do hope so, for her sake, or she may be in the frame herself,' replied Khand, allowing a sinister sounding laugh to escape his crooked mouth, continuing to look Sir William closely in the eyes. Sir William wasn't used to being on the defensive like this, his normal style was that of a bull charging through life pushing others aside, but Khand had him rattled.

'I assume you've heard the news on the radio about that

smart alec, Inspector Hunter? Is it true? Do you think he's out of the picture?' asked Sir William innocently, attempting to change the subject and defuse the tension, of course avoiding any reference to his earlier meeting with Hunter at Guy's Cliffe.

Khand sucked in his breath, playing with something in the pocket of his overcoat. He would play Sir William along for a while, rather than confronting him immediately with the fact of the meeting that had been reported to him.

'I confess that's something I still don't understand. This time it's nothing to do with me and I don't know what's going on, but it does seem to be true. My man saw him being grabbed and then saw the killing while he was trailing Hunter and the gang who had taken him. Maybe it's just a stroke of luck, maybe there's more to it. But in any case apparently he won't be around to bother us further.'

'Indeed, it's a huge stroke of luck, he was beginning to ask some uncomfortable questions,' added Sir William.

'Well, that's exactly why I'm here. There's something about this whole latest episode that I don't like, something fishy. Are you sure you haven't inadvertently said something you shouldn't have about Enigma to the police?'

'Of course not, Khand. I'm in this as deeply as you are.'

'You are indeed,' Khand smiled ominously.

'Look, Khand, this whole thing has to quieten down, you have to keep my name out of it. This business has caused me all sorts of problems. You never told me what was really going to happen and I certainly didn't expect a body on my doorstep. And now with that other murder, the actress and Hunter and this friend of Nadia's – the whole thing's running out of control.'

'Bullshit! You know it had to be done, they were both beginning to ask the wrong kind of questions, you know what that could have meant,' said Khand, the menace returning to his voice.

'Are you questioning my commitment?'

'I'm merely stating the obvious based on the facts as they are.'

'But Christ, why did you have to kill them?'

Khand looked at him intently and brought his own face right up close to Sir William's. He stared at him for maybe thirty seconds before speaking. Sir William felt the barrel of a gun in his stomach as he stared at the evil expression in Khand's eyes. *So that was what Khand was fingering in his pocket, he's got a bloody gun*, he thought. He swallowed hard, wondering what he should do next, not certain at all about how impetuous this dangerous man could be.

> *Thereto the Blatant beast by them set on*
> *At him began aloud to barke and bay.*

Spenser, *The Faerie Queene*

'You've had a remarkably good run in our service, Sir William, but I smell a rat and my sense of smell is usually incredibly good. I'm not sure if I can trust you anymore. Tell me why I shouldn't just pull this trigger right now.'

'Look, Khand, I've done everything you asked me to do, haven't I? Put that stupid thing away and let's talk sensibly about this.' Sir William was beginning to shake uncontrollably; he had not seen Khand like this before. He knew he was dangerous and unpredictable but how much further would he go?

'Tell me now what you've told the police.'

'Nothing, nothing at all, why would I tell them anything?'

'I know you were at Guy's Cliffe. Rohit was there too, what did you tell them about Enigma?' asked Khand with real venom in his voice now. Sir William looked aghast and struggled for words.

'Nothing, that was some stupid stunt that Hunter was pulling. It took me totally by surprise. Anyway how do you know about that?' he eventually stammered.

'I told you before, I have my spies in the police.'

'Look, I've already told you before; we're in just the right place with Enigma. The tender will be awarded next Friday and with the document rewrite and a little lubrication of the process we are nearly home and dry.' Sir William's voice was beginning to crack from the strain of the tension and broke into a sort of grizzled falsetto.

'Hunter had some sort of paper on him,' said Khand, loosening his grasp a little on Sir William's collar, at the same time pushing the gun deeper into his stomach to reinforce his message. 'It referred to Enigma. That can't be a coincidence. There's absolutely no room for mistakes here, do you understand? *He* won't tolerate failure. And as for your loyalty…'

Before he could finish his sentence, there was a knock on the study door and both men turned towards it, surprised by the interruption. Nadia poked her head around the door and Khand moved away from Sir William quickly, hiding the gun under his coat.

'Nadia, I asked you not to bother us,' said Sir William in an irritated voice. She stared at Khand with utter contempt but did not deign to address him. Khand smiled back at her, opening his mouth so that she could see the gold crowns on his teeth.

'You are looking very beautiful, Nadia,' he said in the most obsequious of voices. She ignored his comment and his gaze, turning back to her husband.

'You have another visitor at the front door, my darling,' she said with a false sweetness.

'What now? Can't you see we're busy? Who is it?' he asked, flustered by this news.

'I really don't think it can wait, my dearest, shall I show him in?'

Before Sir William could say anything to stop her, she opened the study door wider and a tall, rather Germanic, fair haired and blue-eyed man entered the room, still hobbling a little on his crutches.

'Hunter!' gasped Sir William, realising he had caught them red-handed. 'You're supposed to be dead…'

Hunter was followed by another three police officers who moved quickly to grab both men. The room descended immediately into chaos. Still in shock, Sir William was submissive and did not offer any resistance, but Khand on the other hand reacted quickly and decisively, struggling free of their grasp. He pulled his gun and fired a shot that winged the officer nearest to him.

There was a cry of pain and Hunter shouted, 'Don't move Khand, put the gun down.'

Without a word, Khand ducked his shoulder to avoid the other officer's hands and span on his heels. With surprising dexterity for a middle-aged man, he launched himself through the open French doors into the garden outside. One officer continued to handcuff the stunned Sir William and read him his rights, while the others gave chase to Khand, out onto the balcony and into the back garden. There were two more shots that lit up the garden instantaneously and the officers were forced to take cover for a second. They shone their torches through the undergrowth to try and locate where Khand was hiding. There was no sign of him. On his radio, the officer holding Sir William gave instructions to direct the spotlights of a police helicopter and sweep the back gardens of the row of Regency houses and the workshops that backed on to them behind.

★

Next door, I saw the sound crew put their thumbs up. Operation 'Pyramus and Thisbe' had worked.

'Got them,' I said. 'With a full confession.'

A second later, I was back on my radio. 'Damn it. Khand's got away, they've got him on the thermal cameras though and the helicopter is trying to track him.'

★

Khand was running for his life now, all his training at the K-company terrorist camps flooding back into his mind. He doubled back through the lane behind the houses, back through the yard of a second hand car dealer. Above him he could hear the throbbing of the helicopter and in the surrounding streets the sound of sirens rapidly converging, the blue lights strobing against the walls of the buildings, obscuring the weaker sodium light streetlights. He paused for breath and tried desperately to think what he should do next.

In that split second of hesitation he felt the cold steel of the silenced barrel of an SV-99 at the back of his head. Instinctively he began to raise his hands, knowing he had only a moment or two to grab the barrel, twist and bring his hands down quickly to redirect the gun towards his assailant's solar plexus while stamping his heel down on his foot to knock him off balance. But before his hands were even past his shoulders, the gun was fired. The shot took one side of his head off completely and his body fell to the ground, instantly lifeless.

★

The Sikh holding the gun was disguised as a police marksman. The silencer on the gun meant that the shot was executed without a sound. He was quick and efficient in packing Khand's body into the boot of his black cab and drove away through the rapidly filling streets, turning off the 'For Hire' sign to avoid being flagged down.

An hour later, the park keeper in Jephson Gardens found Khand's mutilated body as he was locking up. It has been dumped near the group of statues called 'Elephants and Boy', the monument to Sam Lockhart's three elephants, the 'Three Graces'. Every limb had been crushed with a sledgehammer and the remaining half of Khand's ghoulish head was barely recognisable, balanced on the trunk of one of the elephants.

During the Mughal era it was a common mode of execution to have the offender trampled underfoot by an elephant.

G. A. Natesan, *The Indian Review*

*

'It looks like K-Company has done our work for us,' said Hunter, shaking his head when we arrived at the scene. 'Let's get this mess cleared up. At least maybe we'll all get a medal now from the chief.'

'Forensics have just arrived, Sir,' I said.

'Wait, before they start let me see Khand's right hand,' Hunter said, looking at the 'bite' on the web of the detached right hand between the thumb and forefinger. 'As I thought, our friend the Browning,' he added in satisfaction. Alice, already dressed in her protective suit, came up beside us with her forensics bag.

'Hello, Alice,' I said, 'we do seem to be keeping you busy this week. This one's a bit of a mess I'm afraid.'

'Indeed,' said Alice, grimacing at the sight of the crushed limbs and severed head.

Hunter pointed out the mark on the man's hand to her

and said, 'I think we might have the man who fired the Browning, Alice.'

'Maybe, but of course the Browning was not the cause of Troyte's death you know.'

We both looked at her in surprise.

'And in any case, it's Rohit's prints that are all over the stock and his footprints were in the garden, there weren't any others.'

'You mean, Troyte wasn't killed by the Browning?' asked Hunter. He looked anguished by this news.

'No, we believe he died of a massive heart attack, I'd estimate it occurred at least an hour before the bullet wound was inflicted. He was already long dead when he was shot through the head, we can tell that from the way the blood flowed from the wound.'

'So it wasn't murder then?' I asked, totally confused by the implications of this.

'Let's not jump to any conclusions about that,' muttered Hunter, who also looked genuinely perplexed by this unexpected twist.

'I guess it's not surprising that Rohit's prints would be on the gun if he stole it from Baxter,' he deliberated. 'We'd better get him picked up again all the same. Are there any more surprises for us in your report, Alice?' he said, scratching his head. He was clearly irritated that his tidy explanation of events was unravelling with these new revelations.

Alice paused and brushed away the hair flapping around her face in the wind. 'Well yes, the other really strange thing we've discovered concerns the condom we found in Troyte's bedroom. The semen is Troyte's alright; it's a perfect match to his other fluids we tested. But there are no other fluids on the surface of the empty sheath; in fact there is no sign of any female or male contact. It's almost as if it was never used in anger, so to speak.'

'Why would anyone bother to use a condom if there was no one else involved, was it some kind of fetish?' I asked. This was getting stranger and stranger. A thought came into my mind and I reminded the DI about the strange photographs we found in the box in Pearl's safe.

'I think you may be right,' he said. 'But the photos were all part of Miss Taylor's elaborate revenge plot, so I think we've got a pretty full explanation for that now. Is there anything else, Alice?'

'Yes, we got a lipstick and saliva sample from the rim of the champagne glass in Troyte's house. We've run a DNA match and have a result.'

'OK and what is that?'

'There's a match to one of the victims,' her voice sounded somewhat triumphant as if she was proud of her own detective skills. I wondered what else she had up her sleeve, one of my best friends trying to upstage me again.

'A match to Troyte's DNA?'

'No, interestingly there's a match to Nariman. Whoever drank from that glass, and we have to reasonably assume from the lipstick it was a woman, must be a very close blood relative of his.'

'Nadia?' I asked, 'How can that be? She was in the house all day.'

'No not Nadia, Penny, remember there is another woman involved in this whole confused story,' said Hunter. I could see by his changed expression that he was beginning to understand the significance of this new information. 'All the same, I think we do need to get Nadia to give us a blood or saliva sample for Alice to test and it would be good to get something that we know belongs to Miss Taylor as a cross-check.'

'I don't understand. What's Miss Taylor got to do with it?' I asked, my mind racing over new possibilities, but I was by now completely confused.

'I'm afraid that despite my earlier assurance to the contrary, Miss Taylor seems increasingly likely, albeit probably accidentally, to have the code to the whole enigma,' he stated mysteriously.

★

After the police had taken Sir William away in handcuffs, Nadia asked the butler to lock the doors again and went back up to her room. She decided to take the bath that she had promised herself earlier. Despite the arrest of her husband, she felt both a sense of rage and a huge sense of relief at the events of the evening, however disturbing they were, especially once she had heard that they had found Khand's body. Of course they had spared her the more gruesome details of that discovery; however she was still very worried about Rohit. After she had bathed and oiled her hair, she wrapped herself in a towelling robe and sat on the bed watching the unravelling news reports on the TV in her room. It was then that she heard the familiar but unexpected tap of Rohit's signal on her window pane and she hurriedly opened the shutters to see him standing there, silhouetted against the flashing lights from the police cars. They were still searching the garden and lane behind for any further evidence of Khand's flight and his attacker. She embraced Rohit, bursting into tears at the joy of seeing him again, released for a moment from the tension of the evening's trauma.

> *Like gold, indeed, O maiden, is your shining body,*
> *And like sapphire, your fragrant dark hair.*

Abraham Mariaselvam, *Song of Songs and Ancient Tamil Love Poems*

Unfortunately, this time he had been spotted as he made his way along the balcony and their lover's sweet nothings were soon rudely disturbed as two large police officers arrived and were led upstairs by the butler to her bedroom. Nadia protested at the intrusion but Rohit calmed her, saying he had nothing to fear from the police and was quite willing to go with them peacefully. When Hunter arrived a few minutes later, they read Rohit his rights and then bundled him into the car to take him back to the police station for a second round of questioning, this time under caution. Hunter stayed back to speak with Nadia for a few minutes; he had been joined by Alice and another female officer.

'Inspector Hunter, what on earth is going on? Why are you taking Rohit again? I told you he would never have harmed my grandfather,' she said, sobbing.

'I'm afraid this time it is nothing to do with your grandfather's murder,' replied Hunter, 'there is something else that has emerged this evening that we need to question him about. In the meantime, we need to establish something else about your grandfather's medical history. Would you mind terribly if Alice here takes a swab from your mouth as a close relative? It won't hurt and will take only a second.'

*

After they had taken the sample, Hunter returned to the station quickly and went to the interview room straight away with one of his team. Rohit was sitting there with a duty lawyer. He looked calm enough. After the usual preliminary questions, Hunter quickly got to the point.

'So Rohit, it appears you were not entirely straight with me before about what you were doing last Sunday,' he said sternly. 'You weren't hiding in Coventry all day, were you?'

The lawyer whispered to Rohit to explain to him what

he should and shouldn't say. Rohit shook his head and indicated he wanted to answer the question.

'I'm not sure what you mean, Inspector?'

'You paid a visit to a Mr Troyte in Lansdowne Circus, didn't you? We know because you left your prints. Now why would you have gone there, if it wasn't to commit some sort of mischief?'

Rohit suddenly looked very concerned and began to bite his lip nervously. His lawyer turned to Hunter and indicated that his client would not answer the question. Hunter shook his head and looked again at Rohit, repeating his question. The lawyer went to intervene again but before he could stop him, Rohit broke down into sobs and started to answer anyway.

'Inspector, please believe me, it's not what it seems.'

'OK, well I'm all ears,' Hunter pressed him firmly.

'I went to ask him about Nadia,' Rohit replied, falteringly this time. 'I'd found out from my research that he was friends with Mr Nariman at College about the time that Nadia's mother was born and I wanted to know whether Mr Nariman was really her grandfather or not. You see I had my doubts, from the research that I had done, some things in the story just didn't fit. I even had DNA tests done. They were negative; there was nothing, no match, no connection between them.'

'And so what happened when you got to the house?'

'He wouldn't let me in at first. Something had scared him, but when I mentioned Mr Nariman's name and told him that I used to work for him, he opened the door and reluctantly agreed to see me. We sat in his drawing room in silence, while he paced around the room. He was clearly very anxious about something. Eventually he sat down and asked me to tell him the whole story, as I knew it. After I had finished, he just looked at me like a guilty child. He told me it was all a very long time ago and he could not remember very well what had happened. Maybe there had been some sort of mistake, some sort of mix up. In any case, all he knew was that he'd done Mr Nariman a favour by sorting things out for him, but I could tell he wasn't telling the whole truth.'

'And is that when you pulled the revolver?' Again the lawyer tried to stop Rohit saying any more but by now he was in full flow.

'Inspector, I've already told you, I did not have the gun. It had been stolen from my room the night before.'

'Well we'll see about that. So what's your story, what happened next?'

'He suddenly went very pale and started clutching his chest. I realised almost immediately that he was having some sort of attack. I know I should really have called for an ambulance straight away, but I was so scared about what you would think if you found me there. So I got him off the settee on to the floor instead and loosened his clothing. I intended to make him comfortable while I went and called for an ambulance, but he seemed to be fading fast and I was afraid that it might already be too late. I felt his wrist, there was no pulse that I could detect and suddenly he wasn't breathing properly either. He was losing consciousness rapidly. I tried CPR, I've done the training, but nothing happened. I must have tried for ten, fifteen minutes until I realised he was definitely dead. Then I really panicked, I pulled him back onto the settee, closed the curtains, unlocked and then left by the back doors into the garden. I did mean to call you and let you know about the body but I was so frightened I just rode off on my bike all the way back to Coventry and tried to forget the whole thing had happened.'

'You expect me to believe all that?' asked Hunter aggressively.

'Inspector, it's the truth, I was terrified.'

'And what about the message?'

'What message?

'The 'dancing men' message?'

'You found that?'

'Yes, it was in the victim's pocket.'

'OK I didn't put it there. It must have fallen out of my pocket but I certainly didn't put it in Troyte's pocket. I got the idea from that film crew, when I read up about what they were filming. It was just research for one of Baxter's stupid assignments, just a joke. I never intended to give it to him.'

'You really expect me to believe all this?' said Hunter, shaking his head but quietly reforming again his view of the train of events that Sunday afternoon. 'So how was Miss Taylor involved in all of this?' Rohit looked aghast at the mention of her name.

'How do you know about her?' he asked.

'Come on, do you take me for a fool?'

'No, Inspector, of course not.'

'I was wondering if you could tell me if you have another unbelievable explanation about how she came to know that Troyte was going to be in town this weekend. You tipped her off didn't you?'

'Maybe.'

'So what's the connection? This one is intriguing me more than anything.'

'It was pure chance really; I came across her name when I was trying to find out about Mr Troyte. It was a magazine interview she did just after her mother's death; she was talking about her search for her natural father. She did not use his name but referred to an American architect living in Michigan. The article came up when I was googling to research Troyte. It was a pure coincidence really, but I got in contact with her and she recognised the name. It must have been then that I mentioned to her that he was coming to England soon and she got very interested.'

'You've really been very stupid, Rohit, and now you're in a lot of trouble. We'll have to keep you here while we check out this somewhat incredible story. And I need to know right now anything else you know about Miss Taylor's background. Don't withhold anything else from me or it will go badly for you.'

★

Some hours later, I returned in excitement from forensics.

'So tell me, what have they found?' Hunter asked, with a voice that indicated he probably knew already what I was about to say.

'There are two matches on the DNA, and you'll never guess…'

'Actually I think I will.'

'I think Pearl Taylor is actually Nariman's daughter.' I said triumphantly.

'Yes, I had begun to suspect that, by an Afro-American woman called Esther, I believe. Detroit is really 'de Troyte' – that was the clue Esther left to posterity that nobody ever got.'

'How on earth did you know that?' I said, failing to hide my disappointment that he was ahead of me yet again.

'The bit about Esther is on public record, the perplexing thing is why Miss Taylor was so sure that Troyte rather than Nariman was her father. That is still something I need to figure out.'

'And what about Nadia's mother?'

'Presumably the daughter that Troyte thought he had from one of his other numerous liaisons.'

'Yes, forensics thinks her grandmother was probably Native American.'

'And she was possibly a cellist, too?'

'Now you're pulling my leg, Sir. How on earth could

you possibly deduce that?' I asked, quite astounded that he had worked that out as well.

'I've just trained myself to expect the unexpected, I guess. And I have a suspect in our cells, who appears to be a better detective than all of us, someone who had worked most of this stuff out for himself a long time ago.'

'So what are we going to do now?' I asked, still somewhat deflated that he seemed to be one step ahead of me, even after I had made these breakthroughs in the case.

'Well first of all we shouldn't tell Miss Taylor or Lady Flyte about any of this. They don't need to know and we don't need to tell them, not yet at least. Secondly, we still have a murderer to catch.'

'How do you mean, Sir? Khand is dead, isn't he?'

'He's very dead, but it's unfortunately a case of right nationality, wrong man.'

'Rohit then?' I asked. Hunter laughed.

'No, Rohit, isn't our man either, he's both far too scared and far too clever to have killed someone.'

'Pearl then?'

'Yes, you never liked her did you? Now you are thinking more logically, but still not with quite the right instinct, I'm afraid. You are right that Miss Taylor had both the motivation to kill Troyte and the strength of character to carry it through. But I am pretty sure she has already exacted her intended revenge by humiliating him at that conference.'

'Well who then?' I asked, now getting frustrated that he would not get straight to the point as he obviously knew who the killer was.

'We might never be able to prove it, but I am pretty sure Khand tried to murder Troyte because he thought he knew something about this Enigma contract. I expect he had concluded that the timing of Troyte's visit to Leamington was no coincidence and must be connected. Why else would he have come over to meet with Nariman at this time? What

I suspect that he hadn't figured out though, was that when he snuck into Hawthorne House through the garden door to kill him, Troyte was already dead of a heart attack.'

'And Winnie?'

'I believe that was Khand too, trying to cover his tracks. Remember you told me that there were reports of an unidentified consultant in the home that Sunday morning? Someone had messed around with her drugs and they also found that white coat in the laundry. Well I think it was either Khand himself or at least one of his cronies. In any case, Khand must have got spooked when he heard that she had seen everything out in the street from her window. Interestingly, he didn't go after our friend Professor Baxter, but then he did not have the same bird's eye view of the murder that Winnie did. As Khand was clearly being fed information from our team, I suspect that he dismissed Baxter and the other witnesses like Hugh as not worth the risk of taking further action against.'

'So who killed Nariman then, was that Khand as well?'

'The confusing thing there is whether there were one, two or even three separate attempts made on his life that day. The knife attack is fairly clear. There's no doubt Khand paid the Tamils to attack Nariman, they had clear motivation and Khand probably funded them to fly over. We've got the money recovered from the river by Dan and Jack. Further as you told me that first morning, Hugh saw a package, which could have been the money being handed over to them in the car park by someone who matched Khand's description. We might not have a bullet but we certainly have a smoking gun, so to speak.'

'You said three attempts. I can only count two.'

'What if the second possible murder attempt was the heavy metal poison they found in his body? As Alice told us, Nariman was dying anyway, of mercury poisoning. It seems pretty unlikely that that was naturally ingested given his strict religious diet. However, I'm still of the view that this was more likely the result of the medicinal herbs he was using, not a deliberate poison attempt. So at the moment, I don't think there was any intentional poisoning. It is of course also possible that Khand substituted something in the herbal remedies that Nadia was using. Nadia clearly would not have done that deliberately, she loved him too much and she was the one in control of the herbs, and made his tea every morning.'

'I suppose it could have been another member of Sir William's household?'

'I somehow doubt it, unless it was at Sir William's instruction and, nasty piece of work as he is, I don't think he is up to getting his hands dirty like that. He's too much of a coward.'

'OK, so murder attempt number three. What about the sniper? Who was he, Khand again?'

'I agree that that is the biggest open question. Who did fire the shot that actually killed Nariman? Rohit was clearly aggrieved but he had once loved Nariman like a father and had no gun until after the attack. The round was a .22LR calibre, which is commonplace so could have been fired from a number of different kinds of weapon. The Flyte's possibly had motivation as well, and the weapons also, but none of them was there on Saturday morning and they are also not credible murderers in my estimation. Again, it could have been Khand himself, but I suspect given the distance that the shot was taken from that we are probably looking for a trained marksman. And then we have the statement from Mr Baxter about a turbaned man getting out of the cab and then being picked up by a similar vehicle a few minutes later. I think that was almost certainly our sniper…'

'Someone local?'

'Very.'

'You know who?'

'Yes, I believe so. We still have a Sikh marksman to find.'

'The taxi driver, you mean?'

'No, he's a Sikh but he's probably not our marksman as he must have been driving the cab at the time. I suspect that whole thing with the cab and the lamppost was just a nice diversion planned to put us off the scent.'

'So, there is a second Sikh you mean?'

'Yes and given the accuracy of the shot, he is probably a serving or ex-army or police officer as well. And unfortunately, I'm inclined to believe that he was more likely connected to the police given that we clearly have a mole in our team as well.'

'My God,' Alice said. 'What about the officer who helped us at the traffic accident? Of course, he could have gotten out of the cab and taken the shot. Then while the cab waited for him he disposed of the gun in the cab, before joining us to help with the two motorcyclists. I wondered during the autopsy how that artery had been severed so neatly when he was hit by a blunt instrument like a car bonnet. He must have slit it with a knife while we were looking at the other guy.'

'I think she's after your job, Penny,' exclaimed Hunter. 'Alice, you've spent too long watching the team at work. exclaimed Hunter. 'Get Sergeant Singh picked up, Penny. I am going to enjoy interrogating this one.'

It is no longer a violent, exceptional moment of life that passes before our eyes – it is life itself. Thousands and thousands of laws there are, mightier and more venerable than those of passion; but these laws are silent, and discreet, and slow-moving; and hence it is only in the twilight that they can be seen and heard, in the meditation that comes to us at the tranquil moments of life.

Maurice Maeterlinck *(playwright quoted by Elgar when asked about the nature of the Enigma theme)*

CHAPTER TWENTY

ALICE IN NEVERLAND – (ANDANTE) FINALE

'The time has come,' the Walrus said,
'To talk of many things:
Of shoes – and ships – and sealing-wax –
Of cabbages – and kings –
And why the sea is boiling hot –
And whether pigs have wings.'

Lewis Carroll – *Through the Looking-Glass*

'For heaven's sake, Eddie Peterson, can't I trust you for a minute?' Alice demanded loudly as she entered the kitchen. She turned down the volume on the CD player and surveyed the mess covering the kitchen table. Carrie and Eddie had been making jam tarts while dancing wildly round the kitchen to the latest release from a well-known Swedish pop duo. She wished Eddie would not encourage Carrie like this; she was growing up quickly enough as it was. Alice was however relieved that he, for once, was dressed reasonably smartly in a tweed Burberry jacket, twill shirt, rolled-up green cavalry trousers and Converse trainers and had remarkably thought to wear an apron over his best clothes while preparing the tarts. She wasn't sure but she could swear that he was wearing eyeliner too. Carrie, on the other hand, was wearing a scruffy T-shirt and jeans and was almost completely covered in flour; there was pastry, jam and orange marmalade all over the table and more flour on the floor. There was also the distinct smell of burning sugar from the oven. Alice opened the oven door, cursed and then quickly opened a window to allow the smoke to escape.

'I think these might be done,' she said ironically. Eddie, already wearing her pink oven gloves, snatched the tin away and took it over to rest on a tray by the sink, wildly waving the steam away from the tarts with his gloved hands.

'*The knave of hearts, he stole those tarts and took them quite away,*' said Alice, laughing.

'Really, it's not funny, they're just nicely browned, that's all,' he replied.

'Are you ready to go out, Mummy?' asked Carrie, jumping up and down in excitement and smiling up at her adoringly. 'You look so pretty in that dress.'

Eddie nodded in agreement. He returned to the table, held her by the waist and gave her a big sloppy kiss. 'You certainly do, Ms Roberts. Maybe we'll forget the surprise and just stay in for the night,' he teased.

'Get your floury hands off my lovely new dress, Eddie. For heaven's sake, you two, this kitchen is like a bombsite,' she said, brushing herself off and turning to Carrie. 'And if you think I've spent all day getting ready just to stay in then you've got another thing coming. I hope you're planning to clear this mess up when we're gone, young lady?'

It was October 9th, Alice's fortieth birthday. Earlier, while Alice was safely out of the house, Carrie and Eddie had spent most of the day secretively putting the finishing touches to the surprise that they had been plotting for months. At Eddie's insistence and to create the necessary diversion, Alice's sister had been drafted in to take her to the local spa for a facial, hot-stone massage, and a mani-pedi followed by a trip to the local salon to have her hair done, abandoning her normal hippie-mummy mop for a smart 1940s style, her hair swept up and sideways over her forehead in a single large wave that crested above the crown of her head.

She finally returned home at 5pm for a luxurious bath in the evening primrose oils that Carrie had given her for her birthday. She was almost exhausted after all this pampering, but had spent the last hour getting ready, squeezing into the little blue and white flowered dress that had been waiting for her, laid out on the bed when she returned. It had the shortest hemline and was accompanied by the most flattering underwear she had worn in fifteen years; a silk and taffeta birthday surprise from her favourite Park Street shop – she still could not quite believe that Eddie actually knew her dress size – and as for the underwear, her mind had been well and truly boggled by his selection. She suspected he must have had some female help. She had tied a little blue silk bow in her hair to complement the dress.

'I guess I brush up pretty well,' she said, pouting admiringly at her reflection in the looking glass in the hall.

'Mummy, please do tell me where Daddy's taking you,' asked Carrie, jumping up and down again like a little rabbit.

'I've no idea, darling, really this is all still a terribly big secret that your dad's arranged.'

They heard the bell ring. Carrie ran to the front door and shouted, 'It's Penny!' She let her in and then in her quietest voice whispered to Penny, 'she still doesn't know, you know.'

'Well let's keep it that way, shall we?' whispered Penny in reply, putting her fingers to her lips to emphasise the need for secrecy. 'You'd better run off and get ready hadn't you? But don't let your mum see your costume.'

As Penny entered the kitchen, she whistled, taken aback for a second by the sight of Alice in her finery.

'Wow Alice, you look absolutely spectacular,' she said.

Eddie greeted Penny and then pulled her aside, whispering into her ear, 'Everything ready upstairs?'

Penny nodded quickly and then turned to Alice. 'So tell

me, where is Eddie taking you, Alice?' she asked, teasing her further. Eddie dug Penny in the ribs and she giggled.

'I've no idea. This major league rat still won't tell me anything,' she said, looking at Eddie and Penny somewhat suspiciously. She was now sure they were up to something; the knowing glances and the blush on Penny's face were dead giveaways. She decided however to play along innocently for a while and see where this was going.

'Eddie, is it time to go yet? I'm beginning to get really excited,' asked Alice, looking up at the clock.

'Nearly, darling, but before we go I do have one more birthday present for you,' said Eddie, holding out a pretty little glass bottle. Round the neck of the bottle was a paper label, with the words *DRINK ME* beautifully printed on it in large letters.

'Drink me?' asked Alice. 'Is this a clue?'

'No, I'll look first,' she said, 'and see whether it's marked 'poison' or not!' Alice ventured to taste it, and finding it very nice, (it had, in fact, a sort of mixed flavour of cherry-tart, custard, pine-apple, roast turkey, toffee, and hot buttered toast,) she very soon finished it off.

Lewis Carroll – *Through the Looking-Glass*

Eddie smiled and nodded without answering directly and then took her by the arm. Alice issued final instructions to Carrie to tidy up the mess and asked Penny very apologetically if she could give her a hand.

'Of course, Alice, we'll be finished in no time. See you later, alligator.'

'In a while, crocodile,' sniggered Carrie, who had still not left to get ready herself.

Eddie led Alice hurriedly out of the front entrance, looking behind him as he closed the door, mouthing to the two girls to get a move on. They climbed the short flight of stone steps that led from their basement flat up to street level. At the top of the steps he swung open the wrought iron gate, holding it until Alice had passed through and then releasing it again on its squeaking hinges. She walked toward the town a little and waited for him by the pillar box on the pavement. Locking the catch on the gate, he walked forward to stand beside her, pausing for a while, his arm hooked in hers, breathing in the night air.

'So where would you actually like to go?' he asked, somewhat vaguely, staring up at the evening stars as if he had not quite made up his mind where to take her yet. The air was slightly chilled after the warm autumn day, so that their breath escaped into the darkness in quietly swirling coils of moisture. Alice was shivering slightly, either from excitement or from the change of temperature; the goose bumps raised on the skin of her forearm. The scent of late jasmine from the window boxes on Lady Mary's windowsills above them was slightly intoxicating in the night air.

'I'll go wherever you are planning to take me, handsome sir,' she replied, enjoying the game but also getting slightly frustrated with his obvious tactics to confuse her. She suspected she knew exactly where he was taking her. There was a restaurant at the bottom of the Parade that she had noticed he had ringed in the phone book. It had a growing reputation, intimate with exquisite food prepared by the best chef in town but with a faintly exotic-sounding menu. She had walked past it many times wishing they could go there once, because it was certainly pricey. The natural style of décor was one she especially liked; pastel shades, abstract daubs, gilt mirrors and sea-grass flooring.

'Well then, if it's really going to be up to me, then it has to be *second star to the right, and straight on 'til morning,*' he said, laughing.

'Come on stop teasing me now, Eddie, where are we going? Surely you can tell me now,' she demanded. 'And by the way, I hope you're not going to make me walk too far in these shoes.'

Eddie pulled a rather large brass alarm clock theatrically out of his pocket and said in an equally exaggerated voice, 'Ah, we're late, never smile at a crocodile.'

Before she could respond he put one arm behind her back, the other around her thighs and lifted her abruptly into his arms, marching quickly up the steps to the door of No. 5 and rapping loudly on the doorknocker. The door swung open at once, seemingly of its own accord and he carried her inside, putting her down gently in the half-lit hallway. There was apparently no one else around.

In 1932, the original Alice in Wonderland came face to face with the original Peter Pan when 80 year old Alice Liddell Hargreaves and Peter Llewellyn Davies, then in this thirties, met at the opening of a Lewis Carroll exhibition at a bookshop in London.

Based on Wikipedia, *Peter and Alice*

Alice was now very confused. This was not at all what she was expecting. The hall was strangely quiet, only disturbed by the patient ticking of a long case clock, but she was suddenly aware of a white fluffy shape pushing to get past her in the doorway. The white shape (actually a rabbit called Carrie) deposited a little glass box under the ornate Empire console table and ran off into the room at the end of the corridor. Alice, intrigued, stooped to pick the box up and opened it to find a small cake, on which the words *EAT ME* had been beautifully marked out in currants.

'Curiouser and curiouser,' she said, playing along now and smiling broadly, realising that she was clearly the object of some elaborate practical joke. In fact, a second ago, she thought she had heard giggling, followed by a loud 'Sshh'. She followed Eddie obediently down the hall, across the richly patterned carpets, toward the double doors of the main formal drawing room. Her anticipation was building at every step. As soon as he opened the doors, there was a loud cheer, a round of applause and the sound of party poppers and kids' trumpets being blown.

'Surprise!' they all shouted.

Alice found herself immediately moved to laughter in response to the cacophony of sound from her friends. Virtually everyone she knew was gathered in the room and as far as she could tell they had all dressed up in costumes of one sort or another. She looked round at Eddie, who had now ditched his tweed jacket and donned a green tunic and peaked green hat, with an extravagant feather stuck into it. 'Peter Pan,' she said. 'I should have guessed. And I suppose I'm Alice,' she added, looking down again at the dress.

The exquisitely furnished room was adorned with paper lanterns and festoons of party bunting. Scented candles burned in little silver dishes and there was a CD of a very skilled classical guitarist playing on the music system. At the far side of the drawing room were two doors that each opened out onto the balcony and gardens beyond, overhanging with honeysuckle and jasmine. Over the right hand door hung a sparkling sign saying *Neverland*, while over the left hung a flowery sign saying *Wonderland*.

At the table in the bay of the *Wonderland* door, there was a rather grand looking man with a very large hat, which he removed with a low bow as Alice approached, revealing a bald pate and face reddened with rouge. The table was set for tea, with scones and sandwiches and all sorts of little cakes, including a tray of rather singed looking jam tarts.

'No room! No room!' they cried out when they saw Alice

coming. 'There's PLENTY of room!' said Alice indignantly.

Lewis Carroll – *Through the Looking-Glass*

'Gosh, you all look fantastic! I can't believe how much work you've put into this,' said Alice, clapping her hands in amazement.

'Have you guessed the riddle yet?' asked the man with the very large hat, a price tag saying *10/6d* sticking out of its brim.

'No, you idiot, what riddle are you talking about?' replied Alice.

'Why is a raven like a writing desk?'

'Ah, that's easy,' Alice replied. 'I know this one: because he can't crow like a speaking clock!'

'Bravo, well said,' said the Hatter. 'I think we have another joker here, don't we Miss Dore-abella mouse?' He turned to Penny, who was wearing a fake fur stole and animal ears and had sneaked in through the back door to sit beside him at the tea table.

Penny seemed rather breathless, having just rushed up through the garden from the flat below, but smiled and said, 'Happy Birthday, Alice, I hope you enjoy your surprise party as much as we have enjoyed planning it.'

At the other end of the room, underneath the sparkling sign that said *Neverland* stood a rather smart and fearsome pirate with a silver foil hook and a wig of rolling grey hair (she recognised him at once as Inspector Hunter by his steely blue eyes). He bowed deeply to her, doffing his tricorn hat as he did so. Next to him was seated a man dressed as the surly captain's mate, Mr Smee. He had a goatee beard, shorn blonde hair and a rather fetching scar painted across his cheek. He was balancing a rather tall fairy with incredibly long flaxen hair on his knee; Izzie. Izzie, or more correctly Tinkerbell, was stroking Mr Smee's hair in a very familiar way. *Not at all fairy-like*, thought Alice

'And just what do you think you are planning to do with Mr Smee, Tinkerbell? Can I remind you there's a rather sensitive young lady in the room?' asked Alice, pointing at Carrie. Izzie smiled; she was now stroking Penn's beard and landed a huge kiss on his cheek, screwing up her nose.

'Well, Peter appears to have deserted me for the evening for you, pretty lady, so I've got to make do with the next best thing,' she replied.

'Hello Alice, and a very happy birthday from both of us,' said Penn as he kissed Alice's cheek. There was a loud cough behind them.

'Ah, the Darlings have arrived,' announced Captain Hook. Julia and Delia, dressed as Wendy and Nana, entered the room and gave Alice a big hug. Julia kissed them on both cheeks.

'Alice, come with us into the garden,' said Julia, her request echoed by woofs from Delia in her Nana costume. 'There's someone else I want you to meet.'

They passed through the French windows onto the balcony, which was festooned with garlands of flowers. In the planting on the terrace there were lights of every colour and candles in little saucers leading off into the undergrowth. Pink flamingos had been planted in the lawn in the form of a croquet game. A model pirate ship was becalmed on the goldfish pond and strung through the large fig tree were little fairy lights and playing card ornaments. Julia and Delia led Alice along the winding path made by the candles across the lawn to the far end of the garden, where there was a small gazebo, filled with cushions and lit by Arabian-style pierced lanterns. There was a big sign hung above the entrance – *The Blue Caterpillar's Hookah Palace*.

In the corner of the gazebo, sitting on a cushion shaped like a mushroom, was a very blue-looking caterpillar, smoking the advertised hookah. He puffed three times and then took the pipe out of his mouth and addressed her in a languid, sleepy voice.

'So, who are you, little girl?'

'Alice,' she said, flirting just a little bit with her hands and eyelashes.

'Well come and sit beside me, little Alice,' said the caterpillar, smoothing off the cushion for her to sit on. 'May I offer you a drink?' he asked, pouring her a huge glass of champagne. She obeyed and sat down beside him, turning back to look from the garden to the house that was all lit up.

She sighed and announced meaningfully, 'If only you weren't so blue, my sweetheart Hugh.' They sipped their champagne with the Flyte sisters while the revels got going throughout the garden. There was the sound of more laughter from the house.

'This is nice,' she said to the caterpillar. 'I'm feeling very happy. All of my friends are here, a lovely party and a sweetie caterpillar too. What more could a girl want?'

She noticed that the Flyte sisters had disappeared. From the direction of the balcony she began to hear the sound of instruments being tuned up, and then from the open drawing room door she caught a rich and clear voice singing faintly at first and then building more strongly. It sounded like a Negro Spiritual in the sweet night air. She realised it was Pearl Taylor, accompanied in delicate harmonies by Julia and Delia. Eddie was playing keyboards softly and Penn and Bas were playing their acoustic and bass guitars to the restrained and soulful tune.

> *Nobody knows the trouble I've seen*
> *Nobody knows but Jesus*
> *Nobody knows the trouble I've seen*
> *Glory hallelujah!*
> *Sometimes I'm up, sometimes I'm down*
> *Oh, yes, Lord*

Sometimes I'm almost to the ground
Oh, yes, Lord
Although you see me going 'long so
Oh, yes, Lord
I have my trials here below
Oh, yes, Lord
If you get there before I do
Oh, yes, Lord
Tell all my friends I'm coming to Heaven!
Oh, yes, Lord

Samuel Coleridge-Taylor, Traditional song from
the *Overture to Hiawatha's Wedding Feast*

When she had finished, Alice whooped and clapped as
loudly as she could, while the other guests all joined in the
applause. Pearl bowed to them and started to sing 'Happy
Birthday'. Then Mad Jack (dressed as the Hatter)
accompanied by Dan the bulldog got up from their chair at
the Hatter's table and called to the crowd.

'Anyone for the Lobster Quadrille?'
Eddie started into a wild jig on his violin.

'It must be a very pretty dance,' said Alice timidly.
'Would you like to see a little of it?' said the Mock Turtle.
'Very much indeed,' said Alice.

Lewis Carroll, *Through the Looking-Glass*

'OK, people,' shouted Professor Baxter, who was dressed
as a cowboy. 'I need you to form a square with four couples.
Miss Taylor, will you do us the honour of being the first
ninepin? Please stand in the middle.' She nodded, familiar
with this kind of dancing from her childhood.

Dottie and Penny, Penn and Izzie, Hunter and Julia and

Delia and Sergeant Jones formed up into pairs, with Pearl standing in the middle of the circle.

'OK, the four couples should all join hands and circle to the left around the ninepin using eight slip steps, then eight steps back to the right to their starting positions.' They obediently followed Baxter's instructions, giggling as they turned in their circles.

'OK, that's good. Next, the first couple, that's you Dottie and Penny, gallop in hold past ninepin and then back the other side to your original place, followed by each of the other three couples in turn. Ninepin then swings each man in turn and his partner joins ninepin to jig in the centre. Finally, ninepin and the four women circle left and keep circling until the music stops. The one who then fails to grab a male partner becomes the new ninepin. Simple!'

★

Later that evening, Penn took Izzie by the hand for a walk amongst the shadows of the garden, towards the little fountain on the terrace.

'Look at the moon,' said Izzie. 'Isn't it beautiful? Isn't that what they call a harvest moon?'

'Inviting us to stay, for the clouds to fly us away.'

'Maybe,' she said, holding his hands closely against her waist. 'I'm so glad I went down into the park to see who was singing there that night, you know.'

'So am I,' he said, kissing her. She let go of him and danced a slow passacaglia around the pond, twirling her silk scarf around her as she twisted and turned in the moonlight. When she had finished she sat opposite him, wrapping her legs around his thighs so that he couldn't escape.

'So, Tinks, have you heard of the author Washington Irving?' he asked. 'He was one of Warwickshire's most famous writers.'

'I've heard of him, of course, but why Warwickshire? I thought he was American?'

'That's a common but understandable mistake, of course.'

'You do mean the *Rip Van Winkle* Washington Irving, don't you?'

'Yes, the very same, I doubt if there's another author with such a strange name. He was a truly remarkable man, you know, an inventor amongst other things of the Columbus flat Earth theory, Santa Claus, Gotham, the New York Knicks, Sleepy Hollow, the headless horseman and by fact a resident of Birmingham, when it was still part of Warwickshire, for several years.'

'OK clever clogs, so what about him?' she said, passing her foot onto his stomach.

'Well, I've got some news,' he said and then waited, saying no more.

'You can't just leave it at that you tease, what sort of news?'

'I just heard today that I got the part to play Ichabod Crane in the new Fox TV pilot. We're filming in North Carolina.'

'Wow,' she said, 'that's fantastic!' Her face darkened a little, realising the inevitable implication that he would be leaving her in England.

'So I wondered whether you might be interested in coming to America with me.'

'You're joking, me go to America?'

'Why not?'

'Are your sails going to be black?'

'Of course!'

'Then of course I'll come, my darling Tristan Penn, I'll come with you to look for America any day of the week,' and she leaned over to hug him, pushing him to the ground in excitement.

★

And the ancient Arrow-maker
Paused a moment ere he answered,
Smoked a little while in silence,
Looked at Hiawatha proudly,
Fondly looked at Laughing Water,
And made answer very gravely:
'Yes, if Minnehaha wishes;
Let your heart speak, Minnehaha!'

And the lovely Laughing Water
Seemed more lovely as she stood there,
Neither willing nor reluctant,
As she went to Hiawatha,
Softly took the seat beside him,
While she said, and blushed to say it,
'I will follow you, my husband!'

Henry Wadsworth Longfellow, *The Song of Hiawatha*

In another corner of the garden two somewhat older lovers held their glasses touching in the fresh night air. One was the former Wild West hero, Poshizmo Baxter; the other was his Native American Princess, Minnehaha (Dottie) Baker. After his earlier exertions calling the folk dancing, Baxter had demonstrated his lasso techniques to his friends for a while on the lawn, before singing a number of western campfire songs. He was now sitting tired, happy and somewhat philosophical under a mulberry tree, watching Izzie and Penn rolling and laughing together in the grass.

'You seem pensive my dear, are you tired?' asked Dottie

'Not really. I was just thinking about a novel I am planning, after the last month or so I think I have more than enough material. I think those two might make good lead characters.'

'That one in particular. He looks just like you used to when you were younger, my little Poshizmo; blonde, blue-eyed and red-cheeked,' said Dottie.

'Are you sure? That was such a long time ago and we have seen a lot of water go under the bridge since then.'

'Absolutely, you could be father and son.'

'Maybe, but there's something else on my mind too. Let me ask you something, Dottie?' he said seriously. 'Do you still have time in your life for a sad old lost boy like me?'

'Well yes, Mr Baxter, I think I've still got time for you.'

'Ah, that's good. So then I have something that I meant to give you years ago, but the time never seemed quite right until now.'

He opened up a small box and passed it to her. The jewel on the gold band inside was not large, but it was big enough for the rest of their lifetimes.

'Baxter, what's that?' she said, genuinely taken aback.

'It's a ring of course. So will you?' he asked again nervously. She kissed him full on the lips

'Of course I will, you silly old thing.'

> *And they said, 'O good Iagoo,*
> *Tell us now a tale of wonder,*
> *Tell us of some strange adventure,*
> *That the feast may be more joyous,*
> *That the time may pass more gayly,*
> *And our guests be more contented!'*
> *And Iagoo answered straightway,*
> *'You shall hear a tale of wonder,*
> *You shall hear the strange adventures*
> *Of Osseo, the Magician,*
> *From the Evening Star descending.'*

Samuel Coleridge-Taylor, *Hiawatha's Wedding Feast*

Toward the end of the evening when Lady Mary and the Reverend George Dore returned from their honeymoon, they were astonished to see the staid formality of the house transformed by such high jinks.

'What an excess of silliness,' said the reverend, smiling but quietly worrying about the expense of it all.

'For heaven's sake, George, it will be you in the doghouse if you don't join in the fun,' replied Lady Mary with a scowl. She gave Alice and then her two daughters a big hug and reserved a special kiss for Eddie. 'This kiss is shaped like you, Peter,' she said with a wink.

'Ah, my sweet Lady Mary,' he replied. 'But if you'll excuse us for a moment.'

Eddie took Alice's hand and she followed him out on to the balcony, shutting the doors behind them.

★

'So, I hope you liked your surprise?'

'You're a scoundrel, Eddie, if this is what you and Julia were up to all this time. And to think I thought you two were…'

'Sshh,' he said, 'not another word, you really should believe in me more in the future.'

'Don't push your luck, darling, you're still a rascal, if a totally loveable one,' she spoke from her heart, not wishing to spoil the moment.

'Yes,' he said, taking her by the waist and kissing her in a way that felt like they were ten years younger again. 'I'm saving the best till later tonight.'

★

Across the lawn in the little gazebo, slightly merrier now, the blue caterpillar sat thoughtfully by himself on the mushroom, continuing to suck at his hookah pipe. Hugh was watching Eddie and Alice smooching together on the balcony from afar. He felt warm inside to see how happy they were again. Through the steam from his hookah water bath, he spotted Julia coming up to the little garden house to join him. She too was dressed prettily, holding up her gown with her hands, wrapping it around her legs against the dew of the grass.

'Who are *you*?' he asked in a languid, sleepy voice.

> '*I – I hardly know, sir, just at present – at least I know who I was when I got up this morning, but I think I must have changed several times since then.*'
>
> '*What do you mean by that?*' said the Caterpillar, sternly. '*Explain yourself!*'
>
> '*I can't explain* myself, *I'm afraid, sir, because I'm not* myself, *you see.*'
>
> '*I don't see,*' said the Caterpillar.

> Lewis Carroll, *Through the Looking-Glass*

'I think I must be Wendy, the girl who never grew up,' Julia replied.

'Wendy? Not hardly Wendy at all, nor Alice nor Julia neither it seems?'

'I really think I ought to know who I am,' she said indignantly.

'Well that's as maybe but if that is really you, Wendy Darling, Alice seems to have gone and stolen your Peter again. It's all very confusing.'

'It looks very much so, but I agree and I suppose I am glad. Anyway, Mr Caterpillar, is there room for me beside you on your mushroom while I think this all through?' she sobbed theatrically.

'Room? It depends very much what size you want to be.'

He beckoned for her to join and she sat down beside him.

'So are you content now with all your preparations?'

'Very much so, although this mushroom could be a little larger.'

'You'll get used to it in time.'

'So I think you ought to tell me who you are now, Mr Caterpillar?'

'Why?'

'Well it might be polite, but if you're going to be difficult about it,' Julia turned away, the incense-laden steam from the water bath beginning to get up her nose. She pretended to get up to leave.

'Wait,' Hugh called.

'Come back!' the caterpillar called after her. 'I've something important to say!'

This sounded promising, certainly. She turned and came back again.

'Keep your temper,' said the caterpillar.

'Is that all?' she said, swallowing down her anger as well as she could.

'No,' said the caterpillar.

She thought she might as well wait, as she had nothing else to do, and perhaps after all it might tell her something worth hearing. For some minutes it puffed away without speaking; but at last it unfolded its arms, took the hookah out of its mouth again, and said, 'So you think you're changed, do you?'

'I'm afraid I am, sir, I can't remember things as I used—and I don't keep the same size for ten minutes together!'

Lewis Carroll, *Through the Looking-Glass*

'Can't remember what things?' said the caterpillar.

'Who I am or who I came with. Anyway, enough of this, where's Claudia, lover boy?'

'She's with her girlfriend. They came as the White King and the White Queen,' said the caterpillar winking, pointing to Claudia and Jade rustling conspiratorially in the bushes. 'Put one and one together.'

'Sorry, I didn't realise, I thought you were…'

He felt her arms passing round his waist for support as they fell slowly backwards on to the cushions behind. In an instant they were transported back to earlier days and he in turn quite forgot himself and began to kiss her full on the lips, which, to his relief, she responded to eagerly and with total abandon. He felt her hands rushing too onto his body, sending shivers of pleasure up his spine. Her scent attacked his senses, already dulled by the incense from the water bath.

'God, but you're beautiful, aren't you?'

'So are you. This feels right doesn't it?'

'Why on earth didn't I ever do that before?' She kissed him again, so that he could hardly breathe.

'See what you're doing to me?'

How doth the little crocodile improve his shining tail.
And pour the waters of the Nile, on every golden scale.
How cheerfully he seems to grin, how neatly spreads his claws.
And welcomes little fishes in, with gently smiling jaws.

Lewis Carol, *Through the Looking-Glass*

★

'I think our friends are having a pretty good time now,' said Alice, pointing at the shadows of Hugh and Julia entwined in the gazebo. 'I don't think they'll be in for a while, so we'd better not lock them out.' The French doors opened and they were joined by Pearl and Hunter on the balcony.

★

'So Augustus, how are we going to work this out?' asked Pearl as she took a seat next to the slightly intoxicated pirate captain now sitting on the bench on the balcony. She filled his glass with Armagnac from the half-empty decanter in front of them. He looked at the glass, shaking the ice round in a circle and then looked back at Pearl with puppy-dog eyes. *She looks truly sensational*, he thought. Did he dare to take this further?

'Miss Taylor, it's delightful that you were able to join us this evening, your singing was quite enchanting, as ever,' he said, his speech still formal if somewhat slurred.

'I think we should cut the small talk,' said Pearl. 'We need to talk seriously, don't we?'

'Yes I suppose so, Miss Taylor. I'm afraid I think we do. You really were quite naughty the last time you visited us, you know. You realise I should charge you with a whole series of misdemeanours – kidnap, entrapment and blackmail amongst others I could name.'

'Yes, but you won't and we both know why not, don't we, Gus?'

'I guess it's still the same old story.'

'All's fair in love and war.'

'I really don't think that excuses your behaviour though, however delightful an escort you are.'

'Ah, if it's to be your old world courtesy versus my new world justice, an unequal match, I think. It's time to drop the courtly love bit and go with the flow I think, Captain.'

'Revenge is never an attractive virtue in a woman, Miss

Taylor. Would Troyte still be alive if you hadn't been playing your little party games with him?'

'Really not my gig, Inspector, I was done at the gallery. I hurt his pride but nothing else.'

'But you let Rohit know he was coming didn't you? You knew he would take matters into his own hands.'

'Sshh, sometimes, you are a little too smart, Gus, really I am not that manipulative. Rohit approached me, not the other way around. How do you think I knew that Troyte would be here that weekend? He's a clever young man, that writer, and you really ought to think about using him for more than the odd translation.'

'So, you're asking me to break a whole set of police regulations and countless laws and let you off?'

'I'm afraid I am indeed. But I think it'll be worth your while, my Toposcope hound, isn't there a public interest test on prosecutions?' she said, stroking his wig like a dog and blowing him a kiss.

'That's a good point, but not my call. Anyway, what about all that Rule Britannia business?' he said. 'You led us a merry dance there.'

'But you and Penny solved the mystery, didn't you?'

'Yes but possibly not the enigma,' he answered and then paused. The sound of a new song began to rise from the drawing room. That character had still not appeared on the stage.

'Ah, Auld Lang Syne,' she said as they heard their friends celebrating in the drawing room. 'Maybe that's the theme, *friendship*, the signal for us to return indoors.'

★

On the balcony of the house next door, Rohit and Nadia stared down at the frivolity below. They had been cuddling while listening quietly to the music and laughter. That evening she had cooked for him for the first time in the kitchenette next to her room. He'd relished the flavours, the spices, his body crushed by the cinnamon and nutmeg, licked by the sensuous aroma of rose petals and saffron. She had roasted the spices in a very hot pan until they released their oils and aroma, ground and worked them into a lavish paste, scoring and marinating the lamb so that they perfumed the meat. This was the last of the 1001 nights she would be apart from him, now he had been formally released. It was the end of her stories; now he would become slave to her love again.

He stood behind her while she nestled in his arms, snuggling her head in the crook of his neck, feeling ever safer as his strong hands wrapped tightly around the fabric of her sari, rubbing her elevated velvet slippers around his shins. She touched the back of his hand, pressing it closer against her abdomen, breathing in deeply and closing her eyes. She pulled the Mysore silk scarf closer around her shoulders.

'Can you feel it kicking?' she said, telling him now for the first time of her secret growing within her womb.

Her senses were full of the smell of the jasmine flowers she sprinkled in the little copper bowls in her bathroom; the bowls in which she washed her hair before brushing it through with olive oil. She had burnished her skin with yoghurt and turmeric to brighten its glow. He smelled of cologne, manly and western and slightly out of place in her imagined tropical landscape. She turned her face toward him and kissed him on the smoothness of his chin. From the bedroom behind them leaked the bewitching sounds of a qawwalli, art beyond caste, the lyrical sound of the rain and the wind captured in Ali Khan's gentle voice. Rohit stroked her dark shiny hair, which radiated in the light from the moon.

'So, my little prince, let me tell you the last part of the story before the sun comes up.'

★

As Eddie and Alice thanked their hosts for the last time and waved goodbye to Pearl in her taxi back to London, they descended the front stairs with a rather worse for wear pirate. Alice turned to the tall gentleman to kiss him goodnight, too.

'Thank you for everything you did for me this evening, it was such a brilliant surprise.'

'It was my pleasure, Alice. You are truly *our* romantic and delicate inspiration.'

'Thank you. So what will become of Sir William?' she asked, changing the subject. 'I hear you are investigating him on tax fraud as well as the corruption case now.'

'Yes there are quite a few things he is helping us with now. Fraud, using political influence to procure investment for the university, corruption and accessory to murder; in fact we're building up quite a case against him. I think by the time we've finished with Sir William he'll be helping out Her Majesty for some years to come and maybe not in quite the fashion he had come to expect. Yes, I think his dark sayings will be silent for a while longer.'

'And what about you, Inspector Hunter? I was watching you earlier with Pearl. Now that you have truly returned from the grave, do you still have your dinner invitation for your evening with Ms Taylor at the Elgar Room?' asked Eddie.

'Yes, despite being the theme of many enigmas, death is overrated and they say revenge is a dish best eaten cold. I do still have my invitation to dinner and to *dine* again with her will surely be an awfully big adventure.'

Hunter closed his eyes and spoke softly:

And euermore vpon the Goddesse face
Mine eye was fixt, for feare of her offence,
Whom when I saw with amiable grace
To laugh at me, and fauour my pretence,
I was emboldned with more confidence,

Spenser, *The Faerie Queene*